COME AWAY WITH ME

Sara MacDonald was born in Yorkshire and travelled extensively as a forces child. She attended drama school in London and worked in television and theatre before she married, living abroad for many years before moving to Cornwall with her two sons. She has written three previous novels for HarperCollins: *Sea Music, Another Life* and *The Hour Before Dawn*.

Visit www.AuthorTracker.co.uk for exclusive updates on Sara MacDonald.

Carol
11/17

By the same author

Sea Music
Another Life
The Hour Before Dawn

SARA MACDONALD

Come Away With Me

HARPER

Harper
An imprint of HarperCollins*Publishers*
77–85 Fulham Palace Road,
Hammersmith, London W6 8JB

www.harpercollins.co.uk

A paperback original

Published by HarperCollins*Publishers* 2007
1

"Come Away With Me" Words and Music by Norah Jones
© 2002, EMI Blackwood Music Inc/Muthajones Music LLC,
USA Reproduced by permission of EMI Music Publishing Ltd,
London WC3H 0QY

A catalogue record for this book
is available from the British Library

ISBN-13 978 0 00 720157 0
ISBN-10 0 00 720157 5

Set in Sabon by Palimpsest Book Production Limited,
Grangemouth, Stirlingshire

Printed and bound in Great Britain by
Clays Ltd., St Ives plc

In memory of
Nikki, my cousin, who lit up a room.

For Jackie and Pete at Redcoats.

For Toby, Nicola and Phoebe
(Sweet Pea).

With love.

Writing on Water

Single white goose quill
what are you writing

drifting gently on
water's silk surface

making your mark
between liquid and air

leaving behind you an
imprint of movement

the hint of a message?
There's more to writing
than words.

Jenny Balfour-Paul, 2006

PART ONE

ONE

February 2006
Adam felt the hairs crawling on the back of his neck. The familiar nightmarish fear was back. He gripped his fishing rod tightly. The woods rose up from the creek behind him dark and dense. He knew it was up there, watching him, he could feel it.

A moment ago, as he turned and reached for his jacket and glanced up at the trees, he had seen that the shadows had changed, knew the dark shape where light had been was someone, something, up there watching him. Waiting. Waiting until he had to pass it on the path before it jumped out at him.

He started to reel in his line, his ears alert for someone passing, then he could rush to the path and walk behind them back to the cottage. There was no sign of anyone else out on the creek path now. The curve of foreshore was deserted, only the sounds of curlews with their thin, quavering cries and a heron standing on one leg and the mist rolling towards him obscuring the sun as the tide slid inexorably in.

When he had secured his line, Adam closed his tin boxes, gathered his binoculars and made a little pile of his belongings. Now, he must turn slowly behind him to reach for his knapsack. He made himself look upwards into the wood. The shadow had gone. His path was clear. He threw his things into the bag, grabbed his rod and straightened up as the sun broke out again from behind a curtain of mist.

He took a step towards the old barn on the wharf to reach the path beyond it. He jumped violently, as half blinded by the sun he saw something lying against the wall of the building. He stared down at it. It was a woman, curled up on a coat, knees to her chin, wild hair hiding her face. She looked tiny, like a child, her thin arms folded round herself and she was very still. Jenny.

Adam stood frozen. He stared down at her and pity welled up in him, startling him with the power of it. His heart constricted, his eyes pricked at the sight of an adult stricken. His fear evaporated. It all began to make a weird kind of sense. Jenny had lost it. People sometimes went crazy when bad things happened.

He should run back to the cottage. He should fetch his mother, but somehow, he could not leave her lying vulnerable on her own on an old coat like a tramp. He just couldn't. She lay oddly still. He put down his fishing rod, placed his knapsack on the ground and inched nearer to touch her.

She was not dead. Her flesh was warm to his fingers. At his touch she moved and opened her eyes. Adam backed away slightly. He did not know what to say.

Jenny, seeing him, struggled to a sitting position. He saw that her hands shook.

'It's all right,' he said quickly. 'It's OK.'

She stared at him as if coming from some faraway place.

'Adam.' Her voice was husky, as if she had not spoken for some time. She held out a hand towards him. Adam could not quite bring himself to take it. He could feel his heart hammering in his chest. He wanted to run for Ruth. He was out of his depth.

4

Jenny's hand fell to her side. 'I'm sorry,' she whispered. 'I'm so sorry for frightening you.' Her voice was dull, her face bleak.

Adam crouched in front of her. 'Why . . . why were you following me and hiding in the woods? I don't understand.'

Jenny didn't reply and Adam said, 'I'm going to get Mum. It'll be OK. We'll be back in five minutes.'

'I wanted to talk to you, be with you, on your own . . .' Jenny's voice trailed off.

'Why?' Adam was uneasy.

'You are so like Tom. So like him. I somehow thought you were my son; that I was your mother.'

Jenny's eyes looked bruised and her face seemed to have shrunk under her mass of curly hair.

'Forgive me,' she said. 'I must be going mad. I didn't mean to frighten you. I would never hurt you. Please believe that.'

He nodded. 'You're not very well. It's going to be OK. I'm going to get Ruth now.' He hesitated. 'Could you get to the cottage if I help you?'

Jenny shook her head. 'Adam, I'm so very tired.'

Adam leant forward and touched her hand. 'You stay there, Jenny. I won't be long.'

He turned and started to sprint along the path that curled round towards the cottage and his mother. At the bend he slowed to catch his breath. Behind him, he heard the sound of disturbed birds rising noisily from the water, breaking the silence. He turned. Jenny had got up and put on her heavy coat. She was wading purposefully into the water, flowing in fast and black on the incoming tide.

'No!' Adam screamed, as he started to run back, his legs pumping, his breath catching painfully in his chest. 'No, Jenny, no, no, no.'

TWO

August 2005

Rosie lies between us, asleep, fat little bottom in the air; dimpled feet upturned like the inside of pink shells. She is wedged hotly between Tom and me, her face against Tom's arm. Their breath rises and falls in the same shallow rhythm. Asleep, Rosie still looks like a baby; dark curls stuck to her head, cheeks flushed. I have to stop myself putting my lips to those soft cheeks.

Tom is half turned towards us, one hand under his head, the other hand on his thigh, his fingers splayed outwards as if to protect Rosie. His face is buried in the pillow, his short hair sticks up, his face damp from the heat of all our bodies in one bed on a close summer night.

His bare arms and chest are brown and broad. His skin shines with health. He is very fit.

The window is open to catch every breath of wind and I watch him in the yellow light of a street lamp, my body limp with wanting him, with the urge constantly to touch him. I love these snatched moments, these still nights of watching him sleep. I store these nights against the time when he will disappear again.

6

It is the still hour between night and dawn when London stops briefly and in the silence of the dark I can kid myself that I can hear the distant noise of the sea and the seagulls screaming into a new day.

It is not homesickness, but the luxury of happiness. The knowledge that despite living in a city, I have a life here with the man I love. In a house that fits round us and holds all the people I need to be content, to do the job I love. It is not a perfect happiness because that would be impossible. There are these endless leave-takings which interrupt our lives. I never know where Tom is or when he will be home. These are the shadows.

I must have fallen asleep because when I wake the birds are singing and sunlight is pouring through the open window. I hear Flo slowly going up the second flight of stairs to the workroom on the top floor. What a wonderful day it was when she joined us. She will be checking the work schedules for Monday. In a while she will come in with tea for us and exclaim over Rosie being in our bed again.

I stretch contentedly and then reach over Rosie and rub my fingertip lightly over the surface of Tom's arm. It is as smooth as a roll of silk. My hair falls over Rosie's face and tickles Tom and they both stir.

He yawns, opens one eye and seeing me watching him smiles sleepily and turns on his back. He is unconsciously graceful in his movements. He reminds me of a cat.

He turns to Rosie leaning against him and brushes her hair away from her hot little face. He looks at me suddenly, his eyes intensely blue. It is a rare unguarded moment that shakes me with his vulnerability.

I have always supposed our love to be unequal. Tom is everything to me. I am important, but not the whole for him. In this moment I see his raw exposed love for Rosie and me.

I move towards him and he pulls me over Rosie, burying his head in my hair.

Rosie is instantly awake and laughing. 'Me! Me! Dada!'

Tom puts out his arm and scoops her to us, making her squeal.

Flo knocks on the door. 'Tea?' she calls.

We fly apart and sit up. 'Yes, please. Come in!'

Flo comes in carrying a tea tray. She makes a pretend surprise face at Rosie. 'What are you doing there, young lady?'

Tom would leap out of bed, but he has no clothes on. 'Flo, I wish you wouldn't wait on us. It makes me inordinately guilty.'

'Wisht your noise,' Flo says cheerfully. 'I like the kitchen to myself on Sunday mornings, as you well know.' She puts the tray down and holds out her hand to Rosie. 'Danielle is bringing back a present from Paris for a good little girl who eats up all her breakfast.'

Rosie does not want to leave us or the warmth of the bed. 'Ellie coming home?'

'Tomorrow. Come on, darling, let Mummy and Daddy get dressed, then you can all go out to the park.'

That does the trick. Rosie climbs over us and toddles out with Flo, who shuts the door on us. We drink our tea but we don't get dressed. Tom pulls my nightshirt over my head in a practised sweep and we make love with the intensity of knowing we have only seventy-two hours left together before his leave ends.

I bury my nose in his skin and breathe in his smell. His muscular body emanates a faint edge of danger. He has this sexy trick of trying to keep his eyes open all the time he makes love. His eyes become like purple darting fireflies before they roll back and he explodes. The thrill is his wanting to see me, my face, as he climaxes. When we are out and I see women staring, I think with astonishment, *He's mine. He's mine. He's really mine.*

He is holding me so tight against him he is hurting me. 'Tom,' I whisper. 'I can't breathe.'

He lets me go, alarmed. 'Sorry, I'm like a bear, I don't know my own strength.'

'I like it,' I say softly, moving to him again. And I do like it. I love the feeling of precariousness in the coiled power of his body; his constant alertness that lies just below the surface, like a second skin. He is unable to switch off totally when he isn't working or in danger.

One night we were both asleep and were woken by a noise. In a swift, unnerving movement Tom was out of bed and across the room silently as a shadow. He slid open a drawer, took something out and crept across the landing. I sat up and froze at his catlike stealth. I watched as he leapt forward and pounced. I heard a scream, snapped on the bedside light and ran to the door.

Tom had someone in a headlock in the dark kitchen. The man was making grunting noises of fear and pain, but it was Danielle who had screamed. She and a boyfriend had come in from the other side of the house to look for coffee. They were both pretty drunk. The man fled down the stairs and out of the front door at record speed. Tom, furious, rounded on Danielle for being so stupidly irresponsible and creeping around in the dark.

I knew Tom's anger was not entirely directed at her but at himself too. He could have seriously hurt the man. Danielle was equally furious and embarrassed. From that day on the door between our flats was kept locked at night. Tom and Danielle did not speak for three days and then they made up for my sake.

That was the only time I had seen the trained and aggressive side of Tom. It adds a sexual frisson to my feelings for him. Sometimes, in the days before he leaves us again he can turn into a withdrawn stranger and as we grow closer I realise how little I know of his other life.

I watch Tom wheel Rosie across the road towards the park from my workroom at the top of the house. I hate him out of my sight but I am waiting for a phone call from Danielle who is in Paris. Flo could perfectly well take the call but I know that Danielle thinks that I don't take work seriously when Tom is home and it's untrue.

Below me in the kitchen I can hear Flo singing as she moves about, making Sunday lunch. I wander about picking things up and putting them down again, squashing a faint ennui. I start to sketch in a desultory fashion, then, restless, I get up and go to the window.

The pavement is glittery and rain-washed way down below me. It has cooled the air and I can almost smell the wet earth rising up from the garden.

I look right towards the end of the empty road where Tom and Rosie had been a moment ago and panic grips me. I turn and run down the stairs, calling out to Flo that I am going to the park. I wrench open the front door and run down the wide road, cross when the traffic clears and bolt through the park gates.

I make for the pond and when I spot them both feeding ducks I slow down and bend over to get my breath. They are fine. There they are; a large man and a small child, heads together, throwing bread in an arc to a swirling, greedy mass of ducks.

I stand watching them. Rosie feels my presence first. She turns and cries 'Mamma!' and squeals for joy.

Tom laughs. 'You've absconded, how lovely.'

As we throw bread together, Tom says, 'Life here with you and Rosie makes me wonder why on earth I am not a civilian, you know.'

'You!' I laugh at the thought. 'Oh yes! I can just imagine you catching the tube in the rush hour every morning in a suit.'

'Well, it will come to that, I expect, even if I stay in the army. I will get a paunch and have a desk job with the MOD . . .'

Rosie, tired of throwing bread, climbs back into her pushchair and watches the ducks diving. She shakes with laughter at their waggling tails and claps her hands together.

Tom bends to kiss her. 'What a happy little soul you are, Rosie Holland.'

We turn and walk slowly back to the gates arm in arm. A damp little wind brings the pungent scent of wet earth again. It is only August, but I am suddenly reminded of autumn and the end of summer, and I shiver.

Tom pulls me towards him. 'Sometimes, on peaceful family Sundays like this, I wonder what the hell I am doing with my life, Jen. Chasing what?'

I am amused and cynical because I know him so well. 'Family Sundays on a regular basis would bore you absolutely rigid. You'd prowl around like a leopard, driving us all mad.'

Tom grins down at me. 'Talking about predatory, it's been a great leave with Danielle in Paris.'

I sigh. 'That's unkind and she's home tomorrow. I wish you'd try to get on better. You both have to challenge each other all the time. It's become a habit.'

When we get in Flo has done everything and I feel guilty. I wish she wouldn't do so much for us.

'I would have set the table . . .'

'Here we go.' Tom is pouring generous gins.

'My dear girl, every Sunday we have the same conversation. It's not a chore. I *love* cooking Sunday lunch.'

'Did Danielle ring?'

11

'Yes. She's sold everything except those long linen dresses; too long for Parisians, apparently.'

'Damn. She was right then. I'll have to try them up north. Did she sound OK?'

'She sounded as if she was in the middle of a party,' Flo says diplomatically.

'That makes a change then.' Tom lifts Rosie into her high chair.

Annoyed, I defend Danielle. 'She has no family. There's only Flo and me. Don't you see? We are *smug marrieds* to her and when you get pompous you just reinforce her prejudices. You make her worse. Please don't judge her.'

Tom immediately apologises. 'Sorry, Jen. You're right. I catch myself doing it. It's just that she seems to get more promiscuous the older she gets. I do think the way she behaves is irresponsible. I know she has her own flat and what she does with her life is up to her, but I don't have to like it.'

Flo turns from the oven. 'Danielle does have sudden bouts of promiscuity, Tom, and I have talked to her about it because I worry about her safety too. You have to realise it is all about low self-esteem. I know nothing about her childhood, but something happened there. Try to be kind, darling.'

I fill Rosie's little bowl with food and hand it to him. He places it in front of her and cuts it into tiny pieces.

'Now I feel like a pig. Danielle's such a head-tossing sultry beauty that it's difficult to believe she's promiscuous because she lacks self-worth and not because she just likes sex.'

Rosie lifts her spoon and bangs it in the gravy.

'No!' we all say together and Rosie, stunned to hear an almost unknown word, stops, plastic spoon in mid air.

That afternoon we leave Rosie with Flo and go to a gallery opening and then ice skating. After a Chinese meal that Tom insists on, we stumble home.

Tom has drunk too much. 'I'm going to be dry for a long time, darling.'

'Good thing too,' I mutter, heaving him up the steps and getting the key in the door with difficulty. We stumble up the stairs and Tom wants to go in to see Rosie.

'Don't wake her, Tom. I'd like her to sleep in her own bed tonight.'

He watches her for a long time. He seems suddenly sober. 'You don't realise how much you'll change when you have a child. The thought of anything happening to Rosie is . . . unthinkable. I feel so protective of you both. I don't take either of you for granted, ever. When I'm somewhere grim, I think of you and know you're both somewhere warm and safe. *My mainstay*. Without you, I couldn't do the job I do without becoming bleak and hardened.'

We wrap our arms round each other and watch our child sleep. I want to weep because in forty-eight hours he will have flown away again, and the house will be quieter and emptier, and I will have this sick feeling in the pit of my stomach until he phones or a letter arrives without a post-mark and I know he is safe *somewhere* and I can begin to count the days until he comes home again.

THREE

February 2006
When Bea got in from shopping the house was empty and she found a note from James on the kitchen table.

> *Darling, Flo rang from the London house. She is worried about Jenny who seems to have gone missing. Apparently, Jenny met Ruth Freidman again after all this time. Bizarre. Ruth is now on holiday in Cornwall and I have gone down to that creek house at St Minyon to see if they are both there. Try not to worry. I'm sure Jenny must be making her way home. J. x*

Bea's mouth went dry. She picked up the phone immediately and rang Flo. An Asian girl answered. Both Florence and Danielle were with a VIP client at the moment. Could she take a message?

'Would you just say that Jenny's mother rang? If Flo could get in touch as soon as she can, I'd be grateful.'

'Of course. I will tell her.'

Bea went out into the garden still holding the phone. There was a cold east wind and the sea below her glinted fierce and navy-blue. She paced up and down the terrace among the wilted pot plants, a knot growing in her stomach with a chill premonition of disaster.

She turned and looked back at the house and the drive curling round to the gate. *Ruth.* Bea remembered clearly a thin child with fair plaits rounding the corner of the house, her small pale face anxiously searching for Jenny.

Ruth walking up the hill from Downalong each Sunday, desperate for an escape from home and a welcome here.

Bea looked up at the attic window on the right of the house, which had been Jenny's bedroom. She could almost hear the giggles emanating out into the garden with the sound of the seagulls. *Jenny and Ruth. Ruth and Jenny.* The two of them had raced about together for all those years of childhood like odd little twins and then whoosh, Ruth was gone, and how Jenny had grieved.

Bea went inside again and into James's study. She saw that his medical bag was missing.

FOUR

August 2005

Tom wakes with a start. His heart is thumping loudly in the silent house as if he's had a nightmare. If he has, he can't remember it. He turns on his back, sure there is something, some small niggling warning he should recapture from sleep, but he can't conjure it up.

He gets out of bed and pulls on his bathrobe. He goes to the uncurtained window and looks out. It's almost dawn and he watches the pink tinge grow behind the rooftops. He turns back to the bed and looks at Jenny sleeping. He feels such an overpowering sense of love and fear flood through him that he catches his breath.

He moves out of the room and across the landing, flinging the shadows away, swearing at these moods that always come on the last days of his leave. Rosie is curled like a dormouse in her cot, the same wiry hair as her mother, the same way of sleeping, a small clone. He smiles and tucks in her arms, carefully pulls up the covers over her plump little body. Rosie. Flesh of his flesh.

He shivers. The shadows in the room creep nearer, encroach from all sides. He can't turn and face them because

16

he doesn't know from where the most danger comes.

He leaves the room, goes into the sitting room and sits in his battered leather armchair. He loves this house. This marvellous, lived-in Victorian house with its high ceilings and huge casement windows. He loves everything about his life except returning to this nasty little war he is unsure he still believes in. He has to cull these feelings; kill them with one blow before they take hold. He has younger, less experienced soldiers under him, nineteen-year-old boys who rely on him. It's the life he's chosen. He has no right to maverick thoughts, dread or self-pity.

Impatient with himself, he gets up to pour himself a brandy. He'll sit and listen to the silent house move and breathe and creak around him. He'll absorb into himself from the shadows of night the hub of Jenny's busy days. The constant coming and going and chatter and giggles; the sound of the phone or doorbell; the noise of his daughter's small footsteps on the polished floor; the touch of Jenny's hand as she passes him clutching rolls of coloured material, turning back to smile at him, her face alive with love. All these things are the routine of her days when he's away; her enclosed, safe, female world.

Marriage has made everything harder. There's so much more to lose, risks become calculated, less instinctive. It's hard not to grow softer, to lose your edge. He swallows the brandy quickly. *Stop thinking.*

He falls asleep in the armchair and dreams again. Dreams he's getting off a plane in Northern Ireland, or Bosnia, or Iraq. It's pouring with rain and his heart is heavy with the loss of something . . .

There's something he should remember but it dances out of reach, just beyond memory. All he can feel is the icy night rain coming in on a wind that chills him to the bone.

He turns to look at the young soldiers following him off

17

the plane. They shimmer in the heat blasts of the plane warming up behind them. They have a dreamlike quality as they float towards him and he realises with sudden clarity that time as he knows it does not exist. These soldiers, he himself, are shimmering in some timeless zone. They are the soldiers of yesterday and the soldiers of tomorrow. They are smiling, flirting with adventure, dancing with death. They do not understand it will never end, these brutal little wars against an unseen enemy. There they stride with their eager, innocent smiles and their new, squeaky boots and heavy packs, and he wants to shout them a warning. We'll never win. It will just go on and on and on.

Yet, as he moves towards them he sees his own younger face among them, determined and alight with challenge. They move, laughing, through him as he stands facing them on the tarmac and he realises that they cannot see him for he is not there. He does not exist. His time has been and gone.

With relief he wakes. It is morning. He is in England. Sunlight shines across the polished floor. He laughs with relief. Where should he take Jenny and Rosie on this precious last full day of his leave?

FIVE

It was February and the neglected garden was full snowdrops and purple and yellow crocuses. Winter jasmine blossomed in a wave against the fence. Before I left to catch the train I went downstairs and gathered little bunches of snowdrops and dotted them about the rooms as if to leave a shadow of myself in the house. They looked like delicate ballet dancers bunched in white clumps against the stained-glass window on the landing, but they would all be faded and brown by the time I got back.

I was putting off the moment of leaving the house. I did not want to shut the front door behind me and find myself on the outside in the crisp cold air. I felt an irrational dread that something might happen to those left in the house or the high-ceilinged rooms would vaporise behind me.

I sat in Tom's leather armchair and let the sound of the girls' voices and laughter on the cutting-room floor above me filter down. I listened to Flo's deep, soft voice on the telephone. I thought guiltily of how much Danielle had taken on these past few weeks and how it should be a small thing for me to make good the appointments she had set-up for me in Birmingham.

I heard the taxi outside and I got out of the chair and went downstairs. I gathered my bags from the hall and called up to Flo that I was leaving. She came down the attic stairs and stood on the first-floor landing looking down at me. I swallowed the urge to drop my bags and rush back up the stairs and admit that I had changed my mind and Birmingham was the last place on earth I wanted to go on my own.

Something must have shown in my face because Flo started to come down the last flight of stairs to me. 'It's not too late, lovey. Why don't you give Birmingham a miss? Wait until Danielle gets back. A week is not going to make a great deal of difference. I can reschedule your appointments. Danielle will understand.'

I shook my head and lied, 'I'm OK, honestly. I must go today, Flo. Danielle has set up these meetings and I don't want to let her down, it wouldn't be fair.'

Flo sighed and kissed my cheek. 'All right, Jen. I'll ring you tonight.'

I walked down the steps and into the waiting taxi. I waved and Flo watched me out of sight.

The traffic was horrendous and I had left myself short of time. As I hurried along the platform for the Birmingham train a figure ahead of me reminded me of someone. It was the small movement of her head as she walked, the straight back. I had a bewildering lurch of déjà vu; a sliver of memory just beyond reach.

I climbed into an almost empty first class carriage and found a seat. The silence was wonderful. I could do some paperwork.

All of a sudden it came to me who the woman walking ahead of me had reminded me of from behind: *Ruth Freidman*, my best friend at school. We had been inseparable as children. She had practically lived at our house in St Ives. She was one of those girls who was good at everything. She needed to be because she had older parents who were cold and critical of everything she did, and very strict. She was never allowed to take friends home and there had been a myriad rules she must not break. It had made her different, made her stand out from the rest of us.

Bea had instinctively scooped her up into our large noisy family, and away from home, when she was with us, Ruth seemed to blossom. She had been fun and clever. I had loved her very much, but I knew, even as a child, that once she left home she would never return. She was loyal. She never really spoke about her awful parents; she just seemed to accept how they were.

The train gathered speed into the suburbs. I had not thought of Ruth for years and it was strange that a glimpse of a woman's head could trigger memories that flooded back, sweet and painful. I remembered her saying, 'I'm *never* going to get married, Jen. Do you know that my parents have lived in Cornwall all their lives and they've never been *anywhere*? They have no curiosity about *anything* or *anyone*. It's *incredible*. I'm going to fly, free as a bird . . .'

I wondered if she did fly free. Inexplicably, a few months later, as we were both about to sit our A levels, her father, a bank manager, accepted a posting to Toronto and the family packed up in extraordinary haste and in weeks they were gone. *Vanished*. Leaving us all with open mouths.

It had made no sense to pull Ruth out of school just before important exams. It was weird, especially as her parents were always so pushy and expectant about Ruth's academic progress. Bea, anxious that something was wrong, had gone round to see Ruth's parents. She offered to have Ruth to live with us until after her A levels, but her parents had been coldly determined that Ruth was to go with them and take her exams later at the International School in Toronto.

The strangest thing of all was Ruth's odd, robot-like

compliance. She put up no fight to stay at all. When I begged and pleaded with her to remain with us, she eventually became angry. It was the only time she turned on me and told me to mind my own bloody business.

What stung me cruelly was that she left her life and me firmly behind her without as much as a backward glance. She never wrote to me once. We had been inseparable and yet I could be instantly discarded for her new life. Ruth had made a mistake with the box number and all my letters were returned. It took years for the hurt and sense of loss to leave me.

I looked out of the window at the battered little gardens of terraced houses. What did Ruth do with her life? What had happened to her? She had always been a little mysterious and prone to mood swings. It was not surprising with the parents she had, but I wondered, when she left without a backward glance, if I had really known her at all.

I stared at my shadowy reflection in the window. Odd how memory could be jogged by such a frail thing as a woman's back.

Someone hovered near my seat, and then threw their coat on to the rack above me. I hastily fanned out my newspaper. There were plenty of seats elsewhere. I looked up, annoyed, into the smiling face of an elegant blonde woman.

'Jenny Brown! I thought it must be you. No one else could wear outrageous clothes as you do and look absolutely stunning, and your hair is *exactly* the same. It had to be you!'

I stared up at her, startled. Ruth Freidman stood before me. I don't think I would have recognised her immediately, but her voice and laugh had not changed.

'Ruth! Oh my God. I followed the back of your head walking to the train. I just thought it was someone who reminded me of you from the back.'

I was prattling and our eyes met and we both laughed as she sat down opposite me.

'You walked past the carriage window, Jenny. I only caught a glimpse but I was suddenly so sure it must be you and it is.'

Amazed, we stared at each other, fourteen years on, examined the lines and shadows that made up our adult faces. Her tall, athletic body was still slim and effortlessly graceful, but now she had style, was immaculately groomed. Long gone were the thin plaits. Her face was carefully made up, her hair beautifully blonde and expensively cut.

How do I look to her? I wondered, bemoaning, as always, my own small compact body and dark unruly hair that I still couldn't control. I wasn't wearing any make-up and I was sure I had aged more than she had.

I said suddenly, surprising myself, perhaps because it had been on my mind a moment ago, 'You just vanished, Ruth. You just disappeared off the face of the earth. You never wrote to me. We never heard from you again. It was as if you had died.'

A flicker of something crossed Ruth's face, then she shrugged in a movement I remembered. 'I . . . just thought it was best. Look, here comes the coffee, wonderful.'

We fiddled with our small cartons of milk.

'What are you doing on a train to Birmingham, Jenny? Did you get to art college? If I remember rightly you wanted masses of children, like Bea?'

She laughed, taking in my wedding ring. I said, feeling sick and playing for time, 'Which question do I answer first? I'm on a train to Birmingham because I'm working. Yes, I went to Central St Martin's.'

'Did you get your scholarship?'

'Yes. I was lucky.'

'Lucky? I don't think so! You were incredibly talented. So what are you doing now?'

Ruth's terrier-like persistence had not changed. 'I have a

partnership with a French designer, Danielle Sabot. We teamed together for the Royal Society of Arts Bursary Scheme and won. Because of that show, one of the London stores asked us to do some designs for them and it all sort of took off from there. Now we design for various companies here, and in France and Italy. Usually, Danielle does Birmingham. She's a better businesswoman than me, but when she's abroad it's my job.'

'You always were modest. I knew you'd be successful, Jenny. Well done you.'

'So, what about you, Ruth?' I said quickly. 'What did you do in Toronto? When did you come back to England?'

'Hey, not me yet!' Ruth said, equally quickly. 'What about the rest of your life? It can't be all work.'

I looked out of the window as if I could escape. Outside, Lego houses flashed by back to back: tiny gardens, pin-board people going about their days, keeping to their own territories; life rolling inexorably on.

I thought I'd kept my face expressionless but something must have shown because Ruth tentatively put out her hand and touched mine. 'I'm sorry, Jenny. It's none of my business, is it?'

I stared at the slim hand lying near my own. The hand moved and gently placed itself over mine on the table. Grief shifted inside me. I stared out at the fields. Dark, wet earth being ploughed, seagulls wheeling behind the tractor. I said, for a lie was easier, like telling someone else's story, 'My husband was killed in a road accident.' My voice sounded as if it were coming down a long echoing tunnel.

Easier to say it fast, like that. Ruth would not remember or connect those awful headlines and photographs with me.

Her fingers curled round mine and held them. Her voice was shocked. 'Oh, Jenny. Oh, God. I'm so, so sorry. When? How long ago?'

'In August.'

'Only six months ago. I was in Israel. I don't know what to say. I'm so sorry, please forgive me and my insistent prying.'

The small fluttering movement of Ruth's hands on mine triggered a warmth inside me that I thought had gone for good. 'Tell me about your life, Ruth. Tell me about you. How long were you in Canada? When did you come home?'

Ruth searched my face anxiously, wanting to offer me comfort, but seeing my expression she let go of my fingers and leant back in her seat. She closed her eyes for a second. 'I never went to Canada.' Her face was closing, just as mine had done a moment ago.

I stared at her stupidly. 'What on earth do you mean, you didn't go?'

Ruth didn't answer.

'You gave us a forwarding address, even if it was the wrong box number. Your father had a job in Toronto, didn't he?'

Ruth looked up and her face was bleak and expressionless, reminding me of the child she had been. There was bitterness in her voice clear to hear. 'I mean my parents went. I didn't. I was sent to live with an aunt on Arran. I did my A levels by post. I never got to any university.'

I stared at her. 'I don't understand . . .'

'They wanted to be rid of me.'

I looked at her, shocked. 'What do you mean?'

Ruth smiled grimly. 'As you know, my parents had an absolute terror of scandal and were obsessed by what people thought of them. Do you remember that last Christmas before I left?'

I nodded. 'I was in hospital having my appendix out.'

'Yes. Well, I lied to my parents and said that we were both going to a party together. I went on my own and I got drunk and missed my lift home. I was eventually taken home by

25

someone else's father, still far from sober. Unfortunately, he happened to be a clerk in my father's bank.'

She paused and took a deep breath. In her house drink was the devil's brew. 'My father went into a blind fury when he saw me. He told me, before I even had time to sober up, that he and my mother were not my biological parents. That I had been adopted. It was funny, really. My mother stood in front of me muttering darkly, *Blood will out. Blood will out*, like a demented Lady Macbeth.'

I stared at her, horrified.

'A few weeks later my father took a job he previously had no intention of taking and I was deported as fast as humanly possible to the outer regions.'

'I can't believe this. I was your best friend. Why on earth didn't you tell me?'

'Because my father was paranoid and my mother hysterical about anyone knowing what they were going to do. I begged to stay and do my A levels with you. I knew Bea had come round. My father was very threatening and I was scared of him.'

'You should have run away and come and told us everything. Bea and James could have stopped them sending you away. You should have confided in me.'

Ruth leant towards me. 'It's hard to explain now, but the stuffing went out of me. My parents waited seventeen years to tell me that they were not my real parents. They went on and on about how they had saved me from a terrible background. I felt defeated by them, and utterly wicked and valueless.'

'They really were dreadful people,' I said angrily. 'I should have realised you were in deep trouble, I must have been blind.'

'I hid my feelings from everyone. I think I was in shock. I didn't want Bea – any of you – to know I was adopted. It seemed suddenly shameful. Later, of course, I was very relieved I did *not* have the same blood as them.' She met my eyes. 'Truly, I was afraid that you would all think less of me. I needed to remember a place and people where I was loved, *your house*. I needed that to take away with me.'

I closed my eyes and shivered at the random cruelty of life. 'You should have trusted us, known us better. All you had to do was pack your bag and walk across to our house.'

I paused. It did not explain why she had never written. Had she believed she deserved to lose us?

Ruth studied the backs of her hands. 'I've had no contact with my parents for fourteen years. They shipped me out to that Scottish island and they never wrote or got in touch with me again. I haven't heard from them since the day they put me on the ferry at Glasgow and turned their backs. I lived with them for seventeen years and for them I simply ceased to exist. As far as I know they are still in Canada. Anyway . . .'

'They were wicked, cruel people.'

Ruth put her chin in her hand and smiled at me. 'How I loved your warm, chaotic family. How I *envied* you. I don't think I would have survived childhood without your family. I always felt included. It was fun. I could be a child in your house. I always thought of my house as somewhere time stood still; a place with the slow, heavy ticking of a clock that marked the endlessness of my childhood.'

I stared at her. I had taken my childhood completely for granted. 'It's unforgivable that your parents could just abandon you. What happened to you? How did you manage?'

'I managed because of the wonderful aunt on Arran who took me in. She was amazing. Do you know, Jenny, I had more love and support in my years with her than I had in all my childhood with my parents.'

'Could you study on Arran, then?'

'For a while, by correspondence. Then I commuted to the mainland to study. Eventually, I had to leave the island to work and my aunt came with me. I got a job in a big department store in Glasgow, found I was good at selling, became a buyer, got ambitious, did a business degree and began to run my own departments. I also lecture on business management on a freelance basis at conventions. A few years ago I moved from Glasgow and joined the Fayad group in Birmingham.' She laughed and threw her arms wide. 'That's my story!'

I smiled at her. 'Ruth, you're amazing.'

'No, but my aunt was. She was like your mother. Like Bea. She gave me a sense of self-worth and motivated me to succeed, despite everything. She died a few years ago and I still miss her.'

We were both silent. I looked at Ruth's hand. 'You're married?'

'Yes. He's a good and lovely man, very kind . . .'

Kind is a giveaway line. Kind is a word you use instead of love.

As if reading my thoughts, Ruth said, 'Sometimes I suspect my parents might have been right. I'm not always a nice person. I'm driven. I don't make enough time for the people I should cherish.' She fiddled with her wedding ring. 'Do you have children?'

I shook my head and dug my nails hard into one hand under the table.

'God, I'm sorry,' Ruth said suddenly. 'Here I am, prattling on about my life when it's nothing compared with what you're going through at the moment, Jenny.'

'It helps to talk of other things. Do you have children?'

Her whole face lit up. 'Yes. Just one. His name is Adam.'

The sun shone on the dirty train window in a thin ray touching our heads. It turned Ruth's hair gold and reminded me of our schooldays long gone, hiding in a corner of the common room trying to avoid games in the bitterly cold winds that blew straight in from the sea and swept over the playing fields freezing us solid. Light from the coloured panes used to slant down on to the window seat where we crouched, ears straining for a nun's footsteps coming our way.

'Oh!' Ruth jumped up suddenly. 'I get off at the next stop to meet Adam on his way home from school. We both change trains here. We don't often coincide, so it's nice. We live out in the suburbs.'

She was tearing off a used envelope and writing down her address and telephone number. 'My surname is now Hallam. Call me tomorrow, Jenny. Come and see us or I'll meet you somewhere central. I can probably give you some contacts too. Which hotel are you staying in?'

I told her and gave her my card as she gathered her things together. 'You shouldn't be alone in a strange city, you should have company.' She touched my face lightly. 'It's so good to see you again. You never make friends in the same way as when you're very young, when you grow up together, do you?'

'No,' I said. 'I don't think you do.'

I put out my hand and Ruth clasped it. We didn't say goodbye. It felt too final. As she moved away down the carriage I felt a loss at her leaving. I didn't want the numbness of months to wear off, I needed its protection. Her tall figure moved out of the carriage and I turned to the window as the train slowed and stopped.

A lone boy was standing on the platform amid a sea of saris scanning the opening doors of the carriages. He turned my way. My heart seemed to stop beating, so familiar, so beloved were his features and the way he casually flicked his hair away from his eyes. The way he held his head, slightly to the side. The way he moved, darting forward suddenly to Ruth emerging on to the platform, his face lighting up.

'Tom! Tom!' I cried out his name in shock and people turned and stared. The train started to shunt, move slowly forward in slow motion through glass. I saw Ruth run and hug the boy to her. She turned to catch a glimpse of me and waved wildly.

I pressed my face to the window to keep them in sight for as long as possible. Then they were gone, behind me. The train carried me onwards alone, towards Birmingham. I got up from my seat and stumbled into the corridor. My breath came in sharp, painful bursts.

Tom. A lament started deep inside me. I felt the tears streaming down my face. Seeing that familiar face was like glimpsing my love again. I cried out in anguish. I did not understand. I did not understand.

I looked down and saw I still held the envelope with Ruth's address and telephone number on it. I screwed it up violently and threw it away from me down the corridor. I wanted to scream, and I moved quickly into the lavatory.

After a while someone knocked and asked anxiously if I was all right. With a great effort of will I tried to pull myself together. I ran cold water over my face, pulled a comb through my hair, managed to put on some lipstick. My hands shook. I stared at my wild, pale reflection in the mirror. Was I going mad? Did something of Tom live on, but not with me? *With Ruth?*

I felt as if a pane of glass were shattering into a thousand pieces inside me. Then all feeling drained away. Numbness returned. I unlocked the door and moved back into the corridor.

The crumpled envelope still lay discarded on the floor. I bent and picked it up, smoothed it out. *Ruth Hallam.* I opened my bag and unzipped the small pocket that held the photos of Tom and Rosie. I placed the envelope carefully beside them, zipped the pocket shut and closed my bag. It was all I had left.

I looked out of the window. The train was coming into the station. People were pushing past me to get to the door. Everyone had reached their destination. *Ruth has a husband and that boy. She has a home life waiting where life goes on. Where life goes on.*

SIX

I walk away from the noise of the party and lean against the huge trunk of a horse-chestnut tree. Its red blooms stand upright among the green foliage. It is like standing under an exotic, rustling chandelier.

The party is lavish, a PR exercise thrown by Justin, a designer friend Danielle and I had been at St Martin's with. His clothes are a bit over the top, but celebrities and models flock to him for their competitive, reckless little red carpet numbers. He certainly has beautiful women here in abundance.

I watch Danielle networking. She looks like a celebrity herself, a perfect advertisement for our clothes. She is wearing poppy-red chiffon. I designed the dress especially for her. It was deceptively simple, low-cut with a straight silk bodice with floating chiffon panels sewn into the skirt. It looks as if she is wearing a scarlet hanky. Her dark colouring and long legs make her resemble an exotic butterfly.

I smile as I watch her. We need to come to parties like this, to be seen, and she is brilliant at networking. I am better at watching a party from a distance. I can spot emerging trends, get an instinct for the next fashion statement, and it helps to observe how women walk and sit in relation to the clothes they are wearing.

I can see a tall fair man standing with a bevy of women in front of the marquee. He stands like a fish out of water in this showy, arty-farty fashion crowd. He keeps throwing his hair back from his eyes and glancing sideways, as if seeking escape or at least another male. As the place is heaving with girly boys, gay or camp, I can perfectly understand why the women are dive-bombing him like noisy seagulls swooping at their prey, but it's funny to watch.

I see Danielle looking for me, and ease myself away from the tree and walk back across the grass towards the noise and laughter. Danielle made me a classic white dress, cut exquisitely, as only she can, with narrow gold edging. I am brown from a week in Cornwall and I feel cool, simple and restrained.

Danielle had made me swear that I would not embellish it in any way and spoil the effect. It was hard, as I love colour and eccentric clothes, but this feeling of being almost invisible suits my mood perfectly tonight. I am secretly worrying about our premises, which have become too small, and the fact that although we are getting plenty of commissions we do not seem able to balance our books.

As I pass the group with the tall man I see he is looking at me. I smile and walk on. I am not about to become a member of his fan club.

I join Danielle and a group of friends, and we balance plates and drinks, perching on tiny wrought-iron chairs. Maisie Hill, a model Justin and Danielle and I design for, walks over to join us with the tall man in tow.

'Hi, you guys. This is Tom Holland, an army friend of my brother's. I invited them both to the party but Damien's suddenly got posted off somewhere so he had to come on his own, poor thing. Tom, that's Danielle, there. Jenny, Claire,

Joseph, Milly, and Prue. I'll be back in a sec. I've just got to check on the caterers for Justin.'

The man sits down gingerly on a tiny chair, with his plate of food and grins warily at everyone. Danielle and the other women focus on him relentlessly. He has a stillness about him; an economy of movement and a faint air of amused detachment as if he knows he is the interest of the moment, but it will quickly pass because he comes from a different world.

I notice the tightness of his thighs as he balances on the silly chair and the muscles in his arms where he has rolled up his sleeves a little way.

I like Damien, Maisie's brother. He often comes to these parties. She had been worried sick when the Bosnian war blew up and he had been sent with the first wave to monitor the atrocities with the UN.

Knowing even one soldier had changed how we all read the papers and watched the news. I wonder if this man, Tom, had been with Damien out there. How frivolous we must all seem. Danielle is eyeing him under a curtain of glossy black hair. *Oh, leave him alone, Elle. Don't bed and dump this one. He won't know what's hit him.*

When I look up he is watching me. His eyes are extraordinary, purple-flecked and iridescent. They hold mine intently, intimately, as if he is touching me. The blood rushes hotly to the surface of my skin. It is like being hit by a bus.

Maisie calls out to me and I leap up gratefully and walk over the grass. 'For fuck's sake, Jenny, don't just sit there dumb as a daisy. That poor guy has been dying to talk to you all evening.'

I stare at her and fly to the loo, and when I come out Tom Holland is leaning gracefully against a silver birch. I stop in front of him.

'Hi,' he says.

'Hi,' I say imaginatively.

'I'm sorry if it seems as if I'm following you. It's because you are illusive.'

'Am I?'

'Like a ghost. Flitting mysteriously in the distance but never stopping for a proper glimpse.' His laugh is infectious.

'It's what I do at parties. Flit. In case I get caught up or trapped.'

'Very wise,' he says gravely, then adds quickly, 'Am I trapping you?'

I shake my head. We walk across the park together, away from the noise and the music towards the chestnut tree I stood under earlier.

'This is where I first saw you. A small white phantom under a canopy of green. I blinked twice but you were still there, perfectly still. So I knew you must be real.' His voice is addictive, with a lilt of a smile in it.

'I was watching the proceedings from a distance. It's how I sometimes get inspiration.'

'Well, if Maisie's clothes are anything to go by, it definitely works.'

'Maisie would look amazing in a coal sack and bottle top earrings, and I'm afraid we don't exclusively dress her.'

We walk on across the park in the growing dusk as the music and laughter drift behind us and ahead of us lights in buildings come on.

The evening is beautiful, utterly still. The heat has been caught by the day and trapped by the buildings of the city, keeping the air warm, filling the night with the smell of blossom.

I sense Tom Holland does not want to make small talk but draw in the peace of the night and we walk in a strange companionable silence, drinking in the night as if we have known each other a long time.

He looks at his watch suddenly and we turn without speaking and walk back towards the party going on uproariously ahead of us.

'I have to go, Jenny. I'm catching a plane first thing in the morning.'

'To Bosnia?' I suddenly feel bereft. I haven't asked him anything about himself. I thought there would be time.

He shakes his head. 'No, just a training trip somewhere bleak.'

We stare at each other.

'Thank you,' he says.

'What for?'

'For walking with me on a warm London evening in summer and not making small talk, and for giving me a lovely peaceful memory to take away with me.'

'You take care,' I say.

He looks down at me. 'May I ring you when I get back?'

I take my card out of my bag and give it to him. He holds on to my fingers, lifts them to his lips, then he turns and walks away, striding across the grass. My heart hammers like a trapped bird as the distance between us grows.

I call out 'Tom' before I even know I'm going to.

He turns and I run towards him. He scoops me up and turns in a circle with me. Then we just stand holding each other for a moment.

'Please take care,' I say again. I let him go and he walks quickly through the gate. This time I notice his step has a little bounce to it.

SEVEN

February 2006

'You look happy today!' Adam said, grinning at his mother as she jumped out of the train.

'How do I normally look?'

'Stressed, Mum! You're usually in your own little world of work, for at least an hour or so.'

Ruth felt a pang. So this was how she was. She bleeped the car doors open and when they were inside she said, 'It was extraordinary. I met someone on the train I haven't seen for nearly fourteen years. It was weird, Adam, we were best friends at school.'

'Cool,' Adam said. 'You recognised each other then?'

Ruth shot him a look. 'I'm not that old! Actually, Jenny looked more or less as she always did, except . . .'

She concentrated on backing out of the car space.

'Except, what?'

'She was sad. She'd lost her lovely bounce. I was stupid. I was so excited about seeing her that I didn't pick it up, just prattled on asking about her life and then she told me. Six months ago her husband was killed in a road accident.'

Adam turned to her. 'Poor woman.'

'Yes. She's in Birmingham on her own so I'm going to ring her tomorrow. I would have asked her to stay but Peter's back tonight and he's going to be tired.'

'Are we going to the airport to meet him?'

'No, he's on a later flight. He said he'd get a taxi home.'

'We are still going to Cornwall for half-term?'

'Of course we are.' Ruth concentrated on the traffic. 'How was your day?'

'OK,' Adam said. 'Is Peter coming to the cottage with us? It's more fun if I've got someone to birdwatch with.'

'I hope so, Adam, but . . .'

'I know, Mum! Like, why do I have to have workaholic parents?'

He grinned at her to take away the sting, but the familiar guilt was back. She and Peter did work long hours and Adam was on his own too much. Occasionally he brought a friend home, sometimes he went to a friend's house, but it was not the same as having someone there when he got in from school.

The irony was not lost on Ruth. Her aunt had always been the one to be there for him after school when he was small. After that, he had almost always been picked up by someone else or come home to an empty house. The difference was that until his secondary school he had been happy and had loads of friends. Now, they appeared to have dwindled to two or three ostracised loners who had been pushed together.

She thought suddenly of Peter's wistful voice. 'Wouldn't it be great to have another child in the house? I think Adam would like that too. Will you think about it, Ruth?'

Ruth didn't need to think about it. She didn't want any more children. It had taken her years to get where she was. She loved working and she had no intention of giving up. Bringing up Adam had been too hard, even with help. She never wanted to have to juggle work, a baby and guilt again.

In a few years Adam would be at university. She couldn't start all over again. She just couldn't.

Adam had taken her silence as hurt. 'I was only joking, Mum. You worry too much. Most of my friends' mothers work long hours too. It's cool.'

Yes, but most of Adam's friends' mothers worked because they had to, not because they wanted to.

Peter had not been impressed by the huge comprehensive that had been their only choice in the area. He had wanted to pay for Adam to go to a private school. Ruth had refused on the grounds she did not believe in private education. But she knew it was really about whether she and Peter stayed together long-term. If they ever split up she could not have afforded school fees on her own and it would have been cruel to have to pull Adam out of private education. Ruth was not quite so sure she would refuse again. Adam said little, but was obviously fairly miserable at school.

She drove up their leafy road of Victorian terraces and parked. For once there was an empty space outside the house. Adam leapt out and ran up the steps, unlocking the front door and leaving it open for her.

As she walked in and hung up her coat Ruth had an image of Jenny, childless, entering a house where her husband was never going to move through the rooms again. Sadness shot through her. She remembered running, screaming with laughter, with a small curly-haired girl across the sands at St Ives towards the Browns' house with its windows facing Porthmeor beach and the harbour, and her abiding image was of Jenny's happiness, her security in childhood, in life.

If this tragedy had happened to me I might have been expecting it. Even as a child, Ruth had never trusted happiness. It could be wiped off her face in an instant. She had learnt not to show it. All pleasures had to be hidden or hugged secretly to her. She would compose her face on her way down the hill from the Browns' house so that when she walked through the door of her own home her puritan parents would see no traces of joy left on it.

She composed her features into that blank expression she recognised sometimes in children in the supermarket. The closed-in, shut-off features of a child shouted at or slapped too often. Children who knew they could never do anything right and tried to melt into the shadows.

Her own parents' relief that Ruth was out of the house so often and not under their feet making dust did not prevent their jealousy of people who might bring her happiness.

Adam was making toast and humming over his bird magazines. 'Are you thinking of the woman you met on the train, Mum?' he asked Ruth suddenly.

'Yes.' Ruth sat down opposite him, and he cut his toast and Marmite and handed her a piece.

'How did you lose touch?'

'My fault. I never wrote to her when I left Cornwall for Arran. I hurt her a lot. I realised that today.'

'Only today, Mum?'

Ruth met his eyes. She had given Adam the edited version of her early life. 'I thought Jenny would forget me pretty quickly. She had three sisters and one brother. We were good friends, but she had a large family . . .'

'But friends are different,' Adam said firmly. 'Friends are people you make on your own, that are separate from family. They see you in another way. So you become different with them and it's the same for them. Friends are important.'

Ruth stared at him. You learnt new things about your children all the time. Adam was right. He was his own person, not just the person she knew, but another boy she didn't know; a person who acted in a different way when he was not with his mother.

He said now, with butter on his chin, 'Did you explain

about your parents, about Auntie Vi looking after you? About me?'

'A little. I didn't have time to tell her everything,' Ruth said carefully, as Adam watched her across the table. 'But she knew your grandparents and what they were like.'

The phone went and Adam dashed for it. It was Peter. His flight had been delayed. As Ruth listened to them chatting happily she thought with a pang, *I take Peter and the life I have here for granted.*

At seventeen you believed that your dreams might come true. At thirty you tried not to have any illusions; yet the essence of some impossible hope lived insistently on. Somewhere out there was an exciting shadowy figure who could provide all emotional and sexual succour; a soulmate. *Him*.

She did love Peter, they were good friends, but her heart did not leap at his touch. She was not in love with him. He had always known that and Ruth knew she should never have let him persuade her he could change it.

Adam handed her the phone. Ruth listened to his voice, warm and loving and glad to be coming home, and she saw in a flash of familiar angst how little it took to please or make him happy. She understood herself. Childhood had taught her she must only ever rely on herself, never let anyone hurt her again, and the result of that was her inability to commit wholly to a relationship. It was a self-destruct button. Peter loved her and Adam unconditionally. What more could she ask? What more could she *want*?

Look at Jenny, for God's sake. Look at Jenny.

EIGHT

I took a taxi to my hotel to drop off my case. I ordered coffee and a sandwich I could not eat. I got under a power shower. I let the water pour over me and I blanked my mind of all thought in order to get through the afternoon.

I walked to my first meeting. Danielle had done most of the hard selling and the buyers for the department store seemed keen to have both our designs selling on separate fashion floors. Our clothes were quite different. Danielle's work was fairly conventional and classic, the exact opposite of her character. She designed for the slightly older woman. The cut and shape of her work was stunning, with each piece having a small quirky difference that marked out her labels.

My work was mostly for the boutique and high street. I designed for the trendy fashion-conscious twenty-year-olds and my clothes were not meant to last more than a season. I did the bags and belts, the shrugs and the sandals. If I had a gift, it was for sensing what trend was coming next.

Coffee kept me going, but the afternoon seemed endless as the buyers poured through my sample books and decided on exactly what and how many different designs they wanted.

It was dark when I emerged into the street; that horrible

lonely time when all the lights have sprung on and people are hurrying home. A light rain was falling. I got a taxi to my hotel with the familiar sick remembrance of loss churning in my stomach. It felt as if a huge wave continually hovered over my head, waiting to swamp me. I wondered if the loneliness would ever turn into anything I could endure.

I kicked off my shoes as soon as I got into my room and ran a hot bath. I went to the mini bar and pulled out a small bottle of wine, switched on the six o'clock news as background and took the wine into the bathroom. I closed my eyes and soaked, closed my mind.

The wine acted like a sleeping pill. It was still early, but I climbed gratefully into bed.

Snapshots of Tom filled the dark. They seemed to surround me, come from everywhere. Tom throwing his head back, flicking his hair out of his eyes to a backdrop of sea. Tom running across a rugby field, his legs pumping, clutching the ball. Turning to look at me in the garden in London, eyes half closed in a glance that made my heart turn over. Tom in uniform, leaning against a palm tree, blinking from some hot, unknown country.

Had it been a trick of the light, an illusion on that station as I looked at Ruth's boy? For a second I had seen Tom so clearly. A younger, childlike Tom. Was it wishful thinking? The sort of boy Tom must have been before I knew him. Was it just a mirage conjured by my tired mind, like an oasis in a desert?

A frightening enervation crept over me like a shroud. Why was I here in Birmingham? What was the point when I didn't care about anything? I searched for a purpose that would give value to what I was doing and could find none as I lay under the cold hotel duvet.

After a while the telephone started to ring persistently, at intervals. I left it. I let it ring on and after a while it stopped.

43

People passed my bedroom door, laughing, talking and going down to dinner. I lay in an anonymous room, disconnected, floating.

Then I thought of Flo alone in the London house worrying about me. I switched on the bedside light and rang her. I tried to keep my voice light and cheerful. I talked business, talked up my day.

But Flo knew me too well. 'Oh, Jen, you sound so tired. Come home. It's all too soon. Just come home.'

Night came behind the curtains. Car lights passed across the windows and over the walls and ceiling, and I watched the moving lights, mesmerised by their changing patterns. The hotel became still, the traffic outside subsided.

If only I could wish myself backwards to treasure every second that I had in that life I had lost. I fell into a strange half-sleep of feverish dreams and woke early in the morning with a raging thirst. I got up dizzily to put the kettle on and then sat drinking tea until I felt better.

I saw a white envelope had been pushed under the door:

Mrs Holland, we note you are not answering your telephone and trust all is well. A Miss Florence Kingsley has rung twice this evening. A Mrs Ruth Hallam also rang more than once and appeared somewhat concerned. She asks that you return her call.

I took my tea back to bed. The boy on the platform remained absolutely clear in my head. I saw his fair hair flopping over his eyes, his profile sweet, snub-nosed, not yet entirely awkward in adolescence. Fawn anorak over navy blazer. Black trousers, blue-and-red school holdall. I saw him dart forward towards Ruth, his face lighting up.

I jumped out of bed and showered, got dressed and took the lift down to the foyer. I ordered a taxi from reception.

44

As I waited I took the crumpled envelope from the pocket of my bag and smoothed out Ruth's address.

She lived in the suburbs. Eventually the taxi turned into a wide, tree-lined road of large Victorian terraced houses. I made the driver slow down while I looked at the house numbers. When I found Ruth's house I asked him to park a little further back on the opposite side of the road. The driver impassively picked up his newspaper. I sat and waited. I did not know what I was waiting for.

At five to eight a dark man came down the steps of the house and started up his car. After a few minutes he hooted a couple of times on his horn and the boy, Adam, came flying out with his clothes askew, eating toast. Ruth appeared at the top of the steps and, smiling, waved down at them both, calling something to the boy I could not hear.

A sudden, unfathomable anger with Ruth came flying out of nowhere.

I stared at the boy with toast in his mouth. My eyes were pulled to him like a magnet. My heart hammered painfully. *I was not mistaken*. He was a small, immature version of Tom. He got into the car and he and the man waved at Ruth, then she went back inside and shut her front door.

He and Ruth have each other, I thought. *They have each other.*

The car passed my taxi and I saw the boy briefly, talking animatedly, tucking in his shirt and reaching for his seat belt. I stared after them long after they had disappeared.

The taxi driver lowered his paper. 'Are you intending to stay here all day, miss?'

'No. Take me back to the hotel, please.' I clutched my shaking hands and he gave me an odd look, then turned and drove off.

Back at the hotel I picked up my list of appointments. It was hard to focus. I could not drag my mind away from the image of the laughing boy. I had not *imagined* his likeness to Tom. I wasn't mad. It was there and blindingly obvious. How old would he be? How old?

I must concentrate on my day or I would go under. I was unsure when I last ate so I rang room service for croissants and coffee. Afterwards I felt better, picked up the phone and rang Flo. I told her I was fine and we talked briefly about the day's appointments.

My first was at nine forty-five. As the hotel was fairly central to the shopping malls I walked. It was a bright-blue-sky day. The city was busy and still smelt of last night's rain. I walked with the flow of people jostling and hurrying to work. I enjoyed a feeling of anonymity in a place I did not know.

I walked around a new expensive complex of tiny exclusive clothes shops before I went inside to gauge their approximate customer age and income. I compared their prices. I thought Danielle was probably right. They might be interested in my designs, certainly my belts and bags. I had brought a substantial cross-section of sketches and photographs and samples. I just had to make good, to get the orders for us.

The owner of the first shop was around my age and friendly but astute. Over coffee she looked through our portfolio again and ordered deftly and without hesitation. She knew exactly what would sell and kept away from Danielle's tailored and more expensive designs. 'We're a throwaway society and shops like mine obviously have to compete with the chain stores. I have to judge it finely and select clothes that will appeal to the young professionals who need to go upmarket, but still look cool. My first order will be cautious, just to see how we go, but your belts and bags . . . I'll order as many as you can give me. They'll go like hot cakes.'

I took a large order and moved out again into sunlight. As each of the trendy shops in the new mall wanted to market different fashions I also did well with Danielle's tailored designs, especially her deceptively casual summer skirts and skimpy silk T-shirts.

I had to meet a buyer for lunch in one of the big Fayad stores and I thought of Ruth. I got a taxi, as I suddenly felt faint and hot. This buyer was not the easiest and Danielle had always dealt with her. She seemed faintly annoyed that I was here and not Danielle. For a second tiredness overtook me and I was tempted to wrong-foot her by telling her why our normal routine had been shot to pieces.

After a lunch I couldn't eat, we moved round the various fashion departments that marketed our different labels. The buyer went through what had sold well and what had stayed on the rails, and I made notes.

Thankfully, she had another meeting and went off, leaving me with her assistant, who was easier to get on with. I began to feel odd and disembodied but I made myself concentrate for another hour.

She gave me a large order for my belts and bags. We were going to be pushed to deliver on time. I suddenly felt faint and dizzy again. The woman glanced at me anxiously, got me a chair and sent someone to find a glass of water. I apologised profusely and she told me there was a lot of flu about.

I sipped the water and when the dizziness passed I went to the lavatory and looked at myself in the mirror. I saw that my face was flushed and drawn. I felt feverish. I looked a hundred, like a wraith, as if my face belonged to someone else.

Someone ordered me a taxi back to the hotel. I realised my symptoms were physical, not psychosomatic, as I had a raging temperature. I rang and excused myself from the rest of my afternoon appointments. I ordered a bottle of water and some fruit juice, and I was just going to crawl into bed when there was a knock on my door.

'Thank goodness I've traced you.' Ruth, breathless, rushed in. She stopped and stared at me. 'You look terrible. Are you ill?'

'I think I might have flu.'

She felt my forehead. 'God, you're burning up. Right, you're coming straight home with me. I'm not leaving you ill in a strange hotel bedroom. I've been trying to contact you, all last night and again early this morning. You're not to argue. Let's just collect your things and get you home and into bed.'

I was not going to argue. I felt dreadful. And I wanted to see the boy again.

NINE

Ruth put me at the top of her house in the converted attic. 'It's a bit like your room at home, Jenny.'

It was completely self-contained and I lay in bed isolated from the rest of the house, feeling cosseted and safe, listening to the comforting, ordinary sounds going on below me.

Ruth had insisted we drop in to her surgery to see a doctor. He thought I most probably had a virus. I didn't know what Ruth had said to him but he suddenly looked at me closely and asked me if I was depressed. There was no answer to this and he said gently that he thought I should see my own doctor when I got home. I should not battle on my own when there were excellent modern drugs to alleviate clinical depression.

He wrote a note and put it in an envelope for my doctor, and this simple act of caring touched me. He walked me to the door and opened it for me. 'Drink gallons of water, take the codeine and rest. If you don't feel better in a few days come back and see me. Take care, Mrs Holland.'

I slept a great deal and sometimes I forgot where I was. The days seemed to flow into one another. I felt as if I were burning up, but I was dimly aware of Ruth bringing me drinks and pills. When everyone was at work Ruth's cleaning lady came in. She changed my sheets and made me soup and clucked kindly at me in a Birmingham accent I found hard to decipher.

I couldn't remember ever feeling this ill and I wondered why my body was letting me down now. After three days I began to feel better and I sat propped up by pillows, reluctant to join the normal world again. I didn't want to go downstairs and socialise, and Ruth seemed to understand.

She brought her husband, Peter, up to meet me. He leant against the door jamb smiling at me. He was dark and stocky, not much taller than Ruth. He had a kind, open face etched with tiredness and the beginnings of grey in his hair. 'Hello, Jenny. I'm sorry you've been so unwell. Ruth's been very worried. No fun to be ill away from home, is it?'

I smiled back. 'I'm so sorry to be ill in your house. I'm feeling much better now. It's been good of you both to have me and I can leave you in peace tomorrow and move back to my hotel.'

'Please don't. Ruth loves someone to mother.'

Ruth laughed. 'It's true, Jenny. You're no trouble. I'll be hurt if you want to leave.'

'You're being very kind, thank you,' I said. The words sounded formal and hung in the air. All the time we were talking I was listening out for the movements of the boy in the rooms below. I had only glimpsed him when I first arrived and Ruth briefly introduced us. I lay here in the evenings and listened to the noise of his laughter and the muffled sound of a clarinet being played through the open door.

Tonight, he self-consciously carried soup up to me. I could not take my eyes off him. He was so like Tom it was eerie and I felt the hairs rise up on the back of my neck. I had the displaced feeling that I had time travelled and I was his mother looking up at the child Tom, the young Tom I never knew.

'Mum will be up in a minute,' he said, placing the tray carefully on my knees. Then, looking around the room, taking in the silence, an anathema to anyone his age, he asked gruffly, 'Would you like me to bring my radio up? It has tape and CD too. You could play some music.'

Before I could answer he was gone, bounding down the stairs to fetch it for me. He brought back Mozart and Beethoven, Eric Clapton, Bryan Ferry, Handel and Barber. Whose taste, I wondered, Ruth's or Peter's?

As he bent to plug in the radio and CD player by my bed I longed to reach out and touch the back of his neck where his hair curled into his collar, where the small patch of white neck lay vulnerable.

'Thank you, Adam, that's so thoughtful of you.' Longing to keep him, I asked, 'Is it you I hear playing the clarinet?'

He laughed and tossed his head in that achingly familiar way. 'Yeah. I'm not very good yet.'

'You sound good to me.'

'Well . . .' He was moving to the door. 'I don't want to be, like, concert standard. I just love the instrument. Um, I'd better go, I think supper's on the table.'

'Thanks for the soup and the music.'

He stood tall and fair, framed in the doorway where his father had stood earlier. He was half turned to me and I knew for sure that Peter was not the boy's father.

'That's OK,' he said and was gone.

I sat, listening to the sounds of crockery and voices way below me. Ruth would come up in a minute and have her supper with me. She was still a little like the girl I used to know long ago, when we were close as close and swore that nothing would ever come between us, and our blood mingled from the tiny cuts we made on our wrists.

If I closed my eyes I could almost believe I was someone else living a different life here in Birmingham; that I belonged to another family who were caring for me. I felt an acute sense of unreality, as if the past and the future didn't exist. It seemed, as I lay in someone else's attic, that my own life had ebbed away, or was momentarily suspended. I liked it.

Ruth had rung Flo for me. Flo wanted to come down immediately and take me home, but I didn't want that. I wanted to stay here. Soon, I would be well enough to leave, to go back to a hotel or return home, but I liked it up here in my eyrie. I thought about the boy all the time. His image lived behind my eyelids: his schoolboy smell of body heat and biro; his face etched on my brain.

I heard Ruth coming up the stairs. Her steps were slow as she carried up her tray. Smiling, she sat on the chair beside the bed. 'I understand you now have, *like, music*. So sorry I didn't think of it. I've just been ticked off. Is the soup hot enough?'

'It's lovely.'

I wanted to talk about Adam and Ruth was only too happy to discuss him. 'He's obviously not happy at school. It's a worry.'

I played with my soup. 'What does Peter think?'

'Well, he's always thought he would be better off at a private school. The local comprehensive is huge.'

'You didn't?'

Ruth sighed. 'I was against it. I thought Adam would settle, he's bright enough, but that seems to be the problem. We're sure he's being picked on, although he won't say anything.'

'Could he change schools?'

Ruth hesitated. 'Go privately you mean? It's a huge financial commitment. It seems unfair on Peter.'

'But you're working too, aren't you?'

'Not enough for a private education and the standard of living we've got used to, Jenny.'

I was silent. My soup had got cold and I put down my spoon. I couldn't seem to edge Ruth nearer to what I wanted to know. 'Adam's such a sweet boy. You must be very proud of him.'

'I am. We both are.'

'How old is he? You must have got married very young.'

Ruth did not meet my eyes. Colour swept over her face.

I said quietly, unable to bear it any longer. 'Peter isn't Adam's father, is he?'

Ruth turned and placed her tray on the floor. 'No. Peter isn't Adam's father. I've only been married for five years and Adam is thirteen.' She met my eyes.

The heat rose under my skin as I tried to do the calculation. 'You . . . you must have got pregnant soon after you got to Arran?'

She shook her head. 'No, Jenny.' She leant forward, took the tray off my knees and put it on the floor with hers.

Into the silence of the room Adam shouted up the stairs, 'We're off, Mum. See you later.'

Peter called out, "Bye. Back around nine thirty.'

The front door slammed and Ruth picked up the trays and stacked them, arranging the plates all together neatly. 'I'll take these downstairs and bring you back a drink. I won't be long.' She did not look at me.

I got out of bed and went to the bathroom to wash my face and hands. Outside the bathroom window there was a huge chestnut tree hiding the house next door. A blackbird was singing on a branch. It had been raining and the leaves dripped. If I opened the window I would smell the wet earth. I got back into bed. My mind jittered back fourteen years, trying to remember little signals, little signs I should have picked up.

53

Ruth brought back two mugs of tea and sat in the chair again. 'It makes more sense now, does it? The important bit I left out. My parents sent me to Arran because I was pregnant. That's why my father took up the job in Canada, to avoid any scandal and having to deal with me.'

I stared at her. 'How could you leave without telling me something like that? I thought we were so close.'

'What I told you on the train was true. My parents threatened awful things if I told anyone I was pregnant. I was seventeen, traumatised and scared and . . .' Her voice was so soft I only just caught her words. 'I felt I'd let you, Bea, your family, down. I thought that you would all look at me differently. I felt contaminated. I felt unworthy of . . .'

I leant towards her. 'Of our love and support?'

She nodded and as I looked at her attractive, immaculate face I knew with certainty that the feeling would never entirely leave her.

'We all thought of you as part of the family. Families stick together. You should have had faith. You should have known we would never abandon you. Bea could have made you feel so differently about yourself, about everything.'

Ruth smiled. 'Dear Jenny. You talk from the inside of a loving family. I hovered on the outside. I could pretend I was part of your family. I could even have my own bed in your house. But I always knew I had to go home eventually. I knew there were rules even in your household and I had broken one of them. We're talking about quite a long time ago and we were convent girls in a small community. Getting pregnant was still a middle-class taboo. Something that happened to fourteen-year-olds up on the Trelevea estate.'

I was silent. Hindsight was blessed. Ruth was right. Did I really know what Bea and James would have felt and done? They had no right to interfere. Ruth spent more time with us than she did at home, but it didn't give Bea any say in what Ruth's parents decided for her. Bea would almost certainly have been told to take a running jump.

'You should have run back to us as soon as you got to Arran.'

Ruth laughed. 'I probably would have done if my aunt had not welcomed me with open arms. In the end it was a happy outcome. She gave me so much. There was never a question of not keeping my child.'

I avoided her eyes. 'What about Adam's father? Did I know him?'

'No, you didn't know him. He was visiting Cornwall with friends. I met him just that once at the party. It was one of those mistakes that change your life. I had too much to drink . . .'

'What made you drink that night?' I asked. 'You never drank. I can't ever remember you having a drink.'

Ruth fiddled with her wedding ring. 'I don't know. I was stupid. I think I wanted to seem older and sophisticated. He was so different from the boys we knew. He didn't treat me like an adolescent. He talked to me as if I were interesting, and he danced with me as if I were . . .'

She looked at me. 'I couldn't leave him alone. I can't describe how stunning he was. It felt so great that he was taking any notice of me because he was quite a bit older. I led him on. I virtually threw myself at him. I don't suppose he realised I was only seventeen.' She paused and said dreamily, 'It's so amazing, don't you think, that one quick, wonderful fuck after too many glasses of wine produces a child you have for ever; a person who means more to you than life itself?'

And a whole happy marriage can leave you with no child at all.

But Ruth was not looking at me. She was gazing out of the window. She was talking to herself.

55

My hands trembled. 'What happened to the man?' I asked. 'Did he ever know?'

'I've no idea what happened to him. He never knew I got pregnant. I refused to tell my parents anything about him; that's why they were so furious. I didn't see the point of ruining two lives. The boy was at university. He was just starting his career. A month later I don't suppose he even remembered my name or face.' Seeing the look on my face she said quickly, 'It was not his fault, I wasn't being noble. I knew I'd thrown myself at him. I engineered the whole seduction thing and young as I was I got what I deserved. That's just how it was.'

She got up and shook her head as if ridding herself of a familiar demon. 'I have Adam. That's all that matters.'

She looked at me. 'How do you feel about coming downstairs for an hour? Peter and Adam have gone to see a film.'

I nodded and reached for my dressing gown. 'You're right to be proud of Adam, Ruth.'

TEN

Two weeks after I meet Tom at the party in the park I get a postcard in an airmail envelope. Someone has obviously posted it for him in London. It says,

Hi, Jenny. Here, where there is not a tree to be seen, I think of you in a white and gold dress standing under an English chestnut tree. It is a lovely thought. Tom xx

I carry the card around with me in my bag like a schoolgirl. I take it out at intervals to see if the words scrawled across a small space could have multiplied.

There is silence for another four weeks, then Damien, Maisie's brother, rings. 'I have a message from my boss. He is flying home on leave next Friday and he will ring you when he gets back.'

'I thought you were in Bosnia again, Damien.'

He laughs. 'Oh, I'm darting about all over the place, like the Scarlet Pimpernel.' He hesitates.

'What?' I ask quickly. 'Is Tom OK?'

'Tom's fine, Jenny. He wanted me to check that you hadn't vaporised somehow, that you were still there.'

I smile. 'I'm still here.'

'Good. He'll ring you.'

'You OK?'

'Great to have some leave, drink beer and see a woman's face . . .'

I get the feeling he wants to say something. I do not want to be warned off Tom. 'Were you going to tell me something?'

'It's just . . . you're a sweetie, Jenny, and Tom's a lovely officer, but he's training with the *roughie toughies*, which means he'll hardly be in England . . .'

'What do you mean the *roughie toughies*?'

'I'll let him tell you. Maybe keep it cool, Jen? I'd hate you to be hurt.'

I am silent. I suspect Maisie's protective hand. Damien was Tom's sergeant. Was he doing the same work as Tom, whatever that was?

I say lightly, 'I've only met Tom once. How could it be but cool?'

'Cool,' he replies and we both laugh and say goodbye.

Damien had said *great to see a woman's face*? He must have been in the Middle East. Tom must be there too. Roughie toughie? I smile at the thought that Tom needed Damien to check he could still ring me.

ELEVEN

The next day I got dressed and went downstairs. Ruth had been coming home earlier since I'd been in the house and working in the evenings.

In the afternoon I was in the kitchen with her when Adam came in, slamming the front door and calling out he was home. I felt a little thrill. I was getting to know his routine. I was getting to know him. I loved watching him move around in the clumsy way boys have. I loved his sweet boy smell. He seemed so strangely, intrinsically dear.

Ruth had said to me, 'Adam is comfortable with you, Jenny. You're good with him. He can be very awkward with some people; he's got to that age.'

When Peter and Ruth were busy, Adam and I watched television together or listened to his music or played cards.

'I wish you could stay longer,' Ruth said now. 'I know you're better, but you still look frail. Unfortunately, Adam and I are going down to Cornwall; it's his half-term and I promised him we'd go. It's a bit of a disappointment for Adam that Peter can't come. Something's come up and he's off to Israel again.'

'I'm fine, Ruth, and I must get back to work. I've got a

couple of appointments I didn't keep. I can't thank you enough for having me for so long.'

'Couldn't the appointments wait until another time? I wish you'd go straight home. I'd feel much happier putting you on the train for London before I leave. You don't look well enough for work.'

'There are a couple of people I need to see. A night in a hotel, then I'll go home.'

'Then why don't you stay on here? You're welcome to as long as you don't find an empty house depressing.'

'Really? It would be great as long as you really don't mind,' I said, feeling relieved.

'Of course I don't.' She moved to hug me and involuntarily I stiffened.

She looked hurt and I said quickly, 'I'm sorry. I find it difficult to . . . in case I dissolve.'

Ruth smiled. 'It's OK. I understand. I just can't imagine what you're going through. Forgive me if I've been insensitive, talking too much about myself and my child.'

I drew away from her abruptly. *My child. My child.* I walked away and looked out of the window at the wintry garden, and the pain pulled and wrenched at my heart. I said brightly, steadying my voice, my back to Ruth, 'Where are you staying in Cornwall?'

Ruth was fitting bread into the toaster. 'Do you remember my godmother? A rather eccentric old lady who painted?'

'Down in St Minyon? In the thatched house by the creek? She used to take us fishing and give us wonderful teas.'

'That's Sarah. Well, she left me that little cottage. I rent it out most of the time. But we always try to go down once or twice a year. Adam is mad about birdwatching.'

'Your parents always disapproved of her, didn't they?'

'Didn't they just? She disapproved of them too. I could

60

never understand how she came to be my godmother.' Ruth stopped buttering toast and came over to me. 'You know when we met on the train? I'd gone up to London to try to find out about my biological parents. Before they sent me out to Arran my parents handed me my birth certificate. They refused to tell me anything. My real mother's name is not the same as my godmother's, but there must have been some link, don't you think?'

'Couldn't you find out?'

'Yes, I could, but I don't want to know any more how different my life might have been. So, you see, Adam is the one person who shares my blood. Thank God I have him.'

I breathed deeply. 'It's a fantastic place to be left a cottage.'

'I've kept all her things exactly as they were. It feels like my real home. Perhaps when I stop having a career I'll retire there.'

'Would Peter enjoy that?'

Ruth gave me an odd look. 'My decisions in life can't always be based on what someone else likes, only what's right for me, or Adam.'

I watched her face. It was such an exclusive remark. It separated her and the boy from Peter, as if he were not part of their family. Yet he seemed such a kind man and devoted to them both. Ruth, embarrassed, said abruptly, 'That came out all wrong. It sounds hard. Oh God, Jenny, I've been on my own for so long, it's not easy sustaining a relationship. Peter wants to start a family. He would love me to give up work and have babies. But I love my job. I'm happy. I've done the hard times.' She met my eyes. 'I'm ambitious. I admit it.'

'Peter is away a lot, so presumably he's pretty ambitious and involved in his work too?'

Ruth looked miserable. 'I think he's away more than he needs to be because the child issue is unresolved between us.'

That evening round the supper table I watched Peter and Ruth. They talked in a companionable, friendly way, but they were too polite with each other, too careful. They never touched or exchanged a look. They were not like Tom and I had been together.

That night I couldn't sleep. I lay thinking about Adam and about his life in this house. I thought of him lying in bed below me and I had a sudden urge to watch him sleep. I went down the thick carpeted stairs, tense for any creaks. His room was next to the bathroom and the door was ajar. I held my breath, pushed it open and peered into the room.

He lay on his back, one hand thrown out. He looked smaller and younger in sleep, vulnerable in his blue-striped pyjamas. He stirred and turned away from me, pulling his legs up with a little grunt.

I watched the way his hair grew round his face and conviction flared inside me. I turned quickly, pulled the door to and went on down to the kitchen for water from the fridge and a reason to be walking about at night.

Peter left for the airport before I woke. Ruth and Adam were up early, gathering things together for the long journey to Cornwall. They were going to drive away and leave me here.

'Will you be all right, Jenny? I hate to leave you. You must take care of yourself.'

'Why don't you come?' Adam said suddenly. 'It'll be company for Mum now Peter can't come.'

My throat was dry and I couldn't answer for longing to go with him.

'Darling,' Ruth said quickly, 'Jenny has a busy life and people expecting her in London. But maybe one day, when you go to see your parents we could be in Cornwall at the same time?'

'Yes,' I said and smiled at Adam. 'Thank you for asking me. Have a wonderful holiday, both of you.'

At the door Ruth kissed me carefully.

'Thank you for everything,' I said. 'I'll post the keys through the letter box, shall I?'

Ruth nodded. 'I'll call you.'

I watched Adam bumping his knapsack down the steps, his hair flopping over his face. He threw his head back and turned and grinned up at me, and the pain lived and breathed inside me.

''Bye,' he called. 'See you again.'

I watched them until the car turned at the end of the street. I stood on the steps of the house where this boy lived until they disappeared. Then I closed the door.

TWELVE

When the car had disappeared round the corner I moved around the empty three-storeyed house. All houses smell different, they gather the essence and scent of people. I looked at the cork noticeboard in the kitchen. Ruth was very organised. All Adam's activities were carefully pinned up there with her own appointments and Peter's schedules and flights.

I moved up the stairs and stood outside Adam's room like a thief. Then I pushed open the door and went in. The room smelt of boy; of gym shoes and clothes he should have put in the wash. I lifted a football shirt and held it to my face, then folded it carefully and placed it back on the chair. Posters were pinned to the walls: birds and maps and a group photograph of him playing the clarinet in a youth orchestra in Glasgow. I stared at his sweet, concentrated face and Tom stared back at me.

What is it like to have a child of thirteen? To have a child with a formed and independent mind? I don't know what that feels like.

I lay back on Adam's bed slowly like an old woman afraid that her bones might break and I let my darling into my head; just for a second or I would go mad.

Rosie. *I will never have a conversation with you. I will never know what sort of person you would have grown into. You – with your little busy footsteps on the polished floors and your funny, throaty little chuckle.*

I heard myself moan softly in the empty house. How loud it sounded, like an injured animal.

There was an added anguish that would not leave me alone; it burnt inside me like a fever, keeping my body hot and dry. A nagging, persistent little doubt rising up, damaging and relentless, and part of me like a steady beat.

Tom . . . You took Rosie with you. You had my baby in the car. You were always so careful. Were you careful that day? Or were you late leaving the zoo and worrying about the traffic. Were you careless, Tom? Were you?

I lay on Adam's unmade bed and watched the afternoon sun move round and slant across the floor and catch the dust, and I fell into a strange daytime sleep, and the dreams were so vivid that I longed to wake, but when I woke I longed again for oblivion.

I am running across Porthmeor beach in St Ives and Tom is chasing me. He catches me and we fall laughing on to the sand, rolling over each other, getting covered in wet sticky sand. We are kissing each other over and over again. We are playing truth or dare, and I have rolled over on top of him, tickling him.

'Come on, tell! Tell me the most terrible thing you have ever done?'

Tom is twisting away from me, trying to get free and laughing. 'Get off me, woman! I'm getting covered in sand.' He sits up, brushing down his sweater. Then he says, suddenly serious, 'The worst thing I ever did was get drunk one night at a party and I screwed a girl in a bedroom full of coats. She was very pretty and she had been throwing herself at me all evening, so I thought, Why not? She's obviously keen and willing. But I had no idea until later that she was only seventeen and still at school. I felt guilty and ashamed about that night for a long time. Even talking about it now makes me cringe.'

'Did you ever see her again?'

'No. I was at university and in Plymouth with the cadets, doing my obligatory scholarship time. We had driven down to Cornwall just for the party. We went back the next morning.'

'What was she like?'

'Tall and blonde is all I remember in my drunken haze. OK, goody two shoes, what's the worst thing you've ever done? Stick your tongue out at the back of a nun? Ow! That hurt.'

I sat up in the dark and the rage inside me was all-consuming, sucking me dry, making me tremble with anger. *Is Adam Tom's child?* Ruth can't even remember the boy's name or face. *It can't be right that Adam is hers. It can't be.*

As I lay on his bed I knew that I had been guided to Adam. Why otherwise would Ruth and I have met on a train to Birmingham when we'd not met in fourteen years? It was fate. Adam is part of Tom. He is part of my life because of Tom. He is part of me.

I felt light-headed, as if I were floating, as if I might blow away. Like the night of Tom's death I felt curiously out of my body, watching myself from the ceiling. I got off the bed carefully and pulled the duvet straight. I switched on the landing light and went dizzily downstairs. I made tea in Ruth's kitchen.

Tom seemed abruptly near me in this house that belonged to another family. To people he did not know. As if I had conjured him. I looked around at the shadows beginning to fill the empty house and I willed him to stay close to me.

Tom, you have a son.

I walked through to the living room and looked out into the road full of lit houses. The front door of the house opposite was open and light spilled down the dark steps. The family were piling their possessions into a camper van. Up and down the stone steps they ran, laughing and excited, the children in bright clothes like small ladybirds.

They were placing bicycles on the back of the van. They were going to carry their house away on their back. I watched, fascinated, until they were ready to leave, then I wrote down the number of the hire company written in large letters on the side of the camper van.

THIRTEEN

Ruth and Adam beat the traffic and arrived in Truro triumphant. They stopped in the town to have lunch and shop for food, then headed for St Minyon. As they turned off the main street and took the narrow road to the creek, Ruth's heart soared as it used to when her godmother was alive and she knew that for an afternoon she could be completely happy in her skin.

Beside her Adam unwound the window and Ruth heard his small sigh of contentment. As soon as the car was unpacked he would be off with his binoculars heading for the other end of the creek. For a few days he could run free and wild, as she and Jenny had done as children.

The tide was out and the smell of mud and hawthorn filled the air. Ruth backed the car as near to the cottage as she could and they unloaded. Then she parked it neatly facing the water near some upturned rowing boats. Mrs Rowe had been in and opened the windows and made up the beds.

An ancient Rayburn and night storage heaters stopped the house from getting damp, but Ruth knew she would have to put in central heating soon, holidaymakers now demanded what they were used to at home.

Adam looked at her hopefully, then at the wave of shopping bags on the kitchen floor.

Ruth laughed. 'Off you go!'

She handed him some chocolate and a bottle of water, and he shot out of the front door singing like a bird.

From an upstairs window she watched him lift his binoculars to the dense woods on the other side of the creek. Then he lowered them and stood for a moment quite still, looking over the mudflats. Ruth recognised his moment of peace. It brought home to her his carefully guarded misery at a school he had never wanted to go to. She should have listened to Peter. Her work had taken her to a big city and it was a good career move, but it was Adam who was paying the price.

She moved around the cottage touching things as she always did when she first arrived. She loved her city life but as soon as she got here she felt as if she were home; as if she'd shed a skin and somehow become herself.

It was also a rare chance to concentrate on Adam. She knew he liked Peter to come, but she loved having him on his own. *Of course you do. You think you are making up for all the evenings you are working, all the afternoons you are not there when he comes home from a school he hates.*

She went downstairs and put all the shopping away. She stuck wine in the fridge, made a flask of tea, pulled on another sweater and went out to follow Adam down a path she had walked a million times.

Jenny and I – carrying rods home-made of bamboo and string – eating jam sandwiches and drinking Coca-Cola – banned at home. Scary adventures round the lake that leads up to the big house watched by old herons, still as sentinels, who sit in small scrubby trees that surround the water; pretending, when the shadows come, that the wood is haunted and running hell for leather back to the lighted house and godmother Sarah, who has tea and tiny thin pancakes made on a griddle ready for us in a kitchen that is always warm. On the table there is a bright cloth and real butter and honey, and a teapot with a knitted cosy from a jumble sale. Safe . . . safe.

She and Jenny always made a mess and Sarah had never minded. Her fingernails were full of paint and sometimes her hair too. She was vague and eccentric, and Ruth had loved her to death.

In the dusk, if her father had not collected her, tooting his horn from the corner, never coming in or thanking her godmother for having her, Sarah would start up her old Rover and drive Ruth home.

Sometimes, if Jenny was with her, Bea or James drove up from St Ives to collect them. They always came in to see Sarah. They would sit and drink wine together while Jenny and Ruth watched the ancient television.

Sarah had a smoky laugh and long, long hair, which she piled up on her head, and sometimes it escaped and then she looked younger as if she weren't really old at all. When she said goodbye she always held Ruth gently, but very close, as if she were infinitely precious.

Adam was sitting on a bench with his binoculars trained on the incoming tide. Ruth sat beside him.

'Look, Mum.' He handed her the glasses excitedly. 'On that tree . . . no a bit to your right . . . Yes there. Have you got it?'

'A woodpecker?'

'A lesser spotted woodpecker. He's quite rare. Can you hear him?'

Ruth listened to the sound of a small drill. 'I can hear him, he's making enough noise.'

70

They sat side by side drinking tea and watching the waders, and listening to the terns and curlews as the afternoon drew in and the water flowed over the mudflats in small waves. There was only the movement of water and the gentle plop of birds' footfalls in the mud. Ruth thought of Jenny and hoped she wasn't too lonely in their empty house.

'What's for supper?' Adam asked and Ruth heard his stomach rumbling.

'Fish and chips, or scrambled eggs and bacon.' Adam always chose fish and chips.

'Fish and chips!'

They walked home as the last rays of a watery sun caught the incoming tide. People would start to exercise their dogs at the end of the day and the fishermen would arrive in their waders, but for now they had the whole world to themselves.

FOURTEEN

On our first date Tom turns up at the house with the biggest bunch of flowers I have ever seen. It's eight o'clock and I'm not ready. It has been the most terrible day. Our most experienced cutter has gone sick and Danielle and I are behind with our accounts, again, and we are terrified of incurring a penalty. Danielle is upstairs fighting figures while I try to finish cutting a complicated pattern.

I had it all planned for a quick getaway. My clothes are laid out on the bed and an expensive soak is waiting on the edge of my bath. I wanted to feel calm and fragrant when I saw Tom again but when I throw open the door to him I am frazzled and almost tearful.

He grins at me, buckling under the weight of foliage in his arms. 'Hi, Jenny.'

'I'm sorry. I'm sorry. I'm late, I'm not ready. Come in.'

I am mortified. I look a complete mess.

'It doesn't matter. Maybe I'm early . . .' He leans forward and kisses me on the cheek round his acre of garden. 'These are for you.' He hands me the flowers. The smell of them fills the hall, dwarfs me and hides me from his sight. I suddenly want to giggle.

'Heavens, you disappeared.' He takes them back, laughing, and we fill the sink. Suddenly I feel better.

'I'm not sure if I have enough vases . . .' I regale him with the saga of my awful day. I get wine out of the fridge and pour two huge glasses.

'Sorry about your hellish day.'

He raises his drink to me and we clink glasses and I am so pleased this man is standing in my kitchen that I reach up and kiss him on the side of his mouth. 'Thank you so much for my *ginormous*, wonderful bunch of flowers.'

'I didn't know what you like so I got a mixture of everything in the shop.'

'So I see.' We stare at each other, delighted. 'Look, I've got to go back down to the basement to tidy up. I'll be five minutes.'

'May I come down and see where you work?'

He follows me down the stairs and as I tidy and lock up he mooches around in an interested fashion looking at the noticeboard and at designs pinned on plastic models, and the table where I've been cutting out.

'We're a bit cramped, as you can see. We're going to have to look for bigger premises eventually, but it's hard in London. We need to be fairly central for people to get to us.'

'Fairly central means expensive.'

'Exactly.'

'Do you always work this late?'

I laugh. 'This is early, Tom! Danielle and I are self-employed.'

We go back upstairs and an exhausted-looking Danielle is in the kitchen pouring herself a glass of wine.

'I can hear a cork go three storeys up. Hello, Tom.' She holds up her glass to him. 'Jenny, you are not changed. Go at once . . .'

'Look,' Tom says, turning to me. 'You've both obviously

had a pig of a day, why don't I order a takeaway for three and you and I can go out for a meal tomorrow, or another night, when you aren't exhausted?'

Relief floods through me. I have to get up early in the morning. 'Are you sure?'

'I refuse to play strawberry,' Danielle says primly.

Tom and I scream with laughter.

Danielle smiles. 'What? What did I say?'

'*Gooseberry*, not strawberry, Elle. Don't be silly. Where are all our takeaway menus . . . ?'

'Aha. Girls after my own heart.'

We fish them out and I fly upstairs to have a quick shower. Tom and Danielle get on famously.

Tom had to do a bookkeeping course for the army and he glances over our books for us. 'Why don't they teach students the business side of things at art school?'

'I think some art schools do, but not at Central St Martin's,' Danielle says.

'You really need someone to do this professionally for you.'

'We've got an accountant, but we still have to get the books in order for him and it's so time-consuming,' I tell him. 'But you're right, we do need someone.'

Danielle and I smile at each other. 'Actually, we both know the ideal person. We need someone administrative who can also oversee the girls in the workroom, leaving us both free to design. Someone who knows the fashion business inside out.'

'So, have you asked her?'

'It's tricky. She works for a designer we know very well. We'd have to approach her carefully.'

'Headhunt, entice, persuade, inveigle, you mean?'

'That is it.' Danielle laughs. 'Jenny is nicer than me. She worries. I think we should take Florence out to lunch, Jenny,

74

and just ask her. I do not think she is happy with Sam Jackson.'

'He certainly takes her for granted. She's an absolute treasure.'

'We would appreciate her.'

'Of course we would. I've heard he is appallingly mean with his staff, too.'

Tom pours more wine. 'That's the way. Talk yourselves into it. Concentrate on "Operation Headhunt".'

When Danielle has gone up to bed Tom says, 'I'm going to go and let you get some sleep.' But he doesn't leave for another half-hour. We kiss until my mouth is sore.

The following night we make love on the hard polished floor of his flat because we never make it to the bedroom. I see Tom every day of his ten-day leave and when he goes again I cannot even remember what I had done or where I had gone before I met him.

FIFTEEN

The creek lay still and deserted in early evening. The tide was in and the last streak of gold-grey sun slanted through a crack in the darkening sky and lit up the water. The boats were turning in a brisk breeze. The world looked like an old black-and-white film.

Terns swooped like dancers in a ballet or an expert aerobatic team and waders cried out over the water. I sat in the hired Volkswagen camper watching the light go. I loved creeks and inlets. The mudflats were not ugly when the tide was out, but beautiful, full of the patterns of birds' feet and the differing cries of waders. The sound of their cries echoed something primitive inside me.

I pulled the hood of my thick Barbour round me, making sure it hid my face and hair, and stepped down on to soft wet ground. My walking boots sank and I lifted the long coat so that it didn't trail in the mud. I started to walk along the path.

The creek was deserted. People in the cottages had already drawn their curtains and were busy eating or cooking supper. I knew I must not walk too far because the dark would come quickly and engulf me.

I walked fast past godmother Sarah's house where Adam and Ruth were staying. The curtains were not drawn and music came from a lighted window. My heart gave a lurch at the thought of them together inside the house. I was on the outside.

I knew that I could walk up the path to the front door and knock. I knew I could be on the inside of that house if I wanted to be, but I couldn't do it. How could I say anything to Adam with Ruth there? I would have no chance to explain the truth to him: that he was Tom's son and mine too.

The path was muddy and the hedges high and bare still. Small birds scuttled and swooped past my head, gathering and screeching territorially as dusk descended. I reached the lake on the left of the creek where the birds overwintered. It was ruffled and pitted by wind and current, as if a giant had blown on the surface of the water.

I watched a heron fly over my head and land in the shallow water beyond. It gathered its wings fussily round it and became as still as a stone, long neck and head craned away from me as if praying to some unseen god.

Two swans sailed majestically towards me on the tide, like an omen; feet operating like miniature paddle boats as they hoped for bread. I had so many memories of walking here with Dad on shopping trips to Truro or coming here with Ruth at weekends to her godmother. This place had always been eerily magical.

On my right the hedges disappeared and I walked within sight of the creek again. A lone canoeist appeared out of nowhere, negotiating the narrow channel of water left by the tide with speed and skill. The light was almost gone and it was time to go back. The tide was on the turn and the waders strutted in the shallows making complicated footprints I could not see but only hear in little plops on the chocolate mud.

I had a bizarre feeling that I was watching myself noticing

these things. As if I had to note them in order to be here, in order for them to be real. Why *am* I here? I felt fear prickle my skin. I turned and walked quickly back the way I had come.

The only lights now from the cluster of houses were the cracks from behind curtains and I felt an overpowering sense of loneliness engulf me. I looked at the cottage and the closed front door, and wanted to run up the path and hammer on it for Adam and Ruth to let me in.

I got back into the Volkswagen. I was too tired to drive away. I would risk parking here for tonight. My hands trembled as I lit the gas burner to make tea. I climbed into my sleeping bag, pulled back the window curtain and watched the stars.

I could hear the waters of the creek moving gently around me and splashing against the sides of small boats. Curlews wailed their lament, then were silenced by the night. I sat up and stared across at the thatched cottage where Adam and Ruth moved about together inside.

One by one the downstairs lights went off and two lights came on upstairs. I thought I could dimly hear the sound of a clarinet. I imagined Adam sitting up in bed in his pyjamas, playing. Then every light went off in all the cottages. There was only a heavy blackness, as if every light in the world had been extinguished.

I felt as if a thick blanket were enveloping and pressing down on me. I opened my mouth to cry out but no sound would come. I stretched out my hand into the cold dark air to feel the warmth of their hands. Rosie's little hot, sticky one and the large, safe hand of my love. My fingers grasped only air. There was nothing there, nothing to hold on to and my open mouth could not even form a scream.

SIXTEEN

I woke with the dawn and sat crouched and cold in my sleeping bag to watch the sun flare up over the dark forest on the far side of the creek, then rise to touch the water. My spirits rose and swooped and soared in a moment of wonder at the sheer mystical beauty of yellow winter sun rising through mist that lay over the water like a ghostly blanket.

As the sun came up I saw a light go on in an upstairs room of the cottage and I got out of my sleeping bag and pulled on jeans and a sweater. I tied on my walking boots and reached for my Barbour. Then I sat and waited.

The light in the bedroom went off and one came on in a downstairs room. After a minute the front door opened and Adam emerged. He was muffled in green waterproofs, hat and scarf. Outside his coat he carried binoculars against his chest.

He walked quickly down the garden path and turned left up the creek path. He was making for the lake. I waited for a few moments, then pulled up my hood and slowly followed him.

I smiled as I thought of Ruth asleep in her bed while I

was with Adam on the outside of that womblike cottage. I was watching over Adam as a new day began.

The birds were singing as if their hearts would burst and the waders screeched out across the water. Ahead, I could just hear the boy's footsteps. I could not see him because of the mist that lay over everything. He stopped every now and then, and I stopped too. I knew he must be looking through his binoculars but there would be little to see on a morning like this.

When he came to the lake the skies began to lift and lighten a little and I could see his outline clearly. He paused, left the path and moved over boggy ground to the left of the lake where there were large stones he could sit on to watch the waders. Then his outline disappeared. I stopped and leant on a gate leading into a field running parallel to the lake. I strained to hear his movements but there was only silence.

I gathered my coat round me and, holding the hood to my face, moved carefully on down the path between lake and creek, past the point where I thought Adam must have left the path to the far side of the lake. I tucked myself into the undergrowth. The ground was soggy and the stone I sat on was damp.

I waited, waited amid the rustling and swooping and singing of birds. As the sun filtered through, the mist began to evaporate and rise up over the water a few metres like a theatre curtain. The dim shape of Adam started to materialise on the other side of the lake in early morning light. He was crouched on a rock, watching something through his binoculars.

I was at an angle from him so he could not see me as I sat hard against the hedge, but for a minute it seemed as if he stared straight across at me. Then he raised his glasses again and trained them skywards at an egret flying over my head towards him.

He birdwatched for perhaps twenty minutes, then he got up from his boulder, stretched, shook his legs and moved back to the creek path.

I got up too and kept my distance. The sun was beginning to burn off the sea mist. Adam walked slowly but seemed ill at ease. He looked left and right; then he stopped, turned and looked behind him. I stood very still, close to the hedgerow, and hardly breathed. He could not see me, but he must *feel* me here.

He shivered suddenly, then turned and walked quickly on back to the cottage. He almost ran up the path and the front door slammed behind him.

Most of the houses were still in darkness. I got back into the Volkswagen. I needed to drive away before anyone was up. The car engine was noisy and as I turned in the half-light I saw the boy standing in his unlit bedroom watching me.

The car lights flickered across the wall of the cottage before I turned and drove away up the hill. Next time I would park at the other end of the creek where the woods made it easier not to be noticed.

SEVENTEEN

Ruth had been determined not to put a telephone in the cottage. She liked the illusion that she wasn't easy to get hold of in Cornwall. She kept in contact with work by e-mail. Peter complained bitterly because the cottage was in a dip and reception for mobile phones was terrible. Ruth suspected, deep down, that it was really Peter she was avoiding.

Sometimes she dreaded hearing his good-natured, solicitous voice because she imagined it held a veiled disappointment in her. She knew she was being unfair and it was her stubborn unwillingness even to talk about having his child that was unreasonable.

It was becoming a hurdle between them and Ruth did not want to discuss it because she would have to face the moral implications of marrying a man without making it clear she did not want his children. The honourable thing would be separation or divorce. Peter could then marry a good Jewish girl who would bear him the children he and his family in Israel desperately craved.

Peter loved her and Adam so generously. He had married a Gentile against fierce parental wishes and how had she repaid him? With as little of herself as possible. Ruth thought that for Peter any happiness from this marriage was due to Adam, not her.

She went outside and walked a little way up the hill to ring him. Peter sounded so glad to hear her it gave her a guilty ache between her ribs, *where my heart should lie*. She described the alterations to the cottage they had arranged earlier in the year. She told him what she and Adam had been doing. She told him how beautiful the creek was at dusk as she stood talking to him, despite the gloomy weather.

'I miss you, Ruth. I wish I were there with you both. I'm weary of this wretched merger and commuting back and forth.'

'You must be. It seems to have gone on and on. You've got to take a break soon, Peter, or you'll crack. Surely your family realise you are exhausted with the constant travelling?'

He snorted wryly. 'My mother worries about me, as only mothers do. My father and brothers are impervious to anything but getting the right terms drawn up. They certainly don't understand the word compromise in business. Anyway, I'm OK. How's Adam?'

'He's jogging up the hill to talk to you now. Take care of yourself, Peter.'

'You too.' She heard him hesitate, longing for her to say more, or anything that would enable him to say *I love you, Ruth*.

Adam took the phone from her, and she went back into the house and took a bottle of wine from the fridge and poured herself a large glass. The glass misted like her eyes with her wretchedness at her inability to provide the small, normal, loving moments that would wipe Peter's weariness clean away.

My mother worries about me as only mothers do. Oh, Peter.

She went to the door with her wine. Adam's voice, as he chatted to Peter, reached her across the night. He seemed a little subdued, not so enthusiastic about his birds or about being here as he usually was. It occurred to Ruth that he might be starting to outgrow the cottage and his childlike delight in being here might be changing.

He was reaching the age when everything was going to become dead boring and the most boring thing of all would be going anywhere with your mother. Or perhaps it was just the closed-in weather and missing having Peter to birdwatch with.

Ruth started to open cupboards and get out the things she needed to make lasagne, Adam's favourite supper. As she chopped the onions she realised he had come back inside the house and gone upstairs. Usually, when he had been talking to Peter he came and gave her the gist of the conversation.

After a minute the mournful notes of his clarinet wafted downstairs: a James Galway number played tremulously. Anxiety for him welled up inside her. *Why couldn't I, for just once in my life, swallow my pride, say to hell with my principles and accept Peter's offer to pay for a private school?*

She grated cheese over the top of the lasagne and bunged it in the oven. Soon the smell of it filled the cottage. She looked up the television programmes. Thank God there was an aged James Bond. She laid two trays and poured herself some more wine. She was pleasantly bored. She might do some work later on. Tomorrow she would put out bedding plants in the garden, ready for holidaymakers.

Oh God! she thought suddenly, *sometimes I feel forty not thirty-one.* All at once she wished she had no responsibilities at all, that she could jump on a plane, work abroad and answer to no one. Do something exciting. Be free. She prayed the wretched sun would come out, that Adam was not going to throw a moody and that they would not be shrouded in mist for the entire half-term.

After a while the music stopped and following a few thumps Adam came noisily back down the stairs.

'What is it, lasagne?' He sniffed hungrily.

'Yep.'

He grinned at her. 'Wicked.'

Ruth grinned back. 'Could you get some garlic bread from the fridge? There are some green beans in there somewhere too.'

He saw the trays and his face lit up. 'Are we eating in front of the telly?'

'Yes. There's no one to see us slumming and there's a James Bond to watch for the umpteenth time.'

He grabbed a sip of her wine and she batted his hair. He went off, humming, to turn on the television. Ruth was frozen for a second in the fleeting moment of how easy it was to make someone else happy if you really wanted to.

She went and opened the door of the cottage again and listened to the curlews. What a wavery, uncharted line there was between sorrow and happiness.

EIGHTEEN

Danielle rang Flo from Birmingham. 'Is Jenny home?'

'No, she isn't,' Flo said, her heart sinking.

'There is no sign of her here. She still is not answering her mobile phone. I have even been out to Ruth's house. They have all gone away for a break. Her cleaner told me that Jenny was going to stay on one more night in the house after the family left and then she was returning to London. Neither of the buyers at Mason's or Simpson's has seen her.'

'Why on earth hasn't she rung us? Maybe she's on her way home now.'

'Maybe. But Flo, I don't like it. Jenny always lets us know where she is.'

Flo sat down heavily. 'Oh dear. I wonder if she could have suddenly decided to go home to Cornwall, to Bea and James.'

'She would have rung and let us know.'

'Not if she isn't thinking straight. Not if it's all caught up with her. I must ring James and Bea. I don't want to worry them unnecessarily, but it's been forty-eight hours now since we heard anything. Danielle, come home, there is nothing more you can do in Birmingham.'

'Ruth's cleaner told me that Ruth has no phone in the Cornish cottage and there is no reception on her mobile there so we cannot contact her.'

'You've done all you can, dear. Come back to London now. I'll see you tonight.'

Flo replaced the receiver. She wanted to believe that Jenny had suddenly made for home on a whim, as a child does, seeking comfort. She got up awkwardly, a pain shooting up her left leg, went to the landing window and picked up the vase of dead snowdrops that depressed her and threw them away. Nothing could account for this silence. Something was wrong. Flo dialled the Browns' number.

James took the call. He realised as he listened to Flo that he had been half expecting something like this to happen.

'How odd that Jenny and Ruth should meet up after all this time on a train. If it's the same cottage, Flo, I know it well. I'll drive over to St Minyon now. It wouldn't surprise me if Ruth and Jenny were together. They were extremely close as children. If she isn't there and Ruth doesn't know where she is, then I think we might have to do something about it.'

'I'm worried she might be having some sort of breakdown.'

There was a silence, then James said gently, 'Yes. It is possible. Try not to get too anxious. I'll ring you back as soon I can.'

James revved his old car and drove up the hill out of St Ives. It was the most glorious day and the bay below him glittered in sunlight. How often he had sailed with the children out of the harbour and Jenny, the youngest little afterthought, who seemed to have been born happy, would laugh with excitement: *I love the sea, Dad, I love the sea. Oh! There's nowhere in the whole world as lovely as this, is there?*

Bea used to say Jenny had been born joyful. James sighed.

The joy had been snatched away so early in her adult life. Uneasily, he remembered their conversation last Christmas after Tom was killed.

Jenny had travelled down with Flo on the train. The house was bursting with her sisters and their children. Both he and Bea had thought it was what Jenny needed: a time in the centre of her family where she could have all their support and love.

It was a mistake. It had cruelly highlighted the fact that her sisters still had husbands and children, the people they loved. It isolated her, made her anxious that they should not feel guilty. Everyone had subconsciously tiptoed round her as if she had an illness.

Jenny had taken herself off for long walks, getting up early to avoid anyone offering to go with her. She skirted the windy winter town or roamed the cliffs towards Zennor. She sat in her old duffel coat in the shelter of the rocks watching the surfers; spent hours in the tiny Barbara Hepworth museum sitting in the cold but peaceful garden.

On Christmas Eve James had accompanied her on the cliff path to Lelant. They had taken binoculars to watch the birds on the estuary. It was a walk they used to do when she was a child. They would often set off to catch the little single-track train that ploughed between St Ives and the Saltings.

That day, as they walked on the long stretch of beach at Porth Kidney, the wind had buffeted them nearly off their feet. Seagulls screamed and wheeled around them, and the wind was so cold it snatched their breath away. Jenny had marched beside him, loving it, James knew, because the discomfort made her concentrate on that and not on the icy place within her.

He had reached out to take her hand and said, his words torn and snatched by that irritating wind, 'I feel so helpless. I want to do something to make you feel better and I'm powerless. I can do nothing.'

Jenny had turned to him, trying to smile. 'You're *here*, Dad. I'm sorry. I've been trying so hard not to depress everyone, especially the children. It's not fair on them. I would have been better working over Christmas, but I knew Bea would have a fit if I stayed in London. Really, it would be better if I got back home as soon as possible. Without my work I've got nothing. When I'm working I can just think about Tom and the things we used to do together, Tom and me. It's all I want, Dad. It's all I want. I'm trying to be jolly, but I can't.'

'Of course you can't, darling, and no one expects it. If it's what you want I'll drive you back straight after Christmas. But you have to face the future, not just dwell on the past. I'm concerned about your health. You're not eating or sleeping, and it's getting painful to look at you. I hear you roaming about the house at night. Will you let me give you some vitamin injections to build you up and something to help you sleep, just for a while?'

They were moving up into the sand dunes to get out of the wind and Jenny turned to him. 'Yes. OK. But don't let me take any sleeping pills back to London with me.'

James had looked down at her, shocked. 'Oh, Jen, are you that depressed?'

Jenny had been silent before whispering, 'Yes.'

'Then I think you should see someone . . .'

'No, Dad. Come on, I hardly need anyone to tell me why life doesn't seem worth living, do I?' She had tucked her arm in his. 'You mustn't worry about me. I'll be all right. I'll get through, but I'm better when I'm working flat out. There's no point spilling my heart out to complete strangers when I've got you and Mum, sisters, Danielle and Flo . . .'

James had turned. 'If only you would. If only you would weep and talk and get angry and let us comfort you, but . . .'

He had stopped as her face closed against him. 'It's not my way, Dad.'

She had moved off towards the wild sea, leaving foot-prints in the damp sand, which filled with water.

As James joined the dual carriageway he said a silent prayer. He loved all his children equally, but Jenny had been a complete surprise to both him and Bea, and he could still see and hear in his head the funny, happy little curly-haired child she had been, lifting her skirts and running, laughing, through the safe shallows of her childhood.

NINETEEN

Ruth was playing Bach on her CD player: Eva Marton singing 'Ave Maria'. It depressed Adam, sitting in the window seat looking out at the creek. Usually he loved the piece, but today it made him sad and restless. He was not enjoying this holiday and he had been looking forward to it for weeks.

Today, for the first time it seemed as if the sun might come out. There was heavy dew glittering on the edges of the grass outside. It would still be cold, he could feel it in the air. He jiggled his knee up and down, wondering what he would do today.

Ruth sat behind him at the table going through some papers for a lecture. Next time they came he thought he might ask if he could bring Simon or Dave from the orchestra with him. As he sat there the sun broke through the mist and cloud, and lit up a patch of clear blue sky and glimmered on the full tide enticingly. Adam felt his spirits lifting.

He knew why he was depressed. His early mornings had been spoilt by his fear and he despised himself. He had never been afraid of going out into the dark mornings on his own before. Half the excitement of it all was the mystery of the creek at dawn, but that had been before . . .

He felt his skin prickle on the back of his neck at the memory of it. *Before the ghost had come to haunt him.* Then the other voice, the voice that smirked at his nerdiness, whispered, *Ghosts don't live in camper vans.*

Adam looked up to find his mother watching him.

'What is it, Adam? You're very quiet and you didn't go out this morning. Are you feeling all right?'

'I'm OK.'

'Well, something's wrong.'

Adam got up and walked round the room, lifting things and putting them back without seeing them. Half of him wanted to tell his mother about being spooked and the other half didn't want to admit it.

'Do you believe in ghosts?' he asked finally.

Ruth looked relieved. She smiled at him. 'No. What's spooked you?'

'When I go out in the early morning I feel as if I'm not alone. I feel as if someone is following me. I never really see anyone, but it's like I feel them there, watching me. I want to turn round all the time as if someone is behind me and sometimes I see a black shape of something in the darkness.'

Ruth stared at him. 'That's why you didn't go out this morning?'

'Yes.' Adam was suddenly angry. 'I know it sounds stupid, Mum. I know it sounds *sad*, but it's the first time I've ever felt scared in my whole life and that's the truth.'

Ruth got up, came over and squeezed in on the window seat with him. 'Creeks are terribly eerie, you know. We've been enveloped in mist nearly every day since we arrived. It's no wonder you've felt scared. When you go out it's still as black as pitch, with nothing but those mournful waders crying. I'm not surprised you see shapes in the dark. Get up later, when it's lighter. What birds can you see in the mist and dark?'

'It's not so dark when you're out there. Anyway, we've been coming here for years and I've always got up early to go out and I've never been scared before and . . .'

'What?'

'Oh, nothing. Forget it, Mum.' Adam got up. 'The sun's out. I want to get out there and fish.'

'What were you going to say? Come on, Adam, tell me.'

'Only . . . that when I go out in the early morning there seems to be a camper van parked by the boats, or at the other end of the creek. You know, further on from where that special school is.'

'And?'

'I sometimes see this dark shape getting back inside and driving away. I've gone up to my bedroom and watched.'

Ruth's face changed. 'There's nothing very ghostlike about a camper van, Adam. So what are you saying? That someone is following you in the early mornings?'

Adam didn't answer. Then he said under his breath, 'I don't know, Mum.'

Ruth got up and the sun streamed in through the window. 'Right, Adam, I don't want you going out on your own in the early mornings. If you see this camper van again, come and tell me. Is it ever here during the day?'

'I don't think so, but we've been out quite a lot. Once I thought I saw it at Perranporth when we were there, but I could have been wrong.'

'OK. If I see it I'm going to investigate. Where are you going to fish?'

'Down by the old barn at the head of the creek. That's where the locals fish. I'm not nervous in the day, Mum.'

Ruth ruffled his hair. 'I know you're not. In any case there are plenty of people walking dogs out there. If it's any comfort, Jenny and I used to spook ourselves down here as children . . . and you know it might just be another birdwatcher.'

'Yeah, it could be. I'll go and get my fishing stuff.'

'I'll bring lunch down to you. We'll have a picnic.'

His mother was rummaging in the cupboard for old newspapers when he came back. He could feel her watching him as he walked down the path. As he turned the corner he glanced across at the space where people parked their cars. There was no van.

Adam knew his mother would come straight out here as soon as he disappeared, just to make sure. In the sunshine his fears seemed far-fetched and childish, and he wished he hadn't said anything.

TWENTY

I walked the narrow path through the reed beds at the far end of the creek away from the houses. Today the sky was clear blue, cloudless, but the cold bit into me. As I walked, the sun began to reach through my coat and warm me. I felt as light as air, as if I were floating along, as if my feet were not touching the ground; as if I were moving very fast covering the ground without effort.

I stopped at the small bridge where the water tumbled into a small waterfall to join the creek. *Long, long ago Jenny and Ruth played Pooh sticks here. Jenny and Ruth? Long-ago children, happy and carefree.* Pictures of them floated across my mind.

What am I doing here? My heart beat so fast it hurt. I tried to think, but my mind would not clear. I went on walking. I walked on down the path and came to the only cottage at this end of the creek. I remembered it. It used to be derelict, now it was a renovated modern house with a double garage. Strange, it looked, on the edge of the woods; out of place, as if someone had dropped it in the wrong spot by mistake.

I stared at it, remembering the crumbling stone walls with

heavy clumps of ivy clinging to the cracks, and a roof that had caved in and was covered with moss and flowers that grew in the sills. The ruined house never got any sun and neither did this ugly modern house, which looked dark and unloved despite the yellow paint.

I passed it quickly. The path turned to the right and led through the woods. I climbed up the chiselled steps cut into the tree roots on to a higher path that ran above the creek. The trees grew close here, close and dark, and I felt myself melting into them, gliding over fallen brown pine needles as soft as cotton wool until I was at one with the trees, as if I were tree and shadow.

The creek glittered at a steep angle below me and I heard singing. Clear through the wood someone was singing in a high, childish voice although the words were lost to me. When the singing stopped there was a smattering of clapping, then a pause and someone started to play a recorder. Slowly I made my way towards the sound.

The trees grew thinner by a clearing and beyond it there was a small gate in the middle of a hedge. The sounds were coming from the other side. I moved towards the gate and saw the old manor house, which stood on a steep slope facing the wood and creek. A lawn sloped down to the latch gate and not far from the gate, on an even patch of grass like a small terrace, a semicircle of people were sitting on chairs playing musical instruments.

The terrace had been made to catch the early morning sun. The people were swathed in coats and scarves. They were making a lot of noise and seemed excited. Then I saw they were children. The recorder player stopped and made an awkward bobbing bow, and the others put down their instruments and clapped.

I watched them. I saw something was wrong. Their movements were disjointed. They seemed unable to keep still. Some children got up and ran around in circles, their limbs flaying out at odd angles.

A man with a beard called out, clapped his hands for order. He got the children sitting down again and a tall, lanky boy started to play the violin. He played beautifully. The music was haunting and the children swayed and rocked to the sound. He played for two or three minutes, then his concentration suddenly went and he stopped mid piece and stared straight across into my eyes.

The sudden silence shivered, unbroken. I held his eyes and grief rose up in me like an echo. His fear was mirrored in me. I felt the form of his fleeting, terrifying confusion.

The man with the beard touched his arm. So soft were his words to the boy that I could not hear them. The children rushed from their chairs and surrounded the boy. They threw their arms round him, making small noises of comfort and encouragement. They patted and stroked and keened to him until he jerked back into life.

I turned and ran back into the closeness of the trees. I followed the path of soft pine needles as it wound back down to the water and into sunlight. It felt as if the boy's eyes followed me into the shadows. *What am I doing? What am I doing?* Someone tell me.

TWENTY-ONE

Adam and Ruth took the path through the woods. This route was quite new and part of a Job Creation scheme. It didn't lead anywhere but meandered in an arc above the water and came out where the awful yellow house now stood.

Not many people used the new route, they preferred to stay on the open creek path rather than enter the shade of the trees, but it had been a boon for the Manor House, a school for autistic children. The children and teachers could now wander through a little latch gate straight on to the creek.

As they passed the gate Ruth and Adam saw a semicircle of chairs with musical instruments lying abandoned on them, looking poignant and incongruous.

They walked in a circle and came back to the old barn where Adam had been fishing without success. They sat on a bench and finished their sandwiches and apples in the sun. Adam checked his line. Not a bite.

Ruth held her face up to the thin warmth of the sun while Adam took something revolting off his line and put something else on to the hook and cast again. He was humming and Ruth smiled, feeling relaxed.

'OK,' she said after a minute or two. 'I'd better go back to the cottage and garden. Heaven knows when we'll be down again. I'll see you later, hon.'

Adam turned and grinned. 'Don't bank on fish for supper, will you?'

'You've still got time!' Ruth felt relieved that he was happy again.

Walking back to the cottage she saw that the best of the day was nearly over. Clouds hovered and the persistent mist was going to roll in again. She could almost feel its damp hand touching her face and coming up through her feet. She hurried to get her plants in.

Adam was fishing just beyond the ivy-clad barn. He had been fishing for a long time as if he were determined to catch something. I watched him from the trees, just inside the wood where the pine needles were dry. Ruth had gone and Adam was alone again. I stared at the back of his head. It was so familiar, the angle at which he held it, the shape of it, the way the hair grew, just like Tom's. I loved watching him.

There were no walkers on the paths and the sun was sliding in and out of cloud. The warmth of the day would soon slip away.

Adam placed his rod between two sticks and turned. He looked up into the wood where I was sitting and he shivered, pulling a sweater over his head in a swift movement. Then he turned quickly back to his rod, fiddling with the bait on the end of his line. I saw that his shoulders had suddenly become hunched and tense, his movements nervous.

My throat caught. A pulse beat painfully in my head. He knew he was being followed and watched. *I was frightening him.*

I shivered too. The boy playing the violin had hurled me back from some strange place. His eyes, staring straight into mine, had registered the bewilderment of a life he could not quite grasp; a world where everyday actions become a constant battle with fear.

I recognised, for a bleak and startling instant, the dark and lonely place he inhabited. A place where you can no longer control your thoughts or your actions or judge them. A world where it is impossible to relate to anyone; where the simplest decision is too difficult. In the boy's eyes I caught a brief reflection of myself and with horror realised I might be going out of my mind.

I was following and scaring the one beloved person left to me. Ruth and Adam had walked past me as I lay among the fir needles while the fragile rays of the sun touched my face. I could have called out, almost touched them, but I did not. I had trembled with wanting to shout, *Help me. Help me.*

Now I knew there was only one thing I could do. I could not leave Adam frightened. I must reassure him that no one wanted to hurt him, let him know it had only been me following him. *Only me.*

I picked up my coat and moved out of the wood across the deserted path to the small windowless stone barn. Pressed against the wall, I looked at him through the gaping hole. I was so near to him. I would call out to him in a minute. I would call out that it was only me, Jenny, but somehow it seemed hard to find my voice as if it had disappeared inside me.

Adam's collar was caught inside his jacket, exposing that tiny bit of white neck. *I want to hold him. I want to hold him. I am so tired. I will put my coat on the ground. I will rest for a moment, for a moment, until I stop shaking, then I will call out to him.*

TWENTY-TWO

Ruth lifted the primroses out of the orange box and began to plant them under the window. She was shaking the earth out of the box when her eye caught a name in a headline in the old newspaper lining it.

She flicked the dirt away and looked closer. There was a picture of an army officer called Tom Holland. He had been killed by a bomb. It had been placed under his car in London. He had been driving home from the zoo with his small daughter. Ruth looked at the date. It was 20 August 2005.

His good-looking face smiled up at her. Ruth rocked on her heels in shock and sat on the hard ground. *Oh, Jenny.*

Ruth stared down at the photograph and her world receded fast and dangerously in a rip tide. Memory culled, blotted out all these years as if it had never happened, flooded sickly back.

She was once more among the coats, the dusty, sweaty, charity shop smell of them; lying, almost naked, with this man pictured here.

Tom Holland . . . Just a boy when she met him. Here he was, this same man, dead; *murdered*. This was what happened to the man she so casually conceived a baby with in a cold

101

room at a Christmas party. It was Adam's face looking up at her. His face was an older, eerie version of Adam. The face she had taught herself to forget. This man had been Jenny's husband.

Ruth lifted out the paper and turned to the inside page. There were pictures of Jenny. There were pictures of a dark little girl with Jenny's laughing eyes and wild curly hair. Ruth's hands trembled. She wanted to cry out, *Why didn't you tell me the truth, Jenny? Why didn't you tell me you lost both your husband and child in this terrible tragic way?*

She would have understood so much more, Jenny's almost catatonic grief, her sudden illness. Ruth remembered the way Jenny had looked at her, her odd behaviour when she stayed at the house. Her preoccupation with Adam . . .

Oh, my God! Ruth jumped to her feet. *I'm so stupid. I'm so slow.*

She was out of the gate and on to the path running, running, the breath catching painfully in her chest. Through the beat of her heart and the noise of her feet, Ruth heard Adam screaming.

James Brown parked the car by the upturned boats on the grass and strode towards the cottage. The front door of the house was wide open. He called out as he walked down the path. There was evidence of someone recently gardening. A fork and trowel lay discarded on the path. A page of an old newspaper was blowing around the garden and, irritated by it, James grabbed it as it blew around his feet.

He stared down at the photographs of a wrecked car, obscenely mangled. Pictures of his daughter, granddaughter and son-in-law were blowing about in the wind. The world seemed suddenly silent as he stood looking at the images engraved indelibly on his mind. Out of this silence he suddenly heard a woman screaming.

He moved quickly back to his car and grabbed his doctor's bag, then made his way purposefully along the side of the creek towards the intermittent sounds. He was too old to run. It would serve no one if he had a heart attack. As he got nearer to the sounds, two white swans flew over him in perfect unison across the water into the mist. Underneath them the creek shimmered for a moment in late-afternoon sunlight.

From the path he caught a glimpse of movement on the foreshore at the mouth of the creek. It was hard to make out what was going on. As he rounded the corner of the derelict barn and crunched over seaweed and pebbles, James saw a group of people at the water's edge in the mud.

They were bending over someone. A man in waders bent and lifted a small body and carried it up on to the shingle. A muddy, frightened boy was being clasped by a blonde woman.

James broke into a run, his heart racing, towards the fisherman who was splashing out of the muddy water and laying Jenny carefully on to the ground. 'I'm a doctor. I'm her father.'

He turned Jenny on to her stomach but before he had time to pump her free of water she started to retch and vomit. Relieved, James turned her on her side and held her there, realising she couldn't have been in the water long. He bent and felt her pulse, pushed her hair away from her muddy face, laid the back of his hand on the side of her neck. She was going to be all right but she was shivering with cold. He looked up at the fisherman. 'Thank you,' he said.

'Don't thank me,' the man said. 'It was the lad that went in the water after her. I was fishing by the lake, I heard him yelling. I just helped pull her out.'

James took his mobile phone out of his pocket to ring for an ambulance, but abruptly changed his mind. He turned as the boy, covered in mud, walked towards him. He recognised Ruth despite the fact that she too was dishevelled and muddy.

'Is Jenny going to be OK?' the boy asked anxiously, his teeth chattering with cold and fright. His vivid blue eyes stared out at James from his dirty face.

'James?' Ruth said, surprised. 'Oh, thank God you're here.'

'Yes, she's going to be OK. Thanks to you,' James said to the boy, then to Ruth, 'You must get him home, he's frozen.'

The fisherman came back with an old rug. They wrapped Jenny in it and he offered to carry her back to the cottage. 'She doesn't weigh nothing, poor maid.'

James looked down at the small muddy face of his daughter. 'Jenny?' he said softly. 'Darling, it's all right. It's going to be all right.'

Jenny's eyes opened. She stared back with a blank hopelessness that seared him. He felt furious with himself. *I should have seen this coming.*

They hobbled in a strange little procession back to the cottage. He and Ruth got Jenny out of her soaked clothes, put her in a hot bath, wrapped her up with hot-water bottles and placed her in Ruth's bed. James gave her an injection and she stopped shaking as the sedative worked and fell asleep.

Ruth got Adam into the bath and James rang Bea.

When Ruth came downstairs she took one look at James's face and offered him a drink.

'I'd love a stiff whisky, but I'm driving. A cup of tea would be good. How's the boy?'

'Adam. He's shaken, but he's fine. Luckily the tide wasn't fully in. It was terrifying seeing them both struggling in the water . . .' She hesitated. 'You don't think Jenny should be checked over in hospital?'

James smiled grimly. 'I know the system. If I admit her to

a county hospital in this state she will have to be questioned by a psychiatrist. It's possible she could be sectioned. I don't want that. You saw how malnourished and underweight she is; that alone can cause mental problems. I want to help her myself and get the opinion of colleagues I trust before I consign my daughter to psychiatrists.'

Ruth nodded and went to switch on the kettle. James, watching her, asked, 'Has Jenny been staying here with you? What made her . . . what suddenly tipped her over the edge after six months?'

Ruth put mugs on the table between them. She sat opposite James. 'Jenny hasn't been staying with us. We didn't even know she was in Cornwall until this afternoon. I think she's been living in a camper van. She's been out there stalking Adam for days, but of course we didn't know it was Jenny.'

James stared at Ruth, horrified. 'Why on earth . . . ? I don't understand . . . *stalking*?'

'I think you might understand in a moment, James.'

Adam came downstairs, clean but still pale. Ruth went to him and gently turned the boy to face James, who stared. What was he supposed to be looking at? Then the boy flicked his hair back and looked at James out of those extraordinary deep, blue-flecked eyes.

Tom's eyes . . . Of course, the eyes . . . James saw the boy's adolescent likeness to Tom was remarkable and would grow more so as he reached maturity. It was not just the shape of the head and the way the hair grew, but the way he looked straight at you.

James suddenly felt tired and old and sad. He met Ruth's eyes over the boy's shoulder and saw a defensive wariness in them. He looked back at the boy.

'What's going on? I don't understand,' Adam said, moving away from his mother.

That makes two of us, James thought.

Ruth said quickly, 'Now is not the time to talk, Adam. When you've slept, in the morning, I'll try to explain things.'

How would Ruth explain things to Jenny? James wondered miserably. How would she explain away this boy? He took a deep breath. 'How are you feeling, Adam? What you did was very brave. It must have been extremely frightening.'

'I'm OK. Like, I didn't swallow much water. I was only just out of my depth, and the fisherman came to help me.'

'Can you tell me what happened between you and Jenny out there?'

Adam sat at the table and fiddled with one of the mugs. 'I knew someone was watching me this afternoon. They'd been following me for days. I didn't know it was Jenny. I thought they had gone and I was, like, rushing to get to the path home, and I suddenly saw her lying all curled up on her coat.' Adam looked up at James, his eyes anxious. 'It was sad, not scary any more. I knew Jenny must be ill. I woke her and she told me she was sorry she had frightened me. I asked her why she was following me and she said I was like . . . Tom . . . her husband who died and that she had thought she was my mother. She said she must have gone a little mad. I told her I would run to get Mum. I got to the lake and I heard a noise and I looked back, and she was just wading into the water really fast with her heavy coat on. I yelled at her to stop but she took no notice. I went in after her but she didn't want me to . . . pull her out. She struggled and fought. Then the fisherman came to help me. It was awful. *She wanted to drown . . .*' His voice wobbled.

James said gently, 'It must have been dreadful, Adam. You kept your head and you saved Jenny from drowning. That took some courage. Words aren't enough to thank you.'

Adam sniffed, embarrassed. 'Jenny will be all right?'

'I hope so.' James got up from the table and went to get

his bag. 'I'm sorry that you had to go through something so distressing. I'll leave something with your mother in case you can't sleep. Don't be afraid to take it.' He looked at Ruth. 'I'd like to get Jenny home now. I'll go and back up my car to the cottage.'

'But your tea . . .'

'It's getting late. Bea will be worrying. I think it might be a good idea to go to your doctor in the morning and get Adam checked out. The water is undoubtedly polluted.'

James went abruptly out of the front door to get his car. Ruth helped him with the heavily sedated Jenny and they put her in the back seat under a rug. She was feather light and James felt inexplicably and unfairly angry with Ruth. He nodded a curt goodnight, got into his car without another word and drove away up the hill.

The moon swept out from behind clouds and hung dramatically in a navy-blue sky, and James heard again the haunting sound of swans flying in perfect unison over the dark waters that had almost swallowed up his daughter.

TWENTY-THREE

Ruth sat in the window seat of the cottage in the dark. Adam had at last fallen asleep. She gazed out into the thick black night, numb and shocked. The cottage felt cold, and she pulled an old moth-smelling rug round her and tried not to shiver. If she started she wouldn't be able to stop.

She tried to steady her breathing, calm the panicky beat of her heart. She went over and over the moment when she had read the newspaper cutting.

She could not focus on any one thing. Her mind dithered about in alarm, she felt unable to assess the implications of all that had happened in nightmare sequence down on the creek. She felt as if something were slowly breaking inside her and she were falling back down a deep black hole into childhood.

All these years of carefully blanking everything out; all these years of self-induced amnesia had been swept away in an afternoon. She felt like a spy whose cover had been blown and here she was exposed, naked to the world; the reality of her life cruelly laid bare for Adam – for everyone to see like a hideous birthmark.

All the years of love, reassurance and sense of worth

nurtured by her aunt had disappeared in the look James Brown had given her over Adam's head, before he strode out of the house taking Jenny with him. She was flung back to the desperate adolescent she had been and the horror of exposure.

Life had a habit of turning full circle. For fourteen years she had locked Tom Holland behind a heavy door, marked not 'Do not enter', but 'Did not happen'.

The cottage creaked around her as she sat thinking of Jenny. She would never forget the sight of her struggling in the water with Adam. For a second she thought Jenny had been trying to drown him. Her movements had been wild and desperate as Adam hung on to her. It had been surreal.

Ruth got up and, without turning on the light, poured herself a large brandy and carried the balloon glass back to the window seat. It had been terrifying. Both Adam and Jenny could have sunk into the mud and drowned.

To feel so hopeless that you want to end your life. To come to that.

Am I capable of feeling such a loss, such a love? Feeling so bereft that even inching forward to some future holds no power. And dying holds no fear?

Tomorrow she would have to talk to Adam. She would have to explain the unexplainable, tell him that Jenny's husband was his father. That was why Jenny had wanted to drown herself.

Ruth quailed at the thought. God! A totally random meeting on a train had triggered a series of events that would change all their lives for ever. Despair made her limbs feel weak.

What if she had not gone to that party when she was seventeen? What if Jenny had been with her? Could she and Jenny have been rivals over this man?

If Jenny had been with her she would not have got

pregnant, but then there would have been no Adam and that was inconceivable.

She and Jenny could have met on a train to Birmingham when Tom was alive. What would have happened then? Would Tom have acknowledged his son?

Why was she thinking like this? What was the point? The point was the pretence was over. That private part of her life that she hugged so secretly to her had ended that afternoon as she watched Adam pulling Jenny, crazed with grief, from the water.

Adam had been difficult to get to bed. Disturbed and shaken, he had wanted answers and Ruth needed this night to herself before she could give him any. She drank the brandy, let it burn down her throat.

She remembered the heavy feel of the coats on top of them. The excitement of him wanting her and her own over-powering need and desire. She remembered the painful, stinging feel of him entering her; the heady wonder of another body glued warmly to hers and the thrill of his gasp as he climaxed. She felt again the poignant musky smell of sex, the hot rush of semen glutinous and foreign between her thighs . . .

She had trusted absolutely that the boy who had taken her virginity and shared that tremulous, intimate moment would find out where she lived and call her. Naively, she never doubted it.

He had said, *God! What a beautiful girl you are.* He had held her body tight to his. No one had ever held her that close, hot skin to hot skin. The foreign but comforting warmth of a male body pressed to hers. Someone touching her. She was unused to touch, new to tenderness, but here was someone of her very own, loving her.

He had taken her face in his hands so gently afterwards and kissed her forehead. '*I will never forget this evening,*' he had whispered. *'I've got to go now or I'll miss my lift back to Plymouth, but I'll call you!'*

Ruth had relived that evening a million times while she waited day after day, week after week for a phone call that never came. By the time she finally made herself accept the dreadful truth, that he was not going to call her, that she had been a one-night stand, a 'wham bam, thank you, ma'am', she had missed her first period.

It was almost impossible to believe or accept his rejection. How could it have meant nothing to him? What had been an earth-moving moment for her had been a quick fuck for that unknown boy.

Some of the powerlessness and panic of that unbalanced period of her life crept over Ruth now. Terror had made her insentient. With hormones screaming round her thin body she had become uncharacteristically passive. Her parents were able to inflict wounds on a heart already broken. Desolate, Ruth had had no more resources to draw on.

The look James Brown had given her over Adam's head had made her heart jump and her legs go weak. It had brought with it the bitter taste and memory of her beginnings and that dark place of shame that she had resolutely turned her back on.

In its place she had built false memory in order to live with hope, however frail. She had distorted her encounter with Tom into something fantastical and acceptable in order to live with herself. She had changed and enlarged the evening so many times that the truth had been eclipsed from the moment of Adam's birth.

For the rest of her life, Ruth had longed for a man who could sexually arouse her in the dramatic, immediate way that far-off boy had done. It had never happened. Sex was never what she remembered it could be. How could it when she had embellished the moment into something exquisite, with never a second of awkwardness or disappointment.

She could acknowledge that sex with a stranger was obviously more exciting than the reality of a long relationship, but somehow it did not stop her childish yearning for that ephemeral lost excitement. For something more.

Tom's face, looking out at her from a yellowing newspaper, haunted her. The memory of the boy he had been had long faded. It was a shock to see an older mature edition of Adam. Here was the man Jenny had loved and lived with. The man she had shared *her* child with.

A man with crinkly laughter lines on his good-looking face. A man who had died too young, obliterated in one horrific moment with his child on a hot summer evening. She had read the article over and over again, and made herself face the truth of his dreadful death. Then she had carefully put it away in a drawer until she had talked to Adam.

How was Adam going to cope with suddenly having a dead father with a name and a face?

Ruth heard again the horn of the InterCity train as it rounded a bend; heard Jenny's lifeless voice as she told her of Tom's car accident. She heard the background noises of passengers and the smell of coffee. She felt Jenny's small hand tremble under hers.

She lit the lamp, poured more brandy and went back to the window seat. The night seemed endless, as if there would never be a lightening of the sky, no new dawn to come. It felt, in her exhausted state, as if some fissure were opening out in front of her; a crack too wide to leap.

She longed to wail into the empty room, to cry out in anguish.

Life could have been so different. So different. She might have had Tom as well as Adam. She might have had them both.

*   *   *

Adam woke with a jump and lay on his back in the dark. The house was silent, but somehow claustrophobic. He turned on his side, warm and sleepy, pushing aside a little nag of anxiety that was surfacing. Then, with a start he remembered and switched on his bedside light. His head thumped as he moved upright and he waited for it to clear, for his eyes to focus.

Furtively he reached into his bedside table for the newspaper he had watched his mother hide in a downstairs drawer. He had taken it while she was in the kitchen. He had been too dazed to read it last night and now he held it over his knees and carefully smoothed out the creases.

He stared down at a photograph of a mutilated bombed car. There was a smaller photograph of a smiling army officer in uniform called Tom Holland. This man had been in the car with his child. Jenny's husband. Adam turned the page and looked at the photographs of the soldier; of Jenny and of a small, dark child. His hands trembled. He concentrated on the face of the man for a long time in the silent house. He could feel his heart thumping with incredulous excitement, beating against his chest in a startled flurry of recognition.

Those laughing eyes evoked such a rush of emotion in Adam that it hurt. He had to rest the newspaper on his knees as his hands holding it shook. He remembered Jenny's words: *You are so like Tom.*

He knew. He knew without a moment of doubt that this man was his father. The face was a familiar, older version of his own. He recognised the truth without ever having seen him before and he felt a burst and rush of pride. It enveloped him warmly, thrilling him, so that the moment in the dark bedroom at dawn when he first experienced blinding love would always be with him. *This man was his father.*

Was. He smoothed again with shaking fingers the photo

of the dead man between his forefinger and thumb. His excitement ebbed away into a gaping loss. He wept for all that his mother had refused to tell him and for the chance of knowing his real father gone for ever. He wept for the little girl who would have been his half-sister and for Jenny who, without them, had wanted to die.

He heard a strange sound. He got out of bed and went down the stairs. His mother was sitting in the dark in the window seat. Her head was thrown back, her face in shadow. Awful, harsh noises were coming from deep inside her. Adam froze. In all his thirteen years he had never seen his mother cry.

TWENTY-FOUR

Bea left Jenny's side at six in the morning. She had had all night to think about what James had told her and she needed to see Ruth.

As she drove over the causeway her tiredness made everything outside the car appear overbright and sickly. The dual carriageway was empty, the sky in front of her flared dramatically in thin fingers of orange.

Bea drove to St Minyon and down the hill to the water and parked near the upturned boats. The place seemed to have changed little since the days when she and James had collected Ruth and Jenny from the thatched cottage. A hunched figure in a coat stood staring out over the water.

'Ruth?' Bea asked tentatively.

The woman turned. Her forlorn face was familiar, her eyes were swollen and puffy, but it was unmistakably Ruth.

The two women stared at one another as the tears trickled out of the corners of Ruth's eyes in a miserable, unstoppable flow. Bea did what came naturally and opened her arms. Ruth moved automatically into them as she had so often done in childhood, only this time she dwarfed Bea. After a minute Bea held her gently away. 'Come on.

Try to stop. Let's go inside the cottage and make a cup of tea.'

Bea made the tea and Ruth tried to light the fire in the cold cottage, moving quietly so she would not wake Adam. Ruth knew why Bea had come but she had got almost beyond talking. Bea, too, looked exhausted. It was hard for Ruth to look at the Bea of her childhood and see an old woman. They sat in front of the weak fire, clasping their mugs for warmth.

'How's Jenny, Bea?'

'Heavily sedated. There seems so little of her, as if she were wasting away.'

'I'm so sorry.'

Bea looked at Ruth sharply. 'You're surely not blaming yourself, Ruth? I understand from James that it's thanks to your son that Jenny's alive.'

Ruth bent to the fire. 'Adam did react quickly, but so did the fisherman.'

'When James told me about . . . Adam, I realised immediately what must have happened all those years ago. Why you had to leave school so abruptly. Why your parents wouldn't let me see you and why you all left St Ives so suddenly. You were pregnant?'

Ruth nodded and Bea leant towards her. 'Knowing your parents, Ruth, I imagine you had a beastly time.'

Ruth looked up from the fire. 'I didn't even know Tom, Bea. I met him once and I never saw him again. I made myself forget him. To open that paper and find he had died like that with their child was horrific. You know?' Her voice rose, overwrought. 'After that one time with a man I knew nothing about, I've never been able to experience that soaring feeling of love. The only real emotion I can feel is for my son.' Her teeth chattered.

'Come on,' Bea said briskly. 'I'm going to treat you like a child and put you to bed. You're absolutely past it.'

Ruth smiled wanly. 'You've been up all night with Jenny, worrying yourself sick. I should be putting you to bed.'

'Ah,' Bea said, 'but I'm a tough old bird. You have to be with all the children and grandchildren I have.'

Ruth let herself be led upstairs and put into bed with a hot-water bottle. 'You were always kind to me,' she murmured.

Bea sat on the bed. 'Oh, Ruth, how I wish you had confided in us all those years ago. We could have made things very different for you. We would have taken care of you.'

'That's what Jenny said. If I had done that Jenny's life would have been different. I would have spoilt it then instead of now.'

'Jenny *is* going to be all right, Ruth,' Bea said firmly. 'You won't help her by being maudlin about something that's not your fault. A bomb killed Tom and Rosie. Their awful deaths have resulted in her breakdown. I know my daughter and she will come through this.' She patted Ruth's leg. 'I don't believe this is like you, Ruth. You were never sentimental or wishy-washy.'

Ruth laughed suddenly. 'Oh, Bea! You haven't changed a bit. You always made everything seem somehow better.'

'No. I let Jenny down. I should have gone back to London with her after Tom died. I should have sensed this coming. I found it difficult to get near her and I didn't try hard enough. I'm not going to fail her again.'

Ruth closed her eyes. 'I don't know what to do, Bea. For Jenny's sake I should disappear out of her life again fast, but Adam's not going to let this rest. I've only ever told him a partial truth, that Tom was a brief encounter and I remembered nothing about him. Actually, I remember everything about that evening. I just never let myself . . . You should have seen Adam in the early hours of this morning. He was beside himself and very, very angry with me.'

'Disappearing as if none of this has happened is not going to help Adam or Jenny. Her shock and grief are raw but at least they are out in the open now. We will have to help her come to terms with the fact of Adam and Adam will have to come to terms with the knowledge of who his father was. The fact that he can never meet Tom now is going to be terribly hard for him.' Bea paused. 'You do realise that Adam is going to want to find out everything he can about his dead father?'

'Oh yes, I realise. And I don't have any answers.' She met Bea's eyes. 'But, Jenny does.'

Bea held them. 'Jenny does.' She got a pen from her bag and rooted for a piece of paper. 'Give me the number of your mobile. I'll phone you later in the day.' She got up wearily. 'Try and get some sleep.'

She hesitated at the door. 'I'm sorry that James jumped to the wrong conclusion, Ruth. He was too disturbed by events to take in the fact that Adam's age precluded an affair with Tom.'

'It was a natural conclusion.'

'Sleep, now.'

As Bea went down the narrow stairs she glanced at the closed bedroom door where Adam must be sleeping. She longed to see this boy whose likeness to Tom had tipped Jenny over the edge. As she drove away from the creek, doubt crept back like an insidious black shadow: a young boy in thrall to a dead father he never knew; her daughter, whose only lasting legacy with the man she loved, the life she had lost, was this boy; Ruth, so vulnerable and needy in childhood, clinging desperately to the fickle memory of a fleeting passion she mistook for love. Bea shivered. Obsession was damaging, unpredictable and ultimately destructive.

TWENTY-FIVE

'Of course we have to go home, Adam. You've got school and I have to work.'

'I want to see Jenny first. I don't want to leave without seeing her.'

'Jenny's not well enough to see anyone yet. You heard me talking to Bea. She's going to be at St Michael's for a while. It's a small hospital near James. When we next come down I'm sure Jenny will be up to seeing us, but at the moment it's too soon.'

'That really suits you, doesn't it, Mum?'

Ruth looked at him. 'What do you mean, that really suits me?'

Adam stared at her truculently. 'Well, obviously it's in your interests that I don't get to talk to Jenny.'

'Why?' Ruth's voice was dangerously quiet.

Adam coughed nervously and scuffed his shoes on the kitchen floor. 'Why would you want her telling me about my father when *you* haven't told me anything about him since the day I was born?'

'I've always explained to you that I don't know much about him to tell.'

Adam met her eyes for the first time, and Ruth was astonished by the surliness she saw in them and the accusatory tone he was using. 'Oh, so you didn't remember his name was Tom Holland?'

'I remembered his name was Tom, but if I ever knew his surname I certainly forgot it.'

'OK. So you could have told me his first name, couldn't you? You could have told me that.'

'What difference could it have possibly made to you knowing his first name?'

'If you can't see that, then you must be *stupid*. If someone has a name, then they become a *person*, don't they? They become *Tom*. *Tom* is the name of *my father*. You could at least have told me that.'

Ruth picked up her coffee cup and folded her hands round it. She said, in a voice not quite steady, 'Adam, please don't talk to me like that. I know this is a hell of a shock for you, but why are you so angry with *me*? I did what I thought was the best thing at the time. I didn't want to trace your father for reasons that I've already told you, honestly, many times.'

Adam suddenly crumpled and sat down at the table. He put his head in his hands and Ruth, watching his distress, felt like doing the same. He did not cry, he just sat very still. Then he said huskily, 'I've always imagined the day, when I was grown up, that I would secretly go and find my dad. I've thought about it all my life and now I can't. I can't ever see or know the man who was my dad.'

'I'm sorry, darling. I'm sorry. I can't undo my past. I can't make it all right for you. I know it hurts, Adam, but I'm shocked too and I'm not responsible for Tom Holland's terrible death.'

'Jenny's lost everything, Mum, everything. No wonder she didn't want to live. Imagine if you'd lost me and Peter all at the same time. I bet you'd feel the same.'

'What's happened has a huge bearing on how you're feeling, Adam. You were brave and I'm proud of you, but now we both need to step back and establish some sort of normality in our lives. Of course I'm not going to stop you talking to Jenny about Tom. But until Jenny can cope with talking about him you will have to be patient.'

'I've *got* to see Jenny. We don't need to talk. I just want to see her. I can't go back to school without seeing if she's OK. *I can't.*'

Ruth sighed. 'I could ring James and Bea to see if this is possible.'

Adam nodded and got up from his chair to get her mobile.

'Go and get dressed. I'll come and tell you what they say. I'll have to walk up the road for a signal.'

Bea answered on the second ring. 'Ruth! I was just about to pick up the phone to ring you, it must be telepathy.'

'I'm having a problem with Adam. He's insisting on seeing Jenny before we leave tomorrow. I've told him she's too unwell, but he's adamant. I'm sorry, I'm at a loss. I'm wondering if I should get counselling for him after what happened.'

'It's actually what I was going to ring you about. I was rather dreading it. James has organised a private room in St Michael's for Jenny, so she can have some physical tests and an assessment by a colleague. She's very hazy about what happened and she's still sedated. However, she's repeatedly asking to see Adam. Naomi Watson, a psychiatrist friend James has a lot of faith in, thinks it's a good idea for you, Adam and Jenny to see each other at St Michael's to help normalise things and help her assess Jenny's attitude to Adam. Naomi also thinks that Adam might be very disturbed by the incident and it might be helpful if she talked to him. How do you feel about this? It is, of course, entirely up to you.'

Ruth wanted to cry out, *But it isn't up to me! I want none of it. I just want to get Adam home. I want us home and out of here. I'll look after Adam.* But she knew she didn't have a choice and perhaps it would be the right thing for Adam.

Hearing her hesitation, Bea said, 'My dear Ruth, this is very difficult for you. I'm so sorry.'

'It might help Adam. He's hellish this morning, bolshie and aggressive. So, yes, perhaps he'll be easier when he's seen Jenny again.'

Bea thought, but didn't say, This couldn't have happened at a worse age for Adam. He would slowly have stopped being a delicious and easy boy any time now without the added stick of his father to whip Ruth with. It was going to be a long haul for her, but Bea had not expected it to start so soon. 'All right, Ruth. I'll talk to James. When are you heading home?'

'We should leave tomorrow by midday. At a push, we could leave the next morning.'

'I'll ring you back. You may have to bite your tongue and try not to let Adam hurt you. There is a lot for him to take on board, but you know this.'

Ruth laughed shortly. 'I do.'

Walking back to the cottage, she suddenly wished vehemently that Peter were with her. She started to dial his number, but stopped. She had never told Peter much about Tom Holland either, and it wasn't the sort of conversation to have, standing on a gloomy morning with a biting wind coming off the water. If he rang she would have to explain things, otherwise it could wait until they were both home. It was the first time in his life that Adam had spoken to her so rudely and Ruth felt miserable.

She remembered all of a sudden that if Jenny had really wanted something as a child she had gently but surely chipped away until all resistance wavered and gave up under her quiet perseverance and gratitude. James had been a sucker. Bea flintier.

The future seemed abruptly uncertain and Ruth felt powerless in the presence of an imperceptible threat coming from an unexpected quarter.

TWENTY-SIX

James Brown was waiting in the hospital foyer for Ruth and Adam the next morning. He was standing talking to a woman with a long fair plait. He introduced Ruth and Adam to Naomi Watson and they went into a small waiting room to talk.

'How's Jenny?' Ruth asked James.

'She's very quiet and sad, Ruth. She sleeps a lot.'

'Does she remember what she tried to do?'

Naomi Watson leant forward. She was watching Adam. 'I don't think Jenny remembers anything too clearly. It's too soon to hope she'll talk about anything yet.'

Adam said in a self-conscious rush, 'But she's going to get better, isn't she? I mean she'll go back to how she was, won't she?'

Naomi smiled at him. 'She hasn't lost her mind, Adam, if that's what you mean. People get sick, not just physically, but mentally as well. If someone becomes diabetic we give them insulin. If they are epileptic their fits are controlled by special drugs. Jenny is what we call clinically depressed. That is not the same as being depressed, which we all are at times. Jenny needs drugs to help her in the same way as anyone with a physical ailment. She also needs time and a chance to grieve. Does this make sense?'

Adam nodded and Naomi turned to Ruth. 'Jenny has asked to see you both. Are you happy with that, Ruth?'

Ruth, irritated by the way the question was phrased, said, 'Of course I'd like to see Jenny, if she's up to it.'

'Good. I suggest five minutes. Would you mind going with James? Adam and I will join you.'

Ruth did mind, but she went out of the room with James, touching Adam's arm on the way out.

When they had gone Naomi said, 'How about you, Adam? How are you feeling?'

Adam was silent. He did not know what to say or what the woman wanted him to say.

'I understand you were quick-witted and brave. It must have been shocking to see Jenny going into the water.'

Adam looked up. 'Yes. A fisherman helped me.' He started to say something and stopped.

Naomi waited.

Adam swallowed. 'It was terrible seeing her walking into the water. It was scary. It made me really sad. I didn't want her to drown, even though I was really scared when she was following me. I didn't know it was her. I thought maybe it was . . .'

'What?'

'Well, a ghost or maybe a paedophile.'

'That must have been frightening. How did you feel when you realised it was Jenny?'

'I felt . . . like, why? But I was relieved too. Then she told me that I reminded her of her husband and I felt sorry for her. I wanted to help her, get her to Mum. She was a bit odd . . . like, out of it . . .' Adam petered out.

'I understand your mum explained why Jenny had been so muddled. She told you that your father had been Jenny's husband?'

125

Adam's face closed abruptly.

'You don't want to talk about this?'

He shook his head.

'I understand. It's painful.'

Adam looked at his shoes. He was breathing quickly and was obviously upset. Naomi said gently, changing tack, 'Why was it important for you to see Jenny before you went home?'

Adam looked up. 'I wanted to tell her it's all right. She was so worried she had scared me. I want to tell her . . .' He met Naomi's eyes and she saw how intense and blue his were – intelligent eyes. 'I just want to see her.'

'Because she was married to your father?'

Adam's eyes showed a flash of anger. 'Yes, because of that, but because I really like her, too. I liked her from the beginning when she stayed in our house, before I knew anything about my father.'

Naomi stood up. 'I'm glad. Let's go and join your mother. You can't be very long with Jenny, I'm afraid.'

'I'm not going to ask her anything. Can I see her on my own, for just a minute?

Naomi hesitated. It was obviously important to the boy. 'Just for a moment. I'll be right outside.'

Jenny was propped up on pillows like a Pre-Raphaelite painting. Her eyes were dark-ringed in a pale face. Adam heard Ruth say, 'Get well. I'll see you when we're next down. Get better. I'll ring . . .'

Jenny turned as Adam and Naomi came into the room and her face, when she saw Adam, showed relief, broke into a semblance of a smile. 'Adam!'

The blood rushed to Adam's face. He muttered something as he moved nearer, but his face too had come alive. James, watching the exchange, felt disturbed. Jenny held out her hand and after an embarrassed hesitation Adam took it.

Naomi guided a reluctant Ruth and James to the other side of the door.

All three watched through the glass window. Ruth was white and Naomi noticed her hands shook as they saw Adam turn his back on them and bend to hear what Jenny was saying.

'I'm so glad you came, Adam.'

'I wanted to . . . before I went home.'

'I'm sorry, so sorry that I frightened you. Please forgive me. It's all a strange muddle in my head . . .'

'It's OK. It doesn't matter. You couldn't help it.'

'Are we still friends?'

'Yes, of course. Jenny, can I come back and see you again, when you're better?'

Jenny nodded, closed her eyes against the blueness of his eyes. 'I'd like that. I *will* get better, Adam. I will get better now.'

'I should go. I'm only allowed a minute.'

Jenny opened her eyes, let go of his hand and smiled. 'Goodbye, darling boy,' she murmured.

''Bye, Jenny,' Adam said, his heart leaping.

Ruth, James and Naomi could not hear this exchange from behind the door, but the intensity of feeling between Jenny and Adam was obvious. They desperately needed each other, one to hold on to the past, the other to try to make sense of the future.

Turning to Ruth, Naomi said quickly, 'Please understand that your feelings are as valid and as important as Jenny's or Adam's. I hope you might be willing to talk with me?'

Ruth was watching Adam coming towards her. She turned and looked at Naomi with hostility. It was patently obvious that her feelings were *not* as important as Jenny's. It was disingenuous to suggest otherwise. '*I'm* not your patient, Jenny is,' she said abruptly.

'I put Adam and Jenny together in order to see how things were between them. I wanted to make sure Adam was not still nervous of Jenny. It was not to hurt you.'

'Well, that's how it felt.'

Ruth turned to Adam, nodded at James and Naomi, and she and Adam walked away out of the doors to the car park.

James said, 'Oh, poor girl.'

Naomi looked at him. 'Yes. The pull of a dead parent is hard to compete with.'

TWENTY-SEVEN

As soon as he was in the car, Adam put his earplugs in and slumped in the front seat listening to music. It suited Ruth fine, she had no desire to talk as they drove back towards Truro.

Back at the cottage, Adam went straight up to his room and Ruth began to pack things up for a quick start in the morning. She considered setting off immediately, but knew she was too tired to drive all the way back to Birmingham.

She made Adam supper and let him eat it on his knees watching the television. It was better than trying to make conversation. They were both miserable.

In the morning they piled their possessions into the car and left the cottage with relief. It had become too small a place to be cooped up together.

Ruth was not sure if Peter would be home before her. She tried to ring him and eventually left a text message. The last two days felt like a bad dream she could not wake up from. She and Adam had been catapulted from a peaceful half-term holiday to a personal tragedy.

As Ruth drove out of Cornwall the cloud cleared and the sun shone for the first time in a pale-blue sky. She sat on a persistent muted anger. She was now appalled that fate had thrown her and Jenny together on a train. She was resentful with Jenny for not telling her the whole truth about Tom and Rosie, and incensed by that patronising bloody psychiatrist.

She glanced at Adam, slouched beside her, tinny sounds coming from his headphones. She felt annoyed with him too for so suddenly turning, for so abruptly becoming enthralled with Jenny, because of Tom.

She knew she was being unfair. It was her fault. In romanticising his conception and birth, even to herself, she had deprived him of something fundamental to hang on to.

Ruth was used to driving long distances and was aware of her lack of concentration, so she stopped twice to find coffee and something for Adam to eat. When it got dark Adam fell asleep beside her. His face, softening into a child's as he relaxed, moved Ruth with its vulnerability. She drove carefully, longing to get home, yet needing to get her feelings into some sort of order before she arrived.

She began to feel more optimistic about her ability to cope with Adam as they drew closer to Birmingham. Peter was the one person she could talk to about this. Ruth turned into their wide leafy road with relief. She saw that the hall lights were on. Peter *was* back, thank God for that. Adam woke, stretched and got out of the car without saying anything, but he waited to help her with the cases and together they walked up the steps.

Peter had heard them and came out on to the front step to greet them, running down to the car to carry the remainder of their luggage. He had been cooking something in the kitchen and the smell filled the house. Adam sniffed hungrily.

Peter smiled at him. 'Spag Bog. Are you hungry?'

'Starving,' Adam said. 'I'll just put this stuff in my room.'

He bounded upstairs and Peter turned to Ruth. 'You look tired. Bad journey?'

'Not really, just long.'

'I've got a good bottle of cold wine in the fridge.'

'Lovely. But what I'd really like to start with is a malt whisky.'

Peter looked at her closely. Ruth hardly ever drank spirits. 'OK,' he said carefully and went to get her one. Ruth sat at the kitchen table wearily. She couldn't even begin to talk to Peter until Adam had gone to bed.

Peter put the whisky in front of her and went to the stove to dish out a plate of food for Adam, who came crashing down the stairs. Peter turned to Ruth. 'Do you want to eat now or wait a little?'

'I'll wait, but you eat with Adam.'

Ruth listened to them talking together about birds, about the cottage, about the weather. Occasionally Adam's eyes flickered her way, but he said nothing about Jenny. For the first time she noticed how tired Peter looked, grey at the gills. 'What time did you get home?'

'About 3 a.m. But I came back and slept.' His eyes rested on her in a look Ruth could not fathom.

Adam bolted his meal and leant back. He looked at Ruth, his eyes bright with challenge. 'Are you going to tell him, then?'

'Of course I am, Adam,' Ruth said quietly.

Peter was watching them both. He didn't smile or try to defuse the atmosphere with a joke as he usually did.

The room was silent, then Adam said abruptly, 'I'm going to bed.' He went over to the fridge and got himself a bottle of water.

'Goodnight, Adam. See you in the morning,' Peter said.

Adam looked directly at him for the first time. 'Yeah. Goodnight.'

He thumped up the stairs, closed his door with a thud and music played loudly behind it.

Peter got up and shut the kitchen door. Ruth poured herself another whisky; it was blurring the edges beautifully. Peter put some food on a plate for her. 'You'd better eat if you are going to drink seriously.'

'Thank you.' She played with her food, eating small mouthfuls. The whisky began to taste bitter and she pushed it away. 'How about opening that bottle of wine now?'

'You'll regret it in the morning.'

'I have a day off. I'm giving that lecture in London the day after tomorrow.'

'OK,' Peter said quietly. 'It's obviously going to be an evening for talking.'

As he poured the wine Ruth noticed his hands were not quite steady. He was wondering what was coming. There was, all of a sudden, something deeply attractive about his long brown fingers with their sprinkling of dark hair. Ruth felt an unexpected rush of lust. 'Let's take the wine up to the attic flat and talk in bed. We're further away from Adam.'

Surprised, Peter hesitated, then said, 'All right. You go on up. I'll just put these in the dishwasher.'

Ruth picked up her wine, went upstairs and gathered the things she needed, and went up to the flat Jenny had stayed in. She ran a bath and sat with her wine watching the soft swaying of the tree outside the window. She thought she heard Peter way below her on the phone. Adam's music had stopped.

She dried herself and put on a nightdress Peter had given her long ago, which she had rarely worn. It was expensively seductive and she looked at herself critically in the mirror. It was peach, with coffee-coloured lace at the breast and spaghetti straps. It was not a nightdress to sleep in. It was shameful how little she had worn it. Her face was pale without make-up and she had dark circles under her eyes, but she was bone thin and thankful for it.

She climbed into bed. Below her she heard the shower.

Adam or Peter? If he didn't come up soon she would get self-conscious in this nightdress. Ruth suddenly wanted to take it off and put on pyjamas, it seemed such a brazen invitation and unlike her.

It was too late, she heard Peter coming up the stairs. He had the wine bottle and his glass in his hand. He had been in the shower. He poured her more wine without looking at her. 'Adam's asleep already. What's been going on, Ruth?'

Ruth patted the bed, unwilling and almost too tired to talk. Peter took off his bathrobe and climbed in. He looked wary. He did not notice what she was wearing. He never wore anything in bed. Ruth reflected ruefully on all the times he had watched her climb into bed in old PJs and now, when she really wanted him to see her, wanted to have sex urgently, his thoughts were definitely elsewhere.

He smelt good: clean and tangy. He had obviously aired his body near a swimming pool because his skin was tanned. She pressed a nose to his arm and smelt lemon and spice. 'New soap?' she asked. 'It's lovely.'

He looked down at her curiously.

She met his eyes. 'I've really missed you, Peter.'

'Come on, Ruth, what's upset both you and Adam?'

'Let's make love first . . .'

She rolled towards him with her head on his shoulder and put her arm round him. She felt him stiffen slightly. He drew in his breath, hesitated, started to say something and changed his mind as her hand slipped down his body. His immediate arousal excited her and she moved on top of him, kissing his neck and face and his closed eyes, surprising herself with her own urgency. She was behaving unlike herself and Peter responded, rolling her over, entering her roughly and seeming almost angry with her for exciting him. They were both unlike themselves. There was nothing cool or detached about this coupling in the attic, it was the best fuck they had had in ages.

They fell away from each other and were silent for a moment, then Ruth reached for her wine and turned his way.

He watched her as she told him about Jenny; about Tom and Rosie, and all that had happened in their few days in Cornwall. Her words caught and stumbled as she explained that Tom had been Adam's father. She put her hand on his arm for comfort as she spoke about Adam's fury with her and his sudden preoccupation with Jenny because of Tom.

When she had finished Peter said nothing for a while. He went on watching her in a way that made her uneasy as she waited for his careful and measured response. He did not take her hand in his own or bring it to his lips as he sometimes did. 'I'm so sorry,' he said at last, 'that it all happened in that awful way. It must have been traumatic for you both.' The way he said this gave distance to his words. Polite, sorry, but somehow uninvolved. 'I thought Jenny's intentness with Adam was rather odd when she stayed here, but I knew she was still grieving. I didn't say anything because she was your friend and it seemed churlish. I wish I had now.'

He poured the last of the wine. 'Ruth, this thing with Adam's father was going to happen sooner or later, you must have known that. You knew Adam would want to trace him at some point, we've spoken of it. You've got all the details that you could remember about him somewhere, haven't you?'

Ruth looked surprised. 'I'd almost forgotten that. It's with my will. How strange that you should remember.'

'Not really. It's the sort of information that a man stores, especially when he lives in the shadow of that other man.'

Ruth felt a strange falling away in her stomach.

His skin underneath her hand, the hand he had ignored, burnt. She pulled it away quickly. His eyes were sad but resolute as he held hers. 'Shit timing, Ruth. I wish it could be different, but I've wished that for too long. I'm going to go and live in Israel.'

Ruth felt the blood drain from her face and he did put out his hand to her then. 'Ruth, I'm sorry. It couldn't wait. I had to tell you now.'

'Why?' she whispered.

He hesitated. 'I've met someone.'

It was as if he had slapped her. 'Is it serious?'

'I don't know yet.'

Shame flooded through Ruth. 'But you . . . we've just made love . . .'

'Yes. Ironic, isn't it, darling.' His voice was husky. 'The one rare time you initiate sex – and it was wonderful – it's too late.'

'Then why . . .'

'Because it seemed churlish to refuse you.' He closed his eyes and said under his breath, 'That's a lie. I wanted to make love to you one last time, because you are my wife and I've loved you, it seems, for so long . . .'

Ruth looked down at him. She had been so involved with herself this evening that she had not seen or heard or felt *his* distress. As if life had stopped still because something catastrophic had happened to her.

He got out of bed. 'You look exhausted. We'll talk in the morning. Try and sleep.' And he was gone.

Ruth got up and took a painkiller. The drink helped her sleep for a while. She dreamt that she was driving at speed away from Cornwall. She dreamt she was running from Jenny.

When she woke in the early hours she saw that Peter was standing by the window looking out into the dark. He was crying and she understood: he still loved her. He had just given up. Some woman was giving him the single-minded attention he deserved. She thought of his new lemon cologne.

Ruth knew Peter was grasping at the possibility of happiness and he deserved to. 'Peter?' she said softly and when he turned she held out her arms.

He came over and sat on the bed and they wrapped their arms round each other.

'It's all right,' she whispered. 'It'll be all right. You'll see. We'll always be friends you and I. We'll always be friends.'

'I loved you so much, Ruth.'

'I know. I know. But you'll be happy now. You've done the right thing.'

'Have I?' he asked as they rocked together in the dark, cold morning. 'Have I?'

'Yes,' Ruth said firmly, 'you have.' He had always been unfailingly honest and gentle and reliable. She had taken him for granted like background music. She had thrown the life she had lived with him carelessly away and now she must make it as easy as possible for him to leave.

It was too late now to say what she had been thinking driving home from Cornwall. Too late to tell him that she had been jerked out of her complacency in the last few days and had vowed to change. She said what she had to say, in what she knew was her first real act of love and unselfishness. 'You're going to live near your family, in a place you love. Don't look back. Just go forward to all that's coming your way. You deserve to be happy. You've made Adam and me very happy, whatever you might think.'

He got into bed with her and they slept, arms tight round each other, in the same bed for the last time.

TWENTY-EIGHT

It felt as if I were coming back from a long journey where I had been walking outside myself. All the edges were blurred. Sometimes people seemed to be on the other side of a pane of glass. I could see their mouths moving, but I hadn't got the energy to make sense of their words.

Sleep was my escape. I used it often against the anxious faces of my family. I would have liked to sleep for ever but the thread of life that was Adam drew me back.

I fought not to drown. I fought hard to surface. I did not want to become enmeshed in psychiatrists and counselling. Dad understood. He was constantly at the hospital with me, monitoring my medication, questioning my treatment.

The drugs took a while to work and initially I hated how they made me feel. But after a while I had to admit they did blur the edges. They did prevent me looking too far ahead. They did take away the relentless anxiety. Dad was convinced I was malnourished and this could cause chemical changes in the brain. He prescribed daily protein injections and after a while I began to feel stronger.

One day he took me out for a drive. I didn't want to get out of the car but we parked on the old quay at Lelant and watched the sea for a while. It changed colour so many times as the tide shifted and the clouds moved. I became mesmerised by the constant rhythmic movement of water.

All of a sudden a red hang-glider slid into a clear, vivid-blue and cloudless sky and hung suspended over the sea like a human kite. I began to weep. It reminded me of another time, here with Tom. We had been sitting on the beach with my sisters and hundreds of children. Tom seemed happy enough, but I watched him stare longingly up at a hang-glider as it shot this way and that on a thermal in an endless sky, free as a bird.

I knew in a flash that Tom could never be entirely domesticated. He would always have one eye on the air or the sea, the jungle or the desert. It was how he was. He loved me, but I would never tie him down. It was lucky that I never wanted to, that I had my own life.

Spring came slowly and I began to feel stronger. I walked sometimes in the hospital garden full of daffodils and small fluted tulips. When it seemed to me impossible to move forward, I conjured the face of the boy and he anchored me to a future.

One morning I was sitting in a chair by the window of the hospital and I saw on the telegraph wires green parrots and small bright parakeets. They all sat in a row as if they really belonged there, chattering and screeching. My heart thudded. *I was hallucinating. I wasn't getting better. I must be in the grip of incipient madness.* Terrified, I rang the bell.

The nurse came to the window, peered out and laughed. 'Jenny, the birds are *real*. You're not seeing things! They must have escaped from Birds of Paradise down the road. It happens occasionally; I'll go and ring them.'

As she left the room I knew it was time to go home. I was coming out of my trance-like dependency. I wanted to feel normal again. I wanted to be home. I knew how lucky

I had been to have James. I could have been consigned to a mental ward. Instead, my father had let me opt out for a while in a small cosy hospital where everyone knew him. He had protected me like a sheepdog and built me up physically, but most of all he had had faith in my ability to mend.

I could have gone home a while ago, Bea had urged me to, but I had needed a neutral space for a time. Back in Tredrea, up in my old bedroom at the top of the house, it would have been easy to revert to being a child again. Out of the windows the sea glittered and the seagulls swooped and dived, filling the sky with their noise. I longed to feel safe as I had when I was growing up and I knew it was never going to happen. I could never ever feel entirely safe again.

As I slept that terrible afternoon waiting for Tom and Rosie to come back from the zoo, my life had been snatched away. While I slept, my husband was coldly, calculatingly being targeted. It made no difference that he had his child in the car with him. That is the hardest thing to bear. Rosie should have had a whole full life to live, but I knew that I had to stop longing to have died with them.

I lay back on my narrow bed. Ruth and I had spent hours and hours together up in this room playing. Somehow, it was hard to make the connection between the girl of my childhood and the woman who was Adam's mother. I didn't want them to be the same person. I didn't want that.

My bedroom was like returning to a small familiar nest. I realised that for months everyone had been making decisions for me. Now, I made a first irrevocable decision for myself. I did not want to return to London. I wanted to stay in Cornwall. Not here at home; I had to find somewhere to rent for a while.

I needed to be on my own to grieve properly. Maybe I would never be able to design again. Something indefinable had gone. I no longer had the ambition, imagination or wish to create. I was unsure if the feeling would ever come back.

When I told Bea and James of my decision, Dad said gently that I owed it to Flo and Danielle to tell them as soon as possible. I felt I was betraying them both. I quailed at the thought of a long conversation, unsure if I had the energy beyond the basic decision to opt out. I did not know how viable the business would be long-term without my input.

Mum rang and invited them both down for the weekend. Flo had visited me in hospital, but Danielle had wanted to wait until I was home. I talked to them most days on the phone and I knew it would be difficult for both of them to leave London together. They said they would fly down. I knew then that they must suspect what I was going to say.

I wrote notes to Adam but I never posted them. He sent me a postcard once and I had seen him twice at the hospital. He was the sweetest boy. It was not possible to talk about Tom because Ruth was always there, but we would; I promised him that we would.

Ruth had said she would bring Adam down at half-term and we suddenly realised that this coincided with Flo's and Danielle's visit. Bea insisted on inviting both Adam and Ruth to lunch on the Sunday. Flo and Danielle would be here.

'Too many people, Mum, I can't cope.'

'You don't have to, darling. You will have had a chance to talk to Flo and Danielle all Friday and Saturday. No one expects you to sit making small talk. You can disappear when you've had enough. Ruth is bringing Adam all this way for *you* and for *him*. It's hard for her.'

'I know,' I said quickly. 'I know, it's just . . .'

'It's hard for you too, Jen. You've made a huge decision not to go back to London. I think you're very brave and I'm sure both Flo and Danielle will understand completely. Try not to worry.'

I sat down at the huge battered table that had held so many squabbling children squirming for attention. 'Danielle is intensely practical. I think she will have considered what she and Flo might do if I don't go back.'

Bea looked surprised. 'Do you think so?' Then she said, 'I think you need to talk to your father about finances some time soon. I know you have an army pension, but is it going to be enough to live on without you working?'

'I don't know.' I got up. 'There's only me, I don't need much. I think I'll walk on the beach before supper, unless there's anything I can do, Mum?'

'No, darling, you go.'

I heard her sigh and turned as I went out of the back door. 'I'll talk to Dad, Mum, don't worry about me. I won't be a burden on you both, I promise.'

Bea looked sad for a moment. 'None of our children could ever be a burden to either of us. Go and walk, it's a wonderful evening.'

I walked down the hill. It was early evening and the colours were muted and faded, sand and sea melting into each other as the air cooled. There were two little clumps of holiday-makers on the beach, building sandcastles in the last of the day. I sat on the wall and watched them. A tiny fair girl was sitting on her own, engrossed in placing shells on a mound of sand.

I moved nearer to her and she looked up and smiled at me. I longed to crouch to her level but dared not in case her parents thought I was a threat to her. It had happened before and now I was careful.

'What a beautiful castle,' I said.

'It's a fairy castle.'

'I can see that. Are there fairies inside?'

'Of course, but they are sleeping, cos they are tired.'

'I see. I didn't know fairies got tired.'

'Well, course they do. Doin' magic makes you dog tired.'

I laughed. 'Aren't I silly? Of course, it must do.'

The child looked up at me and giggled. I saw her mother get up slowly and walk my way.

'What's your name?' the child asked.

'Jenny.'

'You can help me if you like.'

'That's kind of you. What's your name?'

'Holly.'

'That's a lovely name.'

'Yes, 'cept Daddy's silly, he sometimes calls me prickly.'

I laughed again as her mother reached me.

'Hi,' she said, eyeing me carefully.

'Hi,' I said. 'Well, Holly, I have to go, but that is the best castle I've seen for a long time.'

Holly looked up at me. 'You can help me.' She was bestowing me with her favour like a little princess.

'I'm afraid it's time to go home for supper, Holly.' Her mother crouched down to her level.

'Oh, bollocks,' Holly said loudly and beamed up at me.

'Holly!' But her mother raised her eyebrows at me proudly.

'Daddy says it.'

'I know he does, but that doesn't make it right.'

'Goodbye,' I said. I walked away over the sand quickly before I caught the child roughly to me and whirled her round and round in the sheer joy of her being herself: a unique and definite character.

TWENTY-NINE

The seagulls wake me with their screaming and their great heavy bird feet on the roof. Sunlight arcs across my bed. I sense the heat of the morning, heavy and windless. It is going to be a scorcher. I stretch and remember with a little happy start that Tom is here, lying just below me.

I move swiftly down the attic stairs, circle the house, then open his door a crack and slide into the spare room. He is still asleep. I lift the covers and get into bed with him.

He wakes with a jump. 'Jenny! What are you doing? Get out of my bed! What will your parents think? I'm trying to make a good impression. Go away this instant!'

I laugh. 'No way! I can't believe you are so boringly straight. Hello . . . this is 2001, you know.'

'Straight!' he hisses. 'I should flipping well think so. Rule one: a man does not bonk his girlfriend in her father's house, especially when he's only just been introduced.'

'Oh,' I say sweetly, lying in his bed and yawning. 'What a shame. Dad is such a darling, he would probably bring us tea in bed if I called.'

Tom leaps up. 'Get out of my bed, you little floozy, and stop trying to embarrass me.'

I smirk and relent. 'Bea and James set off at first light. They're sailing with friends in St Mawes.'

'You little punk. Right, you're in big trouble.'

I grin. 'Oh yeah?'

'Yeah!' He jumps on me and I scream for mercy.

'OK. OK. I'll buy you breakfast in St Ives.'

Tom stops tickling me. 'Full English? No wifty-wafty croissants?'

'OK, fatty. Sorry, sorry.'

'Go and get dressed, woman, and stop harassing me.'

We walk across the beach towards the harbour and one of the cafés on the front. I love this time of day. Few people are about and the sea and buildings are pink-tinged. Most places aren't yet open but we find a tiny place next to a small art gallery right on the harbour.

Tom orders a huge breakfast and I have croissants.

'Your parents are great, Jenny,' Tom says. 'Not quite what I imagined.'

I look at him, surprised. 'What did you expect them to be like, Cornish bumpkins?'

'Silly girl! It's just that you dress in a rather . . . unique, dress-designery way and I thought they might be arty types.'

I laugh. 'No, Bea and James are pretty conventional. So are the rest of the family. I'm a bit of an afterthought, so genetically flawed.'

Tom leans towards me. 'Not flawed, just wonderfully, irresistibly *yourself*.'

My stomach does a swoop. I so want to be cool. I do not want my eyes to give away my feelings and it's hard. Danielle says I make it so obvious how I feel about him that she wonders why Tom doesn't take off in fright.

I am terrified he might. He looked so crestfallen when I said I was coming down to see Bea and James that I tentatively told him he was welcome to come if he liked. To my surprise he jumped at it.

He says, with his mouth full, 'James and Bea remind me of my own parents. Comfortingly familiar, with family photographs dotted about in silver frames and their crosswords or golf. With their little routines and air of bewilderment at how the world is panning out. With their gardens and their dogs and their understated affection for us expressed in feeding us until we burst. I love it. We all need great dollops of home to keep us sane.'

His parents live in Singapore and he sounds wistful.

'Tell me about your parents.'

'They are very typical colonial expats; especially my father. My mother is rather beautiful. She's spent her whole life looking after my father, my brother and me, and helping with the family business. She seems to have been happy living her life through us all, but, hey, would I really know?'

He flicks his hair out of his eyes and smiles at me. His eyes turn a deep purple when he's thoughtful or reflective. I think, with a strange surge of excitement, *Here is a man who could never bore you*. There would always be more to know, something interesting to talk about.

We pay our bill and walk round to Porthmeor beach. The waves slide in, the sea as flat as a pond to the disappointment of the teenage surfers standing leaning on their boards.

Tom takes my hand and gazes up at the white columns of the Tate Gallery. 'I'd almost forgotten. I came to St Ives years and years ago for a party. I was a cadet at university and we'd come down to sail at Falmouth . . .' His face changes suddenly as if he has remembered something he doesn't want to. 'Race you to the end of the beach. Come on.'

'You'll be sick. You've just eaten breakfast.'

But he's off ahead of me, sprinting towards the rocks, singing some old army song.

THIRTY

James and Bea sat in the window seat of their drawing room looking out on to the garden. Beyond the wall the sea shimmered on the horizon and small boats scudded cheerfully on the surface, dancing to the wind. It was afternoon and outside, Adam, Danielle and Ruth were playing croquet and Jenny and Flo sat on the lawn talking. It looked so peaceful, a quintessential determinedly old-fashioned English afternoon. For the moment any undercurrents remained safely hidden.

Yet this morning, Bea thought, had resembled a bizarre cocktail party full of disparate people gathered by chance. Everyone was trying so hard to say the right thing that by lunchtime the strain had rendered them almost speechless.

When Adam walked into the house with Ruth, Flo and Danielle had been shocked by his likeness to Tom. Flo had to leave the room. Family photographs lay everywhere in the house and James watched Adam peering covertly at the photos of Jenny, Tom and Rosie on the hall table with barely concealed excitement.

It was good to see Jenny's pleasure in seeing Flo and Danielle again. They had both been half expecting that Jenny would not go straight back to work and they were making it easy for her.

The boy out there playing croquet had abruptly entered their lives and it occurred to James all of a sudden that Tom's parents in Singapore would have to be told they had a grandchild.

Was Jenny ready to accept the stark fact that something of Tom lived and breathed and Ruth was his mother? A piece of Tom survived, but not for her. James felt anxious. He thought it was still too soon for her to absorb all the implications. Naomi Watson seemed to think she could cope, with help, but James knew his daughter and wondered how long she would accept professional help.

The sun shone through the thick panes on to Bea and James as they sat resting together and they closed their eyes and raised their faces to the warmth of it letting go of it all for a minute. They knew each other so well that they did not need to speak.

So many little dramas and tragedies had been played out in this old wind-battered house by the sea. It echoed with years and years of children's voices. With difficult and sad times as well as happy. Bea had had a mid-life crisis. He had been terribly attracted to one of the nurses in his practice. Hard, unforgiving years groping their way back to one another in a house suddenly empty of children.

He opened his eyes for a moment, looked at Bea's face and smiled because even now he could see clearly behind the lines the very pretty, vivacious girl she had been. They were both still together. They still had each other, thank God.

The scent came from a bowl of hyacinths on the table, and from freesias on the mantelpiece and narcissi on top of the piano. The scent was heady, overpowering in the silent room.

'We ought to take tea out into the garden soon,' Bea said without opening her eyes.

'In a moment, Bea. In a moment,' James said sleepily.

Danielle and Ruth walked along the beach, every now and then turning to watch the surfers ride in on enormous waves. People sat or walked along the shore, the wind flipping the hair into their eyes. At Bea and James's tricky lunch both women had felt an instant rapport, had recognised something in the other that distanced them both from the beautifully laid table and the careful politeness of all those round it.

Danielle had been quite prepared to dislike Ruth for the simple reason that she had managed to affect their lives so dramatically, but when Ruth had appeared in the room with the boy, tall, elegant and tense, Danielle had felt a kinship she couldn't explain. Perhaps it was the natural defence for someone caught in a searchlight they hadn't expected. She had watched with sympathy as Ruth downed two gins and tonic in record time.

Ruth, walking into the Browns' drawing room, had quailed at the sight of drinks on the sideboard and cushions plumped. She fought a mad desire to turn and run. It was at this moment that she had caught Danielle's eye and recognised there was another outsider at this civilised little middle-class Sunday lunch.

Ruth wasn't blind to the irony that this had been the intrinsic, principal thing that had made her feel safe as a child when she visited Tredrea.

Danielle was asking her as they walked across the sand how long she had lived in Birmingham.

'Three years. Peter works for a family finance company based in Tel Aviv. He's an accountant. They have offices all over England, but he manages the one in Birmingham. It's

148

convenient because of the airport. He commutes between here and Israel.'

'That must be exhausting. Do you ever go with him?'

'I used to. Last year we all went for a holiday, but as Adam's got older it's not so easy to juggle my career and his schooling.'

'What do you do, exactly, Ruth?'

'I'm principal buyer for the Fayad Fashion Group. I also lecture part-time in business administration.'

Danielle looked at Ruth with renewed interest. 'Pff! You must be good to work for the Fayad group. Jenny and I have designed for some of their stores and they can be difficult to work with until you establish yourself. But if your standard is high they sell a lot of clothes. I am surprised I haven't come across you.'

Ruth smiled. 'I miss being on the shop floor. That was fun. I used to travel a lot, but the trouble is you reach a point when it seems to be mostly paperwork and reviewing other buyers' mistakes.'

They both stopped and watched a surfer shoot into the shallows like a sleek black seal.

After a silence Ruth said, 'Actually, I'm seriously considering changing jobs. I've no need to be in Birmingham any more and Adam hates his school.' She turned to Danielle and gave a short laugh. 'Peter, my husband, has just left me and gone to live in Israel full-time.'

'God!' Danielle stopped walking. 'You are not having a good time. I am sorry . . .'

'Don't be. I don't blame him at all and I think we've managed to stay friends. The thought of upheaval and looking for another job is daunting, but there's nothing to keep me in Birmingham. We only moved there for Peter.'

'I do not think you will have trouble finding work, Ruth.'

'No. It's just with all this . . . with Jenny, I somehow feel . . .'

'Vulnerable? Thrown off the track?'

Ruth smiled. 'Yes.'

Danielle said slowly, 'It is all so sudden. It is hard to believe.'

'It would have been better if Jenny and I had never met again. It was cruel, that chance meeting. Jenny would never have known about Adam. She would be starting to come to terms with Tom's death, beginning to look to the future.' Ruth threw up her arms. 'I so want to disappear with Adam, vanish, but I can't. Adam is naturally intensely curious about his father. God, it's had such a damaging effect on him. He seems on a high all the time. Peter thinks Adam is going to become obsessed with a dead hero.'

'Did you not talk about his father to Adam when he was growing up? Did Adam never ask?'

'Of course he asked,' Ruth said abruptly. 'When he was small, I told him his father didn't live with us. As he grew up I explained that I didn't know much about his father beyond the fact he had been at university. When I thought he was old enough to hear the truth, I explained I'd met his father very young, only once, and I'd never seen him again. I tried to make him understand that I hadn't wanted his father found or told I'd had a child. It was better just the two of us. Adam's always found that hard and it makes him angry.'

She paused and Danielle murmured, 'It is understandable.'

'Adam has always been mature, he's had to be. He's grown up with the story of his grandparents shipping me off to a Scottish island when I was pregnant. I think this has made him more forgiving towards me. When I married Peter he stopped asking so many questions and things were much easier, although he never wanted to call Peter Dad. He said he had a real father out there somewhere.'

150

The sun went in suddenly and the sea looked grey and cold. Sea mist started to roll in and rain hung over the horizon in a deep bruised cloud. Both women shivered and turned back for the house. Danielle did not know what to say. She felt suddenly depressed. None of this was going to go away. Tom's misdemeanour was spilling into all their lives.

'It is hard for you, Ruth.'

'I'm sorry. I've talked too much. It's been strange since Peter left. Just work and then no one to talk to at the end of a day. I think I'm turning into someone I don't like very much.'

Danielle sensed the tears behind the self-deprecation. 'Please, do not apologise to me, Ruth. My work is a success, but my love life . . . Pff!' She laughed and said as they climbed the hill, 'I know you are too high-powered for us, but if you ever want a change for a while, come and work with Florence and me. Jenny is not coming back to London for a while. We will have to take on a graduate designer, but we will need someone to go out there and sell our clothes and be a general PR. I will have to work double time now.'

Ruth smiled. 'That's sweet of you, but you're not serious, are you?'

Danielle stopped. 'I am dead serious in needing someone.' The two women stared at each other excitedly.

Danielle said quickly, 'We would not be able to match the income you must be getting now.'

Ruth thought rapidly. 'There may be ways round that. I get large fees for lecturing and I might be able to get taken on as a consultant, if there is no conflict of interests. Shall I find out?'

Danielle nodded, fished out a business card and handed it to Ruth. 'If you really are interested ring me, but it will have to be soon, Ruth. There is accommodation at the top of the house, so you would not have to pay a huge London rent, just the normal services.'

'I have Adam, obviously.'

'Of course. We might have to juggle our living arrangements, but there is room for him, unless you don't want him to change schools?'

'He hates his school in Birmingham. Look, give me a few days to think this through carefully.'

'Sure. Look, why don't you come up to London and see our set-up and talk to Flo too? Then you can judge if it is a viable proposition.'

Ruth laughed. 'I'll do that! Next week?'

'Next week.'

The rain started in jagged slants. The beach and the sea had disappeared, and the two women bent their heads against the wind and ran for the house.

THIRTY-ONE

James was putting Danielle's and Flo's cases in the boot of his car when Jenny came out and said she'd like to go with him to see them off at Newquay.

Flo sat in the front with James. She had wandered around the garden with Bea, feeling relaxed despite the circumstances. How could she not relax with the sea glittering in front of the house; with the french windows thrown open to a spring garden full of flaring camellias and the last of the pungent-smelling narcissi?

She had felt a pinch of envy for this life far from London and work, where the heavy air made the pace of everything slower, where the days merged into each other seamlessly like the sea and sky. Tredrea weaved its usual magic, yet she knew that as soon as she walked through the front door in London she would beetle happily up to her office to check the coming days' schedules, eager for the chaos and buzz of another week.

It was a sadder house without Jenny and Rosie; without Tom blowing in like a burst of adrenalin, scooping them all up in his great bear hug, causing mayhem and hold-ups in their organised little world. Flo still found herself listening out for his laugh or Rosie's chatter filling the house. How she missed that infectious little giggle rising up the stairs to the workroom.

Flo snapped her mind shut so that she did not undo the pleasure of a weekend with Bea and James. Contentment was no longer taken for granted, but had to be savoured like a delicate taste on the tongue.

Yesterday, she and Bea had gone back into the house from the garden, and found Jenny and Adam sitting on the sofa going through family photographs. Both their heads were bent to the album, oblivious of the two women standing in the doorway.

Bea and Flo had exchanged looks and crept out to the kitchen. They had felt unable to break into that moment of intimacy in the sitting room and change it into something lighter. Jenny and Adam had looked like two rapt children sitting on that sofa together.

The sun hung low in front of the car, a monstrous orange orb in a suddenly clear sky. Flo turned to talk to James.

In the back of the car Danielle touched Jenny's arm nervously. 'Jenee, I did an impulsive and possibly stupid thing earlier. I was talking to Ruth on the beach . . .'

Jenny turned to her, interrupting, 'Adam told me that Peter had gone back to Israel permanently. I wanted to tell Ruth I was sorry, but she left so hurriedly that I didn't have time.'

'Yes, she told me this. She thinks maybe he has another woman.'

Jenny looked startled. 'Poor Ruth.'

'Please listen to what I am trying to say. It is important.' Jenny turned in her seat, alerted. 'Ruth was telling me that there is nothing to keep her in Birmingham and that she was considering changing her job. I say, without thinking, that we could do with someone smart, with contacts to buyers. I tell her to come and see us in London. I practically offer her the job. It seemed a good idea at the time, but now I wonder if I open my big mouth and put my feet in?'

Flo had stopped talking to James and was listening. Danielle watched Jenny anxiously. Jenny was silent for an unnerving length of time. She turned away and looked out of the window, then down at her hands. She was struggling and Danielle said miserably, 'It is not to replace you, darling. Just to help me, to release me from travelling so I can design full-time until you are better. That is all.'

Jenny turned to her. 'It *is* a good idea. Ruth is very successful, I realised that when I was in Birmingham. I'm being selfish.' She tried to laugh. 'I didn't think I would be replaced quite so fast. It's just . . . a bit . . . I feel as if I'm disappearing.' She held up her hand as Danielle tried to speak. 'But I'm being unreasonable. Look, it was *my* decision to take time out. It's what I want to do and that means I'm leaving you and Flo in the lurch. What do I expect? It makes sense to hire someone we know, who could do the job standing on her head.'

Danielle let out her breath in relief. 'That is what I thought.' She leant towards Jenny. 'You know in your heart you can never be replaced, Jenny. We need help with the *selling*.'

Flo turned in her seat and said with edge, 'Can we afford Ruth if she came to us? I doubt it, Danielle.'

'We cannot afford to pay the salary she must be getting, I tell her this, but I tell her also that she can live with us in the house. Flo, please do not be angry with me. You know how it is with me.'

'I do,' Flo said. 'It would have been considerate to have discussed this between the three of us before you jumped in.'

Jenny smiled. Flo was being protective. 'Don't be cross with Danielle, Flo. She has always had to do the majority of the selling. She's carried me for years. I've never done my fair share, we all know that. The business owes Elle a lot and she has a right to be concerned about the future. Ruth was headhunted before. She could be snapped up again by someone else. I won't take any money out of the business while I'm not working; that will help.'

'You have to live, Jen,' James said quietly.

'I don't need much, Dad. I have my army pension.'

Flo drew the conversation to a firm close: 'Let's hold our horses here. Let's see if Ruth wants the job before we discuss this in any more detail.' She looked over her shoulder at Danielle. 'I'm not cross with you, dear, I just don't believe in rushing into things.'

Flo was not an equal partner, but she had a share in the business. She was the elder statesman, the clear-headed, long-sighted, calm member of the team. What she did not know about the fashion industry wasn't worth knowing. The three of them all needed each other to work efficiently and understood this clearly.

'Here we are,' James said as they entered the shabby little airport. 'We've cut it a bit fine, so no time for dallying.'

They got out of the car and Flo hugged Jenny. 'It's been wonderful to see you almost well again.'

'I get bad days still, but I'm getting there, Flo. I know I've done the right thing, not coming home yet.'

'I'm sure you have. We do miss you. I'll ring you tomorrow.'

Danielle kissed her twice on each cheek. 'Forgive me if I am insensitive. I do not mean to be.'

'You are practical and I love you. Go, run.'

Jenny and James watched the tiny plane until it was a dot. James imagined Jenny was thinking of all the times she had been on that plane with them. He put his arm round her. 'Home and a stiff gin, I think,' he said, forgetting.

Jenny laughed. 'I'm on pills, doctor. Would that I could!'

Back in the car James said, 'I was rather proud of you back there with Danielle.'

Jenny smiled. 'My heart stopped for a moment, Dad, it really did. Don't think badly of her, she is just very practical and unsentimental, you know.'

'Well, I do now,' James said drily. 'You've done the right thing, Jen. Grieving is a long process and you need time and space to do it, and selfishly your mother and I think you need to be close to us for a while.'

'I wouldn't have got through this without you and Mum.'

Jenny hesitated and James suspected what was coming. 'Dad, I don't think I need my sessions with Naomi Watson any more, honestly.'

James kept his voice casual: 'Just for a little longer, darling, please. She is so pleased with your progress.'

Out of the corner of his eye he watched Jenny lean back and close her eyes. 'The woman transparently wants to take me back to that terrible afternoon and I don't want to go there.'

'She is an excellent psychiatrist. Try and trust her. I do.'

Jenny pursed her lips but did not argue. James, glancing at her sideways, knew that look of old and did not pursue the conversation. Instead he said, 'You don't have to look for somewhere to rent. Tredrea is your home and has many empty bedrooms. It's quite big enough for you and your sisters' broods when they come.'

'I know, Dad, but I need to stand on my own two feet. You and Mum make it too easy for me. I have to take responsibility for myself. I'm afraid that if I stay I will find it impossible to make even the simplest of decisions.' She turned and punched him gently in the arm. 'Come on, Dr Brown, be honest. After five children and a permanent round of visiting grandchildren, you and Bea relish having the house to yourselves. You know you do.'

James smiled. He loved hearing her infectious giggle again. His granddaughter had inherited the same laugh. 'OK, young lady, you win, but I get to vet your accommodation.'

'Done!'

They crunched up the drive to Tredrea and small lamps glowed from the windows, making a warm sweep of light over the gravel. Bea moved peacefully somewhere within the lighted house.

Evening and lights spring on and you are home and safe. Jenny got out of the car and stood in the dark. *If only there could be a tall figure reflected in the room within, peering out for me, waiting in the light for me to come out of the dark.*

As he drove the car round to the back of the house, James glanced in the driving mirror. Jenny looked small and lonely standing by the front door, wringing her hands. It seared him. However much he and Bea loved her, they could never take the horror or the loneliness away. It would constantly smack her in the face, in the moment of a door closing behind friends, in glancing into lit houses where couples moved, in passing a school playground where the cries of children drowned everything, at night when Jenny reached out to the cold side of a double bed and memory of loss flooded back.

James hoped she would go on talking to Naomi Watson.

THIRTY-TWO

Adam knew his mother was trying very hard to make the half-term fun for him. She had booked him surfing lessons at Perranporth. She had bought him a wetsuit. A part of him was grateful but something in him did not want to forgive her. Why did she need his forgiveness? Adam was unsure and bewildered at where his hard little place of resistance had come from. He ignored her silent plea for everything between them to go back to what it had been. He knew he was shutting her out but he could not help it.

Ruth sat on a rug on the beach in a thick sweater against the wind and Adam felt her watching him as he and six other boys lay on surfboards on the sand feeling pretty silly pretending to paddle out of water.

When the lifeguard took them into the shallows and lectured them on currents and rip tides, it became more fun. However, there was a vicious swell and the waves curled huge and ominous in deep water, preventing them from going any further out. The lifeguard blew the whistle. They would all have to wait until another day to christen their boards properly.

Adam thought the lifeguard cool. He wouldn't mind doing

his job; it must be brilliant to be on the beach every day. He jostled with the other boys in the shallows and wondered at how much easier it seemed to make friends when he was far from Birmingham.

Two of the boys were local and three, like him, had holiday homes. He spent a happy relaxed morning, almost forgetting that Peter really had gone for good and the hated school crouched waiting for him.

Before they went back to the creek Ruth bought him fish and chips and they sat on the sea wall eating in companionable silence. As they drove home they watched the sky changing in front of them. Bad weather loomed and Adam remembered the rough sea, a warning of the incoming storm.

Adam and Ruth both secretly dreaded the cottage in bad weather. The windows were small and they had to switch on the lights during the day. Unlike the three-storey house in Birmingham, neither had any possibility of escape from the other.

Ruth drove back through the town, parked near the video shop and told Adam to choose some DVDs to watch. This would release them both from determinedly strained conversation. The days seemed to hang endless and heavy. Ruth longed to immerse herself in work. She had not wanted to come to Cornwall for half-term and was only beginning to realise how strong a presence in Adam's life Peter had been. How free she had been to do her own thing while they had gone off together.

They had agreed to see Naomi Watson the following day and Ruth resolved to tell her she would continue to bring Adam if she thought it would benefit him, but she certainly did not want counselling sessions herself.

Adam said as they dashed from the car to the cottage in the first burst of the squall, 'Thanks, Mum, for the surfing lessons. They're great.'

'I'm glad you enjoyed the morning, darling. They seemed a nice crowd of boys.'

'Yeah. I'm going to my room to read my book for a bit.'

'Do you want a cup of tea?'

'Yeah, please. Is there any malt loaf left?'

Ruth laughed. 'After fish and chips? You'll be sick.'

At the bottom of the stairs Adam stopped and turned back to Ruth. 'Mum, do we *have* to see that woman tomorrow?'

'Naomi Watson?'

'Yeah.'

'She thinks it might be helpful for you to talk about how you feel about Jenny, about Tom and maybe about me. Because you *are* angry with me, Adam, and I'm sad about that.'

Ruth watched a myriad emotions pass across Adam's face as he scuffed his feet in the dark little hall. His uncertainty and confusion caught at her and she went to him, risking rebuff. She held him with care and for a minute he let her. She understood suddenly how miserable it was making him to be angry with her. How abruptly confused he felt with his life.

She let him go swiftly. 'Go and read your book. I'll bring you up tea and malt loaf. Let's see how we feel, shall we, after we've seen Naomi Watson tomorrow?'

Adam did not reply but went slowly up the stairs. He threw himself on the bed and reached for his book. Out fell the photograph Jenny had given him of Tom Holland. Adam's stomach contracted every time he looked at it. Tom was in uniform, his face serious, red beret on his head. SAS wings at a slant. His eyes held a faintly amused look as if he were ever so slightly laughing at himself. Adam held the small photograph to his heart. When he heard Ruth coming up the stairs with his tea he hastily pushed it under his pillow and grabbed his book, his heart racing with guilt.

* * *

The first thing Naomi Watson did was assure Ruth that these sessions with her were on the National Health, as if somehow this might be Ruth's predominant concern. She took Adam off into her room first, leaving Ruth sitting in the waiting room flicking through a magazine.

Jenny had rung the cottage that morning inviting them to lunch at Tredrea. Ruth had been about to refuse gracefully when she looked up to find Adam leaning anxiously over the banisters nodding his head up and down and hissing, '*Yes*. Say yes, Mum.'

Ruth said, 'It's kind of you, Jenny, but haven't Bea and James had enough of us after last Sunday?'

'No, not at all. Actually, there's a trip out to Godrevy lighthouse this afternoon, if the weather clears, which it usually does in the afternoons. Dad thought Adam might like to go with him. The weather has been pretty foul this week and we've been thinking of you.'

Ruth accepted. Jenny was right; finding things to do with Adam was wearing her down. Not because there was nothing to do, but in the light of his unpredictable moods it was hard to get enthusiastic enough to suggest any.

Adam came out of Naomi's office looking flushed. Ruth went in. Everything about the woman grated on her. The way she set the clock and the way the box of tissues lay discreetly on the table behind her. As if sensing this, Naomi said, 'Ruth, I am here to help you and Adam. It is, of course, your choice whether you talk with me. You might prefer it, or it might be easier for you, if I referred you to a colleague in Birmingham?'

Talk *with* me. Why couldn't she say *to* me? Ruth took a deep breath. 'I'm sorry if I seem rude. I don't believe there's any need for me to talk to anyone. I'm perfectly capable of assessing the difficulties with Adam. I have a horror of airing dirty linen in public and I'm more than used to looking after myself. I'm also sure that all this introspection is not healthy for Adam, he's a private person too.'

Naomi shuffled papers and smiled. 'Adam's still a child. His life has been changed dramatically by the discovery of his father in extraordinary and traumatic circumstances. He has formed a bond with Jenny. She is the only person who can tell him about his father, but he knows this will hurt you and he is torn. All this leaves you vulnerable.'

'I can cope. Adam and Jenny got on well before we knew anything about her life. Adam is also of an age when he needs a father figure. He would possibly be difficult at thirteen anyway. It will pass.'

Naomi made a steeple of her fingers and looked long at Ruth. 'You are right. Adam *does* need a father figure. Have you taken into account the fact that Adam has lost his stepfather too, just after he discovered his biological father was dead?' Seeing Ruth's surprise she added, 'Yes, he mentioned that Peter had gone back to Israel. I gained the impression he was very fond of him, that they had had a good relationship?'

Ruth nodded. She couldn't speak. She was mortified that Adam had confided anything to this woman.

'I wouldn't dream of suggesting that you might not be able to cope with the current circumstances, Ruth. Or that you are unaware of the consequences for you, Adam and Jenny. I am suggesting that it is possible to make them easier for you. In my experience burying things for a long period of time is damaging.'

So who had suggested to Naomi Watson that she had buried Tom? Ruth, angry, heard the defensive tone in her own voice: 'What makes you so convinced, Naomi, that you, as a professional, could possibly be more aware of Adam's needs than I am as his mother?'

'Because as a professional I can take an objective overall

view. I can stand at a distance, something you cannot do immersed in the middle. Adam is struggling, Ruth. He is loyal but totally perplexed about his extreme emotions.'

Ruth was silent. She could not argue with this.

Naomi said gently, 'To help Adam I need to gain his trust. To gain his trust I need to see him regularly or refer him to someone nearer to you in Birmingham.'

Ruth got to her feet. 'We live too faraway for you to see Adam regularly and you can't gain his trust if he prefers not to talk to you. Adam has to want to see someone and to be ready to talk about his feelings, and I don't believe he is yet. If this changes I'll contact you or someone else nearer to us. I don't mean to be rude, I'm grateful to you for offering us help, but it's Jenny who has lost everything and needs your care.'

Naomi Watson got to her feet too and held out her hand. 'That's fine, Ruth, you have obviously thought about it and I respect your wishes. Good luck to you both. Take care.'

Surprised at the suddenness of Naomi's capitulation, Ruth found herself feeling wrong-footed and vaguely uncomfortable as she went back to Adam in the waiting room.

They drove in silence into St Ives and up to Tredrea. Bea was weeding in the drive and waved cheerfully as they turned in. James was mowing the lawn on his tractor and Ruth, watching Adam's face, thought with a pang, *He feels safe here. This is why he loves coming. There is no Peter any more. No grandparents of his own. But here in this house he can pretend these people belong to him.*

Jenny leant out of the window and called down, 'Hi, there, Ruth and Adam. I'm just coming.'

Adam looked up at the attic window. His whole mood changed in a second. He bounded away towards James and the tractor, and Jenny's head disappeared back inside the house. Ruth stood there with the car key in her hand.

Bea came up behind her and put her arm round her waist. 'So glad you could make it. Come and help me shell peas, darling. We'll have a gin and a gossip.'

Walking into the familiar house, Ruth thought back to the days when she and Jenny had been close as close. *Oh, God, here come the terrible twins*, Jenny's older sisters would cry. *Look at the state of you both. Where have you two been?*

Ruth realised how lonely she felt. She ached for that lost, long-ago friendship. Here was Bea, in this familiar kitchen. Scooping her up, just as she always had.

How strange, how chastening, that Adam was being drawn into this household just as she had been, for the lack of something secure and binding to hang on to at home.

THIRTY-THREE

Bea was with Ruth in the kitchen when I went downstairs. Mum had always been good with Ruth. She picked up her moods more quickly than I had when we were children. Sometimes, for no reason that I could fathom Ruth would not want to play with me and she would go and look for Bea. I'd find them together making pastry or tidying my mother's workbox or picking raspberries. Today they were shelling peas. Outside the window Adam was running across the grass, emptying lawn cuttings for James.

I looked down at Ruth and saw how pale and somehow frail she seemed. I remembered the happy, confident woman she had been on the train. She was suffering. Peter leaving her had nothing to do with me, but everything else did.

I thought how she must resent Naomi Watson poking about, wanting to press bruises with her fingertips, trying to discover Ruth's feelings about Tom after all this time, worrying her over Adam and disturbing places best left buried. I sat down beside her and put my hand on her arm. 'I'm so sorry about Peter, Ruth. I'm sorry about everything.'

She let the peas drop from her fingers. 'Thanks, Jenny.'

Her eyes were on my hand touching her. I could feel the

tears way back in my throat for what we had once been to each other. I saw Bea slide quietly out of the back door.

'I miss you,' Ruth whispered.

'I miss you too.'

'Is it possible to be friends?' She looked at me.

I drew away a little. I wanted to be honest. I didn't know. I didn't trust my see-saw emotions. I said, 'Of course.'

Ruth gently pulled a pea pod open and the peas dropped with a plop into the bowl. We stared at each other and the atmosphere was thick with our separate needs. Our once intense possessive love for each other hovered in the room, ambiguous and sullied.

I wanted to run out into the garden. I closed my eyes. I must reassure Ruth. It was important. We had to come to an understanding.

I opened my eyes. 'Think how many hours of your child-hood you spent in this house with us.' I indicated the large kitchen we were sitting in, the whole house, Bea and James outside. 'You were part of us all and now you're back. I'm sorry that you've been pulled in, that you've become involved in my life, but I can't change what's happened.'

We could see Adam and Bea and James walking across the lawn towards us. Ruth said, 'I know. I'm not blaming you for anything. How could I? It's just that the effect on Adam has been catastrophic.'

I looked outside. Adam was lolloping beside Bea and James. 'He's simply getting used to the idea of Tom and of me, that's all. Look out there, Ruth, Adam is relaxed and laughing. Please don't see me or Bea and James as a threat to your relationship with Adam.' I was being unfair. I knew how *I* would feel.

'Of course not!' She put out her hand to me as they reached the kitchen door. 'He loves coming here.'

We smiled quickly at each other and both turned towards

Adam as he came through the door. He greeted me awkwardly, turning pink, before Bea roped him in to help her and Ruth with the unshelled peas that were going to hold up her lunch.

I left the room, went outside and walked across to the summer house. I lay for a moment on the daybed. I found it frightening how much of ourselves we hid from other people. How honest had I been with Ruth or with myself? I did not know the answer. It seemed to me that we never truly know other people and we become strangers to ourselves.

THIRTY-FOUR

James nosed his small sailing boat out of the harbour using the engine. It had been too rough for the boat trip to Godrevy, so he decided to take Adam for a bit of mackerel fishing. Adam sat contentedly at the back, snug in waterproofs and lifejacket, laughing as the spray arced up and over him in the small boat.

They both turned, before disappearing round the headland, just making out Bea and Ruth on the beach waving at them. James headed for the shelter off Carbis Bay and put down the anchor by the lobster pots off the point. Together they unravelled the mackerel line James used with his grandchildren and threw the bait into the inky sea.

Ruth, back on the shore, felt relief. 'This is so kind of James, Bea. I don't know how to thank him. Adam is in his element.'

Bea smiled at Ruth. 'James loves taking the boat out, it isn't a chore, don't worry. When his grandchildren are here he lives in that boat.'

Jenny was back at the house, resting. Bea and Ruth began to walk along the shoreline. 'I remember how hard James worked when we were children. He always seemed to be on duty at weekends but he took surprise days off in the holidays, didn't he?'

'Fancy you remembering that. Yes, he was and still is a wonderful father and grandfather.'

'What is Jenny going to do if she's not going back to London?' Ruth asked.

'She wants to find somewhere to rent nearby. I think she needs to be alone for a while.'

'Is it a good idea?'

'I don't know. She's lived with other people for a long time. However, she's not ready to go back to the London house and at least we're going to be on hand down here.' Knowing that Flo and Danielle were worried about the business without Jenny, Bea said, 'Do you think you might take a job with Danielle and Flo? Are you going to go up to London to see them?'

'I'm very interested. I should go as soon as I can. I've just got to work out the best time. Adam and I are here until Friday or Saturday. Then I'm into a hectic week for the autumn buying. I'd like to go home early, but Adam wants to stay down here the full week. I don't blame him; the house does feel empty without Peter, so I'm happy to stay on.'

They left the beach and began to climb the steep path back to the house. 'Why don't you go up to London from Truro? You could get a sleeper back. Adam could stay with me and James for the day. It would give you more time to think about whether you're interested in Danielle's offer before you go back to work.'

It was tempting. Danielle wanted an answer as quickly as possible. Maybe Adam could go with her? Maybe they could do the Science Museum or something? Ruth dismissed this quickly. Adam would hate to break his holiday for five hours on a train. 'It would be an imposition. I can't take you and James for granted, and Jenny is still supposed to be resting.'

'My dear Ruth, if you feel happy to leave him with us and Adam is happy to stay, it's no problem at all. We have more than enough room and he's the easiest of boys. See what Adam says when he comes back.'

Ruth knew exactly what Adam would say: '*I can stay in St Ives until you get back? Wicked, Mum. No, of course I don't mind you going.*' 'I'm not going to tell Adam why I'm going up to London. He won't question the trip as I go up so often for business.'

James followed Ruth and Adam back to the cottage in his own car. Jenny was still not allowed to drive because of the drugs she was taking. Adam rushed upstairs to get clean clothes, his books, and his mobile phone from his bedroom. Then he dashed back for his fishing rod.

Ruth booked herself train tickets to Paddington. She could get the early train up and the sleeper back.

'Now, don't worry about Adam or anything else,' James said to her when Jenny and Adam were outside, stuffing his things into the boot of the car. 'Adam is a lovely lad and a credit to you, Ruth. Just concentrate on yourself. It's important you make the right decision for *you*, my dear, not to accommodate or please anyone else.'

Ruth was touched. 'Thank you, James. You and Bea are being very kind.'

'Bea and I are very conscious of your feelings in all this. Adam is your son and we'll take great care of him. Jenny will relax about all this, you know. She will get used to the fact of Adam. She will resume her life and so will you, my dear.'

Ruth touched James's arm. 'I know you will take wonderful care of him. Thank you both for being . . . as you've always been.'

James smiled. 'We watched you grow up with our brood. Now, have a good trip.'

He walked down the path and got into the driving seat, and Adam came round the car to say goodbye to Ruth. His face was both eager and anxious, as if she might change her mind about leaving him. He let her hug him, then got quickly into the back of the car.

Jenny wound down the window. ''Bye Ruth. Give my love to everyone.' Her face was suddenly wistful. She hesitated, about to say something else, then changed her mind.

Ruth waved them off and turned back into the empty cottage. She went to the fridge and poured herself a glass of wine. She felt a dormant excitement. She wished to change her life and Adam's. She needed a challenge, something she could build up and get her teeth into. She wanted to work in London with the dark French girl and Florence. She prayed she would like the set-up and that she would be offered a reasonable package. She looked at herself in the mottled hall mirror. Peter had so obviously found someone else, was probably happily mapping a future. Her stomach ached with the hurt of it. She turned away. One way or another, she had to move herself on.

THIRTY-FIVE

Tom and I are lying in the park on a Sunday afternoon, soporific after a boozy lunch with some of his friends. There is a wonderful smell of blossom on the breeze as the day cools. Somewhere there is a concert and music drifts to us with the distant sound of traffic.

It has been a perfect day and I don't want it to end. We lie on our backs under a ceiling of wavery branches that cast flickering light and shade over our prone bodies.

'This is the life,' Tom murmurs. 'How loud and clear birds sing through closed eyelids.'

'Mm,' I say. 'So they do.'

My mobile phone goes. 'Bum,' I mutter and leave it. I thought I'd switched it off. In a second it goes again. I leave it.

'I bet you can't resist seeing who it is.' Tom yawns and stretches.

I root in my bag and find the phone. 'It's Danielle.' I listen to the message: *Jennee. Please answer. This is important. Ring me back as soon as you can. Please.*

'She says it's important,' I say, dialling.

'Of course.' I scan Tom's face for irritation. Her phone is

engaged. Danielle does have a knack of interrupting us. My phone vibrates in my hand.

Tom winks at me. 'Persistence pays.'

'Danielle?' I say.

'Jenny, get yourself over to me as fast as you can. I am between Putney and Richmond. You can get a tube to Putney East.' She is practically incoherent with excitement.

'No way!' I say. 'It's Sunday afternoon and we're lying peacefully in the park. I'm not moving.'

'Jenny, you will regret this if you do not come. Please, do this for me. You have to come and see this.'

'What? What's so important?'

'I have found the perfect house for us. Believe me, I have.'

'Near Putney! You must be out of your mind. Houses over there are way out of our league.'

'It is the house of my godmother. She is ill and has to sell. Please come. Just trust me and come.'

Her excitement is catching. I waver, my eyes on Tom. He is watching me, sits up and gives a mock sigh. 'Where have you got to be? We can fetch the car.' He takes the phone and Danielle gabbles instructions.

Half an hour later we are swishing through the easy Sunday traffic towards Richmond. Tom has put the hood down and I have a really good feeling as we drive over Battersea bridge.

Danielle is waiting for us like a child outside the front door of a beautiful but battered house in a wide, tree-lined road. She runs down the white steps and hugs us both. 'Thank you. Thank you for coming.'

Tom and I look up at the perfectly formed casement windows, at the Virginia creeper curling over the warm yellow stone. We stand quite still, our bodies close, and feel each other shiver, as if some benign ghost has moved softly between us in a moment of excited recognition.

Inside Flo, who has also had to drop everything, is talking

174

to Danielle's godmother. She is an attractive Frenchwoman who has multiple sclerosis and has been forced to live on the ground floor. She has reluctantly decided to go back to Paris to be nearer her family. She pours us wine, wheels herself down into the garden. Her love for her home is obvious. I see her hands tremble as she tells us she can no longer afford such a large house. 'It is crumbling round me. It needs much love and attention. I will only sell to those who have a feel, a respect for the space and the age of the building.' She is watching Tom move silently in a circle taking in the house, a bemused look of enchantment on his face. She says to me wistfully, 'Your man reminds me of a lover I once had just after the war, he too fell in love with this house at first sight. He moved in to paint it and did not leave for six years. Danielle, take them upstairs. Show them all the rooms.'

Danielle too is watching Tom with an expression I cannot read. 'Worth leaving the park?' she asks him in the hall.

He grins. 'Yes.'

The house seems enormous after our flat. Enormous, beautiful and mind-blowing in its possibilities. The four of us walk around in a daze of longing. I think, *Oh, how we could fill this light and space*. I see each room transformed in my mind from the formal very French decor to light, neutral colours so that the house could just be itself and breathe and exist in its own right.

'What's the asking price?' Tom enquires, breaking the spell.

Danielle quails and prevaricates. 'Well, it is cheaper because of the run-down condition and Marie will not sell to a developer. These houses rarely come on the market for long. As a business proposition . . .'

'How much, lovey?' Flo persists.

Danielle whispers the price, not meeting our eyes, and our dreams hit the wonderful once polished floors with a crash. We are silent. Then she says defensively, 'I think to myself, before I ring you both, that if something is right there is always a way to find the money. We would have to make a business plan, go to the bank. We do have a viable growing business.' She looks at me for help.

It is horrible for me to be the practical one for once. 'It would be mad to stake all we have on a house, Danielle, however wonderful. We would be selling our souls to the devil. This is how people go under. We don't have this sort of money.' As I am saying this I feel a sort of panic at the thought of anyone else living here and Danielle hears it in my voice.

We are standing on the landing and I move away into one of the large bedrooms on the first floor. It must have been Marie's once. It is huge and airy, with three great windows looking out on to the wide street. From here I can see the trees in the park. I turn and look at the fireplace, still intact, and up at the intricate cornicing. The others have gone up to the second floor and the room is very still. Dust motes dance in the evening sun. Tears come to my eyes. I stand and experience a strange falling away, a sudden terrible wistful sadness that feels unbearable.

I walk slowly out of the room and cross the landing into a smaller room that looks out on to the side of the garden. A tree makes patterns across the walls as it moves in a breeze. I sit on the small single bed. I know suddenly that I will live here and I shiver violently at the absolute knowledge of this. My mouth is dry, and I run down the stairs and ask Marie if I can get myself a glass of water. I drink it at the sink as I stare out into the trim garden.

Behind me, Marie in her wheelchair says, 'Someone just walked over your grave? It was the same for me when I first saw the house. You will live here, this I know.'

I turn to see if the old lady is doing a sales pitch, but her face is gentle, sad too. 'A house is a place where we do so much of our living and loving; play out our losses and tragedies. No wonder it absorbs into its very walls the essence of ourselves, gives out to us other lives as well as our own. I believe that the past and future are as one really, it is just that we are too feeble to comprehend time. You felt your own life for a second in the heartbeat of the house ready to absorb your life with all its joys and sorrows, did you not?'

I stare at her and nod, choked. I look up and Tom is standing in the doorway. He holds out his hand to me. 'Flo says will you come to the top of the house.' He grins at the old lady. 'I don't think you are ever going to get us out of here, Marie.'

She laughs. 'Is he your lover?' she asks provocatively, knowing full well that he is.

Tom clamps his hand over his mouth. 'This', he says in an outraged voice, 'is my dear little sister.'

'Rubbish,' Marie says, wheeling herself to the fridge for more wine. 'You make a sweet couple.'

'*Sweet!*' Tom mutters as we run up the stairs. 'I'm extremely glad my soldiers can't hear me described as one half of sweet.'

'Just look at this, Jenny,' Flo says at the top of the house. There is a huge room with a skylight in the roof, obviously once an artist's studio.

'Someone has knocked several small rooms into one,' Danielle says. 'One of Marie's numerous lovers, I should think.'

I stare in wonder. 'Workroom!' I whisper.

'Workroom,' Flo and Danielle echo.

We stare at each other. 'Somehow we've got to do it, girls. We've got to have this house,' Flo states firmly. Danielle and I grin at each other. Flo ignores us. 'What we've got to do now is go away and think long and hard about how it might be possible.'

We say goodbye to Marie, who has the insouciant air of

someone who knows we will be back. We make for the river. We badly need food and more wine. As Danielle and Flo talk, I am conscious that Tom has gone very quiet. Flo puts a hand on his arm. 'Dear boy, are we boring you?'

Tom comes from somewhere a long way away. 'I was just thinking. I have an idea, too tenuous to voice yet, that might help you. Can I come back to you?'

Flo laughs. 'Indeed you can. I too have an idea, girls, that is gently percolating.'

'Good,' Danielle says. 'I can't decide whether we ought to ring Terry at this point for advice or if he will behave like a typical accountant and veto our mad schemes.'

'Let's leave him out until we have a business plan,' I suggest. 'I don't have one single idea in my head for conjuring money from nowhere.' I look at Danielle. 'I suppose we could try to sell our bodies to the rich embassy Arabs at the end of the street.'

'Pff!' Danielle says dismissively. 'What would we then do for fun?'

THIRTY-SIX

Danielle, who had been looking out for Ruth, opened the door before she had time to knock. 'I was worrying that you would get lost because we are right at the end of the street. Well done, you found us.'

They kissed twice on each cheek and Danielle led the way into a large flagstoned hall with an impressive staircase leading upstairs. As she entered Ruth felt a leap of excitement.

Danielle took her into the room on the left of the staircase. It was a large sitting room, opulently furnished and obviously for clients. 'We will have coffee,' she said. 'And I will explain the set-up before we go up. Flo is joining us in a moment. I have asked our accountant to come in to go over the financial side of the business with you this afternoon. He will also explain what we are able to offer you, if you decide to work with us.' This was Danielle in work mode. She was playing it exactly as Ruth would have done herself: straight into business. It was better for both of them to remain professional today. It made it easier for Ruth to refuse the job without embarrassment, if necessary.

An Asian girl brought in coffee and croissants, and placed them on a round table in the window.

'This is Molly,' Danielle said. 'She is very talented and comes to us part-time.' Ruth smiled at her. She was extremely beautiful.

Flo came into the room and greeted Ruth warmly. As they drank coffee, both women explained their working day to Ruth. Much was familiar. Ruth had been involved with clothes and designers for most of her working life, if not the expensive and exclusive end of the market.

Danielle explained that she and Jenny were commissioned by chain stores and that they also designed for select shops as well as taking on private commissions. Chain stores were their bread and butter, but their growing success was in designer labels and selling abroad, mainly to Italy.

'If you take the job, you will meet Paolo Antonio. We do a lot of business with him.' She glanced at Flo. 'We had plans to sign up with him under a new label exclusively for the Italian market. We were having lunch with Paolo Antonio that terrible day Tom and Rosie were killed. Afterwards, we lost the heart for it all.' Danielle shrugged in her very French way. 'Pff! I am a little unsure what is going to happen now because it was Jenny's designs he was really interested in. Even so, I still travel to Milan to sell all the time and this is one of the jobs I would hand over to you so that I can concentrate on designing. Right.' She stood up abruptly. 'Let us go upstairs.'

Flo was watching Ruth. 'Would you be happy to travel, Ruth?'

'I'd love it!' Ruth said and thought she sounded too eager. She knew what they were thinking and added, 'Adam is used to me travelling, although I haven't done much just lately.'

As they reached the stairs Flo said, 'You go ahead with Danielle. I'm slow. I have to take my time up three flights of stairs these days.'

Ruth realised as they climbed that the house was in fact two houses.

Flo said behind her, 'When the house next door came up for sale we knew we had to have it. It had been used by embassy staff. Only two of the downstairs rooms and the kitchen had been looked after. It was in an appalling condition, which is how we could afford it. We were limited in what we were allowed to do because the properties are listed. In the end we just took down a wall on the middle floor between the houses.' She stopped to get her breath, leaning on the banisters. 'We made another large workroom and offices, and two separate flats. One is Danielle's and the other one we rent out.'

'The workrooms are Flo's domain,' Danielle said. 'She runs them like a matron in an English boarding school, kind but firm. Nothing escapes her. She sees everything and anyone who doesn't pull their weight or produces shoddy work is out in a flash, with a sweet smile.'

'What on earth would you know about English matrons or boarding schools?' Flo snorted as she reached the top of the stairs.

'I do not know. I pinched this saying from Tom.'

'Did you, now!' Ruth saw the fondness flit across Flo's face for the dead man.

Flo's office on the third floor, with its huge noticeboard filled with orders and snips of material, was immaculately tidy. In the workroom she was introduced to each girl by name. Most were Asian, but the banter was pure cockney. The room was light and cheerful, with a kitchen and a rest area with soft sofas and a sound system if the girls wanted to play their music. Ruth was impressed.

They left Flo and returned to the first floor. Danielle said, 'Students apply to us when they leave art colleges or university. We take on one graduate for a year. They start by making the tea and generally helping out. By the time they leave us they have learnt to put their training to practical use. We emphasise the importance of cut and of studying closely the ever changing market trends. We foster any flourishing talent and we like to make them feel part of the team and encourage them to put their own ideas forward for our commissions. They learn quickly that it is very hard work and luck before they can either expect to earn good money or be recognised.'

Danielle guided Ruth into another sitting room. 'The first floor here was Jenny's and Tom's, although we all seemed to end up here with Jenny and Rosie, especially when Tom was away.' She turned to the window, her back to Ruth. 'With Flo's help we all took turns to look after Rosie. She seemed to belong to all of us.' Danielle's husky voice trailed away.

'It must be so sad for you and Flo. You obviously loved her very much,' Ruth said lamely.

Danielle turned and Ruth was taken aback by the pain in her eyes. 'I adored her. I was the bad Catholic godmother who does not believe in God, but I swear at her christening to look out for her all her life. I could not do this. No one could. You know, she was the happiest child. She loved everybody. She was always laughing. She should not have died. She should not be dead.' Danielle sat down abruptly on the sofa and her sudden anger was startling. She closed her eyes, took a deep breath. 'I'm sorry.'

'You are angry, Danielle?' Ruth sat too, awkwardly, on the edge of a chair.

'Yes, I am angry.' Danielle opened her eyes. 'If you do dangerous things, if you mix with dangerous people you do not take your child with you. You do not risk your child in even the smallest way just because you wish for a day out with her.'

Ruth was shocked. 'How could Tom possibly have known someone was going to put a bomb under his car? He was on leave, he wasn't in uniform.'

'He forgot to look under his car. He was trained to do

this from Northern Ireland. He *always* looked under his car. I used to laugh at him. I used to think he was being melo-dramatic or doing it to impress: the tough soldier. Yet the one time he *should* have checked his car he did not do it. I blame him. Naturally, I blame him. He had his baby with him.'

Ruth said quietly, 'Danielle, a bomb can be small enough to be triggered by a mobile phone. You know this from the London bombings last year.'

'A bomb is not too small to be detected, even if it can be activated by a mobile phone.'

'Tom was a human being. He wasn't on duty. He was just having a happy day out with his daughter.'

Danielle smiled bleakly, embarrassed suddenly. 'I am sorry. Let us leave this conversation.'

Flo came in. 'Can I get you a drink, Ruth? Lunch is all ready in the kitchen.' She darted a quick glance at Danielle and Ruth was unsure if it was a warning.

'I am going to have a glass of white wine,' Danielle said.

'I'd love the same,' Ruth said. 'Can I use your loo?'

'I'll show you.' Flo led her across the landing.

There was an open door to a bedroom and Ruth glanced in. It was so obviously Jenny's room. There was an exquis-ite handmade quilt on the double bed, which had all the hallmarks of Jenny. Ruth paused at the doorway.

Flo said, 'It's very silly, but Danielle and I cannot shut the door on Jenny and Tom's room. It is so final, we just can't do it. We need to feel that Jenny will be back any moment. I think I see and hear Jenny and Tom lying in that bed with Rosie between them, giggling, as Tom sings her silly nursery rhymes.' Flo sighed. 'My dear, don't take too much notice of Danielle. She is still grieving. She simply idolised Rosie and spoilt her rotten, and she did not approve of what Tom did for a living. The bathroom's just here.'

'Where did Rosie sleep?' The words came out before Ruth could stop them.

'The door next to Jenny's room. We keep it locked. Jenny wanted everything to stay just as it was. My dear, we really mustn't get gloomy. I'll go and get us all a drink.'

God, Ruth thought as she shut the bathroom door. *No one can move on. It's unhealthy. No wonder Jenny doesn't want to come back to this house. Tom and Rosie's ghosts are kept alive everywhere.*

'In here,' Flo called as she came out of the bathroom and Ruth walked into a spacious kitchen where Flo had laid lunch on a large battered pine table.

As they sat down Danielle lifted her glass. 'Thank you for coming all this way to see us, Ruth.'

They clinked glasses and Flo said, as if it were obvious what Ruth must have been thinking, 'You must think we are still wallowing in Tom and Rosie's deaths. We are not. We all kept incredibly busy afterwards working closely together as a team, so it was a huge shock to us both when Jenny had such a terrible collapse because she seemed to be keeping it reasonably together.'

'She probably was,' Ruth said. 'It was meeting me and seeing Adam that tipped her over the edge.'

'That was not your fault, Ruth,' Danielle said too quickly.

Ruth suddenly understood. 'It's me being here, isn't it? The sudden realisation that Jenny isn't coming back for a while? That I might be coming here to live in her space? It feels all wrong to you. I've cast a shadow you weren't expecting, haven't I?'

'Not you, Ruth. Not you personally,' Flo said firmly. 'It's just that the reality of having *anyone* else feels infinitely sad. Jenny not coming home is a fact both Danielle and I have to accept, but after many years together we are finding it difficult.'

'Of course it is,' Ruth agreed. 'It must be. Look, Danielle, you offered me a job on a wonderful impulse. I understand completely that you now regret it.'

Danielle laughed. 'But I do not regret it! I have read your CV. I have made enquiries to colleagues. You are what we need at this time. You could do this job standing on your head. We are tiny in comparison with some of the budgets you have handled. We would love you to work for us.'

'We would consider ourselves privileged and blessed,' Flo finished. 'Drink your wine and tell us what you think of us so far.'

Ruth was taken aback and immensely flattered.

'Help yourself to salad,' Danielle said. 'So, come on, what do you think?'

Ruth sighed. 'I'm immensely impressed with everything here. I would give my eye teeth to work with you, but . . .' She held up her hands as Danielle whooped. 'I would have to work out my notice in Birmingham. I would have to look into schools for Adam and I would have to know what financial package you are offering me.'

'Of course. Of course. This is such good news.'

Ruth held up her glass, sitting on her excitement. 'I, too, would consider myself privileged and blessed to work here.'

Flo touched Ruth's arm. 'My dear, don't think you will be working in Jenny's shadow. You are coming in quite a different capacity and doing a completely different job for us. We've badly needed someone like you for some time.'

Ruth knew in that giddy moment of companionship that it didn't matter what they offered her. Compared with loneliness in Birmingham, where she had worked too hard to make real friends, and a chance of living and working in this house with these women, she would take peanuts if that was what they offered, but she knew they wouldn't. They wanted her as much as she wanted them.

THIRTY-SEVEN

I had difficulty waking because of the pills. The sun streamed into my bedroom every morning and I'd lie for hours reluctant to move, with the brightness causing coloured floaters behind my closed eyes. I would drift, feeling as light as air with the sheet tangled round me.

Waking was the hardest part of each day. Memory was instant. Some days my mind veered off to places I did not want to visit, especially when I woke alone in the dark early hours. My brain would keep circling and coming back to the same place.

What had Tom been doing when he died? Where had he been based? What sort of work was he doing? Why was my phone tapped for weeks after he was killed? No one would tell me.

For the first two or three days after Tom and Rosie died the papers played with varying terrorist theories, then the story quietly died. At the time I wondered if a D notice had been slapped on the press and of course I will never know.

It haunts me. Tom was on leave, but there is no way he would have put Rosie at risk. I know this. I do. He was fiercely protective of us both. When he was about to go to

Iraq he warned me that the same rules applied as always in his job: *he would vanish*. Any mail would go through army channels in Baghdad or Basra. He would be permanently on the move and he wouldn't be able to ring me.

Before we married Tom was careful to explain exactly what life with him would entail until he reached the age when he would be put behind a desk. At first it scared me rigid every time he left on a mission to some unknown country. Then I realised that I could not live like that.

I worked like a demon to stop dwelling on the terror of him dying, then gradually, somehow the anxiety was transmuted into my everyday life, there like toothache, but controllable.

When we had Rosie I watched as Tom began to change, to consider the life he was leading and the effect it was having on him as well as me. I thought he might have been working up to the possibility of returning to his regiment, of doing a safer job. Yet I knew he still got that adrenalin rush, the thrill for a life that was precarious.

He told me once that the camaraderie of a small unit of very fit men, living and working in close proximity for a common goal, was seductive and testing in a way that was hard to explain. You had to have blind trust; you had to rely absolutely on the judgement of one another, but in essence you were completely alone.

He said the buzz was a total reliance on your wits and expertise, and how far you could push yourself in hostile circumstances. You had to be a little mad, a little near the edge, perhaps, to do the job you did.

Had he, somehow, got too near the edge, made a terrible misjudgement? Was this why I was questioned for so long and hard? Who had been to the house? Whom had he seen or spoken to on his leave? Had there been any strange phone calls?

Day after day the army and police came, urging me to think about every single day of his two weeks' leave. His movements. My movements. The movements of the whole household.

Then they just went away and left me with this cold dark place that slowly eats away at me. After Tom and Rosie died, these dawn thoughts were so deep, so damaging, that death had seemed the simplest thing.

I see Rosie's small open mouth laughing in her car seat and then, wham! Her small body is blown apart in a second. The fabric of her dress is caught in tiny shreds on the jagged open skeleton of the car. There is nothing left of her to lie in a coffin.

Was there a split second for Tom to be aware of what was happening? Was he singing to Rosie, as she bounced happily in the back behind him? I would never know if he experienced the horror of their imminent death. I hope not.

I kept wondering if there was some small thing Tom did not tell me or a tiny area of danger he overlooked. The pills helped to block out thoughts that sometimes drove me mad.

I knew I must focus on the one tangible thing Tom left me, a part of himself: this sweet boy he never knew he had; a boy who, like me, dreamt of a man he would never see or hear or touch now. But we had each other, Adam and I. We had each other.

Today, lying in sunlight, I suddenly remembered Adam was staying and I picked up my watch anxiously. It was a quarter to ten. I struggled up and went into the shower. This was the worst aspect of taking drugs. Pills helped you sleep, but the mornings were like battling through treacle.

Dad had fixed a kettle for me on the landing with a tray of tea and coffee to stop Mum climbing up three flights of stairs. I suspected she still climbed up to check on me while

I slept. I switched on the kettle and thought of the London house.

Ruth would be arriving in London about now. Flo and Danielle would take her around the home we'd all shared. It made me feel weak and strange. Ruth was considering taking my place in the house. Maybe she would even sleep in the bed I shared with Tom. Don't be stupid, I told myself, Flo and Danielle would not think of it. It was a surreal thought.

I made tea and pulled on jeans and a T-shirt, then I sat on the bed and picked up the phone and rang Flo.

'Jen,' Flo said firmly, 'no one is going to sleep in your bed or touch your room. It stays as it is. This is your home. I don't need a sitting room. We can turn that into another bedroom if necessary. Silly girl. What a thought! As if it would ever enter our minds.'

'Sorry to be neurotic.'

'That's the last thing you are. I'm sure that you've made the right decision to stay in Cornwall for a while, but it's going to be difficult. There will be days when you feel out on a limb. You've worked hard for so long. Designing has been your life. Promise me that when you feel low or lonely you will pick up the phone.'

I smiled. I wasn't sure Flo really did think I'd done the right thing. I think she was convinced that work was the best thing for me; work and resuming my life with those who cared about me in my own home.

I couldn't go back to the house. I couldn't sleep in the bed Tom and I had shared or live a life that was over. That life was now empty of everything that had driven me to work hard. I could no longer bear a house echoing with the sounds of my child. Tom had come and gone like a beloved whirlwind, but Rosie had lived and grown inside me. She had been born in London. She had been part of every moment of every day. *My constant. My joy.*

Without Tom and Rosie the heart had slowly drained out of all that was left. Without them my work seemed vacuous and without value. How could I explain this to Danielle and Flo?

I had never taken my life with Tom for granted in case the worst happened. And it had, the very worst.

'Are you still there, Jen?'

'Yes. Sorry. I promise.' I felt a sudden panic. 'Flo, Rosie's room is not to be touched. I don't want anything touched in there.'

'My dear girl, we locked Rosie's room together. Remember? Nothing has been touched. You mustn't think of Ruth or anyone else as replacing you. We are just getting help with promotion and selling. It's important you remember this. No one can replace you.'

I could hear the sound of the girls trudging up the stairs into the workroom like familiar noisy sparrows. I felt an ache for a life that was gone. It seemed so innocent now, that life, with its plans for the future.

'I must let you go, Flo, I can hear the day going on behind you.'

'I'll ring you tonight.'

I put the phone down. I wondered where my insecurity at the thought of Ruth working with Flo and Danielle had swooped from. But I knew really. Ruth was ambitious and clever. She would promote and sell our clothes far more efficiently than I ever had. It was complete hypocrisy on my part to choose to opt out, then realise I did not actually want anyone else to opt in. At least not Ruth.

I went downstairs. Bea was sitting at the table, peacefully reading the paper with a cup of coffee at her elbow.

'Don't you dare get up and wait on me,' I growled, kissing the top of her head.

'Darling, Adam and your father have gone in to St Ives

190

to buy fish hooks or something. Then they were going up to the Symonses to see if Harry, who is about Adam's age, wants to go fishing with them. James takes him out in the boat sometimes.'

I poured myself coffee and sat down opposite her. 'I feel guilty, I've slept too long. I don't want Dad to tire himself out.'

'He's quite happy. You haven't forgotten you have a session with Naomi Watson at midday. I'll drive you in, and go and do a bit of shopping in Hayle while you talk.'

My heart plummeted. I *had* forgotten. 'Oh, bugger. I hate going. I absolutely loathe going to see her.'

Bea folded up the newspaper. 'Your father has great confidence in her.'

'I know he does,' I said. 'I think he's blinkered.'

'Could it possibly be, darling, that Naomi gets too near the truth of your feelings for it to be comfortable for you?'

I looked at her. 'Mum, should I be made uncomfortable by someone professing to want to help me?'

Bea sighed. 'I'm sure that she *does* want to help you. It's not just about Tom and Rosie's death, darling. It's also about Ruth and Adam. I was so pleased to see you and Ruth talking together yesterday, but it is a tricky situation, especially now Ruth's husband has left her. She always was a funny, mixed-up little girl who longed to have a family like ours and here we are again, easily, effortlessly to her, enveloping Adam into our household, as we did with her long ago.' Bea pushed muesli my way. 'My love, I know you're suffering more than we can ever comprehend. But if you hide the truth of your feelings about Adam being Tom's son, if you are dishonest even to yourself about your ambivalent feelings for Ruth, there is going to be so much more suffering for all three of you. This is why I beg you to go on seeing Naomi for a little while longer, just to help make life more normal, to see the whole from a different perspective.'

I felt the tears coming, swift and sudden as they did these days, and I bent my head on the table and wept. Bea stroked my hair and shushed me gently.

I wanted to be a child again, to have the chance of my young life all over again. I wanted to marry Tom and persuade him to come out of the army. I wanted to have Rosie living and breathing and growing inside me. I wanted my real life to spring out of this nightmare. I wanted it all to go away. I wanted my old life back.

THIRTY-EIGHT

James drove the two boys to Lelant and sat below the old station house watching them lying on their stomachs bird-watching. It was an RSPB reserve, the tide was out and the mudflats exposed, and Adam was in seventh heaven. Harry had borrowed James's binoculars and was catching Adam's enthusiasm. James was impressed with Adam's knowledge and the careful way he imparted his expertise to Harry without seeming a know-all.

James loved this stretch of estuary. He had watched it change over the years. There were modern buildings now at the other side of the water and the village was slowly getting swamped by developments, but so far the estuary and the long stretch of sand and cliffs towards St Ives remained unspoilt.

He had brought his children here, especially Ben and his friends who liked to surf on the beach. James thought of all the times he had been afraid of losing his fearless son in the treacherous waters two minutes from where he sat. In fact, he and Bea had lost their one son to the lure of California and an extraordinarily shallow daughter-in-law.

James felt an ache as he thought of the skinny little blond

193

boy who had been born a bit wild. Sometimes the life he had lived, between a busy medical practice and a house bulging with little girls, seemed now as if it had belonged to someone else.

In summer, at Easter and Christmas, the house was full, not only of various grandchildren but also of step-grand-children and extended families. Two of his daughters had divorced and remarried men with children. Sometimes it was difficult to keep up and remember who was who. You got used to one and suddenly, after endless agonising telephone calls to Bea, a daughter eventually came home with another strained man and more small bewildered children. Really, it was exhausting and James was very glad he and Bea had happily stayed together.

'What's Birmingham like?' Harry asked.

'Crap,' Adam answered.

'Come on,' Harry said. 'It must have some wicked shops and cinemas and stuff. Not like Cornwall.'

'Yeah, the shops are OK. School is crap.'

'Yeah? Big, is it?'

'Huge. I hate it.'

'Are you bullied?'

'Not really. Well, a bit. I'm called a nerd.'

'Why?'

'Because I play an instrument and belong to a music club. It's like a little orchestra. Because I like birdwatching and I fish, and I get good marks and don't like football, only rugby. Because I don't play truant and won't shoplift. So I'm a nerd.'

'Why don't you go to a private school? I do.'

'Do you?' Adam was surprised. He and James had collected Harry from a small house in St Ives. They didn't seem rich.

'Yeah. My teacher at primary school put me in for a scholarship and I got one.'

'You mean you don't pay anything?'

'No, we don't have to becàuse my mum is a single parent. But I think it depends on how much your parents earn.' Adam stared at him and Harry added, 'We live with my grandad, my mum and me. He's retired. Mum works in a delicatessen.'

'My mother doesn't believe in private schools, even though she went to one,' Adam said. 'She thinks one system should benefit everyone and if bright kids are streamed off, state schools will never get any better.'

'Yeah, my grandad's a bit like that, but my mum says that it's not fair to sacrifice your own kids to an educational system that seems to be going backwards.'

Adam was intrigued. 'So what's your school like?'

'Truro School? It's OK. I'd love to board, that would be wicked, but you have to pay to board so I get the train each day. It's a bit of a drag sometimes.'

'How . . . how do you find out about scholarships?'

'I'll ask my mum if you like. There are only so many they give each year. I think all public schools give scholarships. You should ask your mum to find out about schools in Birmingham.'

James called out, 'Would you boys like to go and fish for an hour off the quay? I'll set you up, then come back here to wait for Bea and Jenny to bring our picnic.'

'Yeah!'

'Ace!'

James smiled to himself. He did enjoy the uncomplicated company of boys.

THIRTY-NINE

'It's wonderful to see you looking so much better, Jenny,' Naomi said.

'I am better. I'd like to come off the antidepressants. They make me feel as if I'm buried in treacle until midday.'

Naomi looked at my notes. 'I don't want you to come off them yet, it's too soon, but I'll alter the dose. How are you sleeping?'

'Fine,' I lied.

'Right. Good.' She obviously didn't believe me.

There was silence in the room while she regarded me quizzically. I didn't help her. I knew she was there to help me, but I also knew Dad was paying for these sessions and I couldn't get away from the feeling that she wanted there to be a problem where there was none. I guess that for people who have no one to talk to and don't have families or back-up she must be a godsend, but I didn't need her.

I knew I had given myself and everyone else a hell of a shock. I seriously did not know what I was doing for a while and it had been very frightening. Tom and Rosie's deaths weren't going to go away but I felt as if I were myself again. I hurt, but I wanted to feel that pain; it was a part of being the self I was now. I needed to hurt to keep Rosie and Tom near me.

I decided suddenly that Naomi Watson deserved my honesty. Dad had asked for her help and I was being obstructive. But before I could say anything she said, 'Jenny, you've done enormously well. I admire your bravery, I really do. I am aware you dislike these sessions and perhaps we should review your treatment after this one. How would it be if I don't see you for another three months? However, I would like to talk over a few things with you before we decide.'

I looked at her expectantly.

She continued, 'Tell me how you felt a few months after your husband and child were killed, before you met Ruth on the train.'

'As if I was sleepwalking.'

'You carried on working. You didn't take a break?'

I looked at her. 'I would have killed myself without my work.'

'Were you on any medication?'

'Just sleeping pills.'

'So would you say you were just about coping at that time?'

I knew where Naomi was leading me. 'Yes. I didn't want to see people. I kept to the house and workrooms. I told you, I shared a house with two friends. They were wonderful and so was everyone I work with. If I'd been alone it would have been a different matter.'

'When you got on the train that day, was it your first proper foray into the outside world since your husband and child died?'

I nodded.

'How did you feel when you first saw Ruth after so many years? Were you glad to see her or did you feel you wanted to disappear and to be left in peace?'

I thought about this. 'I was amazed to see her. I hadn't thought about her for years. I didn't feel I wanted to run away. I wanted to know what had happened to her and why she had vanished all those years ago. It all came back in a rush, how betrayed I felt by the fact that she never wrote to me.' I looked at my hands. 'Later, when she began to ask me questions about my life, I felt like running. It was like turning to water. It was the first time I'd had to tell anyone about their deaths. I told Ruth that Tom had died in a road accident.'

'Had you and Ruth always been close as children or were you sometimes rivals?'

'We were close. Dad must have told you, she spent more time at our house than her own.'

'It's not quite what I asked, Jenny.'

I was irritated again. 'I can't ever remember having an argument with her. She used to go quiet. Sometimes she didn't want to play the same things as me and my sisters. At the convent we were in different streams. Ruth was more academic, she went for the sciences and I loved English and the arty subjects. We were never rivals.'

My voice trailed away as a small memory pushed itself upwards like a spring shoot: *What about when you got to the sixth form and boys began to figure?*

Naomi was watching me.

'Maybe, just before she vanished we were a bit competitive over boys. Ruth was tall and blonde so she got lots of attention, but she was very serious and boys don't always go for that. I suppose I was more frivolous. I used to dress outrageously and didn't take anything too seriously.'

'And now, do you think you are rivals now?'

How transparent the woman was. 'We are not rivals over Adam,' I said coldly.

'Adam,' Naomi repeated. 'How . . . ?'

'Look, we've been over how I felt when I first saw Adam. You know perfectly well how devastating it was. How many more times . . .'

'Do you still feel shock when you think of that moment?'

I felt sick with shock, not about my first sight of Adam but what I did later, when I seemed to be someone else, when I didn't know what I was doing. I had frightened him so cruelly morning after morning in the dark. I didn't want Naomi to see my hands shaking so I sat on them.

'Jenny?' she said.

I was suddenly angry. 'Why? Why do you always push and push towards something that you know upsets me? I scared Adam. I scared myself. I wish it hadn't happened, any of it, but I'm not that same person . . .'

Naomi sat there watching me in silence in her unnerving way.

'Now I just feel so lucky to have met Adam. It was obviously meant to happen. Of course Ruth finds it difficult. I was married to the man who got her pregnant and Adam, who knew nothing about Tom, has a need to find out about his father. I've tried to reassure Ruth. We are still friends, despite everything. If you don't believe me, ask Bea and James.'

'I'm glad you and Ruth are still communicating. That's good,' Naomi said ambiguously. 'You talk about Adam's need to find out about his father. What you haven't told me, Jenny, is what your need for Adam is.'

It was such a crass remark. I was furious. 'Adam is my husband's son. Tom never even knew he existed. I want Adam to know he had a wonderful father. It will help him. If Tom had lived, Adam would have come to find him as soon as he reached eighteen. Adam is part of Tom and if you find it strange of me to want him in my life then I think it's you who need help.' My voice broke and I stood up, furious, and stared down at her.

Naomi got up too. She looked upset although she tried to hide it. Her dark eyes held mine relentlessly. 'Of course I understand. But I wonder if you are being entirely truthful with yourself. Sometimes we select a version of the truth. How do you see your future? Is Adam to be part of it? I'm afraid you are telling yourself, and maybe Ruth, one thing while embarking on a dangerous journey to make Adam an important part of your life. You are vulnerable, but so are Adam and Ruth. I am trying to help you to see that *unknowingly* you could hijack their lives in order to preserve your memory of Tom.'

We stood staring at each other. I said, 'You are determined to believe this and nothing I can say will make any difference to your view of me. You haven't got an open mind, Naomi. You've decided I'm still unbalanced. Yes, I *do* still feel frail, I *am* still grieving, but I am not insane, nor do I have an agenda. Ruth, Adam and I will work this out in our own way. I'm sorry if you're disappointed that we can possibly manage without you, but there it is.'

I walked to the door and Naomi's quiet voice followed me: 'I have never for one moment thought you insane. I am trying to give you all the professional help I can. What you have experienced is beyond what most of us ever have to go through. It would be nearly impossible for anyone to be entirely rational having lost so much in such circumstances. You might not mean to use Adam as a lifeline but I want you to be aware of the possibility. Adam had a full life with Ruth and her husband before he met you. He had his own life and Tom can never be entirely real to him as Ruth, his mother, is.'

I turned at the door, put my hand on the frame to steady myself. 'Adam would have become part of Tom's life had Tom lived, and so a part of mine too. He would have found us both and Tom would have been so proud of him. Adam

200

needs to know who he is, find his roots. Everyone does. That doesn't prevent Ruth from being his mother.'

Naomi came from behind her desk. 'I understand Adam's need to learn about his father. What I am asking you is, apart from Adam reminding you of Tom, what is your need of him? You see, he will always be Ruth's son, Jenny. That is who he is. I just hope you have accepted that, because it is going to be far harder than walking out of that door.'

I hung on to the door frame for a moment longer. In that second, I hated her. 'I'm sorry if I've been rude. I'm sure you genuinely want to help me. Please don't send the bill to James, send it to me, I'd like to settle it. Goodbye, Naomi, thank you for your time.'

Naomi said quietly, 'Good luck to you, Jenny. Take care.'

FORTY

Up on the quay, James looked at his watch. Bea was bringing Jenny after her session with Naomi. They should be here soon. He called to the boys that he was going round to the Saltings to meet them. He had just crossed the railway line to the small station car park when they arrived.

Bea smiled at him and lifted her eyebrows, and he looked at Jenny's white set face and thought, *Oh dear. Poor Naomi.*

He kissed them both. Jenny went ahead with the rugs, and he and Bea followed with the picnic.

'Did you by chance buy a beer?' he asked hopefully.

Bea laughed. 'I did. I nearly bought myself a one-man gin and tonic but I thought it was the thin end of the wedge.'

James took her arm. 'Not an unqualified success, are they, our sessions with Naomi?'

'I gather Jenny's knocked them on the head. She hasn't said much, but she's upset. I think she was rude to Naomi and that is rare for Jen, so perhaps Naomi wasn't the right person.'

'It happens,' James said equably. 'It is the loveliest of days, don't let's let anything spoil it. I love my daughter dearly, but she is over thirty. We can do what we think is best for her, but in the end she has to make her own decisions. There has to be a cut-off point of worry for you and me over all our children.' He pulled her close for a second. 'We have a life too, Bea.'

Bea laughed. 'So we do. Keep reminding me at regular intervals.'

They put down the rug on a corner patch of sand below the old Station House. The boys had returned empty-handed. James watched Jenny crouching to the boys as they excitedly pointed out a bird to her. 'Happiness is a conscious decision, you know, not something that just happens. Do you remember what a happy, generous child Jenny was? She and Tom had that in common. They were joyful together.'

'Soulmates. They were simply potty about each other. I know her sisters were sometimes jealous.'

'Jenny and Tom made their happiness. Everything was a positive. They both worked damn hard and rarely moaned. Tom rang me from Iraq at the beginning of the war, Bea, in case he was killed. He was very anxious that I knew that if anything happened to him, Jenny and Rosie would be financially secure. He told me how happy they both made him and how much he loved them. I'd never heard him sound so serious before. Obviously he couldn't tell me where he was going or what he was doing, but it was almost as if he expected to die. I could hear he was low and when he put the phone down I realised he was frightened too.'

Bea turned to him. 'Oh, James. Oh, poor, brave Tom.'

'What I'm trying to say is this. I think Jenny has consciously decided to be as happy as she can. I think maybe she was right and I was wrong to involve Naomi. She wants to get on with her life, to go forward. She and Ruth are both intelligent people who care for each other and they will work it out. I think we've underestimated her. I think Jen has more guts than we credit her with.'

The two boys were shaking out the rug and fooling about. They heard Jenny laugh suddenly as she chased them across the beach, pretending to tick them off.

Adam and Harry, full of sandwiches and pasties, skimmed stones into the incoming tide. All the time they had been fishing Adam had been thinking about schools. 'So what are the lessons like at your school? How many in a class?'

'I think there are twenty in our class. The work's hard and you have lots of homework and there are detentions if you don't behave.'

Adam grinned. 'So you don't have parents stomping in and threatening to beat up the teachers if they give detentions, then?'

Harry laughed. 'Not likely. The fees are, like, thousands of pounds. Parents are more likely to come in and *demand* that their child be put in detention if they're not working.'

'So you're a clever dick, then?'

Harry snorted. 'Don't you call me a dick.'

They fell about laughing and Jenny over on the rug put her book down and called, 'OK, tell us the joke.'

This produced howls of mirth. One of them farted, and they both went purple and had hysterics and shot off back towards the beach.

James looked up from under his panama hat and smiled at Jenny. 'Isn't it absolutely amazing that a fart renders any male on the planet hysterical with mirth?' They grinned at each other.

Bea had gone on home to have time on her own. James put his head back down on the rug and sighed. 'This is nice, darling. Summer is just round the corner.'

'Bliss,' Jenny said. 'Dad, I think I'll take a walk along the Saltings. There was a house to rent in *The Cornishman* down here somewhere. I'll just see if I can find it . . . for interest.'

'Would you like me to come?'

'No, you snooze. I won't be long. Dad?' James opened one eye, knowing what was coming. 'I think I was pretty rude to Naomi Watson.'

'Well, if you know you were then you can write and apologise, but I imagine she's used to it.'

'I'm not, though.'

'Good. Go for your walk before the sun disappears. We'll chat later.'

FORTY-ONE

I vaguely remembered the house. I had come to Lelant sometimes with Bea when I was still at school. She had a friend who lived on the Saltings and we had walked the woman's dog down this road and along the estuary to the beach.

The trees cast moving shadows across the road and scents from the gardens blew towards me on the wind, reminding me of my childhood. The tide was coming in and the water gleamed to my right, silver sparks glinting off the surface like falling stars. I had my first tiny frisson of happiness in being alive since Tom died and I stopped abruptly, my heart pounding at the betrayal.

Into this tranquil afternoon Tom's laughing face slid behind my eyes. I suddenly felt he was walking in step with me as if to discover where I might begin to live again without him.

I rounded a corner and there the house stood, back from the road in a garden that wound upwards full of heathers and small ornamental trees. There were also many bird tables and breeding boxes. Certainly no birds went hungry here. I stood behind the gate looking up. There was the faint incongruous sound of Mahler coming from inside.

I hesitated, wondering if it would be all right to walk up

the path and knock on the door without making an appointment. As I stood there a young woman came out, carrying bin bags full of rubbish. 'Hello,' she called. 'Can I help you?'

'I was just wondering if this was the house advertised to rent in *The Cornishman*.'

'Sure is.' The woman sounded Antipodean. She grinned and deposited her rubbish in the bin by the gate. 'Want to come in and take a look?'

'If it's OK.'

'Sure. You'll have to take us as you find us, we're doing a mass clear-out. Hi, my name's Maggie Bruce.' She held out her hand and I took it.

'Hi, I'm Jenny Holland.'

'This was my aunt's house. She's just died. My mum is not well enough to fly to England at the moment and I was over in Europe with my bloke working, so we've copped the job of clearing up. Come on in.'

The house was in chaos, there was stuff heaped everywhere. A bronzed male surfer type nodded at me from a floor covered with old newspapers.

'Jeez, Maggie, the old girl never threw anything away!'

'Don't I know it?' The girl grinned at me. 'This whingeing man is Dean. I reckon when we go to bed the fairies fill up the cupboards and shelves again.'

'You looking for somewhere to rent, then?' Dean asked.

'Yes, for at least six months.'

'That would suit us great,' the girl said. 'My aunt was unmarried and she's left the house to all her family. We're not sure what to do with it yet. Mum might decide to sell but she's sort of sentimental about the place. She used to come over every other year to spend some of the summer with her sister. So we thought we'd rent it out while we decide.' She pushed some boxes out of the way. 'Come and have a look. It's pretty small and it looks tacky inside, but we've had all the main services checked and everything's good. The outside of the house has been painted, but I guess the old girl was too much of a hoarder for anyone to attempt the inside.'

It was not a pretty house inside. The rooms were small and somehow awkwardly angled so that the windows caught the sun, but it was as if they had been added as an after-thought. The house felt as if it had been plonked down, laid out and the architect had thought, *Whoops! I should have laid it thirty degrees to the right.* I thought he must either have had limited imagination or wasn't an architect at all. But the house was south-facing, with only the road between the garden and the wonderful rolling expanse of estuary. As I stood there I could hear the long, undulating sound of curlews and I shivered, for the noise was as familiar as breathing.

Dean turned to a small CD player and Mahler's Fifth flooded the little house. I stood there rooted. It felt like a sign.

'How much rent a month are you asking?'

She looked surprised. 'You're the first person to like this place! A few people, men mostly, have said they'd pull it down and begin again.'

'Well, it's not a pretty house, but the position is heavenly.' I looked around. 'It could easily be improved if a wall or two came down.'

'Aunt Nelly was a bit of an eccentric. She came to England to teach in the war and never returned home. She fell in love with Cornwall on a holiday. I think she sort of built this house herself and added bits she'd got wrong.'

'That'd be about right!' Dean said.

'To answer your question,' Maggie said, suddenly anxious, 'we were sort of hoping we could start with a reduced rent and maybe the tenant could do the inside decoration. Problem is we have to leave in ten days' time. We're musicians and we have to join the rest of the ensemble in Vienna. We split up for the summer to play different venues. Thing is we have to practise a lot each day and clearing up this house is taking for ever.'

'I swear I'll go out of here on a Zimmer,' Dean said.

'Oh, shut up,' Maggie said.

'So how much rent were you thinking of?'

'Oh, well, we thought about £350 a month. That's quite low.'

'It is,' I said, 'but at the moment the house isn't really live-able in.' I stood in the main room and looked around. 'You would have to get all the electrics and services inspected properly and up to date by law before you could rent it out legally. You're not with an agent, but if you were, he would tell you that to get a decent rent it would have to be pretty immaculate, then you could probably ask £550 or £600. Decoration and repairs alone is going to cost you quite a lot if you have to pay someone because it's been so neglected inside.' I smiled at their dejected faces. 'Can I put a proposition to you?'

'Fire away,' Dean said hopefully.

'What if I did all the repairs and decoration inside in lieu of rent for, say, three months or until the house is in order? After that I'll have it valued by a letting agent and pay you the going rent from then on. In that way it will be an ongoing proposition for your next tenant.'

The two Australians stared at each other gleefully. 'Jeez, Maggie, it gets us off the hook. The sun shines out there and the surf calls.'

'Why don't you go through everything, pull out the nice pieces of furniture, the things you think are worth keeping, then get a house clearance firm in?'

Dean grinned at me. 'You an angel who just fell from heaven or something?'

Maggie said, 'There are one or two OK-ish pieces. I suppose you wouldn't consider keeping them on in the house, would you?'

'Sure. I don't want to bring anything from London so I'll beg, borrow and steal what I need for a while.'

Maggie looked curious. 'Have you got a job down here for six months or something?'

'No. My parents live in St Ives. I'm just taking a break from London for a while.' The music was building to a crescendo and I found it unbearable. 'God, this Mahler is sad.'

'Sorry.' Dean snapped it off. They both stared at me.

'I'm sorry. It's a beautiful piece, but . . .'

'It makes you want to go wade in the sea up to your head!'

Maggie saw my face and gave Dean a warning look.

I looked around. 'Just one more thing: I know you'll have to think about what I've said and talk to your mother, but you see this wall? If it came down, you could have one lovely big main room instead of three poky ones. The kitchen would be lighter and the dining room no longer a triangle.'

They both looked around. 'Yeah. See what you mean. Are you an interior designer?'

I smiled. 'No. I'm a dress designer, but we converted two flats in London and I'm quite practical. Look, I must go. I've left my father and two boys up the road. Could you ring me? I know I've jumped this on you.'

They took down my address and telephone number, and Maggie walked me to the gate. 'I'm really sorry about Dean's remark about wading into the water. I saw your face.'

I smiled. What a sensitive musician she must be. 'It's all right. It was just a bit near the truth. Listen, I quite understand if your mother wants to go another way.'

Maggie snorted. 'My mum is not here doing the clearing

up. I'm not losing my sexy, restless boyfriend over a house.'
She grinned at me. 'Take care. I'll speak to you soon.'

The tide had swept in up to the sea wall while I was in
the house, filling the late afternoon with the slap of water
on a flood tide. I hoped the boys had been watching the tide
or they would have to walk the long way round, over the
quay and back down the road.

I wasn't worried; I knew Dad would have checked where
they were. I felt excited. I could make something of that ugly
little house full of sun. I could imagine myself inside with
new peach walls and empty rooms. I saw myself there and
I saw Adam visiting me and cataloguing the birds the old
woman had enticed into her garden.

It was a house I could live in quietly until I stopped hearing
the sounds of a child playing everywhere, until I stopped
listening out for a man whistling somewhere in the depths
of a four-storey house. It was a place where I could begin
to tell Adam about his father in peace and privacy.

FORTY-TWO

I wake in Tom's flat and see him at the window looking out.
It is still dark but I can hear the birds singing. I lie watching
him for a moment, feeling like a voyeur. His back is to me
and he's wearing just a pair of shorts. His body is brown
and smooth and I love the very sight of him, but something
in the way he stands alerts me. 'Tom?' I whisper.

He turns, his face is serious, perhaps sad, I can't tell in
this light. He comes slowly over to the bed.

'What is it?' I ask.

'Oh . . .' He half smiles. 'I'm just having a dark night of
the soul. Sorry if I woke you.'

It is the first time I've ever seen Tom down. I put out my
hand. 'Can I help? Am I invading your space?'

He shares this flat with a pilot friend and I know he loves
it when he has the place to himself. We were together all
day; maybe I should have gone home.

Tom laughs and gets back into bed. He pushes my hair
away from my face. 'Where on earth do you get this amazing
hair?'

'Bea's sister. Spanish forebears.'

He bends and kisses my nose, my forehead, each cheek,

my chin and finally my lips, chastely, like a monk. 'You', he says softly, 'could not invade my space if you tried.'

He lies on his side, propping his head on his arm. 'I'm in a dilemma,' he says, watching me with his startling blue eyes. 'I love you, Jenny. I love every single thing about you.'

'So sorry it's a dilemma.'

He puts his finger over my lips. 'You've ruined my carefully laid life plan. I go to a party I'm not keen on to please Damien. I'm surrounded by stunning women whom I find strangely boring. What is the matter with me? I say to myself. This should be fantasy land. Then I look up and see a girl in a white dress edged with gold. She is walking away from the party and she stands under a tree looking down at everyone and I think suddenly, *There she is, my future wife, the mother of my children. There she is*. It was like being struck between the eyes.'

Tom's voice is thick with emotion. Tears slide out of the corners of my eyes in blessed relief at the sound of those words. Tom has never once spoken of the future. I knew from the beginning that I wanted him above all things and I have been terrified by his silence and a little bewildered. All the signs were that Tom felt exactly the same, yet he had given no indication of where our future lay.

He dabs the flow of one tear with his finger. 'Every moment with you, Jenny, has been like coming home from an arduous journey. I have longed to rush with you to a castle and pull up the drawbridge and yell *Get off! She's mine* to every man who looks at you. I've wanted to say every time I see or kiss you, Marry me. Marry me.'

My tears are soaking the pillow. I can't stop them.

'I've stopped myself, because of the job I do. I *can't* ask you. I love you, but it would be unfair. I've chosen to do a risky job and I love what I do. I'm selfish. I don't want to stop. I can't stop. My work is a part of what I am. I'm bang in the middle of a career I love, but it doesn't go with marriage, darling. Lift your head, I'll turn the pillow over before we both drown.'

I start to laugh and we hold each other tight. 'I love you so much it hurts,' I say into his neck. 'I know you've got to go off and do the things you do. I would never try to stop you. It is what you are and it is what you do. My terror is not having you. Not being with you. I can bear anything but the uncertainty of not knowing you feel the same.'

'I could be injured or killed.'

I stare at him. 'How is that less bad if I'm not married to you, Tom?'

'Because I wouldn't be *your* burden, *your* problem. You'd find a nice man.'

'So,' I say, getting mad, 'you were standing at the window thinking. *OK, I'll tell her we've got to split up in case I get killed, in case I get maimed. So sorry, I love you and you love me but goodbye, I'm off to the front, so forget me.* Just like that!' I pause to take a breath. 'I have never ever heard anything so feeble or melodramatic or self-serving in my life. If you can't or don't want to make a commitment, just be honest and say so; don't wrap it up in angst and make your job an excuse.'

Tom starts to laugh. 'Tell it as it is, girl, don't mince words!'

I hit out at him, still angry, and he holds my hands together in one of his like a trapped bird. 'Listen, you. What brought all this angst on was seeing that house yesterday and the fact we have nowhere to go where we can be sure of being on our own. Your flat has Danielle. This place has Simon coming and going.' He stops. 'Are you awake enough to come into the kitchen and look at my night plans?'

We get up and I throw on a shirt of his, and we pad into

the kitchen and make tea. On the table is a notebook with lots of figures. I sit down, fighting a growing excitement.

'It's only an idea,' Tom says eagerly. 'You may think I'm being presumptuous and muscling in on your world, but I wondered if I came in on buying that house whether it would help all of us. We could maybe make a little flat together there, couldn't we? Somewhere of our own.'

It was a brilliant idea. I trembled with the thought of it.

'I've been trying to work out all my assets. Simon isn't going to be too pleased, but if I sold this flat . . .'

'It's *your* flat!' I ask, incredulous.

Tom grins. 'Yep. My parents used it when they were in London. They gave it to my brother and me when they got too old to make the journey often enough. I bought him out as he lives and works in Sydney. I'm not sure of its exact value, but maybe £350,000, do you think?'

'At least. It's tiny but it's central.'

'I've also got a few savings.'

'Tom, you can't put everything you have into the house.'

'Why not? I think you would have to suggest that I came in with you all, as a last resort, to Danielle. It's her godmother's house and I know how I'd feel in her position. It's also possible that Flo and Danielle might not want me involved. They might think that if I have a stake I could limit what you want to do with the business. I wouldn't, of course, but we'd have to tie it all up legally. It would have to be done tactfully for it to work between us all. If they were against the idea I would be disappointed, but I would respect it.'

'They want the house as much as we do, Tom.'

I grab his pen and do some scribbling of my own. Danielle and I have a mortgage on our flat, that we have been paying off regularly. What would a three-storey house in Hammersmith be worth now, with the large basement space we renovated? Probably £400,000.

I look at Tom, feeling pale. 'You know, it might be possible to have that amazing house. I mean really possible?'

We laugh like overexcited children. 'Will you marry me, Jenny Brown? House or no house?'

'I'll be the worst army wife in the world.'

'I know, but I'm not marrying the army.'

'*Promise* I won't have to do wives' clubs?'

'Promise.'

'Promise I won't have to wear frilly shirt collars and sensible clothes?'

He tries to keep a straight face. 'The mere thought of it is hysterical.'

I am serious for a second. 'I'll always want to work. It's what *I* do, Tom.'

'I know it is. Why on earth would I want to stop you? I love what you do.' He grins. 'In any case if we buy that house we'll all have to work until we're eighty.'

'True,' I say, 'if not very romantic.' I lift his hand to my cheek, press my mouth to his palm. 'OK, then. I *will* marry you.'

FORTY-THREE

Ruth got off the night train at Truro, picked up some croissants and coffee and went back to the cottage for a shower. She waited until nine o'clock to ring Tredrea in case she woke anyone up. Bea answered. 'I'll come over and pick Adam up. It's been really good of you, Bea. I hope he's been no trouble?'

'No trouble at all. He's made a friend and had a whale of time.' *Oh dear*, thought Bea. *Should I have said that?*

'Oh?' Ruth's voice was guarded.

'Just come when you're ready, Ruth. Adam will be pleased to see you.'

'Where are Adam and Jenny?' Bea asked James as he came into the kitchen. 'Ruth's back in Truro.'

'Down at the end of the drive by the gate, talking to two Australian musicians in a camper van who seem to be giving them tickets to some concert or other. Adam has disappeared inside it, fascinated.'

'It really is good to see him relaxing and happy. It was a stroke of genius introducing him to Harry, James.'

'I rather thought they might hit it off. Harry's a strange little boy who spends a lot of time on his own, too. I don't think

Adam's in any great hurry to go back to Truro, Bea. I just hope he doesn't show it when Ruth comes to pick him up.'

'Oh, Lord. So do I,' Bea said.

Jenny came into the kitchen with Adam behind her. 'Those Australians are completely barking but very sweet. Listen, you two, I've got the cottage if I want it. Isn't that amazing! And on my terms. I can hardly believe it.'

Adam grinned at her. 'They just wanted to go off surfing. They would have done *anything* to offload the cottage, you could tell.'

'Jenny!' Bea said. 'I hope you haven't said you'll clear the rest of the junk out of that cottage?'

'Well, yes, but Mum, it's in my own interest to get on with it. Besides, it's a project for me. You know how I love projects.'

'I do,' Bea said drily.

'They've given us six tickets to their concert in St Ives Church tonight. You'll love it, Dad. It's mostly Mozart. Adam's very excited because Dean plays the oboe, Adam's favourite instrument.'

'Jenny, Ruth's just rung,' Bea said quickly. 'She's coming over to collect Adam. We don't know what plans she has for the rest of the day.'

'She would probably like to come to the concert,' Adam said hopefully.

'I'm sure she would. Let's talk to her when she gets here. Adam and I are going into the town, Mum. I have to go to the bank. Do you need anything?'

Bea made a short list. She said under her breath, 'Please don't be long. I think it's better if Adam is here when Ruth arrives.'

'You're worrying unnecessarily, Mum. Ruth didn't say exactly what time she's coming, did she? We'll be half an hour at the most.'

'And with that she swept out,' James said. 'Remember what we said yesterday, Bea, about leaving grown-up children to get on with it?'

'Good in theory, hard in practice,' Bea said crossly. 'I'm going out to dead-head my roses and pretend I'm a nun.'

James snorted. 'You must have one hell of an imagination, having borne me five children!'

Bea gave him one of her looks and stepped out into her garden. She snipped at the heads of her old roses and worried. Poor Adam, caught in the middle. Was either Jenny or Ruth capable of imagining what the other must be feeling? Of course not. Pain is all-consuming and selfish.

Adam was a biddable and polite boy. Bea had watched him relax and respond to them both, but especially to James. He had been deprived of two sets of grandparents and Bea was conscious of the hole she and James were filling for him. Adam felt safe and secure here, and undeniably he was, at heart, a country boy. She had seen him with Harry yesterday; he was literally in his element.

If Ruth took the job in London with Flo and Danielle, how would Adam adapt? She knew James would say *Darling, it's not your problem*. He was right, it wasn't, but Ruth was vulnerable and alone, and was going to have to make some difficult decisions.

Cornwall was so far from Adam's real life and his real life had somehow to resume its natural rhythm with Ruth, wherever that might be. Bea sighed and snipped.

After lunch in the garden Adam walked down the hill to ask Harry if he'd like to go to the concert with them that evening.

'I hope we're not outstaying our welcome,' Ruth said to Bea.

'Of course, you're not,' Bea said. 'I know you probably

219

wanted to get home, Ruth, but Adam seems very keen to go to this little concert.'

'It's fine. I had nothing particular planned. Adam really misses going to concerts with Peter, so it's great he has the chance here.'

Jenny said, 'Tell us how you got on in London while Adam's with Harry.'

'I was impressed by the whole set-up. You've got an amazing team up there.'

Bea and James excused themselves and went off to read the papers in the conservatory.

'Do you think you'll accept Danielle's and Flo's offer?'

Ruth saw in Jenny's eyes a sudden darting anxiety; a fleeting uncertainty. 'I'm considering it, but I must discuss it with Adam.' She paused. 'I would only work in London if *you* were happy that I should.'

Jenny got up and poured more coffee into their cups. After a minute she said, 'It feels strange, the thought of someone else working with Flo and Danielle, but it's important we have the best person for the job and we all think that's you.' She handed Ruth her cup. 'But you mustn't feel you've been steamrolled into something out of the blue. You may have second thoughts about leaving Birmingham. So be very sure before you accept.'

'I *am* sure. I'm absolutely sure.' Ruth laughed. 'I think everything else – finding a school for Adam, the logistics – will fall into place once I've made the decision, but I will wait until I have a formal offer.'

They got up and walked across the grass. 'I saw some of your designs. There was one of a wedding dress that took my breath away. You're too talented to be away from designing for long. I'm sure of this. I wouldn't necessarily expect to stay once you were well.'

'You don't have to appease me. I don't think of you as

220

replacing me. Even if I'd remained in London we would have needed a good PR. Someone who can sell and promote us successfully.'

'It's much easier to sell other people. I could sell my own grandmother. You know how persistent I am, but I can't design clothes, so there's no competition, is there?'

No, Jenny thought. *Except you will be living in my house. In Tom's and my space.*

They stopped and faced each other. Jenny said, surprising herself with a shadow of a memory, '*Were* we competitive as children? I can't remember that we were.'

Ruth laughed. 'Not when we were small. Maybe a little as we got older. Everyone's slightly competitive. Danielle and Flo feel bereft without you. I envy you that sort of friendship. I've never seemed to have the time, or maybe the facility.'

They moved on and sat on a garden bench facing the sea.

Jenny caught the regret in Ruth's voice. 'Well, the London house works as a team and Flo and Danielle wouldn't consider you if they didn't like you or think that you could be part of the team.'

'Thank you,' Ruth said quietly. 'That's a nice thing to say.' Across the rooftops the sea glittered in the arc of the bay below them. 'Do you remember how we used to have somersault races down this lawn to the gate?' she murmured.

'Yes. Doesn't it seem a long time ago? And yet . . .'

'Sometimes it seems like yesterday. As if we could close our eyes and slide back to childhood.'

'But we can't,' Jenny said. 'We can't.'

Harry said, 'I've got the bumph on Truro School here for you. It tells you about different scholarships and things. Mum says your mum can ring the bursar, too, for information.'

'Don't say anything about it in front of my mum. I want to read up everything first. She's just been up to London. I don't know whether she's going to change jobs again, but if she does, that's when I'll tell her.'

'What if she doesn't change jobs and you stay in Birmingham?'

Adam's face closed. 'I'm going to tell her anyway. I'm going to tell her how I seriously hate that school. Peter made it a bit better. He was away a lot, but he coached me at home and he took me out to the cinema and concerts and things, and I could talk to him. He never wanted me to go there. I think he offered to pay for me to go to a private school.'

'So why didn't your mum let him?'

'Because he was my stepdad, not my real dad. Anyway, he left in the end.'

'Why? Did they argue?'

'Nope. Hardly ever. But they never kissed and that either.'

'No lovey-dovey to make you puke?'

Adam laughed. 'Never! What happened to your dad?'

Harry kicked at a tin can. 'He died. He was a lifeboat man and he drowned when I was seven.'

Adam caught the bleak expression that flitted shadowlike across Harry's face. 'I'm really sorry.'

'Race you to the Sloop.'

The two boys ran, swerving past the people on the pavements. Harry won. He said, breathless, leaning against the sea wall, 'They were always lovey-dovey and soppy, my mum and dad. I used to put a cushion over my head, it was *so* embarrassing.'

As Adam listened to the concert in the parish church that evening he felt acutely affected by the passionate playing of the Australians. He was aware of nothing except the music. He felt as if he were curled inside a closed warm shell of sound. Dean, the oboe player, coaxed out sounds that Adam only dreamt of. The music trembled off the walls and rafters, hovered hauntingly like floating gulls in the thick hot air. Adam held his breath in awe, consumed.

The church was candlelit, the audience rapt, and packed to the altar and choir stalls. The Australians belied their faded, sun-drenched appearance. They were young and intense, as if their very souls were in their music.

Maggie played a Mozart violin piece that sounded to Adam almost perfect. A side door had been left open because of the heat of the crowded church and Adam could hear the rhythmic sound of the sea. Longing caught and tore at his heart. He was unaware that he was crying. Tears silently flowed down his cheeks in the darkened church and as the aching sound of the violin shivered through him he prayed: *Dear God, please help me. I want to live in Cornwall. I want to go to school with Harry. I love my mum but I don't want to live in Birmingham or London. I want to live near the sea. I want to know everything about my father. I want Jenny to tell me and there is never time. Please make it so these things happen and I get a scholarship and my mum lets me and lives here too near James and Bea. If you help me I will try not to ask anything again. Thank you, God.*

FORTY-FOUR

The house in Birmingham seemed cold when Ruth and Adam
got home. Ruth shivered, it had never felt cold before. She
had told Adam about the job in London on the drive home.
'I know it would mean a change of schools for you, Adam,
but you're unhappy where you are. London has so much to
offer and the good thing is that I would see more of you
because I would be living and working from Jenny's house.'

'When you weren't away, travelling,' Adam said flatly.
'You've just said that they need you to promote their business and sell their clothes. That means you going away, like
you've always done, doesn't it?'

'Well, yes, Adam, sometimes.'

'So I'd be left in a house in London with people I don't
know. No, thank you.'

'Adam, listen. We'd have our own private rooms in the
house. We'd go up to London and look into schools together.
This is such an opportunity for us both. This house feels sad
without Peter. You've never settled in school here. We can
both move on. I really believe you'd love London and all it
has to offer.'

'Have you said yes?'

'Well, I'm waiting to have a formal offer from Danielle and Flo.'

Adam stuck another tape in his CD and prepared to put his earplugs back in his ears. 'Will you get more money? Is that one of the reasons you want to move?'

'No, it's not the money, Adam. This is a great chance for me to work for a small business, build it up and make my mark, like I used to in Glasgow.' Ruth heard her overweening enthusiasm and knew her pitch was entirely wrong.

Adam looked at her with his unnerving, clear-sighted blue eyes. 'You're going to take the job. It doesn't matter what I think or feel. You always do what *you* want.' He put his earplugs back and closed his eyes, shutting Ruth out. The rest of the journey was spent in silence.

Ruth felt a little core of anger growing inside her. He had been sweet with Bea and James. His sullen act seemed to be entirely reserved for her.

On Monday Adam returned to school. On Tuesday morning she had a letter in the post from London offering her the job. Ruth's heart soared. *Yes!* The money was better than she had expected. It meant that if she and Peter sold the house and got rid of their mortgage it would make her significantly better off.

Before accepting, she rang Peter to ask his advice about Adam and to discuss the sale of the Birmingham house. It was good to hear his voice, but he sounded tense and tired. 'How are you?' she asked.

'So-so. Adjustment is difficult, isn't it?'

'Yes,' said Ruth. 'It's bloody difficult.'

'Problems?'

Ruth explained about the job in London and Adam's resistance.

'Well, it's not an ideal age to move schools. Is he any happier at that school, then?'

'No. It's change per se, I think.'

'I don't suppose Adam knows what he does want. You're the adult, Ruth, you may have to make the decision for him and hope he is happier in a London school. You know what I think of the school he's at now. You can only do better for him, but if you jump from a prestigious and well-paid job and sell up Adam's home to live in someone else's house, you've got to be very sure it *is* the right thing for you. Then everything else will fall into place.'

'Thanks,' Ruth said. 'I didn't listen to you about schools last time, so I will this time.'

'If I could, I would offer to help with private school fees, but my circumstances have changed and I'm not in a position to do that any more.'

'For heaven's sake, Peter, that's not why I rang. I wouldn't accept then and I certainly wouldn't accept now we are divorcing.'

'Actually, I haven't started proceedings yet, I've been so busy.'

'Oh.' Ruth was taken by surprise. 'Right. It will be a relief if I do put this house up for sale, won't it? I expect you would like your share, whatever you said before?'

'Well, yes. I need to sort out some accommodation of my own over here. I've had a few problems.'

'I'm sorry to hear that.' Ruth waited to see if he would tell her what sort of problems, but he didn't. 'I'd better go,' she said. 'I should be working and you must be busy.'

'I was going to ring Adam anyway. He might offload to me. I miss him.'

Ruth heard the regret in his voice for a life gone wrong. 'He misses you too. Thanks, Peter. Take care,' she said gently.

'You too.'

Ruth was working from home and as she replaced the receiver the telephone rang again immediately. 'Mrs Hallam?'

'Yes, speaking.'

'This is the school secretary here. Mr Hastings is taking a class but he asked me to ring to find out if Adam is unwell or if you were still on holiday as Adam has not returned to school after the break.'

Ruth felt her stomach plummet. 'What do you mean? I saw him get on the school bus this morning. You mean he was not in school yesterday or today?' She could hear her own panic.

'No, I'm afraid he wasn't. You've always notified us if Adam was going to be absent and Mr Hastings overheard two of the boys talking, and he thought we ought to ring you.'

'Talking about Adam? What were they saying?'

'Apparently, that he wasn't coming back to school at all.'

'Oh, God. Are George Woo and Darren Singh in school? Those two and Adam are good friends.'

'Yes, they're here, but if they know where Adam is they are not saying.'

'Look, I'm going to come down to the school. They might talk to me.'

Ruth grabbed her car keys and ran out to the car. Surely this wasn't happening. Adam roaming around Birmingham when he should be safe in school, at the mercy of pimps and addicts and . . . She snapped off her mind and concentrated on her driving. She had no idea where he had been yesterday because she had worked late.

At the school Mr Hastings, a tall, weary man, was waiting for her with George and Darren.

'If it had been anyone but Adam I probably wouldn't have worried you, but Adam is not as streetwise as some. This isn't like him. Have you any idea what's worrying him?'

'Yes, I'm afraid I have. I might be moving to London to take up a new job.'

Mr Hastings smiled thinly. 'I would have thought he might welcome that, Mrs Hallam. I don't think he's entirely happy here. A bit of difficulty fitting in.'

'Why do you think that is?' Ruth felt a flash of anger. 'Is he bullied?'

'We have zero tolerance on bullying.' As he spoke Ruth heard the irony in his voice. He was obviously parodying the headmaster. 'Adam and the two boys sitting over there are brighter than most. They enjoy learning and they are articulate. Being verbally adept here threatens the intellectually challenged who, I am sad to say, are in the majority in this school. Your son is not flourishing. If you can afford to send Adam anywhere else, I suggest you do so. George Woo is off to boarding school and Darren Singh is returning with his family to school in India. This could have a bearing on Adam's two-day absence.' He turned and guided Ruth towards the two boys sitting on chairs at the end of the corridor. 'We have never had this politically incorrect conversation, unless you wish me to be unemployed and my pension halved. See what you can get out of these two. I will be here until five thirty, if I can be of any assistance. I'll be glad to know when you've found him.'

Darren Singh broke first. George was made of sterner stuff. 'He was going to the library looking up stuff.'

'What library? What stuff?'

'Dunno.'

'Was he upset when he knew you two were leaving the school?'

'Yeah, sort of, but excited too.'

'Excited?'

'Yeah. Like he had this plan.' George kicked Darren hard.

'This is not a game,' Ruth snapped. 'You know what Adam's like. He did not grow up in a big city like you two, he's not streetwise. If you are really his friends you will look out for him, not put him at risk.'

'He had this plan about some school he wanted to go to. He wanted to find out all about it before he told you. He is dead miserable because he thinks you won't let him go there. You'll make him go to London.'

Ruth felt suddenly dizzy and sat down beside them. *No. Please no.* 'Which library, boys?'

The boys were alarmed. Adam's mum had gone dead white.

'County Library on Fairfield Road, I think,' George said quickly.

'Thank you. You haven't been disloyal to Adam, either of you.'

Ruth turned and hurried back to her car. She got her map from the glove compartment and when she found the library she parked and sat for a moment taking deep breaths.

Adam was in the reading room poring over heavy books. Ruth let out her breath with relief. He had pulled an old Aran sweater over his school clothes. His hair was flopping over his face and he looked, in the empty room, thin, angular and defenceless.

Ruth, watching him, felt wretched. She remembered, as a child, how she used to cry out to her parents when she was endlessly berated, *I didn't ask to be born. I never asked to be born.*

Adam hadn't either and his fears and his yearnings had to be listened to. He was floundering suddenly in an insecure world where there were no absolute certainties.

Ruth knew herself. She was too selfish to turn down the job in London. She could not do it. So she must try to make it all right for Adam. It was all she could do. She was not going to let him drown, whatever the cost to herself.

She slid into the seat beside him.

Adam laid out all his research on the kitchen table. Warily, he put Harry's prospectus for Truro School next to it and

229

started to explain to his mother what he'd found out about various different scholarships and what they were worth. Ruth, hiding her misery as her worst fears materialised, made herself look at them. She read them all carefully for three-quarters of an hour while Adam had a bath.

When he came down again Ruth said brightly, 'I'm impressed, you've been very thorough. Did you notice that you can take a scholarship for any Methodist school in any county, not just Truro? That includes London.'

'I know. But Truro School does five music scholarships a year, Mum. I could try for a music scholarship *and* an academic scholarship based on the entrance exam. Then I get two chances.'

'What if they give preferences to local boys and what if you're disappointed? I mean, the competition will be stiff. We have to be realistic here.'

'Harry's uncle coached Harry in his weakest subjects and went over old entrance exam papers with him. And music is the one thing I've always kept up. Please let me try. *Please.*'

Ruth sighed. 'OK. I'm not promising anything but in the morning I'll ring the bursar of Truro School. We'll find out more and look into all the possibilities. In return, will you at least come with me to London and look at some private schools there that also award scholarships?'

Adam bit his lip for a moment and then, reluctantly, nodded.

Ruth smiled. 'Give us a hug. Please don't give me a fright like that again.'

Adam went over and hugged her. 'Sorry. Thanks, Mum. Thanks a lot.'

'Darling, just don't get your hopes too high.'

When he had gone to bed, Ruth poured herself a drink. There was no way she could commit herself to four years of school fees. If Adam didn't win a scholarship, and he certainly hadn't been stretched here in Birmingham, what was she going to do?

What had made her so selfishly pigheaded that she had refused Peter's help with Adam when she had been married to him? It seemed inconceivably selfish now. What had she been thinking? That Adam was bright, so he would prosper despite the handicap of a vast class? It had been something far more selfish than that. She had wanted a get-out if her marriage to Peter failed. She had not wanted to be financially tied or indebted to him. Well, good for her. With a bit more financial dependency she might have worked harder at her marriage to a perfectly nice and loving man, and Adam would have felt safe at home instead of dreaming of Harry Potter boarding schools miles away from her.

She thought that in the morning she might ring Mr Hastings to see if Adam could get extra coaching from somewhere. She went up to her bedroom. The stars glittered in a cloudless night sky. This was the house and the life she had so carelessly taken for granted and devalued. Her life with Peter had not just been hers. It had been Adam's and Peter's lives too.

What goes round comes round. What a bloody little homily that was. She had misjudged Adam's feelings about a father he had never known; over Peter leaving; over Adam's small everyday uncomplaining life in a school he hated. What did she expect, for God's sake? Of course he looked towards the settled, stable lives of Bea and James; to the routine and comparative safety of a small school in Cornwall; towards the vulnerable, warm Jenny, the only person in the world who could talk to him of his father. The one human being who could breathe life and breadth into the central shadowy figure that had dominated his childhood dreams.

Tom. A figure Ruth had always fantasised as bursting into their lives again. And he had.

FORTY-FIVE

When I'd had the little house cleared completely, Bea and Loveday, who had cleaned for Mum for as long as I could remember, came to help. I wanted the place scrubbed and bare before deciding what major alterations needed doing. In good Cornish fashion we kept it in the family and Loveday's son Roger, who was a builder when he wasn't a fisherman, came and gave me advice.

Dad was worried about me spending too much money, but he saw that the walls needed to come down and relaxed when he realised none of them was load-bearing. In fact, the house had been built like a child's Lego toy. One large room had been partitioned into four tiny rooms with flimsy wallpapered walls that looked substantial but were not.

Roger pulled them down in a week and threw them into a skip. He laid a basic pine wooden floor for me, then Dad and I set about painting the inside with strong Italian powder paints I mixed in a bucket. I was left with an open-plan living and kitchen area, two small bedrooms and a bathroom, which we made lighter by knocking it into the loo next door.

I gave up trying to stop Bea and James helping me, they seemed to enjoy it and I got a kick out of surprising them with my mix of colours and showing them how they could work together. In a few weeks the place was unrecognisable. I took photographs of each stage of the refurbishment to show the Australians.

I was grateful to be so busy, and so exhausted by the time I fell into bed that I slept. I cherished this time with Bea and James. We were such a large family that it was rare to have them to myself.

The weather could not have been more perfect. It was a baking hot June and July, and we spent days working on the cottage. Dad barbecued in the evening and we drank icy white wine in the garden full of birdsong. Mum snoozed under a Philadelphia tree and Dad went off for a spot of fishing.

Before we sent the photographs we had taken to the Australians, Dad suggested that I got in an estate agent to value the house again. I had watched how the sun moved round and the light changed. I had painted peach walls that changed to terracotta towards the kitchen at the far end. At the back, where the branches of the trees practically touched the windows, I had a leafy green against an arch of rusty Tuscan red. With the pale pine floorboards and bigger windows it all worked, and I was quietly thrilled because I knew I could live here.

The estate agent's mouth fell open when he saw it. He thought I had added at least £50,000 to its value. Dad thought I should offer to buy it and so did the estate agent. We worked out what I had spent, then we put in what Dad considered a fair offer. Tom had taken out life insurance, and Dad thought I should invest the money wisely and that the house would be a good investment.

I had my answer from Maggie's Australian mother almost straight away. She jumped at it as if she couldn't believe her luck.

'Was it mean not showing her what we've done to the house?' I asked Dad. 'She sold it to us on the memory of how it was.'

Dad and Mum raised their eyes to the ceiling.

'Oh Jen! They could have spent money on doing the house up if they'd wanted to. What's the difference between this transaction and you buying the place in an awful state and then doing it up?'

I saw that, of course. It was just that making obvious changes, looking at things in a certain way, knowing instinctively how to cut certain fabrics or what colours and textures of materials would work together came easily. I felt that erroneously, I had made a quick buck. I had liked Maggie and Dean.

Dad laughed and shook his head. 'I'll never make a businesswoman of you.'

He wouldn't. I knew I was occasionally taken advantage of. It had driven Tom and Danielle wild sometimes. I also knew where I got it from: my parents. They would give the shirts off their backs and often had. My father could only be businesslike for his children.

When I was alone at the house, I would sit on the step in my paint-splattered shorts in the sun and listen to the curlews out on the estuary. I felt like someone else. The height of summer slid slowly by. As I worked, I felt Tom was with me. I thought of the London house we had all worked on together so long ago and I tried to see my improvements here with Tom's perfectionist eye. I sent postcards to Adam and Ruth, and they sent tired, busy city postcards back.

Now the house was nearly finished I began to put off the moment of moving in and moving on. I could not admit to anyone that I was afraid of being alone all of a sudden. I sometimes shook with the thought of going to bed and waking to an empty building. I had never been alone in a house in my life.

I was afraid of the small ghost of my child filling the spaces with her presence, pulling me back into that heavy blanket of darkness. I was afraid of my body, which ached for Tom, and of his voice, which would come to me, catching me unawares in quiet moments.

I had ached for so long to be alone with the two people I had lost and now I was afraid of it. I saw that somehow, in my skewered imagination, I had Adam here with me. I knew from Flo and Danielle that Adam and Ruth had been up to London looking at schools for him.

Danielle said Ruth was being given a hard time working out her notice in Birmingham and a harder time selling her house. I thought of Adam finishing his last term at school. I worried about him. Change is so hard when you are his age.

Both London and Birmingham seemed impossibly faraway to me. I had spoken to Adam on the phone only once. He sounded tired.

One morning a postcard arrived of black-necked gulls. It said,

Dear Jenny,
  I hope you are well. I will see you very soon. Mum and I are coming down to Cornwall soon and we will come over to see you if that is OK. Please keep your fingers crossed for me (it's a secret). I have e-mailed Harry to tell him that I'm coming too.
  Lots of love,
  Adam.

FORTY-SIX

When I tell Flo about Tom's offer to come in with us to buy the house, she thinks it is a brilliant and sensible idea, especially if we are going to get married. I can tell she is delighted. She agrees with Tom and we say nothing to Danielle until she has exhausted every option with every bank.

Even I know that no bank or mortgage company will sanction the amount we need to borrow. If they did we would be saddled with a crippling amount to pay back with no room for mistakes or a bad business year.

Flo puts her house on the market. She will be able to contribute far more than Danielle and I can scrape together. It is only when I find Danielle in despair that I tentatively put to her the idea of Tom coming in with us. Her reaction is totally negative. She insists on viewing it as a business venture and would rather borrow from the bank.

However, her godmother's health deteriorates and it is only after a bleak surveyor's report and the realisation that we are in danger of losing the house that Danielle begins to waver. Flo's lovely house in Chiswick sells quickly, so does Tom's flat. Between them, financially, she and Tom make the reality of buying the house outright, possible. Then Danielle

voices her concern about Tom putting in the greatest investment which she thinks will make the rest of us vulnerable.

From the moment I told her I was going to marry Tom I
began to realise that Danielle had developed a problem with
him. She doesn't want him in our lives and I wonder what
he could have done to alienate her because he is working so
hard to make sure the legal side is tied up in our favour.

Without Tom, the house would have remained a dream
only. Danielle knows this. Because of Tom, we are going to
have prestigious business premises and a huge leap in cred-
ibility. When I ask her what her problem is she says, 'Divorce
is messy enough for two. If things go wrong the four of us
will be involved.'

It is the first time I see Flo lose her temper. She sends me
out of the room and I go off into town to see a friend, miserable. It all feels suddenly like a pack of cards; none of it is
going to work if we cannot live together in trust and harmony.
I am glad Tom is away on a course. It's wounding when
someone doesn't seem to like the person you love.

When I get back, Danielle is in bed with a migraine.

Flo tells me that they've had a long talk. Danielle is frightened of losing me; losing the business; of things changing
between us. Of Tom spoiling our working relationship and
friendship. 'Basically,' Flo says, 'she resents Tom's intrusion
into our little female enclave. She is a mass of insecurities.
I've told her you and Tom are an item and she will have to
get used to it, whether we buy the house or not. I don't think
she knows herself whether she is jealous of you and Tom
being wildly in love or jealous of Tom taking you away from
her or the business.'

'This way', I say, 'Tom does not take me away from anyone
or anything.'

'I pointed that out,' Flo says drily.

I have never fallen out with Danielle and the following

evening we go out together and talk. She apologises. She says she has never liked change and just wishes the two of us could have done it all on our own. She tells me she has always been scared of big commitments and tying herself to anyone or anything. *Of course* she doesn't have anything against Tom; or all of us living in the same house. She wants me to be happy. She wants us all to be happy. As we totter home in the dark, arm in arm, we vow never to argue again.

Six months later it is ours. The four of us walk round the empty house quailing. Without the heavy French furniture the extent of the work is frighteningly apparent, as the surveyor's report had warned. We commission an architect for the structural changes and a builder we trust.

In a year, Tom is in Oman for six months and in spite of still living with builder's dust and chaos on the ground floor, in spite of all we still have to do, none of us can remember living anywhere else. In two years the house swallows and nurtures us seamlessly. We all have our place, separately and together. It has worked. It has really worked. Tom returns from Sierra Leone. In two years and three months I am pregnant and Tom starts to decorate the small room next to our bedroom. I do not know who is more excited, me, Tom, Flo or Danielle. This baby is going to be spoilt.

FORTY-SEVEN

I moved into the house with its odd sticks of furniture that week. I made sure I was cheerful in front of Bea and James. I *was* moving on, but it was not as easy as I thought. I knew I had to find a reason for getting up in the morning. I knew that I could still sink like a stone. Bea and I launched ourselves into bookshops and I bought a huge amount of fiction as well as art books, pencils and plain paper.

I watched myself eagerly buying, but I knew in my heart that I wouldn't use any of them for a while. It was like a strange game I was playing with myself.

Bea was sneakily wise, though: she drove me into Truro and we bought rolls of pale muslin in primrose and cream with tiny flowers for curtains. As I bunched the delicate material in my fingers I felt an instinctive stirring of pleasure in the thought of making it up.

On my first day in my new home a huge bunch of flowers arrived. They were from Paolo Antonio. Danielle must have told him. I was touched that he remembered I loved white lilies, despite their poignant connotations.

Bea wanted to stay the first night with me, but I knew I had to do this alone. Dad brought champagne and Bea lovely great prawns and French bread and salad, and we toasted the house and the future. I fell into bed in a blissful champagne stupor and woke to sun streaming over my bed, and it was all right. It was more than all right.

Ruth and Adam arrived on Saturday morning, surprising me. I was shocked at how thin Ruth was.

'We couldn't ring you, but Bea and James told us you were here,' she said as we touched cheeks.

'The phone's coming next week. Are you OK, Ruth? You've lost a lot of weight.'

She smiled. 'I'm fine. Life's just a bit relentless at the moment. The Fayad group are working me into the ground to pay me back for giving in my notice. The Birmingham house is not selling, and Adam and I are frantically busy packing our possessions into crates.'

I turned to Adam. I was so pleased to see him that tears came to my eyes. He came and hugged me fiercely and I realised that in just a matter of weeks he had grown taller than I was.

I put on the coffee and they walked around my tiny domain exclaiming.

'Wow!' Adam kept shouting. '*Wicked!*'

'It's lovely,' Ruth said. 'It's amazing, Jenny. You still have your flair for putting things together. You make me feel totally unimaginative.'

'Pff!' I said, imitating Danielle. 'I've heard about some of the business ideas you've put to Flo and Danielle. They're thrilled that you're so organised and thinking ahead.'

I turned and saw that Adam was bursting to tell me something. I grinned at him. 'OK, give! What's this secret you mentioned in your postcard?'

He laughed. 'Guess what, Jenny? Last week I went to Truro School to try for a music scholarship. I had to play two instruments, piano and clarinet, and take a written exam

240

which was quite hard. Yesterday, I went back to take the entrance exam. That's why I told you to keep your fingers crossed, but I probably won't know how I did for ages.'

I stared at him, speechless, then sat down abruptly and turned to Ruth.

Her face was devoid of expression. 'Adam wanted to come to Truro School as a boarder and I agreed to him trying for a scholarship as long as he looked at London schools with an open mind. I would much rather he were in London with me but at least I have the cottage down here and I can drive down regularly to see him, if he does win a place.'

I heard James outside and Adam rushed out to tell him his news.

'It's important that Adam is happy and settled,' Ruth added, looking miserable.

'What happens if he doesn't win a scholarship?'

She shrugged and smiled. 'A scholarship, with my income, will only be worth twenty-five per cent of the school fees. Adam doesn't realise. I will have to use the money from the house sale. I've had huge problems with Adam. If I hadn't agreed to him trying for a scholarship he would have gone off the rails. I didn't have a choice. There is little hope he will agree to even a private school in London. He's made up his mind he wants to be in Cornwall and go to school with Harry.' As Dad and Adam came up the path she added quickly, 'I think Adam has a good chance of winning a place. He's worked ferociously. His form master has been wonderful and has given him a great deal of extra tuition, and he's also had extra music coaching. He's practised assiduously every day for hours.' Suddenly the tears were streaming down her face.

I jumped up as James got to the door. 'Dad, could you and Adam go on home to lunch? Ruth and I will catch you up.'

Dad took in Ruth's crumpled figure, nodded, turned round

and said heartily to Adam, 'Girl talk! Let's go and find Bea and tell her your news.'

I went to Ruth and tentatively put my hand on her arm. She was very stiff and she couldn't stop crying. 'You're tired,' I said. 'You're very, very tired, Ruth.'

She nodded. 'Sorry. This is so bloody unlike me. Or it used to be.'

'Why have you been battling with Adam alone? Why didn't you ring us?'

'It's *my* problem, Jenny.'

I went and got my tissues. 'Why don't you lie on my bed and sleep for a couple of hours as you're so exhausted?'

'Could I?'

I smiled. 'Of course you can. Go on, get under the covers, I'm going to make you some soup; it's my staple diet.'

She went into my bedroom and when I went in later with a tray of soup she was lying on top of the bed in her slim jeans, grey with fatigue.

'When you've had this,' I said, 'sleep as long as you can.'

'I'll try, but only if you leave me to vegetate and go and have lunch with your parents and Adam. Please. I'll sleep if I'm alone. It will be bliss.'

'OK,' I said. 'You've got your mobile?'

'Go.' She smiled. 'Stop fussing.'

'My turn to fuss.'

I ran down the path to my car. It was as if a shadow had passed over me and I was in the light again.

FORTY-EIGHT

Peter flew into Birmingham to sign the contract for the imminent sale of the house and to organise the removal of the rest of his things. It had at last sold to a widow who wanted to buy it for cash, but needed early completion. Neither Ruth nor Peter wanted to lose the sale.

He looked guiltily at the stripped walls devoid of pictures and the packing crates in every room. He was met by a pale, exhausted Ruth and an overwrought Adam, and he went straight to his old study to use the phone. Half an hour later he came into the kitchen. 'I'm sorry, Ruth, I'm not taking any argument. I've booked us all into a spa hotel on the Helford. I have a week's sailing down there with a friend. Adam and I will go off all day and you can spend a whole peaceful week doing absolutely nothing.'

Ruth, surprised, opened her mouth to protest.

'Think of it as a thank you. You've had the hassle of putting the house on the market and all the packing up. I should have flown home and helped you and I'm feeling guilty as hell about it. It would also be great to spend some time with Adam. He needs to unwind as well.'

Oh God, it would be bliss. She needed a break before she started work in London. Adam was thrilled by the idea but anxious about the letter that should come any day from Truro School sealing his fate. Ruth rang the bursar, and gave him her mobile number and the name of the hotel.

Her phone rang one afternoon as she lay by the swimming pool facing the sea. Listening to the voice at the other end congratulating Adam, she felt a burst of undiluted pride that took her by surprise. She heard herself laughing out loud. Adam deserved this, he really did. He had worked so hard and the odds had been stacked against him. She went and ordered champagne.

When Adam and Peter got back, sunburnt and salty, the first thing Adam asked was: 'Did anyone ring, Mum?'

Ruth signalled to the waiter and stretched. 'Did anyone ring? Um . . . Oh, yes. You', she said casually, 'have just won the Daniel Hammett Music Scholarship outright against stiff competition!'

Adam went pale and sat down abruptly. 'Honestly? Do you mean it, Mum? You're not joking?'

'I'm not joking! I mean it. Look, here comes the champagne to prove it. A letter from Truro School will be waiting for us at the cottage.' She went round and hugged him. 'Clever, clever boy! I'm so proud of you, Adam. You were so determined and you did it!'

'I wonder who on earth he takes after,' Peter said and poured the champagne. They lifted their glasses. 'Well done, Adam! That's a prestigious prize to win.'

Adam grinned, embarrassed, and could not stop grinning. He drank his champagne in a gulp, choked, turned green and made a dash to the lavatory where he was sick. He leant against the cubicle and trembled with relief. He knew that if he had failed he would have had to agree to go to a London school. The school fees were astronomical without boarding fees on top. He could not have let his mother even try to pay them.

Ruth, waiting for him to emerge, knew that if the answer had been different she would have had to watch Adam's life unravel in front of her.

When Adam had disappeared to shower and ring Harry, and, she guessed, Jenny, Peter asked, 'How will you feel living without Adam for the first time?'

'Miserable, I expect. I made a huge mistake in insisting he went to his last school, Peter. I have to try and put that right and think of what Adam wants now, and Cornwall is what he wants. He's achieved it by sheer will and hard work, and I have to respect that.'

'He's certainly a country boy. You should see him on the boat, binoculars at the ready, happy as the day is long. It's been great watching the tension disappear. The scholarship is obviously a help, but with boarding fees it's going to be a bit tight, isn't it?'

'I'll manage. I'll invest my half of the house, and Danielle is paying me well.'

'It means you end up with no home. What if this job doesn't measure up and you want out?'

Ruth laughed. 'I have my Cornish cottage.'

Peter smiled. 'So you do. Shall we swim?'

For a week Ruth lay by the pool and read and slept. She had every spa treatment going and felt wonderfully spoilt and decadent. She started to put on the weight she had lost and she could feel the exhaustion slipping away from her. She found herself smiling for no reason.

Adam grinned at her one morning. 'You're happy, Mum. I've never seen you do nothing before. It's spooky.'

Ruth thought, *How self-perpetuating happiness is. I must think back and remember because unhappiness is catching too and can become a habit.*

On their last night at the hotel there was a dance and Adam went off with some American teenagers to have a barbecue on the beach.

Peter said suddenly and astutely, 'Make the future work, Ruth, for both you and Adam. The new job sounds great but you're going to be living in Jenny's house with Jenny's friends and work colleagues. Adam is probably going to see more of Jenny and her family in the term-time than you. Realistically you're not going to be able to travel down to Cornwall every exeat he has and Adam will need to get out of school. Are you prepared for this? Have you thought it all through?'

Ruth, moving to the music, wasn't sure she had. The shadows were back, like distant voices from another room, faint but insistent. She was avoiding facing the reality and consequences of what Adam's award really meant. She was avoiding exploring her feelings about something that seemed to have happened so fast.

Peter said gently, 'You must get it all clear in your head. I feel responsible in a way. I left you and it's dictated the decisions you've made.'

Ruth looked at him. 'You left me because I didn't make you happy and . . .' She stopped.

'You would probably have left me anyway,' Peter finished for her with a dry smile.

They went back to their table, picked up their glasses and made their way out into the hotel's tropical garden. The air smelt of herbs and seaweed, and the crickets sounded loud in the dark beyond the pool.

'How are things with you?' she asked. 'Your family must be over the moon to have you with them.'

Peter did an amusing imitation of his Jewish mama, then he said, 'I'm going to buy my own house. I'm too old to live back at home despite my mama's pleas.' He sighed. 'It's hard forming new relationships as you get older. Perhaps I'm set in my ways. Anyway, let's say things haven't gone quite as I hoped. Sharing space is difficult.' He closed his eyes and took a deep breath. 'I just want that old-fashioned thing, a wife and a child. It doesn't sound complicated, but it seems to be.'

Ruth felt sad. She didn't know what to say. Peter took her hand suddenly. 'I've just been lecturing you to make your life work. Now you know why. I have to make mine work too or what has it all been for? What's it all been for?' They stared at each other in silence. Then Peter jumped up. 'Come on, let's have one more dance, then we'll go and find Adam.'

As they danced, Ruth said, 'Thanks for this week. It's been an absolute godsend. We're still good friends, aren't we, Peter?'

'We are indeed.' He was smiling down at her as they danced.

'Why are you smiling at me like that?'

'Because actually, you are still my wife as well as my good friend and I still fancy you like hell.'

Ruth grinned. 'Don't tempt me! It would be bad move, Peter. I'm only your wife on a piece of paper. We both have to move on. You know this. Don't let's risk spoiling the week. You've already told me that we must make our lives work.'

'So I have.' Peter kissed the end of her nose. 'So I have.'

As they made their way to the beach, Ruth said, 'Pete, don't make me or our marriage into more than it was in looking back. It's easy to do, especially when things are going wrong. We're probably closer now than we ever were when we were living together.' She stopped walking and turned to him. 'You know, by not starting divorce proceedings you will make anyone you are with insecure and doubtful of what you really want.'

Peter looked guilty. 'I know. I know I should get on with

247

it. Somehow, I just thought I'd leave it for three years and then divorce is automatic.'

'But one of your reasons for leaving me was to be with someone else.'

'Yes,' he said miserably.

Ruth reached up and placed her cheek against his. 'Listen, you. Go back and start divorce proceedings. Go back and try again.'

'Thank you,' Peter said. He sighed. 'It's been a wonderful few days, Ruth. It's what I needed too.'

Adam, catching sight of them, waved. He looked flushed and happy. Watching him Peter thought, *I do want children of my own. I must make things work out there. I must; but letting go of these two is hard. So hard.*

FORTY-NINE

I woke early in my house and would lie in bed listening to the curlews and the songbirds in the garden. I could see them hopping over the tiny lawn and exploring old Nelly's numerous bird feeders.

In the next-door garden there was an enormous macrocarpa tree. Its huge branches were bent at angles by the relentless wind and some must have split and been lopped as there were gaps in the trunk like missing teeth. The spread of the tree was so wide that it was if it were stretching in all directions to fill the sky. It was staggeringly beautiful with its top branches flattened by the prevailing winds. It looked like an African acacia in the middle of the desert. In the evenings as the sun set behind it the branches turned silver. I was so afraid someone would try to fell it. It was what happened all the time. City people bought a house or developers came and all they could see was a tree that blocked a vestige of their sunlight or whose trunk took up room for another dwelling. They did not even pretend to care that trees hundreds of years old had more right here than the relentless race to turn each village into a uniform suburbia.

It was a long time since I had listened to the sounds and

sensations of a day waking up. It cleared my spirit, made way for a quiet peace, but it also made room for sorrow.

In my cloistered first few weeks in the house I felt an indefinable growth and expansion as if, sub-consciously, I were beginning to accept that the pain I carted around with me was never going to go away but would become a part of who I was. My thoughts were often stark and vivid as I began to edge forward towards a future without Rosie and Tom, the two people who had anchored me to such happiness, a happiness I had never dared take for granted because of the job Tom did.

September came and the light began to change, the leaves faded and curled, their edges turning brown. There were only a few hardy holidaymakers left, sitting in clumps on the beach watching the high neap tides.

Sometimes I would get up early and walk on the deserted estuary still bleached of colour, black and white with the sun trapped behind mist. Seabirds rose up in feathered clouds in front of me and wheeled away in a circle like miniature silent jets.

The sea was pewter, still as glass. I would love to trace my feelings on the surface of the water, knowing that when I turned away my dark thoughts would disappear like a ripple, sink without sound into the endless depth of this space in my life that I was trying to make sense of.

Every day Bea or James, Danielle or Flo would ring me, not quite trusting my ability to endure alone. Even in the darkest moments I appreciated my luck in having them. It was this unfailing love that warmed me and gave me the same sense of wonder as my tree, or the aching, undulating sound of curlews. Or Adam.

As I thought back over my life with Tom, as I did all the time now that I was at last alone, it felt like a precious and sacred story I was preparing for Adam. I wanted it all there for him, no piece left out, so that it stayed with him for ever, a vivid, indelible picture of his father.

The day we get married in St Ives parish church there is a heatwave. As the wedding car drives down Tregenna Hill the streets are lined with people. Everyone knows James. He has lived in St Ives for the whole of his working life. Most of the older generation have watched all of his children grow up. In this car we feel a bit like the royal family. I wave on one side of the car, Dad on the other. We both get the giggles.

The doors of the church are thrown open against the heat. The church is bursting with people and so are the narrow streets outside. It seems that everyone, holidaymakers and locals all thronging the town, has decided to join in cheerfully from the doorways and edges of the church.

Danielle designed my wedding dress. It is deceptively simple and exquisitely cut, like the dress Tom first saw me in. This time Danielle, Flo and all the girls have scattered millions of tiny pearls all over it and sewn narrow silk ribbon in a cross band round the waist. The tiny pearls catch the light and I feel as if I am floating out of the car like a mermaid, bright blue sky above me, intense blue sea caught in a glimpse as I walk into the church.

My hair is too wild for a veil and it is hardly appropriate, given the amount of time Tom and I spend in bed. Danielle has made a little tiara of white silk roses and dotted more on clips in my hair.

As I walk into the church where I was christened and confirmed, with my two little blonde nieces as bridesmaids in similar dresses, there is a gasp and I hope fervently that Danielle hears it. I lost count of the midnight hours she spent working and worrying about these dresses. A selfless, sweet labour of love.

251

When I reach Tom I see that his hands are trembling. I am late. I am always late. Did he think I wasn't coming? His incredible purple eyes widen when he sees me. *How I love him*. I hold out my hand. He takes it as if I might break and as we turn to the altar he sighs.

The church is full of the scent of white lilies and incense; of white and pink roses, all my favourite flowers. Bea and my sisters have decorated the church and it is amazing. I float through the service and it seems that in one trance-like moment we are married. I want to do it all again and take in every second of the wedding mass.

We walk out through Tom's guard of honour, who are causing quite a stir in dress uniform and spurs, then hand in hand we walk through the crowds down to the harbour beach for some wedding photographs, closely followed by his best man, and other officers who bolt straight for *The Sloop* and a beer.

'Don't even think about it!' I murmur.

'Perish the thought, wifie,' he says.

I watch Tom's parents as they pose for pictures with us. His father is rather bluff and alarming, but his mother is tranquil and easy. When the bridesmaids are being photographed with me on the harbour wall, I see Tom walk over to Danielle. He bends and says something to her, then suddenly pulls her to him and hugs and hugs her. He is telling her how beautiful my wedding dress is. I watch her face flush with pleasure. I watch her hug him back and see what she hopes no one will notice: tears have sprung to her eyes. I turn away, choked. The best wedding present I could have is that my best friend and my husband are friends.

We traipse up the hill to Tredrea and the marquee in the garden. Bea is having a panic about the caterers and James is calming her down. The dreamlike day whirls into evening and when the dancing begins Tom and I watch our friends getting off with each other and giggle. We are smug marrieds now. All that is behind us.

We move alone to the bottom of the garden and watch the sun set over our wedding day. It has been so perfect. The weather, friends and family getting on together; the food, the speeches. Everything.

Tomorrow we fly to Malaysia with Tom's parents. We have ten days on our own on Pangor Laut Island, then a treasured week for Tom with his family, playing golf and going to the Club with his father, snatching precious time with his mother.

As soon as we get home Tom leaves for Northern Ireland. Monitoring the activities of IRA members reluctant to be part of the peace process, I guess. He has been home working in London for a few months and it's been wonderful. How will I bear his going away again?

Tom hugs me. His voice is thick with emotion. *This has been the most wonderful day of my life*, he says. *I have every-thing and everyone I most love in one heavenly unforget-table place. How lucky we are, darling Jen. We must never forget that. How very lucky we are.*

I can bear any absence, I think. I can bear any absence because of the joy and certain knowledge that I have just married someone very special.

FIFTY

Ruth drove Adam down to Cornwall to talk to his house-master and have a guided tour of the school before the begin-ning of term. Cornwall was at its wettest and Adam dared not admit to Ruth how nervous he felt as the first day of term loomed.

As they walked round the school buildings up on the hill overlooking the city he recaptured his sense of excitement and disbelief that he really was coming to this school. It was only when they reached the dormitories and he was con-fronted with the reality of communal sleeping that Adam felt sudden irrational panic.

The dormitories were set in the grounds, in separate houses with a housemaster and his wife who lived in. There was a communal room with microwave and toaster. The rooms were small, with three or four beds. Not as he'd imagined, great rows of them but there was no real privacy, hardly an inch of his own space. Adam felt the sweat break out on his forehead. He had never shared a room with anyone in his life and at thirteen it seemed a totally alien, claustrophobic concept.

Ruth had been watching him, and when his housemaster sent him off with his music teacher she said, 'I think Adam's going to find the boarding bit difficult. He's an only child and used to his privacy. He's always spent a lot of time on his own.'

'It's obviously going to be harder for Adam to adapt to boarding school than if he had come to us a bit younger. The first few weeks of any new place are difficult for all pupils until they make friends. Try not to worry. Adam's a bright boy and I'm sure he'll fit in quickly.' The housemaster poured Ruth coffee. 'We do suggest that parents leave it two or three weeks before they take their children out in order to let them settle into a school routine.' He smiled at her worried face. 'Please don't worry, Mrs Hallam, boarding – being away from home for a while – is an excellent thing for boys without siblings. It allows them to integrate fully into the life of the school and experience a more male-orientated world.'

Ruth knew that what he really meant was 'boys without fathers', boys anchored to single mothers, and she felt mildly irritated. It reinforced all her prejudices about boys' public schools even though it was now co-educational.

Adam came back grinning, thrilled by the choice of music for next term. The music master shook Ruth's hand. 'I'm afraid we're going to work your boy hard. There will be music practice each day on top of his school work, but your son is talented and enthusiastic, and we're very glad to have him with us.'

As they said goodbye, Ruth repeated that although she would be working in London they had a holiday cottage the other side of Truro and she would be down to take Adam out regularly. She had already explained about Bea and James, and given the school their address in case of an emergency.

'Is that Dr Brown who used to be a G.P. in St Ives?' the housemaster asked.

'Yes,' Ruth replied. 'I lived in St Ives as a child and they were very good to me.'

'I know the family. Their boy came to the school when I was just starting out as a teacher. Ben, wasn't it? He was a wild and personable boy in a sea of girls. He was quite a character. I imagine Dr Brown and his wife were very sad when he emigrated.'

'I was friends with their youngest daughter, Jenny. Ben was older and I didn't really know him. He was always surfing or at uni,' Ruth said. 'I'd almost forgotten that everybody knows everybody else in Cornwall.'

'Indeed!'

The housemaster shook her hand and as they drove back to the cottage, Adam said suddenly, 'Funny, isn't it? If you had a job in Cornwall I could practically walk or bicycle home every night.'

Ruth looked at him. 'Darling, are you having second thoughts?'

'You are joking, Mum. I can't wait. You saw the music room. *Wicked.* I'm just not into sleeping with other boys with their smelly feet, or listening to them fart and snore.'

Ruth laughed. 'What a charming picture you paint!'

When they were inside the cottage and Adam was making toast, Ruth said, 'Adam, you do realise that I couldn't earn enough money to live down here. I hate the thought of you living away from me, it's going to be so hard.' She watched sudden wariness cross Adam's face in case she was going to become sentimental or wax lyrical about the possibilities of weekends and half-terms in London again.

They had stayed in London briefly after the holiday in Cornwall. Danielle had moved out of her flat so that Ruth and Adam could spend time together. Ruth had been able to ease herself into working in the mornings because Adam stayed in bed late reading and when he did emerge he practised his clarinet for hours.

In the afternoons Ruth had taken him off sightseeing.

Adam had been polite, interested, but not overenthusiastic about anything. As soon as they got back to the flat he would disappear into the bedroom and pick up his book or instrument. Ruth had the distinct impression he was determined not to enjoy himself; that he purposely wanted to detach himself from her life in London. He did not want to be part of it.

In the end Flo said gently, 'Ruth, take Adam off for a week somewhere he wants to be. When he's settled in school, come back and start properly.'

Ruth had taken him to Spain. She had an old friend with a villa and pool. With the house in Birmingham sold, she had felt rootless and vulnerable. Adam had been quite happy, but obviously marking time.

He grinned at her now and said, 'It's OK, Mum. You know you're a townie. Just because I want to go to school here doesn't mean I think *you* should live in Cornwall. It just seems rather funny the cottage being quite near to the school, that's all, and . . .' He paused. 'I get worried about you having to pay boarding fees. I wish you didn't.'

Ruth poured out two mugs of tea and handed him one. 'Well, don't worry, there's no need. The house sold well in the end, so all is absolutely fine.'

She heard a note she hated creep into her voice. 'You're going to be incredibly busy, darling, but I hope you'll miss me just a bit. You living here while I live in London is going to feel very strange.'

Adam crammed toast and Marmite into his mouth, and muttered something she couldn't hear. When he had swallowed he said, 'Of course I'll miss you, Mum. It will be, like, strange for you at first until you get used to it, but I could tell you like being there with Flo and Danielle. You wanted that job really badly and you love London and that, so it will be all right. Don't worry about me. I can . . .' He stopped

257

himself and got up from his chair. 'I'm just going outside to get a signal. I think I'll ring Harry. Can we go to St Ives tomorrow when we've done the rest of my uniform?'

'I don't know how long that will take, but yes, when we're done.'

Adam automatically picked up his binoculars and slung them round his neck. He shut the door behind him and turned left towards the lake. He felt guilty. The days, since their holiday with Peter, had hung heavy and anticlimactic. He wasn't sure why, but he did not want to have anything to do with his mother's London life. Even down here in the cottage he felt restless. *He wanted to get on with his own life*. He wanted Ruth to go and start *her* new life, to be happy. He was afraid of hurting her. He had only just stopped himself saying *I can go to Jenny's*.

He sat on a bench by the lake and dug his phone out of his pocket, but he dialled Jenny's number, not Harry's.

Jenny answered, breathless. 'Adam! How lovely.'

Adam laughed, relaxing. 'Have you been running?'

'I was in the garden. It was extraordinary. I saw something out of the corner of my eye and it was this huge fox just watching me a few feet away. He didn't run away, just stood there looking at me. We were eyeballing each other.'

'Oh, wicked! Maybe the old lady fed him or something, like she fed the birds to bursting.'

Jenny laughed. 'Tell me how you got on today.'

'OK. The music teacher's ace. I met the headmaster again and my housemaster and stuff. We've got some of my uniform from the school shop. We've just got to get my blazer and socks and name-tags and things tomorrow.'

'Tell Ruth that Bea and I will willingly help her sew in your name-tags if she runs out of time. Are you coming over tomorrow?'

'Yeah, I hope so, after we've got the rest of my things.

Thanks, sewing isn't Mum's thing. I think she might get stressed out. We've got my trunk to put everything in . . . Jenny?'

'Yes?'

'You know your brother went to Truro School. Did he board or did he come home every night, like Harry?'

'Ben was a weekly boarder. He came home every weekend. Dad knew he would have been out with his friends or surfing every night if he'd been a day boy.' Her voice softened. 'He was a bit of a naughty boy, Adam, but he was very charming so he got away with murder. How do you feel about boarding? I'm sure it'll be fun.'

'Did your brother find it fun?'

'No, I'm afraid he hated being cooped up or confined anywhere, but he wasn't academic. You'll be fine.'

'You don't have to be academic not to want to sleep with a lot of smelly boys. I think I'm too old for it.'

Jenny laughed again and he added seriously, 'I wish Mum lived in St Ives and I could come home every night with Harry.'

Come home. Jenny caught the desperate note in his voice. She paused, then she said softly, 'Adam, you *could* come home every night with Harry.'

Adam shivered with hope but dared not speak.

'Have you told Ruth how you feel about boarding?'

'Mum knows I'm not keen, but it was me that, like, started all this. I wanted to come to Cornwall to school. She's paying a lot of money for me to board, how can I say anything?'

Jenny was silent. Then she said, 'How would you feel about living with me and travelling in to school every day with Harry? It might be a great deal more boring than living with boys of your own age . . .'

'No, it wouldn't. It *wouldn't*, Jenny. Really it wouldn't. Could I? I mean, do you mean it? I mean, is it possible?'

259

'Slow down. Slow down. I do mean it and it is possible. But only if Ruth agrees to it. Do you want me to ask her tomorrow?'

'Yes. Yes, please.'

'How do you think she'll feel?'

'I don't know,' he said. 'Maybe if she knows I really feel freaky about being cooped up with other people . . . I didn't expect to feel like that but when I saw the smallness of the rooms. I just, like, came out in a terrible sweat.'

'I think you had a little panic attack. You're going to have to be honest with Ruth, Adam, and tell her how you feel.'

'What, before you talk to her?'

Jenny thought for a moment. 'You might have to play it by ear. I'll think about how I might suggest it. I don't want to hurt her. She's going to miss you enormously and the thought of you living with me might be worse for her than if you were in school with a lot of boys.'

'Yeah, I know, but she's going to be living in your house and you could feel weird about that couldn't you?'

'Truthfully, I think I do, sometimes. Go back to your mum now and have a nice evening. I'll see you tomorrow and don't worry, we'll try and sort something out.'

'I want to live with you in your house more than anything, Jenny. I wouldn't be a nuisance, I could help you with things and . . .'

'Adam,' Jenny said gently, 'whether you live with me or not, you are now part of my life and we *will* talk about your father. I have so many things to tell you. We have plenty of time now you're in Cornwall, all the time in the world. Goodnight, darling boy.'

Goodnight, darling boy. Adam ran back down the path jumping the puddles, choked with happiness. *All the time in the world to talk about your father.*

*   *   *

260

Ruth woke in the night and heard Adam moving around. She lay for a moment, reluctant to get out of her warm bed. The cottage was cold, autumn was edging in fast and she wanted to be back in London. The job was going to be challenging and as she listened to Adam restlessly awake her spirits plummeted. Was this all going to go suddenly catastrophically wrong?

She got out of bed, pulled on her dressing gown and went into his room. Adam was sitting in the window seat wrapped up in an old faded eiderdown that had lain on the bed all her childhood.

'What is it, Adam?' she asked.

The light from the landing streamed into his room but Adam kept his face turned towards the window. 'I'm sorry, Mum.'

'What are you sorry for?' Ruth went nearer and sat on the end of his bed.

Adam made himself turn to look at her. 'I know I hurt you not wanting to be with you in London, wanting to come to school here.'

'What's brought all this on? Of course I'd prefer to have you in London with me, we've always been together, but darling, I understand about city schools and I understand the lure of Cornwall for you.'

Adam looked at her and wondered what she meant by this. Did she just mean what she said or was she thinking of Jenny?

'Come on, Adam. Tell me what's worrying you. It's perfectly normal to have last-minute nerves about going away to school. It would be more abnormal if you didn't.' Adam looked out of the window again without answering. 'I can't help you if you don't talk to me.' *Please God*, she thought. *Don't let Adam say he has changed his mind and wants to be a day boy in London after all. I can't cope. I really can't. I've got to get a grip on this job from the start. I can't go through the school thing all over again. Flo and Danielle have bent over backwards to accommodate me.*

Adam took a shaky breath and turned to face her. 'I don't want to board. I don't want to share a room with other boys. I want to leave school at the end of the day like Harry. I'll work like I've never worked before. I promise I won't disappoint you. I want . . . *please,* I want to live with Jenny in the term-time.'

Ruth stared at him. She felt the skin on her face tighten in shock as the blood drained from it. *No. Oh, no. This isn't fair. This is too much. This is too bloody much.* She had always known, deep in her heart, the impossibility of travelling down to Cornwall every weekend. She was not going to be working regular hours; she would literally be living with her work. Danielle and Flo had been generous with their financial incentives but they expected a lot of hours from her. She had acceded to everything Adam wanted, knowing that Jenny would have easier access to him, and now . . . She had made herself imagine Adam and Jenny getting together to talk about Tom and she had tried to rationalise her feeling of panic that she might lose Adam to the lure of the past, to the life Jenny had led, and to the comfort of Bea and James and that wonderful house by the sea. Now he wanted to live with and go home every night to Jenny. Not her, Jenny.

'Mum . . .' Adam leant towards her. 'Mum, please, *please* don't look like that.'

Ruth focused on his face. Tears welled up in his eyes. He looked wretched, but she could not speak.

'I really love you, Mum. I do. I'm sorry, I'm sorry. It isn't that I don't want to be with you, it isn't. I just don't want to be in London.'

262

But Ruth knew it wasn't true. Adam didn't want to be with her at this particular moment in his life. He wanted to be with Jenny because of Tom. My God, if she had known that sleeping with the youthful Tom under a load of coats would bring this pain fourteen years later she would have run out of the house howling.

'Mum? Are you all right?'

'You're asking too much of me, Adam. You're asking me not to mind you going home each night to someone else. It's just too bloody hard. It's like a slap in the face.'

Hot, fat tears rolled down Adam's cheek. 'I know. I know it is. I'm just desperate. I feel stupid about freaking out at the thought of boarding with a load of strangers. I just never thought about that. I'm so used to being on my own.'

Ruth wanted to ask, *Are you sure all this angst isn't because you just want to live with Jenny?* But she daren't.

'What makes you think Jenny would have you, Adam?' Ruth asked pointlessly. 'I thought she wanted to live on her own; that's why she moved into the cottage.'

Adam didn't answer.

Ruth got up from his bed and moved to the door. 'I'm tired and I'm cold. We'll talk about this in the morning, Adam. Go back to bed.'

'Are you angry with me, Mum?'

Behind Adam the sky was already lightening, edging towards a new day. 'No,' Ruth said. 'I'm not angry with you. Get some sleep. We'll work something out.'

As she shut his bedroom door she heard him say, 'I didn't want to hurt you.' Well, he had. Ruth went downstairs and switched on the kettle. She made tea and sat at the table. The kitchen with its ancient Aga was the warmest room in the house. She thought of her godmother who used to sit here at all hours, sleepless, in an old candlewick dressing gown with her mass of hair plaited like a German Frau. Anger simmered, saving her from tears. She felt duped, tricked. By Jenny? Could Jenny be capable of this duplicity? Of course not. It was Adam who was having a crisis of confidence. This was nothing to do with Jenny. 'What do I do?' she asked the empty room.

Her godmother's presence filled the kitchen.

It's time to let Adam go. He's not a little boy any longer; he doesn't need you in the same way. This space between you would have opened up even if you were living together. He would start to grow away from you. It's what happens, Ruth. Let him get Tom out of his system and Jenny too. Leave them to it. You've done all you can. Go back to London and seize with both hands this rare chance to be fulfilled. Think of it positively. If Adam is in a dormitory full of boys, you would inevitably worry about him. With Jenny you will know he is well looked after and content. It releases you. Try to think of it like that. You were determined to take the job in London. None of us can have everything we want in life. You chose your life. Adam is choosing his. Accept it. Move on. You will only lose Adam if he thinks you want to come between him and knowledge of Tom. Play the long game and revel in the freedom to think only of yourself for the first time in thirteen years. You have the chance of a new life and happiness. Take it, Ruth, and don't look back. Take it.

Ruth smiled. How strongly Sarah's sane voice came down the years. She closed her eyes and the kitchen was full of the smell of baking and Sarah grumbling: 'I don't understand it. Ruddy cake's gone down in the middle. I did everything they said. Let's make lumpy icing sugar and throw little silver balls in, then we can hide the hole. We will be the only ones to know it's not a perfect cake.'

Ruth got up and leant against the Aga. *Make it work,*

Ruth, Peter had said. She switched off the kitchen light and went up the stairs. She bloody well would make it work. She had no choice but to leave Adam to the life he wanted for a while and she must not look back.

PART TWO

FIFTY-ONE

Adam stood stamping his feet in the cold damp morning waiting for the little one-track train to pick him up. As he waited he lifted his binoculars and looked across the Saltings. Redshanks bustled in little groups. Large flocks of knots stood on their short legs on the smooth unmarked mud, all facing one way like little old men playing bowls.

Adam felt like laughing out loud sometimes. *How many boys get to wait for trains in the middle of an RSPB Reserve?* He heard the train coming and glanced back to the small copse and the house that lay behind it. Jenny would still be sitting at the table hugging her coffee. He sighed. It was great having someone in the house when you left for school and still there when you got back. It made him feel warm in the pit of his stomach every single day.

Jenny had asked Danielle to send down some of her family photographs. She and Adam were going to sort them out for a collage on the dark wall between the bathroom and kitchen. Each day as they talked together he learnt a little more of Jenny's life in the London house with his father. He found it peculiar thinking of his mother living in Jenny's house and leading the sort of life Jenny had once led.

He wished he had explored the house where Tom and Jenny had lived when he had stayed there with Ruth. He wished he had looked into all the rooms. He wished he had sat in Tom's leather armchair and studied the shelves where he kept his CDs and books, but he had been too busy freaking out. His overwhelming emotion during his time there had been his abject fear of Ruth changing her mind; making him live in a London she appeared to be hard-selling to him in their frenetic afternoons sightseeing.

The train chugged noisily in and Adam got on. Harry nodded his head and grunted as Adam sat beside him. Harry did not do mornings. He did not like to wake up or talk before they reached Redruth. It suited Adam; it gave him thinking time or extra time to check his homework.

He had expected his life to be difficult for the first few weeks of the new term, but it hadn't been at all. There was no misery, no taunts from other boys. The workload and catching up made him anxious, but he found when he asked a master for help he got it. No teacher here felt threatened by oversized bullies. No member of staff lost control of a class and few boys were disruptive.

The children came from all backgrounds and countries, and were competitive. The classes were structured and the emphasis was on academic achievement. There were the clever dicks who played for laughs or argued a point to death with a teacher, but Adam was never going to be mocked for being articulate or curious. The classes were so different from his school in Birmingham that it seemed to him that he was on another planet.

Until he had started to live with Jenny, Adam had not fully realised how the Birmingham school had affected his life. Casual cruelty had been relentless and dominated his days. Worst of all had been hiding it from Ruth. Peter had

270

suspected and had tried to make it easier for him, but after he left it had been unbearable.

Harry asked suddenly, breaking his morning silence, 'What's it like going back home to someone who isn't your mum? Don't think I'd like it. Do you have to be on your best behaviour all the time?'

'Nah,' Adam said. 'It's cool. Jenny makes cakes and stuff for when I get home and . . . well, she's just, like, easy. She doesn't tell me what to do or anything. She's got me this desk with lights and everything, and I use her London laptop; it's wicked, faster than mine.'

'Lucky bastard.' Harry was impressed. 'My computer is so slow I can make tea while it switches itself on. What about telly? Do you have to watch girlie stuff?'

Adam laughed. 'We don't have a telly.'

Harry was astonished. 'What do you *do*?'

'We walk and birdwatch for a bit after school if it's light enough, or we walk on the beach. Then I do homework and Jenny cooks supper. I do more homework, and then we talk and listen to music and stuff before I go to bed.'

Harry was silent for a long time. 'I can't make up my mind whether I'm sorry for you or dead jealous. It's, like, hell sometimes trying to do homework to mum's *EastEnders*. I was thinking the other day our house is never silent. There's always the radio or the telly on. I don't know what the sound of silence feels like.'

'You can come and stay any time, Jenny said so.' Adam grinned hopefully. 'Especially when it's physics homework. I've got bunk beds, proper sized ones.'

Adam had never talked to Harry about his connection with Jenny. Harry just thought that Ruth and Jenny were friends. It was something private between him and Jenny. He could not explain to Ruth his new sense of well-being, either. He had waited to be homesick, waited for

271

the dull ache of missing her, and it had not come.

Of course he missed her. But it wasn't painful. Ruth rang most nights before he went to bed to say goodnight and they swapped news of their days. His mother seemed busy, flying off to Italy or France with Danielle. She sounded happy too. Adam was careful what he said about school because he knew Ruth's ambivalent feelings about private education.

Ruth would stamp on any suggestion of elitism he might feel and he was secretly, guiltily, revelling in this feeling of being safe with his own kind. He was aware that he was enjoying an easier more privileged life with Jenny. He loved Bea and James's house in St Ives and always felt welcome. He loved having proxy grandparents and most of all he loved with passion living in Cornwall with Jenny. He felt he had fallen into a life that was as familiar as breathing. All of a sudden he fitted into his own skin and the comfort was euphoric.

Jenny had given him a small box of photographs of Tom in uniform. Each night he took it from under his bed and allowed himself to look at one or two. He needed to ration himself because these photographs were all he had of Tom. He stared for hours at Tom in combat fatigues, in any army uniform. When he looked at these pictures he could feel his heart swell with pride and a slow-burning ambition to lead the sort of life his father had led.

Jenny still found it hard to look at any photographs of her child or of Tom and Rosie together. He knew the big brown envelope from London was full of pictures of Rosie. He had seen Jenny's face when she took it from Shaun, the postman: so abruptly bleak he had wanted to comfort her. She had placed it in her room and it had remained unopened.

When he looked at her, she seemed so small and fragile sometimes. He had never forgotten the afternoon by the creek or the days preceding it when Jenny had followed him. In

272

that moment of him turning and seeing her lying on the ground broken, everything had changed. He had felt an overwhelming need to protect her and this feeling had never gone away or diminished. In that scorching moment an instantaneous bond had sprung up. When Jenny had lain sick in the hospital, Adam's heart had throbbed with anxiety that something might happen to her. He was so happy and he loved his life so much that he had to pinch himself to make sure he wasn't dreaming.

Out of the train window he spotted a bird of prey just above the trees, hovering on trembling wings. Adam lifted his binoculars. Wicked. It was a sparrowhawk riding the thermals, swooping free, soaring alone in acres of clear blue sky. Adam grinned. Free, free as a bird.

FIFTY-TWO

Danielle raised her glass to Flo and Ruth. 'What a bizarre day!'

'Possibly one of the most bizarre we've ever had,' Flo said.

The three of them were sitting in their favourite Italian restaurant demolishing a carafe of red wine. They looked at each other and burst out laughing.

Ruth said, 'I couldn't believe my eyes when I went into the fitting room and found the honourable Daisy Monkton snorting coke through a ten-pound note on your antique desk.'

Danielle rolled her eyes. 'You should have seen Ruth's face, Flo. She shot back into the room with eyes like saucers, making Lady Monkton stop dead mid sentence. "What *is* my daughter doing in there?" she demanded suspiciously. "How long can a fitting take? Has she lost *more* weight?" Ruth stood there, her mouth opening and shutting like a goldfish.'

'I was trying to be subtle and signal a warning to you.'

'Warning! You were squeaking like a mouse. "I'm afraid Daisy is feeling a little unwell. We have not tried the dress yet." Pff! It was so funny.'

Ruth laughed. 'Lady Monkton barked, "Do tell Daisy to get a grip. We have a charity event this evening and she is on the catwalk." I think she must have thought I'd developed a twitch.'

'Well.' Flo grinned. 'It's the first time I've ever heard something like panic in Danielle's voice. Anyway, the day was saved with Molly's exotic sandwiches and a frantic glass of champagne. Her ladyship was diverted until you both got Daisy upright.'

Danielle snorted, 'The stupid girl was blissfully floating around the room with her eyes rolled back, in just her headdress and knickers, giggling. It took us ages to get her into the bloody dress, which will have to be taken in *again*, by the way. I had to pin it drastically at the back.'

Flo began to laugh once more. 'I wish I could have photographed you emerging with the honourable Daisy beaming vacuously and hanging on to you both. She looked a picture of loveliness, but still had distinct traces of white powder in her nostrils and on her upper lip. When Lady M started to tick you both off for plying her daughter with too much champagne . . . your faces . . . It was absolutely hilarious.'

'Thanks a lot,' Danielle said drily. 'I do not take kindly to being spoken to like a schoolgirl when I have another fitting any moment and my desk is showing remnants of illegal substances.'

'Do you think Lady Monkton is really so dim that she doesn't notice her daughter's addiction and dramatic weight loss?' Ruth asked.

'Yes,' Flo and Danielle said together.

Flo sighed. 'It wouldn't have been so funny if we'd had a cancelled order. If Lady Monkton had lost face, we wouldn't have got a penny. She would have insisted we had the stuff on our premises and, untrue or not, mud and adverse publicity stick. Come on, let's order before we all get past it.'

Ruth felt a surge of contentment. Life was fun. She felt she was edging somewhere safe.

Flo, half listening to Ruth and Danielle chatting and laughing, thought of Jenny and her rippling infectious giggle, which Rosie had inherited. She missed her presence in the house and the bounce, energy and happiness Jenny had once exuded. They ordered their food and she let her eyes wander around the Italian restaurant. 'Goodness,' she said suddenly, as a man moved towards them. 'It's Antonio.'

Ruth turned as a dark, stocky man approached their table. He beamed down at them. 'Florence, Danielle, how good to see you.' His eyes wandered curiously to Ruth.

'This is Ruth Hallam, Antonio. She's just joined us. She is our wonderful new PR.'

Antonio bowed and smiled at her across the table. 'Another beautiful woman. I am pleased to meet you, Ruth.'

He kissed their hands and lapsed for a moment into rapid French. Then he turned to Flo. 'Please, tell me how is Jenny.'

'She's better. She's doing well. I think she made the right decision to stay in Cornwall for a while. We're all going down there next weekend to see her.'

'You must miss her. We also in Italy miss her designs. Please, tell her that I ask after her, that I send her my love and best wishes. Ah, here is your food, I will leave you.' He looked at Danielle. 'May I call you tomorrow? I am here for only a few days and I hoped to meet with you. Fate brought us to the same restaurant, I think.'

Danielle looked pleased. 'Of course. I look forward to your call.'

Ruth noticed her raised colour and wondered if she fancied the Italian.

He was certainly not classically good-looking. He was neither slim nor tall, but he had a sensual magnetism and his eyes and his voice were delicious a 'close your eyes and die' voice.

As Antonio left, he turned and said softly in a quite different voice, 'Tell Jenny that she has remained in my thoughts and in my heart.'

When he had gone, Flo said to Ruth, 'Antonio was part of that dreadful, dreadful day.'

'Jenny and I were having a working lunch with him the day Tom and Rosie were killed. She had planned to go with them. If Antonio had not asked us to meet him, Jenny would be dead too.'

Danielle shrugged grimly at arbitrary fate and Ruth shivered.

'He was amazingly kind to Jenny,' Flo went on. 'Undoubtedly he likes to do business with us, but he proved himself a loyal friend, too. After Tom's death he invited Jenny to his house in Italy with Danielle, to get away, to rest.'

'He has this most beautiful house near the Amalfi coast,' Danielle added. 'I had only known him as a business colleague. He turned out to be a wonderful host and friend to Jenny.'

Flo and Ruth thought they heard a note of regret in her voice. Danielle instinctively, possibly unaware that she did so, used her sexuality all the time, even with the waiter who hurried over with the obligatory vast pepper mill. She was used to men falling at her feet. Antonio obviously had not. Ruth could not help wondering if Danielle had ever tried it on with Tom.

As they got out of the taxi in front of the house Flo said suddenly, 'You see that grey Audi parked over there? I could swear it's the same driver who was in a red BMW last week. He just sits there all day reading a paper.'

Danielle and Ruth looked. A man was sitting in the driving seat with a newspaper hiding his face.

'Can he read the print in a dark car without the light on?' Ruth asked.

'I do not think so,' Danielle said, paying the taxi driver.

He handed her a piece of paper through the window. 'I've written that bloke's car number down. I'd ring the police if I were you. Nice houses around here. Diplomats, MPs. I've carried them all. Don't want to get yourself burgled, do you, love?'

As Flo locked and bolted the door behind them she said, 'Even if I look a bit of a fool and it's a private detective on the trail of adultery, I think I will give the police a call.'

'I think you should, Flo,' Ruth agreed. 'It would be awful if something happened and we'd done nothing. It's funny, none of us ever really thinks something will happen to us, always to other people.'

'I do not think that any more,' Danielle said quietly. 'I agree, Flo. You are very observant.'

When Danielle had undressed she glanced out of the window down to the street. The car had gone. Leaves blew about the street. The black cat sat on the wall of the house opposite, as it always did, its eyes glinting witchily under the yellow glare of the street light.

She stood at the window, cold, hating this moment at the end of each day when the world stopped and remembrance of the small warm child she had loved slid into the night with her.

She folded her arms round herself and shivered. Only one thing ever helped with the memory of bad things: sex; a rough, raw, uncomplicated fuck with a stranger banished her demons. At the moment her sex life had come to an abrupt halt by sharing a flat with Ruth. It was one of the reasons she had offered to share with Ruth. It would limit her opportunities; help her, like overcoming addiction.

If only she could go back in time and relive the life she

had once had here, relive the completeness and the small things of each day she had so casually taken for granted.

Danielle drew the curtains and leapt into bed, pulling the duvet up round her head. In the safety of the dark she let images of Rosie into the warmth with her; tried to recapture her little cheerful voice; felt the weight and heat of the child on her hip, carrying her around the house as she worked. *Dat colour, Ellie? Rodie come too? Ellie carry. Why, Ellie? Rodie can't sleep.*

Rosie, the child she had shared with Jenny. Almost her own flesh and blood. The child who had slept beside her in this bed; the child she dressed and hugged and bathed and sang to. A child who had managed, with consummate ease, to reach and melt her sometimes empty heart.

FIFTY-THREE

Danielle stands with her luggage on the pavement looking for her house keys. Is Boy Wonder still here? The atmosphere of smug self-satisfaction when Tom is home tends to make her nauseous. Flo is just as bad, complicit in her adoration. It makes Danielle feel cynical and combative.

She finds her keys and lugs her case up the steps. Inside she can hear Rosie laughing and her face lights up. She calls through the letter box, 'Rosie, Rosie Holland, I can hear you.'

The laughter stops for a moment, then, 'Ellie . . . Mamma, Ellie back!'

The chuckling starts again. 'Rodie coming. Rodie coming.'

Small footsteps patter disjointedly down the stairs and as Danielle pushes open the front door Jenny lets go of Rosie's hand and she rushes to her. Danielle gathers her up and turns to shut the door, hiding the softening of her face from Jenny as she hugs the child to her.

'Hi, Danielle.' Jenny is standing on the bottom step, the sun from the landing window catching her wild hair. 'So glad you're back. I've just made tea, or . . .' She scans Danielle's face. 'You look as if you need a drink.'

280

'Definitely a drink. The plane was delayed two hours. Very tedious.' Danielle smiles at Jenny. 'Has true love disappeared again?'

Jenny makes a face and laughs. 'Afraid not. He leaves the day after tomorrow. Watch your jacket, Rosie's been eating a chocolate biscuit.'

Danielle tries to hold a clinging Rosie and lug her case up the stairs.

'Give me your case, you'll both fall downstairs, you soppy couple.'

On the landing Danielle whispers to Rosie, 'I have a present for you.'

Rosie claps her hands. 'Now, Ellie?'

'I will bring it down in a minute, *chérie*. You go with *maman* and make Ellie a drink while I wash my hands.'

She picks up her case and goes up to her flat, stopping to talk to Flo on the way. In her flat there are six messages on her machine. She smiles and leaves the anticipation for later.

When she goes back downstairs, Flo is in Jenny's kitchen and hands her a large gin and tonic. Danielle sits at the table watching Jenny spoon scrambled egg into Rosie. Rosie's eyes widen as she sees the beautifully wrapped parcel Danielle is holding.

'This is for you, my darling, as soon as you have finished all your egg.' She continues, wondering where Tom is, 'I knew I was right about the length of those skirts, Jen. Parisian women like to show off their legs.'

'The cut was so beautiful. Obstinate, aren't I? I think I'll have a go with Jaeger or we could try them in Brum.' Jenny wipes the wriggling Rosie's hands and face, and lifts her out of the chair, and she rushes for Danielle and the parcel.

'Elle, you spoil her,' Jenny protests.

'Pff! Rosie has not yet got to the age of spoilt. It is unknown to her that word. She is still pure in her feelings of pleasure.'

Jenny and Flo grin, Danielle is always very French when she returns from Paris, but they know exactly what she means. Rosie is still unspoilt. Jenny wonders why Danielle rarely shows this side of herself in front of Tom; the nice, gentler side that she and Flo see often. Danielle lifts child and parcel, and they go into the sitting room.

The phone rings. It is Tom. Danielle watches Jenny's eyes light up. When she replaces the phone she grins indulgently at Flo and Danielle. 'Tom's met a friend in the gym. They're off to the pub for an hour or so.'

Rosie sits on the floor, tearing at the tough, bright paper, her eyes shining with excitement. Her small tongue is held between her teeth as she concentrates. Inside the paper is a box, inside the box is a small exquisite doll. Rosie squeals with delight. Danielle leans forward and pulls a little cord in the doll's back. The doll's mouth begins to move as she sings a French lullaby. Rosie's mouth falls open in an 'Ooo!' of wonder.

Jenny leans forward, enchanted. 'Danielle! What an amazing doll. I covet it myself.'

'Look at Rosie's face!' Flo murmurs.

Bemused at suddenly owning something so beautiful Rosie sits, fat little legs splayed, with the doll in her lap pulling the cord again and again each time the song finishes. Danielle bends to kiss her. Rosie's arms snake up round her neck and she rests her hot cheek against Danielle's, speechless with gratitude.

When Flo finally takes doll and child away to bed Jenny says, 'That is the most wonderful but seriously expensive doll. I wish you wouldn't spend all your money on Rosie.'

Danielle shrugs. 'Who else do I have to buy presents for?'

Jenny hugs her. 'You're very generous. Come into the kitchen and talk to me while I do supper.' She opens a bottle of wine. 'Give me the gossip. See your many old boyfriends this trip?'

'I was too busy.' Danielle grins and tosses her glossy hair. 'But I did meet this businessman on the way out.'

'Nice?'

Danielle considers. 'Mm, so-so. Quite sexy, but oh, so English. Polite chat-up, then dinner. I think he likes me, but very strange, Jenny, he did not ask me to go to bed with him.'

Jenny claps her hand to her mouth. 'OMYGOD! How *terrible* for you, Elle! He did not want to sleep with you on a *first date*. Oh, write him off, he has got to be *gay*!'

'Oh, shut up!'

They both burst out laughing. 'So, how is Tom? Have you had a good leave?'

'Great.' Jenny sighs. 'It's gone so quickly.'

'Back to Iraq?'

'Yes. After that Afghanistan.' Danielle hears the tight note in Jenny's voice.

'Tom can look after himself, darling.'

'I hope so. Is quiche and salad OK for supper?'

'Flo and I will disappear. You will want Tom to yourself.'

'He'll be ages. I'm pretty sure he'll grab an Indian or something with the guy he's with.'

After a minute Danielle says, twisting her glass in her hands, 'You still love Tom as much as ever, yes?'

Jenny looks up from the sink. 'Afraid so. *More* than ever.'

Danielle sighs. 'Marriage amazes me. What is there to say, to do, to feel that is new every time. How do people keep the mystery of each other? Of course,' she adds drily, 'it is a little different for you, Jenny, because Tom is away so much doing *dangerous things*.'

Her voice holds a veiled sarcasm that Jenny has learnt to ignore. It always surfaces when Tom is home. She tosses the salad. 'I guess the first excitement changes into something of

283

more depth. I suppose life for most people is mainly mundane and routine, Elle, but the comfort and warmth of getting close to someone more than makes up for the loss of mystery. I haven't spent enough time with Tom to be bored or irritated yet, but I often wish I had. Sometimes it feels like living life in the fast lane and I long to pull over to a steady pace; to live a more ordinary life and have Tom come home safely every night.'

'Maybe you have the secret. Do not daily live together. Do not make a conventional marriage.'

'No fear of that with you, Danielle. Hey, you could marry a long-haul pilot! That's a good idea. Maybe you wouldn't get bored then?'

'No! I do not think that I will ever marry.'

'Don't you sometimes feel you want a close or permanent relationship? Someone who doesn't care about the size of your bottom or that you forgot to shave your legs? Someone who cares about you because you're *you*? Don't you get tired of the effort of attracting different men all the time and never really getting to know them?'

Danielle laughs. 'You do not have to know a man to have good sex with 'eem.'

Jenny raises her eyes to the ceiling. 'You can have amazing sex with a man you do know.'

Danielle sits at the table playing with her glass. 'Anyway, no one could put up with me on a permanent basis so I make sure it never happens.'

Surprised at the tone in her voice, Jenny stops chopping tomatoes. 'Whatever do you mean? Why do you say that? Don't be silly.'

'Not silly, Jenny. You know perfectly well that I am promiscuous. Are not promiscuous people supposed to have a very low opinion of themselves? Is this not what they say?'

Flo has come back into the room and stands quietly listening.

Jenny stares at Danielle, upset; this is unlike her. 'Why should you have a low opinion of yourself? You are beautiful and talented and successful. You are practical and funny. You have everything going for you.'

Danielle gives a hard, short laugh. 'Except my sharp tongue and bad habit of going for the jugular, darling. Men don't like to be laughed at; their egos are too frail.' She smiles over at Flo. 'I am tired and the wine is going to my head. Take no notice of me. Let us change the subject, please.'

Flo gathers up cutlery from the drawer. 'My dear girl, don't let a wretched childhood fuck up the success you're making of your life.'

Danielle is startled at the f-word coming from Flo. 'How do you know that I have a horrible childhood?'

'The signs are unmistakable. Exorcise it. I was considerably older than you before I was able to do so and it spoilt many years I can never have again.'

Danielle and Jenny stare at her in silence. Flo has never, ever mentioned her past.

Flo laughs at their faces. 'Old as I might seem, I did have a childhood, you know. I even had a life before I arrived here. Come on, where's my supper? Let's talk of cheerful and important things like work schedules for tomorrow.'

In bed, Danielle lies awake thinking of Flo. The most unlikely people have secret pasts. She thinks of the few men she has really liked as well as fancied. Tom, for instance? She closes her eyes tight against the memory of his cold rebuttal many years before. *I am destined to that no man's land, to the lonely half-light of a stranger's back.*

She thinks of Rosie with the doll. Her secret longing for children is a physical ache in the pit of her stomach. Pity you need a man to create them. How wonderful if you could create a child out of your own love and longing.

Flo lies in the room below Danielle. Maybe one day she will tell her how she wasted twenty naive, childbearing years of her life on a man who, in the end, never left his wife. *When the children are a little older. When they have finished their exams. When Betty is a little stronger. When the children leave home . . . When hell freezes over.*

She had settled for second best because it was what she believed she was worth. Her parents' voices had dominated her young life. *Florence will be lucky to get a man. Face as plain as a pikestaff. What man is going to fall in love with Florence?*

A married man, that's who; but not quite enough. Florence Kingsley decided she would place a *Mrs* in front of her name anyway, like a Victorian housekeeper.

All those Christmases and bank holidays alone. Until she came here. Maybe one day she will say to Danielle, *Your young life is precious. Don't throw it away. Happiness has a way of surprising you. Look at me now.*

I lie entwined with Tom, sleepless again. A wind smelling of rain moves the curtains and rattles the windows. There is going to be a storm. It seems a waste to sleep. Tom holds me, one leg thrown over my hip as if I might escape. Lying skin to skin I burn the moment into me. Loving the weight of him, I breathe him in.

Rosie wakes twice in the night crying and when I pick her up she clings to me, sobbing. I rock her in my arms. Perhaps it is the wind that is gusting outside making the old casement windows rattle. The second time Rosie wakes I take her back into our bed. It's fast becoming a habit that is going to be hard to break.

I lie holding her trembling little body, listening to the wind tearing the leaves off the trees before they are ready. We are safe in this strong old house and it feels wonderfully secure and settled around me.

I wonder if our house in St Ives is being battered by the same storm. I find myself straining, as I did in childhood, for the sound of the maroon going up for the lifeboat. I remember the shiver and wriggle down the bed as I listened for the second firing, which meant the lifeboat had been launched safely. For a moment I can almost hear the swirl and crash of the sea outside the window.

Rosie is hot. Maybe she got too excited over the doll. She turns over and burrows into Tom's back, draws up her legs in a foetal position, like a small animal. She reaches out to touch Tom's back with a small crab hand, and sticks the thumb of her other hand into her mouth and sleeps again with a little shaky sigh. I curl up next to her and try not to go on and on doing a countdown. One more whole day together. I wonder anxiously if Rosie is getting to the age when she can sense when Tom is about to leave us again. What nebulous unformed horrors can a child of two have that make her cling to me and scream out in such terror?

FIFTY-FOUR

When Adam had gone to school I would go and walk on the estuary in autumn sunlight. There was an old heron who sat on a rotten log all day and the gulls and crows constantly mobbed him. They would circle and dive-bomb him, crowd and jostle him like playground bullies who instinctively zoom in on the weak. He was old and scruffy, with loose feathers hanging like a tattered coat. I was worried that he had given up and the other birds knew it, although Adam told me that was not scientific.

It was so peaceful with the tide creeping in over the stones in little sucking movements. I wondered how I could have contentedly spent so many years in a city.

My days here with Adam began and ended with the birds. Adam's enthusiasm was catching. It made me appreciate all that was around me in a special way. Until I lived in London, I took everything that I had on my doorstep for granted. Adam gave me new eyes. I began to view the world with a wonder at all the small things I had missed.

I carried a small pack on my back with my sketchbook and pens, pencils and binoculars. I had started to draw again, just for my own enjoyment. I jotted down the colours and textures I saw each day. I collected small pieces of driftwood and seaweed, and carried bags of pearly pink shells home from the beach.

I could sit for hours in the shelter of the sand dunes, watching the wind catch the top of the waves in a white mist. Ideas began to come to me thicker and faster than I could get them down.

I had sloughed off the city like a dusty discarded coat, now I drank in the changing luminous sea and sky as I had done in childhood.

In the evenings, if the tide was out, Adam and I crunched along the shoreline, and over the old quay where the locals fished in the evenings and on to the beach. St Ives lay shimmering in the distance, haloed in a cloudy lustre of pink light.

'In the summer we could bring one of those disposable barbecues and cook sausages up in the dunes as the sun sets,' I said to Adam.

'Cool,' he said. He could watch the windsurfers for hours. They seemed fearless, flying behind their huge colourful kites in a gale and sometimes having to be rescued.

When Adam was in bed I thumbed through my fashion books and my books on the V & A. I drew ideas for dresses and skirts the muted colour of seabirds. I made lists of materials for accessories. Belts of shell and leather and rope, and bright canvas bags beaded with shells: summer seaside clothes.

I was suddenly full of ideas. They tumbled over themselves in my head. It was strange; I had given up work because I was empty and just living, and being here had released something inside me as if it had been waiting to burst out of me.

I had no plans to show my work to anyone. I was doing this for myself and for Tom. I used to show Tom my rough drawings for designs. I would fix small pieces of coloured material to the sketches so that he had some idea of what I did and I could hear his voice saying, *Wow! I really like that and that one. Stunning. Not sure about that . . . and that one is a bit over the top, for me. That evening dress is fantastic. How come someone so talented and trendy married a boring old army man?*

I had no idea if what I was experimenting with was any good. I only knew that it released something in me, some fundamental need to make something out of each day. I thought it might be a little like writing a poem; bleeding a small piece of yourself into each line or stitch in order to feel alive.

I felt as secretly excited as I did before a collection. In the hospital I thought I had lost every creative urge. I thought it had died with Rosie and Tom. Being with Adam had rekindled it like a miracle, a rebirth. It made going to bed alone a little easier. It made waking without Tom manageable.

I knew that soon I would have to tell Adam about the day Tom died and I dreaded it. I had to relive it to tell him. I knew it was necessary for both of us. Adam wanted every small detail of our lives. I knew he stored all that I told him carefully to make a patchwork of my memories, of our lives and the way we had lived, Tom, Rosie and I.

I think he squirrelled these details in a special separate part of himself, carefully building up the life of a man he had thought about all his childhood.

When we were sorting out photographs, Adam would sometimes place his finger on Tom's cheek, his face eager, full of longing. It hurt watching him. I wanted to pull him to me and rock him as I used to do with Rosie.

One evening, as the wind blustered and blew outside the house, I carried the parcel of photographs that Danielle had sent from London into the sitting room.

Adam looked up from his book. 'Are you OK?'

'It's time I opened this up, Adam. These photos need to

be out of their box and around the house, full of the happy times. I'd rather do it with you here and I will try not to get upset.'

'Doesn't matter if you do,' he said gruffly. 'It is . . . upsetting.'

We sat on the floor, and I cut the tape from the padded envelope and pulled out a large and a small box of photographs. I felt sick. I wanted, but dreaded, to see Rosie photographed over and over in black and white, in vibrant colour. I quailed looking down at the markers of her short life: photographs taken on her birthday; summer in Richmond Park; Christmas in St Ives. We had all taken hundreds and hundreds of photographs of my indulged but not yet spoilt little girl.

I was frightened of the horror I fought to keep at bay when I had to face, admit, accept her innocent terrible end in the car seat behind Tom. I held hard to the memory of how they had been together, Tom and my sweet Rosie. Close as close. *My two women*, Tom would whisper. *My two lovely women.*

Adam touched my shoulder. 'Wait,' he said. 'Wait a moment.'

I heard him in the kitchen and he came back with some red wine in my favourite glass.

I smiled, touched. 'Thank you. This will help, darling.'

I opened the boxes and together we fanned out the photographs on the floor, in a sweep like a pack of cards: Tom throwing Rosie up into the air in the garden; Tom, asleep in the chair holding her as a baby, with Rosie peeping out curiously at the camera as if to say *I think I should the one who has fallen asleep.*

There were her first wobbly steps on the polished floors, in one of the little dresses I made for her, arms raised to balance herself, looking anxious because her small chubby legs were proving unreliable. There were all the photographs of me and Rosie that Tom had taken; our wild curly hair dominating each picture. We were so alike, she a tiny version of me, a vital, fundamental part of me.

How many times can a heart break? My hands trembled. I could not speak to Adam as I turned the photos over on the floor one by one. The happiness of those lost days filled the room, staring up at me; my child's life in lucent memories. All that I had. All that I lost.

It could never heal, this loss, it would live on and on in me for ever, making all I did pointless, just an exercise in diversion. How could I have thought my urge to create again was anything but a diversion, a manic grabbing of straws? How could I?

Adam whispered, 'Jenny, Jenny, please don't cry. Don't cry. We can put all the photos back in the box.'

I looked at him. I did not know I was crying. He was very pale. I opened my arms, and he came and wrapped his arms round me on the floor and I smelt his young schoolboy scent. We rocked for a moment and I felt his emotion fighting for control in his chest. I knew he wanted to say something comforting but could not find the words.

I held him away. 'I'm so sorry. I should not be putting you through this, Adam. I'm going to bed now. We'll talk in the morning.' I kissed his forehead. 'Goodnight.'

I leave him with the kaleidoscope of my life. I don't put the light on, I don't have a bath. I throw off my clothes and pull on old pyjamas and climb into bed in the dark. Once I let go I cannot stop. I muffle my crying with a pillow. I lose all sense of time as my body heaves around the bed. Now I have started I cannot stop.

I want to feel and touch and smell and hold Rosie and Tom. I want to hear their laughter and their voices singing around the house. I want them back. I want my life and all I had back. I want this to be a terrible mistake. I want to wake up and find this is only a nightmare and I will laugh with relief, laugh that I could have such a dream. I want my life back.

FIFTY-FIVE

Adam sat among the sea of photographs on the floor unsure what to do. He did not feel he had the right to touch them or to return them to the box. He let his eyes roam slowly over them, peering down at the laughing faces. Everyone looked so happy. Everyone in that London house seemed to laugh all the time and yet he knew that no one took photographs of sad or angry people. The camera caught the special times. Lives could be distorted by what you saw, not what was actually being lived out.

He wished he could have been part of the life in that house. He wished he had known the time when Jenny was happy and carefree. He did not know how it would ever have been possible for him to share in lives that had not been linked to his own. But he knew that reunions did happen, usually when you were grown up. Estranged or adopted children did walk into their parents' lives. It was too late for him. He had always planned to do it, but now it was too late.

What if his mother had given him little pieces of information about Tom that he could have followed up years and years ago? Like with the Salvation Army or someone. Then he could have made contact secretly, could have got to know Tom and they would have talked and talked, and he would not have been a stranger any more. Jenny and Tom would have told him how glad they were that he had found them. He might have been a part of all that he now looked down on. If only his mother had not made a secret of Tom.

Dimly through her closed bedroom door Adam heard the sound of Jenny's weeping. It went on and on and on like a disturbing Gregorian chant. He knelt in the still house where the curtains were not yet drawn and black night deep and violent gathered outside. There was only the sound of Jenny crying and the curlews calling out an alarm into the windy night, adding to the long lament that filled the house.

Adam got up and drew the curtains against the dark. He had a shower and then listened outside Jenny's door. She was still crying. Somehow he had to stop her. She would make herself ill again. She might even have to go back to hospital.

He went into the kitchen and switched on the kettle. He made a mug of tea and added milk and sugar. Sugar helped in a crisis, he seemed to remember. He knocked on Jenny's door then, without waiting for an answer, opened it and went in. The room was in darkness and Jenny was huddled in the double bed, her head buried in the pillows. 'I've brought you some tea.' He stood awkwardly in his pyjamas by the side of the bed. At least she had stopped crying. Carefully, he placed the tea next to her and tiptoed out of the room in case she was asleep. He turned off all the lights and checked that the doors were locked, then he went to bed.

He heard an owl somewhere in the small wood beyond the house and it made him feel very alone. He heard Jenny running a bath as he slipped into sleep and felt relieved.

He woke in the night from a frantic dream full of sneering, laughing faces that got bigger and bigger, and swooped towards him threatening to smother him in hysterical mirth.

He sat bolt upright, sweat breaking out on his forehead. Outside the night seemed suffocating, intense and endless. He was afraid to go back to sleep in case the faces returned to haunt him.

He got out of bed for a glass of water and saw there was a thin slit of light under Jenny's door. He knocked lightly and Jenny called, 'Come in, Adam, I'm not asleep.'

He opened the door and went in.

She was sitting up, reading. 'You can't sleep either?' She smiled at him. 'I'm not surprised. I'm so, so sorry to put you through that, darling. I should have opened those photos alone.'

'No, you shouldn't. I wanted to be there. I'm glad I was. I just had a nightmare.'

Jenny patted the bed. 'Come and talk to me. Shall I make you a drink?'

Adam shook his head.

'Do you want to get your dressing gown? You're going to get cold.'

Adam hesitated. 'Can I get in? I don't want to be on my own, Jenny. I know the dream will come back. Can I stay with you?'

He could feel his face flush. He knew he was far too old to be saying this, but it was true. Jenny hesitated, stared at him for a long moment, then without answering she turned over the duvet to the other side of the bed.

Adam got into the warmth beside her and sighed. He burrowed into the pillow and closed his eyes. 'I think I might sleep now.'

'Good.' Jenny bent towards him and gently pushed the hair from his hot face. 'If the dream comes back I'm here, right beside you. Sleep now, sleep, my darling boy.'

FIFTY-SIX

When I woke, Adam was still beside me. He looked so young and vulnerable asleep. His long blond fringe hid his eyes and I had to stop myself reaching out to smooth it away from his face.

I felt, as I lay there, a fierce joy in him. I wanted to protect him from all cruelties that lay in wait for him and I knew that I could not. I had not been able to protect Rosie and I couldn't shield Adam from the world either. It made me sad. How close joy and sadness were. Like light and shade.

I got out of bed quietly. I did not want him to wake beside me. I knew he would be embarrassed and confused. We both knew he was too old to get into my bed and yet, in all adolescent boys a child still hovered full of insecurities. I had seen it in my sisters' children.

I went into the kitchen to make tea. I wondered if living here with me and the weight of my sometimes crippling pain was affecting him. Yet I knew we were happy, Adam and I. I was sure of it in his broad smile as he caught sight of me from the train or came into the kitchen to watch me cook; in our walks; in just being together. Adam was so easy to love, so easy to be with.

When I remembered our first meeting in Ruth's house in Birmingham I realised, even before he knew who I was, that Adam and I had had an instant rapport.

I carried my tea into the bathroom. Adam was still fast asleep. In the shower a cold little voice whispered, *From the moment you first met him you gave him your undivided attention, you listened carefully to him. Ruth was too busy to give him that level of rapt attention and his school was failing him. You came along at exactly the right time . . . No.* I closed my eyes against that inner voice. I loved Adam at first sight, as I did Tom.

I wrapped the towel round me and stepped out. I was trembling with an intense emotion I didn't quite understand. I needed Adam near me, with me, here. He was a part of Tom and so a part of me. While he was with me Tom's face remained vivid, clear and alive.

I did not want to return to my bedroom for my clothes and disturb him so I pulled my pyjamas on again and went back into the kitchen. Through the open bedroom door, I heard Adam get out of bed. 'Hi there,' I called. 'Like some tea?'

Adam came to the kitchen door avoiding my eyes and mumbled, 'Yes, please.'

I made him a mug, carefully concentrating on the tea while I prattled to try to put him at his ease. Luckily, it was a Saturday. 'What are you up to today? I'm going to make an enormous carrot cake to try and impress Flo, Danielle and Ruth. They're coming here first, because Danielle and Flo want to look at the house.' I handed him his tea.

Adam sniffed and began to relax. 'I think we're going fishing. Harry and James and me,' he said.

'OK, honeychile. In that case I will make you bacon and egg, the wind out there looks vicious.'

'It's all right, Jenny, you don't have to. You never eat bacon and egg.'

'Ah, but I am *wicked* at making it, aren't I?'

Adam grinned at me. I grinned back. 'Go and get dressed. It will be ready in two minutes.'

Relief that everything was normal between us lit up his face. He turned and made for his bedroom.

When he came back I sat down with my coffee while he ate. 'Is James picking you up?'

'I think so. I *think* he said he'd ring.'

'He'll probably ring any minute, then. Where are you fishing?'

'Well, it depends on the weather.' Adam looked over my head. 'I don't think we'll be going out in the boat in this wind, so we might fish down below the ferry house.'

'Will you make sure you're back here by four when they arrive?'

He looked up at me. 'Oh. OK. I don't think Mum would mind if I wasn't.'

I did. I said, choosing my words, 'Probably not, but I think she would love it if you were waiting for her. I know I would.'

He met my eyes and I said lightly, whisking away his empty plate, 'I want this weekend to be really happy, especially for Ruth, darling. She must miss you terribly.'

I dropped the plate into the sink and turned to him, leaning against it. He was listening but wary. 'I don't know what plans Ruth has for you this weekend, but you will both want time to yourselves. She might want to go and have some peace with you in the cottage in Truro.'

I stopped as Adam's face fell. 'But what about the party? I've asked Harry. I thought everyone would stay at Bea and James'.'

'That's tomorrow night. There's tonight . . .'

'I want to stay here. I want to stay here with you. You might need me.' His voice was husky.

I swallowed my hypocritical and treacherous joy. I went

behind his chair and put my arms round his neck, my face against the top of his head. 'Adam, we have every day together. Your mother is only here until Sunday afternoon. It's very important not to hurt her or make her feel I've in some way replaced her. It's difficult enough for her. She agreed to you being away from her because she loves you. Now is the time for you to show how much you love her and how happy you are to see her. That's only fair, isn't it?'

Adam was silent. Then he said, 'Yes.' He looked up at me. 'I do love my mum, Jenny.'

I kissed the top of his head and moved away. 'I should jolly well hope so! Make sure she knows it too. Oh look, there's Dad. Rush and get ready while I make him coffee.'

Dad hugged me. 'Coffee sounds great. Bea had me chatting at four in the morning over tea and toast; fun at the time, but I couldn't really get back to sleep.'

Adam appeared with his fishing gear and James said, 'OK, let's go and pick up Harry. He's getting the train, he wasn't dressed when I called. I take it you'd like Adam back before they all get here?'

'Definitely. Adam's got his orders. Have fun.'

''Bye, darling.' James made for the front door in his vague fashion and I noticed he had developed an old man's wide walk. *Oh, Dad, don't get old.*

Adam was following James out when he suddenly dashed back to me. 'I will be back in time, I promise.' Suddenly he reached up and kissed my cheek.

'What was that for, darling boy?'

'I love my mum, but I love you too, Jenny.' Then he was gone and the front door slammed behind him, and I was left in the stillness of the house.

FIFTY-SEVEN

Ruth, driving along the Saltings, saw a familiar figure outside Jenny's house. He was carrying his fishing rod and his old green fishing bag was slung over his shoulder. She smiled and slowed behind him and called out.

Adam turned and grinned when he saw it was Ruth. 'Hi, Mum!'

'Hi, Adam. Oh it's so good to see you.' She leapt out and hugged him as Jenny emerged from the house.

Flo got out of the front seat stiffly. Long journeys were a bugger now. Danielle slid out of the car and kissed Jenny on both cheeks. 'My God, each time we come by car I forget how far away it is.'

James, who had been following Adam down the road with Harry, greeted everyone before he got into his car and drove back to Bea.

'Just in time. Skin of teeth!' Jenny hissed at him before he disappeared.

Flo and Danielle were intrigued by the odd little house full of Jenny's touches.

'This is so *you*, Jen. I'd know it was you living here even if it were in the middle of the Sahara,' Flo said.

Danielle turned and gazed around with a professional eye. Everything was casually put together with Jenny's effortless hand, with the natural instinctive flair for colour and texture she used in her designs. Relief flooded through her as she padded around, looking and touching. *Pff! If Jenny can do this her imagination is not dead.*

'Come into the kitchen. I've got an old-fashioned tea all ready for you.'

Jenny's cake stood in the middle of the table. A work of art.

'Oh, wow!' Adam exclaimed.

'My goodness,' Flo said, laughing. 'How spectacular! Tiny egg sandwiches too. What a welcome, Jen.'

Danielle stared at the table, remembering the amazing cakes Jenny had made for Rosie's two birthdays.

Ruth became very still. *This is all too perfect. Adam leading this charmed and magical existence without me. It is like life in a film. I am on the outside watching it all on a screen. I can't compete with this.*

They sat round the table all talking at once. Ruth watched Adam helping Jenny get milk from the fridge, hand out the sandwiches. She tried with a great effort of will to blank out the furious, persistent and damaging little voice that threatened to drown out her joy in being with Adam again.

She was bitterly jealous. She had never made Adam a cake in his life. Yet Adam sat down next to her, making sure she had something to eat, grinning at her contentedly, making it obvious he was glad to see her.

Jenny leant over the table. 'Ruth? You're very quiet. Are you OK?'

For God's sake enjoy this precious weekend. Don't spoil it.

Ruth mentally shook herself and smiled. 'Sorry, I'm fine. I'll get my second wind in a bit.'

'Jenny?' Flo asked. 'Did you manage to book a table some-where to eat tonight? I don't want Bea to have to cook.'

'Yes, with difficulty. Bea thought it a dreadful luxury, but is secretly looking forward to it. I booked a table for eight o'clock.'

She turned quickly to Ruth. 'You probably have plans for the weekend. We don't want to hijack you and Adam. Bea just wanted you to know that your old room is there if you didn't want to go all the way back to Truro. Or, of course, you can stay here if you don't mind a bunk bed.'

Jenny's voice was warm and considerate, so why did Ruth feel she was being reeled in? She turned to Adam, caught his anxious face and knew instantly that he wanted to stay in St Ives where the action was. She thought quickly. 'A meal together tonight sounds great. Would it be OK if I stayed here with Adam tonight?' She turned to Adam. 'I've got to go and check out the cottage while I'm here, Adam. Maybe we could do that tomorrow? A friend of Peter's wants to rent it for a while.'

Relief made Adam expansive. 'Of course, Mum. We'll go in the morning. We'll open windows and stuff.'

Danielle had wandered away and found herself at the other side of the kitchen in a rudimentary conservatory. It was here she found Jenny's first tentative designs. She was examining them when Jenny flew in, flushed. '*Danielle*! I didn't want you or anyone to see these. I'm just fiddling about trying things out for my own amusement. Please don't look.'

'Jenee, if you are doing these for your own amusement, please will you do some for my amusement? They are very good. Believe me.'

Jenny seemed genuinely surprised. 'Are you sure?'

'Well, I *am* a designer and I have worked with you for a long time. Trust me! I had lunch with Antonio last week.

He still wants us to go in with him. He still wants to market your designs in Italy.'

'Danielle . . .'

'Listen. Antonio knows the situation. He knows you are taking time out but please may I take a few of these drawings to show him? It does not commit you to anything but it does show you have not lost your touch.'

Jenny shook her head. 'I'm not ready. It's too soon. Antonio will take your designs, you can adapt to meet his needs.'

'I cannot compromise my work, Jenny. We are very different designers, which is why our partnership works. Antonio wants your work, not mine. I am so reluctant to take on another designer . . .' Danielle saw Jenny's face and closed her eyes. 'Sorry, I am doing what I promised Antonio I would not do. I am putting pressure on you. Forget it, darling.' She smiled. 'I felt so excited when I walk in here and see you are working again. It blew me away.'

Jenny saw how tired Danielle looked. So did Flo and Ruth. They were all responsible for keeping the business afloat because she had decided to opt out. 'You've always wanted to work with Antonio, haven't you?'

'Yes. It is the way forward for us. I am sure of this.'

'I'll think about what you said. Just *think*. OK?'

'I will not say another word. Thank you. Thank you.' She kissed Jenny on both cheeks gleefully and lowered her voice. 'Is everything all right in there with Adam and Ruth?'

Jenny nodded. 'Yes, we've got it organised. Ruth is staying here tonight and I'll sleep at home so Ruth can have Adam to herself.'

'Great!' Danielle linked arms. 'We can get drunk together and gossip like the old days. We had better get to St Ives and settle Flo in. She might need a sleep. Her arthritis is getting bad. The stairs are not helping.'

'I noticed as she got out of the car. I might elicit James to help persuade her to see someone.'

'She will never retire. She would die.'

'I know, but we are always going to be around to look after her.'

A full moon hung dramatically over the sea as they all ate together looking out on the harbour. Ruth began to relax. Adam was happy. She loved her job. What had she been fussing about, for heaven's sake? Life was good.

Back in Jenny's house Ruth revelled in having Adam to herself. He chatted about school and Harry. He told her about the teachers and his music. He seemed more confident and obviously had no trouble making friends. He also talked about Bea and James fondly, but he seemed oddly careful what he said about Jenny.

When Ruth asked him if it was all working out, living here in this small house with Jenny, he said quickly, 'Everything's cool. You know it is, Mum, or I'd have told you. How about you? Are you OK in London?'

Ruth laughed. 'Apart from missing you, I love it.'

'Yeah, but I have to work really hard during the week. I have tons of homework and music practice. We'd probably never have time to talk to each other because you work late too. Anyway, tons of kids are at boarding school at my age, so think of it like that.'

He grinned at her and Ruth said, 'Oh so rational and clever we have become at public school!'

Adam looked at her quickly, wondering if he heard something in her voice, but he saw that she was laughing and he relaxed.

Adam had had a broken night and was exhausted. He fell straight into bed without even cleaning his teeth. Ruth wandered around the house. She had been worrying about

305

nothing. She hummed softly in the dark and hearing the seabirds, she shivered as the ghosts of her childhood revisited her.

Were they dead or alive, those impostors of parents? Did they ever find happiness? In old age did they lose their terror of not conforming to some distorted image of respectability? She would never know and it was better not to think about them.

She went and watched Adam sleeping. The light from the hallway shone into his room. Ruth was exhausted but did not want to go to bed.

Just the two of us. Like it used to be. She longed suddenly to go back to the small close world of his babyhood. Then she remembered that she had never truly been alone with Adam. Her aunt had predominated in his first years. She had worked. She had always worked. Then Peter had come along. It was a myth she had made in her head that she had ever had Adam completely to herself for any length of time.

Adam was happier and more settled at school than he had ever been. He loved his life here in Cornwall. He had been truly pleased to see her and in time he would enjoy his holidays in London with her too. What more could she ask of life than that her child was healthy, secure and happy?

Nothing, she said to the moon as she climbed into Jenny's bed. Nothing at all.

FIFTY-EIGHT

The next morning Danielle and Jenny walked down into St Ives to shop and look around the myriad small galleries.

Flo was sitting with Bea and James in the kitchen drinking coffee and reading the papers when she lowered the colour supplement she was reading and took a deep breath. 'Something rather odd happened last week.'

Something in Flo's voice made James put down his paper. 'Oh?'

'I noticed a man sitting in a car in the road outside the house. The car changed and so did the man, but it looked as if someone were watching our house or the house next door. No one else seemed to have noticed him but when I mentioned it to Ruth and Danielle we all agreed that we should ring the police, in case of a potential burglary. As you know, there are quite a few diplomats in the road.'

Flo paused. James was watching her intently. *I think he's ahead of me*, Flo thought.

'I rang the police and instead of a polite lack of interest a Detective Inspector Wren came round immediately. He told me they were monitoring the movements of a nameless diplomat in the road and watching the comings and goings

307

of everyone entering and leaving his house. I told him that it seemed to me that it was *our* house that was being watched. He assured me that I was mistaken and that surveillance officers have to change around. He seemed concerned that I shouldn't interfere with their investigation and that I should keep what he told me to myself. I would have believed him except I knew I had seen him somewhere before and I suddenly remembered: it was when Tom was killed. He was one of the detectives who came to the house. I knew he was lying and I could see that it annoyed him. At the front door he said. "You're an observant woman, Mrs Kingsley. It's in the interests of Tom Holland's widow not to jeopardise or put at risk an ongoing investigation." Then he left. I told Ruth and Danielle what he wanted me to say. That one of the diplomats in the road was being watched.'

James and Bea stared at Flo in silence.

'I didn't see any point in mentioning this to Jenny. She's just finding her feet again and there is nothing tangible to tell her. Am I right?'

'Of course you are, Flo,' Bea said quickly. 'We have no idea what these police inquiries or investigations mean. There's no point whatsoever in mentioning it.'

'I agree,' James said. Justice for Tom should be paramount but it seemed unlikely to him that the police would find who was responsible at this late stage. The nature of Tom's job made the possibilities endless. 'There's no point in Jenny knowing that the police are still investigating his murder. I'm sorry. It must have been disturbing for you.'

'Well, I'm a tough old boot. My father was a policeman and he used to make me play that game of remembering how many objects there were on a plate. It made me observant.'

'I'm glad Tom's death hasn't been forgotten,' Bea said.

'Thank you for telling us, Flo. Now, weren't you two tough old boots going to meet the girls at the Tate?'

'What are you going to do, darling?' Bea asked.

'I'm going to potter blissfully on my own in the garden.'

Flo reached for her jacket. 'I think that's our cue to be off and leave him in peace, Bea. He is rather overwhelmed by women this weekend.'

'My dear Flo, when have I not been overwhelmed by women? It has been my lot these thirty years.'

'You've enjoyed every minute,' Bea said unsympathetically, reaching for her coat from the back door and pecking him on the cheek.

'This poor old cottage is beginning to feel damp and unlived in.' Ruth threw open the windows. 'If I keep it, I shall have to get rid of the night storage heaters and put in central heating.'

'You're not going to sell it, Mum?'

'I don't want to.' She looked at Adam. 'But, maybe you . . . we . . . have outgrown it. I should be practical.'

Adam shook his head. 'No,' he said seriously. 'It's your heirloom, you have to keep it. Do what Peter said and rent it out for a while. If you put central heating in, maybe you could get a new Aga that works when we are not here and then it will keep the house dry.'

Ruth tried not to laugh. 'You're right it is my heirloom. Maybe that's what I'll do. Use a bit of our Birmingham house money. Let's open the windows and then walk over to Polmarrick and have lunch at The Egret.'

Going into his own room to open the window, Adam stopped and looked over at his bed and at his books stacked on the shelf above it. What a baby he had been when they all came to the cottage. Now he felt so grown up. It seemed like remembering someone else. Yet how simple it had been, too. Just fishing and picnics and Mum and . . . often Peter. A shadow slid across his horizon for a second: a pang of regret for Peter who had given Adam unselfish years of himself. 'You can't sell this place, Mum,' he called. 'It's part of my heritage.'

He heard his mother give a snort of laughter. 'Is it indeed? I'm glad to hear it, darling.'

On their way back to St Ives in the late afternoon, Adam got out his mobile and dialled.

'Who are you ringing? Harry? You'll see him in a couple of hours.'

'No.' Adam went pink. 'Hi, Jenny. Yeah, great. We're on our way back. What time shall we come over to St Ives? Yeah? OK. See you later. I was just telling Jenny we were on our way back,' he said to his mother unnecessarily.

'So I gather,' Ruth said drily.

Danielle and Jenny stood looking over the harbour wall, watching the clouds of seagulls following the fishing boats back in.

'It is very beautiful, Jen, and there are lovely galleries and some interesting shops, but do you not miss the buzz of London? For a holiday it is perfect, I think, but to live, pff, I would soon be bored.'

Jenny laughed. 'You're a city girl, that's why. This is my home, Elle. For now this is as perfect for me as it gets.'

Danielle turned her back on the sea. She picked up the 'for now' and took heart. 'Of course it is. It is different when you grow up in a place. I selfishly miss you, that is all.'

'But it is working out with Ruth?'

'Oh, yes. She knows her stuff. She is clever at marketing, very much the PR girl and she has found us many new contacts. She is also very nice, but you know this, you grew up with her. And you, it is working with the boy living with you?'

310

They turned away from the harbour and began to walk home. Bea had sent them on ahead to turn up the Aga.

'Oh, yes. It's working perfectly.'

At that moment Jenny's mobile rang. She smiled as she talked. 'Hi there! Have you had a good day? Oh, come about six thirty or seven, whenever you're ready. OK, love, I'll see you later.'

'Not too perfectly for Ruth's peace of mind, I hope,' Danielle said, watching her.

Jenny glanced at her sharply. 'Surely Ruth must be relieved Adam is happy, which he is. I know I would if he were my son.'

Danielle stopped herself from saying *but he is not your son* and linked arms. 'Darling, do not get defensive. It is a tricky balance for you both, is it not? I see it from a distance, from a position of . . .'

'Neutrality? Objectivity?'

'Both. Let us change the subject.'

After a moment Jenny said, 'I don't miss the city but I do miss the house and you, me and Flo working together. I miss the life I had and sometimes when you or Flo ring and I can hear the buzz of the day behind you I feel great loss. It all suddenly seems strange, this life I have now. As if I have stepped into another world and become another person.'

'You are Jenny and you always will be. You will come back to us. I know this. You will come back when you are healed and ready.'

'Maybe.' Jenny smiled. 'I've been thinking about what you said. I feel guilty about leaving you to carry the main responsibility for everything on your own. The trouble with grief is it makes you self-centred without realising it. It's like being in a bubble and nothing is real outside your bubble. If you truly do want to take a few of those sketches to show Antonio,

311

go ahead. It won't be enough to interest him, though. I'm just feeling my way back.'

Danielle gave a whoop of gratitude. She had dreamt for a long time of a business union with Antonio.

She saw Jenny was grinning at her. 'Do you fancy Antonio, Elle?'

Danielle changed colour. 'Of course I do not! It would not make any difference if I did. It is you he has always had the eye for! You can do no wrong.'

'What utter, utter rubbish you talk. He likes my designs, that's all, and he was extremely kind to me after Tom died. He's a really nice man.'

Danielle laughed. 'Yes, he is. And he is going to be a very grateful one when I show him your ideas. You see.'

'I won't hold my breath. Come on, we'd better hurry and turn the oven up or we will incur Bea's wrath.'

To their left the sun hung low, blood-red and dramatic over the sea as the day eased slowly into black and white.

That night, after Bea's dinner and hours of inebriated charades, everyone stayed at Tredrea, squashed in organised fashion into all the bedrooms. Ruth woke in the early hours with the image she had fallen asleep with still embedded behind her eyes: Adam and Jenny filling the dishwasher together. She had entered the kitchen carrying plates to see them kneeling over the open door of the machine, faces close together, as they chatted and laughed about something. So easy with one another, so somehow intimate.

Harry had rushed in behind her with more dishes and the spell had been broken, but Ruth had seen them. Seen what? There was nothing to see. Ruth knew in the depth of her being that Jenny was taking Adam away from her; casually, with love and kind words. Deliberately, as she looked Ruth in the eye, Jenny was forming an impenetrable bond with *her* child.

312

Ruth got up in the dark and walked silently up the stairs to the next floor where Harry and Adam were sleeping in the attic room next to Jenny. Both boys were fast asleep, but Jenny wasn't. She heard Ruth and pushed her door open. She was making a cup of tea on a tray in her room. 'Come and have a cup of tea. I've woken up early too,' she whispered.

Ruth shook her head. 'I think I'll try and go back to sleep. It's a long drive home to London.'

'OK. Look, take a cup back to bed with you.' Jenny handed her a mug.

'Thanks. See you later.' Ruth turned and went back down the steep stairs. She knew Jenny was watching her puzzled, maybe hurt, but she did not care.

FIFTY-NINE

I knew I should try to talk to Ruth before she went back to London.

I got my chance in the afternoon before they all left. Adam suddenly realised he needed a bird book for an English essay he was writing. Ruth drove Adam and I followed with Danielle and Flo so they could all head straight off on the dual carriageway back to London.

Ruth wanted to walk along the creek before the long journey home and we followed the path up to the stream, leaving Flo and Danielle reading the papers in the cottage.

I felt odd walking this path again. After a while we sat on a bench in the sun. The narrow twisting channels of mud the tide had left made the creek interesting for Adam. He watched the birds, passing his binoculars back and forth to me and Ruth.

To our left, on the foreshore, lay the old barn with the backdrop of trees behind it. I shivered involuntarily. I would not have come back here by choice. I saw Adam swing his binoculars towards the barn and I knew he must be remembering. Ruth too.

Adam glanced at her but she remained as silent and cold

as she had been early that morning. Feeling the atmosphere, he took off, crunching along the foreshore to look around the lake.

I turned to Ruth. 'Thank you.'

She looked at me curiously. 'What are you thanking me for?'

'For still being here. For not taking off and putting yourself and Adam a hundred miles from me. For letting Adam stay with me after all that happened down here.'

'I certainly wanted to take off.' Her voice was husky.

'Do you still?'

'Sometimes. I wish I could go back to how it was; the three of us, Peter, Adam and me in that house in Birmingham. Ironic that you don't recognise contentment until you no longer have it.'

'I'm sorry. I buggered up your life, didn't I?'

She looked at me without smiling. 'Well, I buggered up yours by appearing out of the past.'

A little flock of lapwings turned and swung into the sun, their white underbellies catching in a flash of white. Ruth's voice was suddenly low, hoarse: 'I wish we'd never met again on that train to Birmingham.' It was like the suddenness of a slap. She was facing away from me towards the water.

'I don't know what to say. I thought it was working out for you in London. I thought you were happy.'

'I love the job. I love working with Flo and Danielle, but neither of those things compensates me for not having Adam with me.'

I turned to face her, puzzled and annoyed. 'You blame *me* for that? It was your decision to let Adam come to school in Cornwall because he was so thoroughly miserable where he was. It was your decision to work in London. No one twisted your arm. I only stepped in at the last moment when Adam threw a wobbly about boarding.'

Ruth turned to me, her face closed and hostile. 'It was a done deal. Adam acquired a dead father who was a hero and a vital link with that father, *you*. He discovered *your* loving, warm family to identify with. What could I offer in comparison to all this . . . this Cornish paradise . . . ?' She threw her hands out towards the water. 'This permanent holiday atmosphere, this seductive, safe dropping out. I could only offer a broken marriage, a city life with people he didn't know. No competition.'

I was shocked by her bitterness. She could not look at me. She stood stony-faced, staring straight ahead at the mud and the water creeping in, and the sun sparkling on the incoming tide.

'Why are you so determined to believe you've lost Adam? He could have been a boarder at Truro or any school. Would you have talked about loss then? How often did you have time to spend with him in the evenings in Birmingham? How much free time do you have in London? I know the hours we work, Ruth.'

I had touched a nerve and she turned angrily. She began to say something that sounded like *It's turned out all right for you*. Then she stopped and started to stride away from me back towards the cottage.

I followed slowly, feeling miserable. I was worried that Adam might have heard us.

Suddenly she stopped walking and waited for me to catch up. She said in a quieter voice but with considerable effort, 'I'm sorry. I'm tired and I'm hung-over. Look, I'm grateful for all you do for Adam. He's happy and that's all that should matter. Please let's forget this conversation.'

'Is it this place? Is it that you can't forget what happened over there? Despite everything, do you think I'm still a threat to Adam? Do you think I'm still unbalanced or mad or something?'

Ruth stared down at me. 'I've never, ever thought you were mad, Jenny. But you know what I do think? I think you're not being honest with yourself. Adam is your last link with Tom. Each time you look at him you see the image of the man you loved. That's why I feel threatened. He's *my* son. *My* flesh and blood. *Mine* . . .'

Her voice broke, came so jaggedly from within her and was such a pitiful cry from the heart that we stared at each other in horror. A curlew rose up, giving its strange wavering cry, and we walked in a tense unfinished silence towards the cottage, where we could see Flo and Danielle coming towards us.

SIXTY

By Wednesday morning Danielle had had enough. She went to find Flo. 'I cannot stand much more of this, Flo. I am unused to moody people.'

'Is Ruth still morose and monosyllabic? Oh dear. I've no idea what happened between her and Jenny, but it's bound to be about Adam.'

'I can see that it is hard for her. Jenny maybe has a blind spot over him, but he is a very contented boy. I thought the weekend was happy. I think she is making a problem . . .'

'You want me to have a word?'

'Yes, please, Flo. Her misery is affecting everyone. This has always been a happy workplace. We are too small for bad atmosphere. Jenny was always like sunshine in this house. I like Ruth. She is very good at what she does, but I cannot be doing with undercurrents and atmospheres.'

'I know you can't, dear. I'll try and catch her this morning.'

'If I do it I will get it wrong. I am annoyed and do not feel sympathetic.'

Flo caught Ruth alone in her office at midday. 'Have you got time for a quick word, Ruth?'

'Of course. Would you like coffee?'

'No, I can't stay. Look, obviously something's wrong. You've been upset since the weekend. Can I help?'

Ruth shook her head. 'No, thank you. I'm fine.'

'But you clearly are *not* fine and you are affecting the whole household. It's making us all miserable and it can't go on.'

Ruth coloured painfully.

'Do you have misgivings about the arrangement you have with Jenny over Adam? If you have regrets, Ruth, if you think you've made the wrong decision or are unhappy with the way things have turned out, it's never too late to do something about it. If living without Adam is too painful, perhaps you should think about being in Cornwall. Perhaps this is not the job for you after all.'

Ruth looked stunned. 'But Flo, I love this job. I love working with you and Danielle. I've worked hard all my life for an opportunity like this.'

Flo stared at her in a way that made Ruth uncomfortable. 'Most things in life have a price, Ruth. This job entails gruelling hours and a lot of travelling. You are away at least three nights a week. If Adam were here with you he would have been left in this house with Danielle and me, as well as contending with a new school. Adam seems happy. You can see him often. What more do you want? How else could you do a demanding job with us?'

Ruth shook her head. 'I don't know.'

'I think you'll have to try to curb your understandable jealousy about Adam living with Jenny if you're going to have a successful career with us. Adam so obviously loves you. That's never going to change. You have to adapt and move on. It's the only way.'

Ruth tried to smile but Flo saw she felt hurt and isolated. She said gently, 'Until this weekend you seemed to be very much enjoying your life with us. Danielle and I love having you on board. You have been a breath of fresh air. You are doing the most marvellous job for us.'

Ruth's face lit up. 'Am I?'

'You know very well you are.'

'I don't want to leave, Flo. I know everything you say is probably true. I'm sorry, I didn't realise I was upsetting everyone.'

'You have absolutely nothing to apologise for. Angst and guilt go with being a mother, I'm told. Now, are you going to cheer up and start enjoying life again?'

'Yes. I understand. Shape up or ship out!'

Flo laughed. 'My dear Ruth, I don't think I was quite as blunt as that!'

Adam was sleeping but I couldn't sleep. I walked barefoot around the house listening to the birds down on the estuary and watching the shape of the huge fir tree in the dark. The house breathed around me. The wind blew the branches across the skyline and the thin wavering shadows crossed the window, moved over the floor in gusts like invisible footsteps.

I could not get Ruth's words or her face as she uttered them out of my head. Disturbed, I kept pushing them away, not wanting to explore the truth that lay subterranean and complex between us.

I thought of Adam, his small, eager face so like Tom's. I thought of the pleasure he gave me within the close circle of this house we shared.

My guilt lay in the ease with which it had all so seamlessly come about. I did not think I had been calculating, but I knew my empathy with Adam had made me understand, deep down, that this was always what he wanted. Now, I felt blessed each day because he was with me. I thought everything had worked out for everyone.

320

How very convenient, a little voice inside me muttered. I curled, chilled, into the chair. Something else had occurred to me as the days passed. Had Ruth's rage and bitterness been solely about Adam, or did it go deeper, back to our childhood?

When she spent all those hours at our house, year after year as she grew up, did she secretly, subconsciously, harbour feelings of rage and bitterness at the life she had been given, the parents she had? Did she long for Bea and James to be hers? Did she long to be me?

I looked out into the dark. Did *I* mind *her* living in the house Tom and I had shared? Suddenly I felt deeply lonely for adult company.

The phone rang, making me jump and I grabbed it before it woke Adam. I thought it would be Flo or Danielle, but it was Ruth. Her words came out in a hot rush. I wondered if she'd had a drink before she rang me. 'I wanted to apologise, Jenny. I have a lot to thank you for. I'm jealous Adam is so settled with you and jealous that you get on like a house on fire. There, I've admitted the nasty side of me I hardly knew I had. I remembered today how jealous I used to be of you over boys.'

'But Ruth, you were the one with the long blonde hair and legs to your armpits!'

'Maybe, but it was *you* the boys went for, you and your crazy clothes. You were always giggling and bubbly and fun. I was too serious.'

'We had each other. We never paired off or fell out over boys, did we?'

As I said it I thought, *But we would have fought to the death over Tom.*

'No,' Ruth said. 'We never did. I'm off to France tomorrow with Danielle, but I wanted to ring you before I left.'

'I'm glad you did.'

321

'Give my love to Adam in the morning. 'Night, Jenny.'

''Night, Ruth.' I climbed into bed. I knew what that phone call must have cost her and she had an absolute right to be jealous.

SIXTY-ONE

'Jenny, come and see what I've found,' Adam called, his voice muffled. I went out of the back door and saw him on his stomach, his feet protruding from the undergrowth. He manoeuvred himself out backwards holding a plaque, his hair covered in small yellow leaves. 'I was wondering if the hedgehog was in there,' he said. We had been leaving bread and milk out for a hedgehog that amused us by slurping it up noisily every night. Adam brushed the earth off a small earthenware plaque with a dirty hand and stood up. I went to look. Together we read:

Prayer of Socrates, O beloved and all ye other gods of this place grant to me that I be made beautiful in my soul within, and that all external possessions be in harmony with my inner man. May I consider the wise man rich and may I have such wealth as only the self-restrained man can bear or enjoy.

'Cool. Is it very old, do you think?'
'I guess it's probably Victorian. What a find.'
Nelly must have been an interesting old woman because

323

we kept finding odd little bits and pieces of treasure in her garden. I got the impression that she had placed objects she liked to look at in the garden and then they got overgrown.

'I'll go and wash it.' Adam was as pleased as if he had returned from an archaeological dig.

'Treat it gently. I'm not sure it was meant to stay outside.'

Adam cleaned it up in soapy water and we propped it up on the wide window ledge in front of the sink where we could see it every day.

Out of the kitchen window I suddenly saw the sky. 'Adam, just look at that weather coming in.'

We went into the sitting room where we could see that the sky was like a livid bruise hanging low over the water, making the day suddenly dark, shutting us into the small house. I shivered. 'Let's light a fire.' It was a Sunday and we had been shrouded in low mist and cloud all week.

'I'll get some logs.' Adam dashed outside to the pile in the corner behind the back door.

It took a while to get the fire going, then I switched on the small table lamps. I felt like drawing the curtains and shutting out the day, but it was a bit early. 'I'm going to get out those photographs of Rosie. It's time I made that collage for the passage outside our rooms, time that I had them out of their boxes and up on the walls. Will you help me?' I asked Adam.

'Of course I will.' Adam turned from the fire, one cheek red from the flames.

I went and got a large piece of white cardboard and laid it on the floor. 'We'll sift through the photos and place them on here. We'll try various combinations first before we use paper glue. I bought some glass the other day. We'll make our own frame, thin, I think, like bamboo. Or maybe we could raise the middle section, a square plinth for contrast and paint the surround white to bring out the photographs. Let's experiment.'

'Are we just going to use the black-and-white photos?'

'Yes. The sharpness of black and white will look good. This wouldn't work with colour, it would just look tacky. Let's find a striking central photograph and we'll work a side each and see what it looks like. The whole thing has to have balance.'

Adam looked at me nervously. 'I've never done anything like this before. I might spoil it.'

'No, you won't. We'll be juggling photos for hours. It'll take us ages to be satisfied. We'll probably have to go away and come back to it.'

I went to put on some music. The fire had caught and the room was suddenly warm and full of light. I smiled at Adam. 'What shall I put on? You choose.'

Adam thought for a moment. 'Norah Jones or maybe Mahler's Symphony No. 5.'

I stared at him. 'Both those CDs were Tom's. The Mahler was one of Tom's favourite pieces.'

Adam sat up, his eyes bright. 'Was it? Cool. It is melancholy, but it sort of gets inside you and you go on hearing it in your head for ages afterwards.'

'Tom used to play it over and over before he had to go away again. It always reminds me of his leaves ending. I love it, but maybe we'll play Norah first.'

'Sure,' Adam said. He looked down at the photographs of my laughing child. 'Doing this is going to make you sad again.'

'Yes, but it's easier than it was, Adam. I want to do it. I want to see Rosie's smiling face in this house. She was such a happy little thing, always laughing.'

Adam smiled down at the photo in his hand. 'She looks like she giggled a lot. She's really like you. I used to wish I had a brother or sister. Peter wanted children. He and Mum used to argue sometimes. Mum didn't want any more. I think it was hard having me so young and she didn't want to be tied down again. I think that's why Peter went and got a girlfriend in Israel.'

'Oh,' I said, interested. 'I didn't know all that.'

We lay on our stomachs in front of the fire and began to sort through the piles of black-and-white photographs. Occasionally Adam hummed a lyric under his breath and I wanted to hug him for the companionship and sense of peace he gave me. What a shame that sweet young voice would break soon and his eager innocence fly with it.

We picked for our central photograph a picture of Tom holding Rosie above his head. Rosie was reaching down with plump little arms to catch his nose. They were both screaming with laughter.

We looked down at the photo for a long time. Tom and Rosie seemed so vibrant and alive. I could almost believe they might be in the next room. How difficult death was to accept with every part of you. How hard not to be imbued with a terrible sense of futility and disbelief.

The fire crackled behind us and Norah Jones whispered, *Come away with me . . . in the night. Come away with me and we'll kiss on a mountain top . . . in a field of blue . . . on a cloudy day. Come away, come away with me.* I heard Tom's voice in my ear and the smell of coffee, and Rosie laughing.

I swallowed. 'Come on, darling boy, help me make something beautiful and memorable.'

For two hours we turned and sorted and manoeuvred the photos into a symmetry and order and form so that the joyful captured moments of Rosie's short life and the people who had been part of it told their own special story.

The wind was so strong that it bent the trees and prevented Jenny and Adam from hearing Bea opening the gate and coming up the drive with a cake she had made for Adam.

The sitting room was alight in the dark afternoon and Bea looked in at the two figures lying close together in front of the flickering fire, surrounded by a sea of photographs. Their bodies were almost touching and it was the natural ease with which they lay side by side that made Bea marvel in a not entirely comfortable way. She remembered how Tom and Jenny had sprawled on the floor together playing board games or cards. It felt like watching a replay of something disturbing but without being able to say precisely why.

Before she knocked and went inside, Bea wondered if her misgivings about the innocuous scene caught at her because nothing was deemed entirely innocent in the world any more.

Both Adam and Jenny looked up, startled, as she came into the room. They had been so immersed in what they were doing that Bea felt she had interrupted their peaceful afternoon.

'Mum! You gave me a shock.' Jenny got up dizzily, as if she had been sleeping.

'I've brought you and Adam a cake. It was such a foul afternoon I thought you might need cheering up.'

'How dear of you. I'll put the kettle on.' Jenny followed Bea's eyes. 'What do you think? It's not finished yet.'

Bea looked down at her dead granddaughter and the pain was unendurable for a minute. She sat down abruptly. 'I never knew you had so many photographs. What an enchanting collage you're both making. It's like being surprised by joy. Our wonderful, happy little Rosie . . .'

Jenny went over to Bea and they held each other silently. Adam slid out of the room into the kitchen. After a second he thought about putting the kettle on. Bea and Jenny joined him a minute later.

Bea smiled at him. 'I hope you're hungry, Adam. I'm experimenting on you. This is my try-out death-by-chocolate cake. I need your opinion on it.'

Adam grinned. 'I've never eaten so many cakes in my life until I came to Cornwall.'

Jenny laughed. 'I might tell you *I* did not have this many cakes in my childhood, they were strictly rationed. It is only since Bea became a granny that her cake repertoire has expanded. Darling, could you get another couple of logs, the fire's getting low.'

As they sat in front of the fire Bea said to them both, 'I'm very impressed by your will-power, but don't you two both miss television, especially in weather like this?'

Jenny turned to Adam. 'Speak first. Be honest.'

'If it was here, I suppose I would be tempted to turn it on for the things I used to watch. But I definitely get more work and music practice done in the week. I've never thought I wish we had a television, not once.'

'Good,' Jenny said. 'I don't miss it, Bea. None of us was a great watcher in London. Because I was always sewing, I preferred the radio. I enjoyed watching films with Tom. Men always watch more, I think.'

As Bea was driving home she thought about the function of television and how it dominated and distracted a household. How it brought the world and other lives into a house. If it was a mixed blessing, it did at least provide contrast, politics and debate. Without its intrusion into their daily lives it was possible that Jenny and Adam were evolving into an isolated, safe and reclusive world devoid of normal, real, humdrum social interactions. Once they shut their front door, closing themselves in and everyone else out, they seemed wrapped together in the world they were effortlessly making for themselves. It did not seem quite right and it could not last. Bea, describing the scene to James, found it difficult to voice her rather formless anxiety.

James said slowly, 'If Jenny were Adam's natural mother and they were as close, enjoyed being together so much, we would say it was unhealthy and the boy should mix with other boys more. We'd tell Jenny to let him go; that they both needed to lead more separate lives. But, Jenny is not Adam's real mother; the circumstances that have drawn them together are not normal, but they are very powerful. The complexities of Jenny bringing up Tom and Ruth's son *is* disturbing.'

'Is that why you take Adam off regularly and try to get him and Harry together at weekends?'

'Yes.'

Bea held out her hands to her own fire in a house that settled around her like a familiar cloak and closed her eyes. James was good at seamlessly translating her amorphous feelings into something both coherent and soothing.

'They were making an extraordinary montage out of hundreds of photographs of Rosie. It was beautifully done from the heart like a patchwork quilt of memories celebrating Rosie's short life. It wasn't a lament, James. It was a miraculous thing of joy. That's what they were doing when I arrived.'

SIXTY-TWO

I had the most wonderful dream. Tom, Rosie and I were walking in a park. Rosie was running ahead of us in small red Wellington boots, scattering brown crunchy sycamore leaves. She was laughing as she stamped her small feet and Tom, pushing her empty pushchair, ran after her kicking the deep piles of leaves into the air. As we ran our breath made small clouds in the cold air and I thought, *Oh, God, I had a dream that they were dead, Rosie and Tom.*

Then I woke in a strange house with the rain lashing the windows and streaming down the outside walls, and the sound of the gutters overflowing, and I lay motionless, knowing that running together among autumn leaves was the dream and this, now, here was the reality.

I got out of bed, pulled on socks and an ancient cardigan over my pyjamas and went into the sitting room. The fire was dead but the room smelt of pungent apple logs, reminding me of Christmas and childhood and feeling safe.

I switched on a small lamp, and crouched on the floor and gazed down at my lost family. They gazed back, caught in moments of happiness, of being. I thought, *I can never take a single moment of my life for granted ever again.*

Tragedy hovers, ready to strike. It seemed to me in the still room that it was not a case of *if* it ever strikes, but *when*.

Tomorrow I would mount the picture and mould a frame, and put it up in the passage that Adam and I passed a hundred times a day, and they would be part of my life again – never lost.

I sat in a chair and watched the sky lighten over the water. The curlews warbled and the house creaked round me, and Adam slept with his door half open as he always did, and I felt his presence in the house, a warm, sweet nearness that kept hopelessness at bay. It was time to tell Adam about the day Tom died. It was time that he knew, because it was a fragment of a story he wanted and needed to be part of. Then we must put it behind us, the memory of violent death. I must put up the living reminders we made yesterday to celebrate the lives Rosie and Tom lived beside me. I made tea and crawled back to bed.

As I did so Adam appeared at the door rumpled with sleep. 'Are you OK, Jenny?' he whispered.

I nodded. He stood quite still in the doorway, shivering, hopeful at five in the morning.

I lifted the duvet. 'Get in,' I whispered back. In one quick movement he was under the covers and we both slipped back into sleep, comforted and warmed. The night before Tom and Rosie died there had been a storm like this. When we woke I would tell Adam about the morning after the storm, the day Tom died.

SIXTY-THREE

I wake early and get out of bed carefully so that I don't disturb the still sleeping Rosie and Tom. We want to take Rosie on her first trip to the zoo and I don't want her to be tired. I go into the kitchen, switch on the kettle and climb up to the empty workroom to check the workload for the day. I don't want any crisis to hold up my last day with Tom. I leave notes for Flo and general instructions for the girls.

Danielle and I are lucky. All the women who work for us are enthusiastic and dedicated, and I try to banish my guilt at taking a whole day off during a busy week. This time tomorrow Tom will have his kit packed and will be roaming the flat restlessly. He will already have gone in spirit.

After the storm last night, the day is strangely still, the streets below washed clean, everything quiet, as if still sleeping. I go to the window, open it and lean out to breathe in the smell of rain. Great wet patches lie dark on the houses opposite and there are leaves and branches strewn across the road and pavement below. Poor little damaged town trees. I feel unaccountably happy and stretch like a cat at the thought of the day ahead.

When I go down to make coffee for Tom I hear him in

the bathroom with the shower on. As I carry two mugs across the landing there is an outraged little bellow from Rosie, waking in a large empty bed to find both her parents missing. We appear in the doorway together, laughing at her until she giggles and climbs on to Tom's knee.

Looking at me over Rosie's head, Tom says, 'I thought I'd go and collect the Mini early, then if there's a problem with the MOT I can borrow or hire a car from the garage.'

'The garage hasn't rung, so I guess it must have passed all right.'

Tom looks down at Rosie. 'I'm going to get the car, little pudding, then we are going to the zoo with Mummy. How's that? Will you put your best dress on for Daddy?'

'Are you walking?' I ask, lifting Rosie from his knee.

'It's too nice to catch a bus. Anyway the garage won't be open yet.'

He pulls on jeans and a T-shirt, and plants a kiss on the top of my head. 'See you both later.'

I have just got into the bath with Rosie, who insists on getting in too, when I hear the telephone ringing upstairs. Danielle answers it, then the girls blow in the front door and clatter noisily up to the machine room like baby elephants. I start to sponge a giggling Rosie when Flo knocks on the bathroom door. 'Jen? Danielle needs to talk to you straight away. Shall I finish Rosie off?'

I get out of the bath, wrap a towel round myself and go into my bedroom. Danielle is pacing up and down, impatient and excited.

'What on earth's happened?' I ask, drying myself.

'That was Antonio on the phone. He is here for a flying visit and he wants us to meet him. He has a business proposition.'

'You already do business with him. He exports some of our clothes.'

'No, no, this is different, Jenny. He wants to meet *you* this trip. I am sure he wants us to design for him. A contract with an Italian company is what we have been waiting for. We can expand! There are endless possibilities for overseas export. We could really make our mark.'

'Wait, wait, Danielle.' I reel away from her enthusiasm this early in the morning. 'It's very sudden, isn't it? We hardly know him.'

As I dress, Danielle sits on the bed eagerly explaining. 'I have spoken to him many times when I meet him in Milan. I tell you he likes the clothes we produce. I have checked him out. He has a good reputation. He says your label has sold well in Milan and he likes some of the pieces we do together. I thought he might approach us but I did not say anything to you because it was silly to get our hopes up.' She pauses for breath. 'It is *your* clothes he is really interested in. He thinks they are perfect for the young Italian market.'

'Well, it's flattering, but . . .'

'He is in London and he wants to meet us. He had a cancelled meeting. We are to ring his hotel and leave a message if we can make lunch.'

'Oh, *no*, Danielle, not today.' I pull on jeans and a shirt.

'He is only here for one day. This is so important.'

So is my day with Tom. My heart sinks. I have never seen Danielle so excited. 'Oh, bloody, bloody hell,' I wail. 'Why today? Why not tomorrow? Any day but today.'

'I could go alone, but it doesn't look good. He wants to meet you before he makes a decision, I know it.'

I give up, sick with disappointment. 'OK, Danielle. I guess we can't afford to throw up a chance like this.'

I hear Tom's key in the lock and he comes bounding up the stairs calling, 'Jen? The car's fine.' He stops as he sees Danielle in our room and takes in our faces. He knows the signs, it has happened before and it will happen again. 'Don't tell me something's come up?'

Danielle disappears and I explain.

His face falls. 'Oh, Jen, what a pity. Our last day together. Damn.'

'I'm so sorry. I don't know what to do.'

Tom says quickly, '*Of course* you must go and meet the Italian. You deserve this break. You all work incredibly hard and I know you are the best designer in London.'

I smile. 'Biased or what?'

'Absolutely not! You will be rich and famous one day. Look, darling, we'll get up early and go off somewhere for an hour or so tomorrow morning before I go.'

He is trying to make me feel better. 'It's not the same. I feel so guilty. I'm sorry . . .'

'Sh. It can't be helped.' He puts a finger on my nose.

'Will you and Rosie still go to the zoo?'

'Of course! We've got a date, haven't we, sweetheart?' He opens his arms to Rosie who has just come into the room squeaky clean in a new dress, all shiny and pink. 'You look delicious!' He swings her up under his arm. 'Come on, let's have coffee together, then we'll disappear and you can regale me with your triumphs tonight.'

I watch them from the top step. Tom straps Rosie into her car seat. Rosie turns and blows me kisses with a little fat hand and I blow them back to her. Just before he bends double to get into the car, Tom runs back to me, hugs me again and again, turning me round and round, kissing me, laughing. 'See you tonight. We'll bring back fish and chips and a huge bottle of wine. Have an exciting day.'

'And you. 'Bye, darling. 'Bye, Rosie. Be good.'

Tom's long legs disappear into the tiny car. I watch them in warm sunlight until the Mini sounds its horn and rounds the corner. Leaves from a sycamore tree float down, dance round me and land at my feet. I bend, feeling the dry, crumbly, brown-green texture of them. I feel such a surge of happiness in the life that I have that I close my eyes in sudden gratitude. Then I turn and go running up the stairs yelling for Danielle, wondering what on earth I should wear for this important lunch.

SIXTY-FOUR

Paolo Antonio is a thickset, compact Italian with an amazing smile. For some reason he is always known by his surname. He is dark, with body hair covering his arms and hands. He reminds me of a gangster out of a Mafioso film, but his smile and voice more than make up for his physical limitations. He speaks beautiful, almost perfect English.

He flatters both Danielle and me outrageously, in typical Italian fashion and I notice that there is a certain amount of flirting between him and Danielle. I smile to myself, wondering how much talk-talk has been discussed in bed.

'Jenny, I will explain my proposal. I have been exporting your clothes to Milano under your own label. They have sold very well indeed, but it is an expensive way for me to get your clothes into Italian shops. I cannot afford to sell your clothes in bulk and you cannot afford to design just for me. So this is my proposition. I would like to start a company near Milano making and selling expensive and exclusively English designs. I will put up the money for the sole right to sell your designs in Italy under the Antonio label.'

Antonio is watching my face carefully as he talks. 'Initially,

I would start with a small workforce making up your clothes to test the market. Milano is full of wealthy young Italian women with a penchant for casual English designs that are different. Labour is cheaper in Italy and fashion is taken seriously and considered big business. We have far less bureaucracy than you have here.'

He pauses. 'I have studied the market carefully. It would be more cost-effective to make your clothes from Milano than go on exporting on a regular basis from London.'

'For you, maybe,' I say. 'At the moment all our overheads are in one place and we can ensure the quality of the clothes we manufacture.'

'But your little workforce could not cope with the quantities I have in mind. You are both successful designers. Eventually you will be forced to expand, so why not expand in a place where you have a healthy growing market?'

Danielle is watching me anxiously. She has seen the potential for growth straight away, but she knows that somewhere in me there is a reluctance to take on more because of Rosie and Tom. 'We would not lose anything by designing under the Antonio label, Jenny. They will still be our designs.'

'We would lose our independence, our autonomy.' I turn to Antonio. 'Do you propose to market both our work?'

He hesitates. 'You design for a quite different market. I would concentrate on your work primarily, Jenny. It is the more modern, cheaper end of the market, for the young. Once established, I would introduce Danielle's work to a different age group of woman. I know that you have input into each other's work. This is why all your clothes are so beautifully detailed. You work together. Danielle has done a wonderful job of establishing a European market for you both. I will be capitalising on this. The way your clothes are beginning to be snapped up by wholesalers makes me realise that the potential for business is enormous.' He gives me his beautiful smile. 'I do not throw my money away, Jenny. I am a careful businessman.' He leans forward and touches my wrist tentatively with a forefinger. 'Think how you can give rein to your wonderful imagination. We can send round the world for any fabrics you need. Thailand, Singapore, anywhere! My money will give you more freedom in your work, not less.' He is very persuasive. 'Make use of my knowledge, my business sense. I know my market. If I put capital into this, what have you to lose, my dear girl?'

Safety. I love my tiny manageable workforce. Change is risky, frightening, but I have to think of Danielle. It's her business too.

As if reading my thoughts, Danielle says, 'Jen, we are getting more work than we can handle. We have been over-loaded for weeks. By transferring our overseas market to Italy we would be solving problems we have been putting off.'

I know she's right. We've had to take on more girls and convert one of the second-floor rooms.

'Danielle is the ideal person to set-up the project for me. She knows Milano well and of course she speaks Italian. Could you manage without her, Jenny?'

'It would be difficult.'

Danielle shrugs in her expressive way. 'Pff! It would not be for ever. I would so much enjoy the challenge of helping to set-up a business again from scratch.'

'Would we be able to support our regular high street market without you designing? Because, as you know, they are our bread and butter. It's taken years to build up that market, those contacts.'

'There is no reason why I should not design from Italy even if I cannot produce the same volume of work. We are talking about a short flight, less time than it takes you to go home to Cornwall.'

I grin at her. 'That's true. You really want to go for this, don't you?'

Danielle leans towards me. 'We could take on a student, a young designer straight from college to help you. We could afford it now.'

I shake my head to clear it. 'Oh God! I hate huge decisions.'

Antonio pours the last of the wine. 'My dear Jenny, you cannot make a decision instantaneously. You must go away and think about my proposal and let me know. Talk to each other and then ring me in Milano.' He touches my arm again. 'I would love to have you designing for me.' His hand lies square and dark on the arm of my cream jacket. Long dark hairs run across the top of it. I am unsure whether this repulses me or gives me a small frisson of sexual excitement. He wants my designs and Danielle's business acumen.

Finishing the last of my wine, I think of Tom and Rosie and wonder where they are. I suddenly have this overriding urge to run out of the restaurant to find them. I glance at my watch. It is nearly three o'clock. Will they still be at the zoo?

I would have loved to have seen Rosie's expressive little face as she gazed at the animals. Regret suddenly surfaces for this missed day with Tom. It feels overwhelming, like a form of sorrow. It is the wine. Too much wine at lunch always makes me maudlin.

SIXTY-FIVE

When we get back home, Danielle and I sit in the conservatory drinking coffee and discussing Antonio and his proposition with Flo.

Full of wine, I fall asleep in the sun and I only wake up when the girls clatter down the stairs at five thirty. Tom should be back by now and I wonder where else he could have taken Rosie. I go upstairs and have a shower to wake myself up. Rosie will be getting very tired unless she's had a nap.

I go up to my office and pretend to do some paperwork. I make a few phone calls, then I come down again to make tea, still feeling heady and hung-over.

By six thirty I am anxious. What can they be doing? Tom sometimes forgets Rosie is only two. Why hasn't he rung me? I try his mobile but it's switched off, not even voice mail.

Flo, coming into the kitchen and seeing my face, says calmly, 'The traffic's going to be awful out there if Tom has misjudged and hit the rush hour. Don't worry. They'll be back any minute. Rosie will be fast asleep in her car seat.'

I take my tea into my bedroom and lie on top of the bed. I want them home. I want them to come home now. I have a sudden thought and go to Tom's desk. His mobile phone is sitting there. He so rarely forgets to take it. He can't even ring me if he's stuck in traffic.

Faraway across the city the wail of a police siren starts up, followed by another and another and another. My blood runs cold. Please God, not a major accident while they are out there. Tom should have headed home before the rush hour. My heart hammers with anxiety.

They must be nearly home. At any moment they will turn the corner into the road and Tom will sound the horn and park noisily. He will carry a tired little Rosie in and complain about the traffic, and apologise and pull his hand through his hair and look guilty and dishevelled. Any moment. Listen, there's a car now.

I jump off the bed and go to the window, but it is another car in the road below. I look down the wide, tree-lined street, willing the small car to appear, but it does not.

The wail of sirens seems to be coming from all over the city. The dusk is full of this one heart-stopping sound. There will be nothing Tom can do if he is caught up in an incident. He will know how frantic I am and he'll be swearing at himself for leaving his phone. I lie on the bed again with a throbbing headache and somehow, despite my anxiety, I doze off in the quiet house.

I am woken, jerked out of an unnatural sleep, by the door-bell. Before I can gather myself I hear Flo going downstairs. I struggle upright and switch on the lamp. Eight thirty. I leap off the bed in panic. This has to be Tom and Rosie. He must have forgotten his key.

I reach the bottom of the stairs as Flo opens the front door. A policewoman and a policeman stand on the doorstep. 'Mrs Holland? Mrs Tom Holland?'

Everything is going into slow motion as I watch myself walk towards them in the doorway.

Flo gently pulls me to one side to let them come in. She puts her hand under my elbow. I stand facing them. A sick, curdling sensation rises in my stomach. I can still hear the sirens. The blood pounding in my head is so loud that I clutch Flo dizzily. I can't speak, I stand frozen, staring, trying to read what has happened in their faces.

The policeman clears his throat. 'Mrs Holland, could you just confirm that you or your husband owns a vehicle with the registration WH20VTT?'

I nod. For a second I grasp at hope. *Maybe the car's been stolen. Maybe Tom's been booked for some traffic offence.*

'Was your husband driving the car today?'

Why is he asking me that?

'Yes, of course he was driving the car.' I am trying not to scream at them. 'My little girl is with him. Will you *please*, for God's sake, tell me what's happened?'

The policeman turns away and speaks into his phone. The policewoman moves nearer to me. 'I'm very sorry, Mrs Holland. I'm afraid your husband and child have been involved in a bad . . . traffic accident. We had to be certain it was your husband driving.'

I am not listening to her words. I just want to go wherever Tom and Rosie have been taken. I circle both police frantically to get to the door, clutching blindly at the large glass knob. 'Take me to them. How badly are they hurt? Where are they? Quickly, *please*, we're wasting time. I must go to them.'

The policewoman puts her hand out to stop me. 'Mrs Holland, I'm so sorry. Both your husband and child were killed instantly. Death was immediate. I assure you they could have felt nothing. I'm very sorry.'

I back away from them and shake my head violently. I know it's not true. They are hurt but they are not dead. They are not dead.

'Come upstairs, darling.' Danielle is suddenly on the other side of me and she is whispering to me in French, and she and a policeman gently propel me up to the sitting room. They sit me in Tom's chair and Flo brings me a brandy. She tries to place it in my hands, but her own are shaking too much. Danielle kneels in front of me, folds my hands round the glass and makes me drink. Her face is like a ghost.

I sit clutching the brandy glass, my eyes riveted to the policeman's face. In a moment I will wake up sweating and clinging to Tom in the dark, explaining this terrible nightmare, and he will hold me, comfort me, smile at my horror. I will wake up. *I will. I will.*

I close my eyes and beg, 'Please, please tell me it's not true.'

The policeman says, 'I'm so very sorry, love.'

I can hear the policewoman in the kitchen making tea. I am up on the ceiling looking down at us all.

'What happened?' I whisper.

The policeman hesitates. He can't meet my eyes. 'At the moment it's not clear what exactly happened, but it seems an articulated lorry went into the back of your husband's car. He didn't stand a chance. The petrol tanks went up in both vehicles. So far we don't know why. The police are still on the scene. I assure you it was too quick for either your husband or child to know anything.'

I stare at his face. I watch his mouth making comforting but meaningless words. *Rosie, my Rosie in the back of the car, skull crushed like an egg. Tom, for a second frozen with horror, looking back in the driving mirror. Then wham. It's all over.*

'Did the lorry driver die?'

344

'I'm afraid so. A cyclist and two pedestrians were also badly injured.'

There is silence in the room. Danielle and Flo are sitting on the arms of Tom's chair beside me. It does not feel real. None of this seems real. Flo gets up and goes into the kitchen to help the policewoman. I think how old she looks.

I stare at the policeman. 'Where are they? Where are my husband and child?'

He swallows and cannot answer me, and I grow cold as ice. 'Do you know?' I whisper to him. 'My husband survived the war in Iraq. He survived Northern Ireland and Bosnia, Kosovo and Afghanistan and I have no idea where else. For all those years I was terrified he would be killed and he dies with my child, in a traffic accident, when he was supposed to be safe.'

The policeman's face changes. He walks towards me. 'Mrs Holland, which regiment was your husband with?

'He's with the SAS. He was on leave . . .'

The policeman wheels away from me and leaves the room. He calls out something to the policewoman, then he is running down the stairs and out of the front door to the police car. Danielle and I look at each other. We get up and go to the window. The policeman is holding his car radio, gesturing with his arms.

The policewoman moves out of the kitchen, talking urgently into her radio phone. As she too runs down the stairs I hear the words: 'Alert all units. Tell forensics . . . Special Forces . . . Bomb . . .'

It is the moment I know for sure. I go back to Tom's chair and look around our sitting room with its elegant fireplace and high ceilings. I examine closely the beautiful cornices Tom and I painted together.

I understand, what I already suspected in some part of me, as soon as I heard all the sirens, as soon as Tom and

Rosie did not come home. It is not a bomb in some foreign land that has killed Tom, but a bomb here in London, a few miles from me, when he had my child with him.

I wish I had gone with them this morning. I wish I had died with Tom and Rosie. I wish we had all died together.

SIXTY-SIX

We sit huddled together as the house fills with plain-clothes policemen and army personnel. They go over our home inch by inch. They dissect the phone, make lists of all the people who enter and leave this place.

An army doctor comes and gives me some pills. I won't go to bed. I curl up in Tom's chair and Flo brings me a rug. It is like seeing everything from the wrong end of a telescope. I hear, from a long way away, Danielle and Flo being asked endless and repeated questions about the car and the garage; about Tom's movements that morning. It seems to me pointless.

Danielle lights a fire and we spend the night in front of it, close together for comfort, our chairs in a circle as men come and go around us, as if the house belonged to them. It goes silent for a while. Danielle and Flo sleep. As it gets light I get out of my chair and weave dizzily to the bathroom. There are two policewomen in the kitchen.

I splash cold water on my face and move back on to the landing, holding on to the walls.

One of the policewomen comes out of the kitchen. 'Are you all right, love?'

All right? I nod.

'I'll make you a cup of tea,' she says.

I walk back into the sitting room, open the curtains a little and look down into the road. There is a policeman guarding the front of the house. What do they think is going to happen?

Then I see that at the end of the road there are television cameras and a mass of photographers camped behind police tape. I go back to my chair and curl into it with my head under the rug. Tom's death is news. An off-duty soldier is murdered in London with his child on a summer's afternoon.

I shake my head to release me from the image of Rosie in the car. I moan and beg God to take the image from me. *It is not bearable. I will not be able to bear it. My tiny innocent Rosie.*

Flo looks old in sleep. Danielle looks sallow and ill. I notice her angular thinness. The three of us will never be the same again. Our lives have been taken from us. I drink my tea, sleepless, my eyes heavy and dry. It is still early when the regimental army padre who married us arrives.

Suddenly, running up the stairs comes Damien, Rosie's godfather. I know immediately that he and Tom must have been working together. I run to the door and he catches me up and rocks with me in the thin grey morning of another day. He cannot speak and neither can I.

I cling to him. He is big and solid and safe. 'Why? Why Tom, Damien?' I whisper.

He lets me go. 'I don't know. Tom was always incredibly careful. Something went wrong. We'll find out who is responsible. No one is going to rest until we've got them. Maisie is on her way. She'll stay with you as long as you need her.'

'You really don't know?'

His voice breaks. 'I really don't know.'

Everyone tries to stop me watching the news or seeing the papers full of the blown-up car and the pictures of Tom and

348

Rosie alive and well. How do they get these pictures? I look down at the other people who died too, merely because they happened to be passing at that moment.

As the days pass, I can only wonder at the sheer cruelty of fate that prevented me from dying too. The three of us should have been together. I think constantly of how I can put this right. It keeps me occupied. It keeps me sane.

Hundreds of flowers have been placed at the roadside where Tom and Rosie died and I brave the cameras to go with Flo and Danielle to look. I am touched by the small bunches placed by children with sweet and simple messages. I recognise the names, too, of the Muslim girls in the workroom. I crouch behind my sunglasses reading them.

The lorry driver's wife writes to me. She tells me that her husband was once a soldier who did his time in Northern Ireland. The irony of his death does not escape her.

I have so many touching letters from army wives and mothers who have lost their husbands or sons. They write poignantly from the heart and I don't feel quite so alone. The army close ranks round me and protect me night and day from the persistent and merciless press. It is something they do well. It is as if, for a short while, the world mourns with me in shock and breathes in my grief.

The house is stilled of laughter and of small pattering footsteps. The girls in the workroom no longer play their music. I need to keep working but when they see me their gentle faces fill with sorrow. Each day there is a small gift left for me in my office.

The trees begin to lose their leaves in the London parks. There is the smell of bonfires as winter crouches round the corner. Life grinds on in a strange faraway existence. Neither the police nor the army know yet who placed the bomb under Tom's car. They do not know or they cannot tell me. Suicide bombers are easier to identify by group. A home-made bomb under a car could be almost anyone.

The world moves on. Another tragedy happens to someone else.

I watch Flo's grief but cannot help her. She gave up her flat and her privacy to move in with Tom and me and help me with Rosie. We are her family. She loves us all unconditionally. I watch her stifle her anguish; hear her walking about at night; see her diminished and lost by their deaths.

Danielle's refuge is in an anger she cannot completely hide from me. She is furious with God but she is also furious with Tom because of Rosie. She believes that Tom put Rosie at risk. I don't know why, but she does. It upsets me, unsettles me. It makes me go to places I do not want to go.

I sit night after night in the window seat of our bedroom staring out at the night sky. I watch people in the road getting in and out of their cars, going out, doing normal things. The world has not stopped because Tom and Rosie are dead. It is busily going on down there. I feel a strange surprise that this can be so.

I go into Rosie's room. I lie on her small bed and see what she saw on first waking: the beautiful French doll within reach; a blue rabbit with a chewed paw; a large fawn bear Tom had bought her; small fabric dolls I had made out of odds and ends.

On the floor is a beautiful doll's house that Tom's parents bought for her when they were in London. It is hardly used because Rosie was still too small to manoeuvre the tiny catches. Her small hands were not yet dexterous enough to make the tiny furniture stay upright. Her toys lie scattered on the floor where she left them. Open 'Mr Men' books lying on her bean bag. Mrs Tiggy Winkle and Peter Rabbit. Wooden bricks lie in her little cart. I want everything to stay exactly the same, just as she left it. I bend to her duvet and close my eyes and breathe in her warm baby smell, the very essence of Rosie. I see and hear her everywhere in the house.

Before he leaves to fly back to active duty, I ask Damien the question that keeps going round my head: 'Could Tom have known there was even the slightest danger that day? I know he checked the car that morning before he put Rosie in it.'

'Tom couldn't possibly have known he was being watched. He would have stayed well away from you if he had thought there was any danger to you, Rosie, or his household. He was a true professional and he would never have taken risks. He was in London. How many of us would think someone would place a bomb under our car while we are taking our children to the zoo?'

'I know that really. I just had to ask.'

'Doing the job we do carries some risk, Jenny. I check my car every morning, it's habit, but not every time I get out of it. Do you think we would ever come home if we thought our wives and children were in danger?' He holds me to him for a moment. 'Tom was the target, not Rosie. That is the double tragedy and the despicable crime. However careful we are, we cannot prevent betrayal.'

'Is that what it was?'

'With the work we do it's possible. We'll find out.'

I know I cannot ask him more. I do not really want to know.

I watch him climb into his car and drive away. Apart from Damien, the army part of my life with Tom has gone. However kind people are we will drift apart. The wide street is empty except for curled brown leaves like small dormice blowing hither and thither. I feel as directionless and pointless as those scattering leaves.

SIXTY-SEVEN

'Then you found me,' Adam said hastily, because Jenny's face was pale and desolate. He put out his hand and closed it round her arm gently.

Jenny smiled. 'Then I found you.'

Adam turned on his back and closed his eyes. That was his father's last day on this earth. What had he been doing on the exact day that Tom took Rosie to the zoo? A familiar sorrow started up in him. He turned to Jenny, propping his chin in his hands. 'Why did the house fill up with policemen? Why were they searching your house?'

'It's what happens when someone is killed. In Tom's case they wanted to see if the phone had been tapped. If there was anything in his papers that might give a clue to why someone had put a bomb under his car. They didn't find anything but it all took a long time because we have so many people working for us. People come and go in that London house all the time and . . .'

Adam waited.

'Most of the girls who work for us are Muslim. It was awful for them, Adam, they all had to be investigated, all their families. Not one of them left us. Not one of them complained or was bitter. It was humbling.'

Adam nodded. No wonder Jenny had been strange when he first met her. No wonder she had nearly gone mad with grief when she saw him.

'I don't want you to dwell on Tom's death, Adam. I didn't tell you to make you sad. I told you because we've been talking so much about his life and his death is a part of how he lived his life. Darling boy, you've helped me so much. You are a part of him and you make me want to go on living, and I am so grateful for having you in my life. But now we move on, together, don't we?'

Adam nodded.

Jenny looked at her watch. 'I need to sleep for a while. It's your home study day, isn't it, so you must work and practise. Then I shall take you into St Ives and buy you and Harry fish and chips. We won't talk of Tom's death again. OK?'

'OK.'

Adam knew Jenny meant him to get up and go to his own bed but he could not leave her. She turned over away from him and pulled her knees up to her chin with a tired little sigh. Adam looked at her mass of curly hair on the pillow and felt strangely choked. She was so small. He wanted to stay guard in case she needed him.

He slid down the bed and lay still. After a while he thought she was silently crying. Unsure how to comfort her, he turned away, moving slightly towards the middle of the bed so that she could feel the warmth of his back. Then they both slept.

SIXTY-EIGHT

Danielle telephoned me as she ran to catch a flight to Paris with Ruth. 'I must warn you, Jen. Antonio rang me to ask if there was any chance of you meeting him in London. I told him no chance. I think, maybe he plans to come down to see you in Cornwall.'

My heart jumped. 'Danielle, did you make it clear . . . ?'

'Yes, I made it quite clear. I do not think he has any intention of pressurising you. I have to go now.' Danielle's words jumped as she ran.

'We – are – back – tomorrow – night. Be – nice – to – Antonio, Jenny.'

I went out into the garden to feed the birds. I wished now that I had never let Danielle take my sketches to show Antonio. I did not want the outside world coming in. I wanted life to roll gently on in just the way it was doing. I had my own plans.

The morning was heavy with grey cloud. The days were winter short and melancholy. I turned and went back into the house. When the phone rang I knew it would be Antonio. He asked if he could fly down to see me for a day. I had had time to think about what I was going to say. 'Antonio,

I don't want you to waste your time. I have no intention of working seriously.'

'You think these designs I have in my hand are not serious? I do not come to put pressure on you, merely to talk for a few hours if you would be so kind as to grant me your time.'

I could hear the amusement in his voice. For Danielle's sake I could not be churlish. I told him I had to be at Newquay airport on Friday to put Adam on the plane to Gatwick. I could meet him on the incoming flight, if that wasn't too early.

He assured me it was perfect. It would give us time to talk and he would return to London in the evening. I heaved a sigh of relief. One whole day was not too bad an invasion.

It was half-term and Ruth was taking Adam to Birmingham. They were meeting Peter, who was there for a conference. Peter had booked for a concert by the visiting London Philharmonic and Adam was over the moon. He was looking forward to seeing Peter and I was glad. He was also secretly excited to be flying on his own.

We stood together at the tiny airport at Newquay waiting for the passengers to disembark from the incoming flight. Antonio was as distinctive as some exotic animal as he walked across the tarmac.

Adam grinned. 'He looks very Italian. How long is he staying?'

'He's only here for the day.' I hugged him. 'Listen, you, have a good time. See you next week. Take care. Stay put when you get to Gatwick so Ruth doesn't miss you.'

'Yeah, yeah, yeah. I'll ring you, Jenny. I'll tell you what I'm doing.' He ran backwards, laughing, then shot off after a trail of passengers and I turned to greet Antonio.

He beamed at me. 'It is so good to see you again. You are lovely as ever.'

He kissed both my cheeks and we walked to the car.

'So, this is where you bury yourself at the end of England.'

'Afraid so. It's good of you to come.'

'It is my pleasure.'

Antonio was quiet as we drove back to the house. He looked out of the window with interest but he did not prattle or try to talk business. It was still early and as we reached the causeway the sea on our right was a rough royal blue against a dramatic sky. He sighed, leaning forward to gaze at the flash of coastline.

We turned for the Saltings. There was a flood tide and as I stopped outside the house seabirds called out into a day shiny and fresh from early rain. Antonio stood silently facing the swollen water, listening, seemingly captivated. I felt myself warming to him.

Once inside the house I felt suddenly awkward. Antonio smiled at me as he took in the small rooms. 'This is charming, Jenny. I am beginning to understand your need to be here in this little house by the water, full of small calling birds and changing sky. This is the place for an artist.'

We smiled at each other. 'I'll put the coffee on. If you want to wash your hands or anything, it's just through there.'

I set out breakfast in the kitchen and worried about the strength of the coffee. We sat opposite each other eating croissants and Antonio amused me with stories of mutual acquaintances in the fashion world. I thought as he only had one day in Cornwall I would take him in to St Ives – in summer it was a little like the Amalfi coast. And I could see if James or Bea wanted to join us for lunch. I might run out of things to say to Antonio by then.

After breakfast we moved into the sitting room and Antonio got out my designs from a beautiful pale pigskin case. 'Your belts and bags. I can sell unlimited numbers of these, I assure you.'

I took him into the tiny conservatory and showed him some belts I had made the previous week. Flo had sent down some of my tools by parcel post and the sheer pleasure of using my hands again had taken me by surprise. I took a breath and turned to him. 'I've met a little group of artists and we've formed a small co-operative to sell our work in Cornwall. The talent down here is amazing. Many of the artists and craftsmen sell worldwide, but choose to live and work down here. There is some prodigious talent, young, as yet unknown, painters, ceramicists, glass blowers, potters. The jewellery is exquisite.'

Antonio was listening intently.

'I decided to join them, partly to test the market, but also I wanted to discover local people who could make up my designs. These belts and bags are young and seasonal. Next year they will be last year.'

'But in Italy they can be next year. So from where do you sell? Where is your shopfront?'

'Everyone shares the rent of a shop in St Ives. There is a small workshop at the back. The local arty shops around Cornwall come to the workshop, see what they like and order from us direct. I only joined them last week. There are six of us so it means we can pool our resources and also employ local people. I don't want to get too involved, but it is a way of . . .'

'Establishing yourself down here?'

I hesitated. 'Maybe.'

'Do Danielle and Florence know?'

'No. Not yet. I've only told my parents. I will tell Danielle and Flo. It's just . . . they'd both like me to go back to London and perhaps I need to prove that I don't have to be there in person to design or contribute to the business. Do you see?'

Antonio started to laugh. 'Jenny, where has this story come from that you no longer have any ambition to design? Danielle gives me a lecture on not putting any pressure on you to produce work for me.'

'She's right. I'm not really sure of anything. I'm still feeling my way. For now, this feels OK, manageable.'

Antonio turned away and looked at my sketches pinned up between the windows, then down at the work I was experimenting with. He must have been wondering why he was here. I would not be able to produce work fast enough for him and a local market. In London they were working at full capacity with expensive designs that brought in big money, not the equivalent of peanuts.

I thought suddenly that both Antonio and Danielle were humouring me in the hope that I would get back to full-time designing. Maybe I would. I just didn't know. I walked back into the kitchen to make more coffee.

After a moment Antonio followed me. 'Do people down here know what a well-known London designer you are?'

'Well, I grew up here, so some people know my work.'

Antonio sat down at the kitchen table and loosened his tie, and suddenly he looked younger and attractive, and for a flash I was back in his villa after Tom died. I felt the colour flood to my face and moved to fix the filter on the jug.

When I turned back to the table Antonio said, 'Well, darling, it seems to me that you are being very sensible. You wish to prove to yourself, quietly out of the limelight, that you have not lost your touch. Down here you can design gently. You can please yourself. You are politely showing me that you are not ready yet for the pressure of me and Danielle?'

I smiled and sat down opposite him. I had forgotten how nice he was. 'Poor Danielle. She will be very cross with me. It is kind of you to be even remotely interested in these very simple designs.'

'I am not being kind. I know what sells. How would you

358

feel if I were to have the bulk of your Cornish designs made up in Italy under a separate label? Would you be willing? It would be less remunerative.'

It was a good idea. I said, after a minute's thought, 'Yes, I would be willing, but don't sell them under a new label. Market them with the clothes you export to Italy under the Danielle Brown label. Then it is all under one umbrella. Danielle and Flo will be happy that I am designing for you and I do not feel I have deserted the business completely.'

Antonio laughed. 'Done! We will talk later, darling. May we walk by the sea? Will you show me a little of your world?'

I took him in to St Ives. I showed him the tiny co-operative shop on the front by the harbour and he bought some lovely jewellery. For a girlfriend? I wondered. I knew he was not married. We roamed around the small galleries and I took him to the Tate, then the Barbara Hepworth garden. He was easy to be with because he was so genuinely enchanted and interested in everything.

James and Bea walked down to meet us for lunch. We ate at the Elba, which had once been the old lifeboat station. It was sophisticated and Mediterranean, and I wanted to show him that Cornwall had much besides its seductive coastline.

Bea was enchanted with Antonio and practised her terrible Italian on him. It made Dad and me wince, but Antonio flattered her efforts with a straight face and inimitable charm.

After lunch I took him to the island, across Porthmeor beach and up to Clodgy Head and the cliffs.

We went back to Tredrea for tea and Bea and James showed him round the house and garden, and I sat in the window seat above the harbour and opened a text from Adam: 'Plane cool. Mum at Gtw. Luv A.'

Antonio was very relaxed with my parents. I supposed he must be around forty, but he seemed younger when animated.

He and James became immersed in a conversation about English war poets.

Dad was the first to notice the bad weather coming in and rang Newquay airport to check on the early evening flight to Gatwick. He was told that all flights in and out of Newquay that evening were cancelled.

Bea and James immediately told Antonio that he must stay the night. He was anxious and embarrassed. 'No, no, I will not put you to trouble. I will go to a hotel.'

'Well, if you'd rather. But you are very welcome.' Bea and James disappeared into the kitchen.

Antonio was looking out of the window, nervously jiggling the coins in his pocket. 'How quickly the weather changes, Jenny. It is rather alarming.'

I smiled. 'Please don't feel trapped. I should have warned you about the vagaries of flying from Newquay. Will you miss anything important?'

He turned from the window. 'Nothing my assistant cannot handle. I am embarrassed. I do not want to outstay a wonderful day with you and your parents. I think a hotel will be less trouble for you all.'

'This is a big house and my parents will love having you, but if you prefer to go to a hotel to work or chill out they will not be in the least offended.'

'Oh no. I *hate* hotels. Then I thank you for your kindness.' He bent quickly and lightly kissed my hand with a smile of relief. 'I see why this place is right for you and how it must fire your imagination. Colours change in a moment and the elements must get into your soul.'

Dad came in with drinks on a tray and I went up to the top of the house to make up my bed with clean sheets and lay out towels. As well as a view up here Antonio would have his own bathroom. I would sleep downstairs tonight so that I could drive him early to Newquay.

James took him to the pub while Bea cooked and I laid the table.

'He is utterly charming, Jen. I do like him.' Mum was pink and happy. She loved new people.

I hugged her. 'Maybe it's because you can practise your execrable Italian?'

'You're very rude.'

She insisted we used the Venetian wineglasses she and James had bought on honeymoon. Dad and Antonio came back slightly merry. Antonio had been introduced to Cornish beer. I should have warned him.

The house was warm, the table flickered in the candlelight. The harbour below us was full of small glittering lights in the rain, signalling an inhabited outside world, while we were comfortable and secure up here in our eyrie. I used to think when I was a child how lucky I was. I still felt it.

I looked at my parents' faces in the candlelight, ageless to me. Home was a refuge that never changed or faltered in love, welcome and security. What would I have done without Bea and James these last months? I watched them chatting happily to Antonio, a man they had only met today but decided they liked unequivocally.

I raised my glass, suddenly overcome by love for them. 'Bea, James, to you!'

They turned to me, surprised, and I added quietly, touching their glasses, 'Just to say thank you, in case I ever forget.' I laughed, embarrassed, and they laughed too.

Antonio raised his glass to them as well. He met my eyes and held them. They showed regard and something impossible to read. 'Why do you sometimes call your parents by their Christian names?'

Dad laughed. 'She grew up with a little friend who obviously called us Bea and James. She started to do it too and it became a habit. She doesn't know she's doing it!'

After supper Antonio insisted on helping me clear up. Bea and James went and watched the news, and we talked business as we filled the dishwasher. If the weather had not lifted by tomorrow Antonio would have to catch a train to Paddington as he had an evening flight back to Milan.

I took him up to my room. 'I hope you've got everything you need.' I showed him the tiny bathroom and went to draw the curtains.

'Leave them, darling. I like to see the sky and hear the sea.' He came to the window and looked down at the hundreds of lights spread below us round the harbour. 'A bewitching place . . .' He turned to look down at me.

'I'll say goodnight.' I felt awkward. I had drunk quite a lot of wine.

'Goodnight, Jenny. I fear I have taken your room. I shall sleep well.'

Antonio's voice was like a caress. He bent to me and as I raised my cheek for his goodnight kiss I wobbled and had to hold on to his arms. They felt warm underneath my fingers, warm and surprisingly strong. Desire shot through me and I had to fight an instinctive intake of breath.

His mouth hovered for a moment near mine as if the belt of sexual tension had been mutual. He caught the side of my mouth with his. I felt his hands tighten on my shoulders and I could not move away. I felt the pressure of his fingers and his mouth stayed quite still against my own. I drew away, shaking, met his eyes, whispered goodnight and fled.

I threw off my clothes and fell into bed. I thought of Antonio above me still standing by the window looking out at the closed in night sky. I had wanted him to throw me on the bed and just take me. Just take me. Fuck me quickly without words.

I tossed about on the bed, my treacherous body betraying Tom, burning me up. *I want to feel his dark square body*

362

on top of mine. I want that soft voice in my ear urging me on. I want to crawl up those stairs step by step and see him waiting for me. With a moan I sat up. *I'm drunk. In the morning I'm going to die a hundred mortified deaths for having these thoughts.*

I got out of bed, wrapped an old eiderdown round me and went and sat in the window. This bedroom had a view of the island and the cross on the tiny chapel was illuminated in the cloudy night. On the horizon the ocean moved like a thin snake.

I remembered with rising embarrassment that I had once slept in the same bed as Antonio in Italy. I had blanked it from my mind. It seemed so improbable now and long ago. As if it had happened to someone else.

I stood up. If I had climbed into his bed once from loneliness and need, could I not do it again? I went to the foot of the stairs and looked up. Not a sound came from above. The house creaked and breathed around me. My courage deserted me. I turned and went back to my cold bed.

I miss Adam's sweet warmth. I did not like sleeping alone any longer.

SIXTY-NINE

Antonio's villa stands on a hill facing the sea. Between the house and the water lies a path through trees to the beach. It is all so beautiful and unexpected that Danielle and I are momentarily speechless. We knew Antonio had a plush modern flat in the fashionable quarter of Milan and we had imagined that his house in the country would be split-level and modern.

The house is old and surrounded by a formal garden and vineyards. I am somehow unprepared for a home full of elegant comfort. Antonio has kept everything simple in natural woods. The floors are polished and uncarpeted, with Persian rugs in bright colours. The furniture is light oak. There are no curtains at the windows, only shutters, and the house stands serene in dappled sunshine.

I feel warm for the first time in weeks. Antonio is watching me anxiously. We came by water ferry and it feels like being transported to another land completely, a world without nightmare.

'What an amazing house. It's perfect. Thank you for inviting us.' How strange my voice sounds.

Antonio takes my hand and I see that his face is tinged

with pleasure. 'While you are here, darling, this is your home also. I want you to rest and heal and swim and lie in the sun.'

'Thank you. You're very kind.' I turn to the open windows. 'May I explore?'

I step out into the heat of late summer and pray they will let me walk away on my own. The sea glitters in the distance. I turn down the hall to my room to change into my swimming things, then make my way down the path to the sea leaving Antonio and Danielle wandering around the house calling out to each other in Italian.

Antonio comes to the french windows and shouts to me, 'It is safe to swim, darling, but do not go too far out. In a moment we join you.'

I raise my hand in acknowledgement. I want time alone to soak up the beauty of this place. As I walk the heat presses down. There is only the sound of crickets and a slight wind through the trees, and that of my footsteps.

The small cove is deserted and the sea is warm, breaking in small waves, comforting, like home, like Cornwall. I swim out a little way and tread water looking out to sea. I feel that if I turn and look back at the villa I will see two figures watching me anxiously from the terrace.

The water is clear, tiny fish swim up in shoals beneath me. I kick out and swim up and down trying to close my mind to everything but the velvety touch of salt water.

Up and down, up and down through the pale-blue sea I swim, letting the sun warm me through the water. I swim into the shallows and let small waves break over my back and legs in little slaps. A heat haze hangs over the water, merging sun and sky. I close my eyes.

Mama, Mama. Hold hand. Jump! Jump wave, Mama. I look up, rise out of the water with joy to catch Rosie to me. No child runs towards me. No man follows, chasing his daughter in the shallows. There is no one at all in the deserted landscape. The beach lies before me curved and empty.

I put on a light-green dress that Danielle made for me. It is so wispy, so light that I can hardly feel myself within it. It has two panels of multicoloured silk that float out from the shoulders like wings to fly away. It took her two days in the workroom; two days and two nights. A little act of love. Tom would have approved. It is classic but it has that edge of difference.

I do not have Danielle's amazing olive skin that tans instantly, but I am brown from the summer and I think my face is less pale after three days here in Antonio's house in the sun.

Antonio is having a party. He says it is partly business and partly pleasure; a late-summer gathering for his friends. I have put off going downstairs for as long as possible, but now I must steel myself or I will seem rude. I think of home. I miss Flo. I ring her on my mobile.

'Jen!' Her voice is anxious.

'I'm fine.' My voice cracks.

'You're homesick. You're wondering what on earth you're doing there?'

'Yes. What on earth made me agree to come? It's too soon. I'm not ready. Antonio is having a party and I don't have the courage to go downstairs.'

'You have more than enough courage. Sweep down in Danielle's exquisite dress. Pretend you are playing a part. Well-known dress designer about to become rather famous . . .' Flo, faraway in London, pauses. 'It will get better, my love. Just moving forward one pace at a time will get easier. Danielle and I will help you get through this.'

'Thanks, Flo,' I whisper and say goodbye.

Flo and Danielle hide their own grief in order not to

compound mine. I look in the mirror. A thin, wiry-haired creature stares back at me. *Pretend you are playing a part.* I take a deep breath and go downstairs. Antonio is hovering at the bottom for me like a suitor.

He takes my hand and kisses it. 'Darling Jennee, you look ravishing.' He grabs a drink from a passing tray and hands it to me. 'I know how very hard all this is for you. I thank you from the bottom of my heart for coming downstairs. I was not sure if you would be able to face us. Some of these people are important to us and some are my very good friends. Come, I will not leave you alone. If we get separated, come and find me instantly.'

I smile. It is rather like being a child again. I take frequent drinks from the many passing trays. I sail round on Antonio's arm and smile vivaciously. I answer questions about work, about London. I flirt. I laugh. I take another drink from another tray. I think I am doing very well. I watch myself being a success.

I catch sight of Danielle circulating. She is stunning, all in white, her long glossy dark hair loose and sexy. Every time I look she is surrounded by more Italian men. Occasionally she frowns at the glass in my hand and gently shakes her head. Then she comes over and whispers, 'Be careful with the wine. Do not take my example. I have the capacity of an alcoholic, as you know.'

I smile. She is worried that I am going to embarrass myself, burst into noisy drunken tears or suddenly fall on the floor or start to slur my words. But I'm not at all drunk. The wine appears to be having no effect at all except to blur the edges and make things fractionally better. *I am merely playing a part.*

When it is time to eat I cannot face the buffet table full of food. I slip away and make my way out of the french windows and down the steps to the lower terrace. The light from the house spills over me as I move into the shadows. I hold out my hand to the light as it shines on old flagstones and my hand becomes pink, translucent and strange. I gaze at it curiously.

What am I doing away from home so soon after Tom's death? I let my hand fall and turn to face the sea. I can hear the faint hiss if I strain and I wonder if I have enough energy to walk and stand by the edge of the water. I stand staring out at the purple strip beyond the fruit trees. Every so often the surface of it is disturbed by little breaking white waves.

Tom would love this. The smell of the night unmistakably Mediterranean, highly scented. The sound of cicadas, the whiff of olive oil.

From behind me the sound of the party comes in small bursts of voices and laughter. I want to melt and be part of the night, part of the stone step I sit on. I want to adhere like a shadow to the old stone balcony I lean against. In the light spilling from the room behind me I study moss on the ancient uneven bricks, little hairs protrude like prickles on an old man's chin. It is spongy to touch and damp, revealing a ladybird deep in its depths. I have disturbed it.

I want, above all things, to go to bed but I seem unable to move. I am overcome by a powerful lethargy. I go on sitting on the cold step. I hear someone come out of the windows behind me, then Antonio is beside me. He crouches down to me. For a moment he says nothing. I sense his alarm but still I cannot move or turn my head. Slowly he places the back of his hand to my arm, gently, like a question mark. 'You are getting cold. Will you come inside now?'

I can't find my voice and he puts his arm round me tentatively. 'You are tired, darling. Let me take you up to your room.'

I nod and he helps me up as if I am ill or old. He guides my stumbling legs round the side of the house and into a small side door, which leads up some back stairs. I can feel my legs buckling and I clutch on to him. Once inside, he lifts me, carries me as if I am weightless up the stairs and into my bedroom, pushing the door open with his foot, and placing me on the bed. 'Get undressed and into your bed, darling. I go for a warm drink and some bread.'

But somehow I cannot summon the energy to get undressed. Everything is faraway and I am watching myself. I turn dizzily on to my side and bring my feet up to my chin. Antonio returns. He mutters something in Italian and I see he is with an old woman. She tuts at me and sits me up. My dress is pulled over my head, then I am under the quilt.

'Drink a little of this, Jenny.' Antonio holds my head on his arm and I sip milk with something in it, nutmeg or herb. Then he lets me go. He sits with his beautiful sad eyes looking down on me. The old woman speaks rapidly to him and leaves. When she has gone Antonio hesitates. He does not know what to say to a guest in his house who wishes she were dead.

I hear my voice, reedy and thin with fear: 'Don't leave me, Antonio.'

He looks down at me and I hold his eyes, pleading, desperate, like a child. He sits down on the bed again, heavy, and I am warmed by the relaxed feel and shape of him. He radiates an animal warmth and kindness. He smiles. 'I will go and say goodnight to my guests. I will make sure all is well with my staff and then I shall return to you.' He picks up my hand and holds it to his lips. 'I will stay with you all night. Do not be afraid, I will not leave you alone. I will be here to comfort you. I will not try to make love with you.'

'I don't mind,' I tell him.

'But I do,' he says softly. 'Come now, try to sleep. I will be back soon.'

I lie in the dark, waiting for him. Voices gradually cease

and the distant sea becomes louder, reaches me in a faint monotonous hush, like listening to the sound from a curved shell. Antonio comes back so quietly I hardly hear him. As he throws off his robe his shadow on the wall seems suddenly huge, like a gorilla and I feel panic and freeze as he gets into bed beside me.

He lies on his back moving carefully, thinking I am asleep. I relax as his breathing slows down into sleep, glad to have someone in my bed, relieved not to be alone for one night.

I sleep until the sun edges into the room and I wake abruptly with the familiar horror of memory. *Tom and Rosie are dead*. I burrow instinctively towards the warmth of the man in the bed. Sleepily Antonio pulls me to him, strokes my hair away from my face, tucks me into the crook of his arm and I fall asleep again comforted.

I wake to find him watching me, his face very close to mine. He speaks to me softly in Italian. I do not understand the words but the tone is unmistakable. I meet his eyes and my stomach leaps. As our eyes lock, neither of us moves. I wait for him to touch me, but gently he moves his arm from under my head, leaps from the bed and goes into the bathroom. He comes back to smile at me from the doorway, a towel safely round his middle. I smile back. Later, I will be grateful.

SEVENTY

Adam wanted to visit Gloucester Cathedral for a school project while they were in Birmingham. From beneath its beautiful high carved ceilings he darted ahead of Ruth and Peter, examining with keen interest the inscriptions to dead soldiers of two world wars. The names of the regiments were inscribed in marble and he ran his eyes over their names, wondering what age they had been when they died.

In the atmospheric arched cloisters the flagstones were worn shapeless, the inscriptions under their feet long smoothed away and faded back into stone. It seemed to Adam, in the damp, echoing silence, possible to hear the echo of a Gregorian chant and feel the swish of rough woven cassocks brushing against the grey stones of vaulted corridors.

Peter watched him. The boy was happy. His contentment seeped out of every pore. He had an almost permanent grin on his face and a bounce to his step. Adam had always been a rewarding and uncomplaining boy, but now he positively glowed with the possibilities life had brought him. It was as if in finding his father he had found another dimension to himself.

The only thing that disturbed Peter was Adam's constant preoccupation with war and death and all things military. He quizzed Peter about the Israeli army and what level of force they were allowed to use. He showed an unhealthy interest in suicide bombers and how many mutilated bodies Peter might have seen. He was also surprisingly informed about modern warfare methods and the differing roles of American and British servicemen in Iraq. Peter tried to draw him back to his birds and fishing. He noticed Adam was canny enough not to talk about the army in front of Ruth.

Ruth had arrived in Birmingham looking triumphant, but strained and determinedly jolly with Adam. She was making a conscious effort rather than just being his mother. It made Peter uncomfortable. It was as if she were trying to woo Adam back to her like a jealous lover, as if she now felt grateful for time with her son, and Peter wondered what difference it might have made if he had not left them both so suddenly for Israel and a fated bid for happiness. 'How do you fancy a pub lunch with a roaring fire, then a long walk?' he asked her.

Ruth turned, her eyes crinkling with happiness in a way he loved. 'Bliss, Peter, I'm having such a lovely few days, thank you.'

'Don't thank me. I am too.' He laughed. 'We all are.'

That afternoon they walked up on the Malvern Hills. The world was spread out below them like some huge map. Counties melded into one another, stretched into distance and mist; yellow and green fields, blue rivers, church spires and rolling forests of trees. Gloucester, Tewkesbury and Worcester were to their left, Hereford and the rolling hills towards the Black Mountains on their right.

Ruth said, 'Odd, how the sheer size of these hills rising up around you makes you dizzy and unbalanced; as if you might fall. I feel like an ant on the edge of a wall.'

Adam grinned. 'I know what you mean. It's like the scale of everything is suddenly all wrong. We've shrunk; we have become too small.'

'Or', Peter said ponderously, 'nature dwarfs us and we need to be reminded occasionally. How would you both like to come out to Tel Aviv for a holiday? Maybe after Christmas, or in the summer holidays?'

'Wicked! Can we, Mum?'

Ruth met Peter's eyes. 'It's a seductive thought.'

'Then bear it in mind.'

When Adam ran ahead with his binoculars she turned to Peter. 'Why haven't you signed the divorce papers? What's going on in your life?'

Peter was silent, then he said, 'Things haven't worked out quite as I hoped in Israel. That's life, but I don't see the reason for divorce. We're separated, we lead different lives, but we're friends. I miss you and Adam inordinately, Ruth. I don't think sharing time with you both is hurting anyone, is it?'

'No,' Ruth murmured, thinking there was a danger that they were both filling in the cracks for one another from habit. Ruth knew they would make love before the holiday ended. Sex had gained a frisson by being technically forbidden. They were both suspended in the present, neither knowing the absolute direction of their separate lives. It was, Ruth thought, like living in a temporary oasis: comforting but not a permanent solution.

As they lay in Peter's bed that night, he asked, 'What's eating at you, Ruth? You love your job, so it must be Adam. You seem overanxious to please him the whole time. You're not yourself with him. It's painful to watch.'

Ruth edged away so she could see his face. 'Is that how I seem? Oh God. I'm totally inconsistent in my feelings towards Jenny. Adam is so happy with her and at that school. I should be unutterably grateful, yet I feel huge resentment.'

Peter was silent.

'Say something,' Ruth whispered.

'I was wondering if your ambivalence is not to do with Adam living with Jenny, but with Jenny herself.'

'What do you mean?'

'How did you feel when you saw Jenny again on that train?'

'I was thrilled to see her again.'

'Yet within a week you discover that she's been happily married for years to the father of your child, to the man you would never speak about, and that this man had been brutally killed.'

'I don't want to go into all this again.'

'I think it needs to be said.'

'No, Peter, it doesn't.' Ruth started to get out of bed.

'OK,' Peter said quietly. 'Run away, Ruth. You always did at any mention of Adam's father.'

Ruth hesitated. 'That's not true.'

'Isn't it? Then, tell me what you felt when you saw those photograph cuttings of a dead man who had loved, married and had a child with Jenny. Not you. *Jenny.*'

Ruth suddenly sat down on the edge of the bed. In a while she said, 'After the initial shock, I was plummeted back to the seventeen-year-old schoolgirl I had been, waiting for a call that never came. It really was like falling back in time.'

'You were so young,' Peter said gently.

'I remembered all over again that terrible feeling of self-loathing, the terror of what my parents would do when they found out.'

'Yet you protected Tom from them, didn't you? Why?'

'Because I knew I had thrown myself at him. I had enough insight, even then, to understand I was needy.'

'How lonely and frightened you must have been. I wish

you had been able to talk to me when we were married. It might have made a difference.'

Ruth turned to him. 'It was the hardest lesson I ever learnt, Peter. That you can do something so intimate with a man and it can mean absolutely nothing to him.'

'He broke your frail heart and you protected him, preserved his life and forfeited your own. My lovely, brave Ruth. All you got in return was anguish, pregnancy and banishment.'

Ruth stared at him, abruptly angry. 'You think it's a good idea to remind me of it all, do you, Peter? Make me go back to something I buried with good reason. Why spoil a happy week? I don't want to hear all your psychological counselling crap.'

Peter ignored her. 'You froze the whole Tom episode slowly out of your life. As if it never really happened. You tried to banish him from your heart and mind in order to go forward and to survive, but you couldn't quite manage it, could you?'

'Peter, just stop it!'

'He lived somewhere inside you, a little gold hero you dared not take out in case he became tarnished. You refused to even discuss him with Adam. All your life some little piece of you has hoped that Tom might by some miracle walk into your life again. Aren't I right?'

Ruth shook her head furiously. 'Rubbish! I don't understand why you are doing this. You are way off beam.'

'Am I? You work your guts out and make a success of your life. You meet a nice boring Jewish accountant who gets on with your son. It's enough. You marry me. It isn't enough. I can't get near. I cannot even *begin* to get near.' Peter was surprised at his own anger flying out of nowhere. 'When the ghost of Tom surfaced like a phoenix, did you secretly think that it should have been you who had all those wonderful years Jenny had with the father of your child?

375

Did you wonder why Tom should fall in love with Jenny a few years later and not you?'

Ruth had gone pale but Peter made himself go on. 'Jenny seems to have it all, doesn't she, Ruth? A loving family and talent as well. Is it possible you have always, sub-consciously, even as a child, resented as well as loved Jenny, for always, even in tragedy, seeming to have everything she wants? Have you asked yourself why you handed Adam over on a plate?'

Ruth was shocked by Peter's anger. He seemed intent on unflinchingly unwrapping her life like a parcel.

'Ruth,' he said tiredly, 'be honest with yourself just for bloody once. You let Adam decide for you. It solved your conscience about a job you fully intended to take, despite having Adam to consider, despite any consequences.' He got out of bed and pulled on his dressing gown. 'You made a choice. Jenny made it easy for you. Now, you are riddled with jealousy over Adam's easy relationship with Jenny while she pursues her career from a backwater. You got what you thought you wanted: a place and a job in Jenny's household. Adam is blissfully settled and well-adjusted in the life you agreed for him. What more can you ask? Or is it this that is your nightmare?'

Ruth pulled her wrap round her. She walked to the window and turned her back on Peter, lifting the curtain and looking down on to the road. Peter's words felt like a betrayal of every personal conversation she had ever had with him. No wonder she did not do so often.

She heard him getting miniature bottles of spirits from the fridge.

'I don't enjoy hurting you, Ruth. I'm desperate for you to examine your motives for resenting Jenny so fiercely.'

Ruth turned. 'Have you examined yours for resenting me, Peter?'

He met her eyes. 'Touché. My own bitterness over your

376

unknown soldier caught me unawares.' His tone caused Ruth another glancing blow.

'I hurt you. I spoilt your life.'

'No. I've done that for myself, Ruth, in a bid for love and children that failed miserably. Poetic justice, I think it's called.'

They stared at each other, appalled at the damage.

Ruth said quietly, 'Perhaps everything you say is partly true. I admit my feelings about Jenny are complicated and can consume me, but I feel with every instinct of my being that Adam is being subtly drawn away from me.' She thumped her chest painfully with her fist. 'I feel it in my heart and guts, and nothing you can say can change what I feel.' Her voice broke, which was strangely dramatic for Ruth.

Peter went over and wound his arms round her. 'Maybe you and Jenny should talk this through with someone qualified?'

Ruth shook her head. 'God, no! I'll work it out. I'm trying.'

'Things change between mothers and sons. The gap would have widened between you and Adam anyway. Be happy, Ruth. Don't ruin your life. Don't become obsessed. You haven't lost anyone.' He smiled at her. 'Not even me. I love you and that's never going to change. I don't know what the future holds but I'll always be around somewhere in the background, if you want me to be.' He handed her a small glass of brandy and she drank the burning liquid in one go, as he had done. It warmed her.

Peter knew that there was always more than one truth. He had wanted, partly, to protect Adam. He'd had a sudden fear that Ruth might, like a kamikaze pilot, make Adam choose between herself and Jenny and in doing so destroy them both.

SEVENTY-ONE

Christmas came and Adam and I decorated the house with hundreds of candles. We bought a tiny fir tree with roots so that we could put it in the garden afterwards. Adam also went over and helped Bea and James decorate Tredrea and the big tree that needed to be ready for an influx of grand-children. We were touched that he was not too old or too cool to enjoy doing this with us.

Two of my sisters were coming. The third was living in America with a new husband none of us had met. Adam was amused that Bea and James ran Christmas like a military campaign, constantly losing their copious lists.

This Christmas could not be sadder than the previous one, but it felt more poignant. I accepted that Rosie and Tom were gone. I knew I could never have that life back. I knew I was, with guilt, moving on without them and it felt like a betrayal of sorts. Like the first day you think with a start, *Oh, God, I haven't thought about them for an hour.*

Flo had always come home with me and Tom for Christmas. Danielle loathed Christmas and invariably went off to Paris to stay with a single friend. I was afraid Ruth might want to whisk Adam away for Christmas with Peter, but Adam made it perfectly clear in his excited chatter to her on the phone that he wanted to be in St Ives.

I left Flo and Bea to talk to Ruth. I was afraid I might sound patronising or somehow possessive or smug. I was afraid I would say the wrong thing. I felt for her and didn't want her to arrive and feel the outsider in all the preparations.

Bea said Ruth sounded exhausted and only too happy to come down with Flo and stay in St Ives. She had been far too busy even to think of an alternative Christmas. The run-up to Christmas in London was always gruelling. I knew Flo and Danielle were also working flat out. It was the same every year, it was the party season and people suddenly demanded dresses overnight.

It was the time Danielle and Flo would miss me most and I felt guilty, especially when I rang and their voices cracked with tiredness.

I planned to contribute more to the business next year. I could build up my work from here. The little co-operative shop had sold everything I could make over the Christmas period and I was quietly excited.

Ruth had been upset that she could not get down for Adam's school concert, so James told her that he would video it and she could watch it over Christmas.

On the evening of the concert Bea, James and I made sure we got there early armed with the video camera. Bea and I sat near the front, and Dad positioned himself at the back. Adam was weary with constant rehearsing. Harry's mother and I had taken turns ferrying the two tired and tetchy boys to Truro at the weekends and picking them up after school in the evenings.

All the scholarship boys had had to practise incredible hours. There were children of professional musicians at the

379

school, which kept the standard high but was totally unnerving. Adam missed the musical Peter, who had supervised his practice and given insight into his playing.

Bea and I both felt nervous when Adam began to play his clarinet. It was Weber's virtuosic Concertino, a solo piece and he was as white as a sheet. Biased, we thought he played wonderfully and he got an ovation. Harry played Mozart's Piano Concerto in D Minor like an angel and there were four ambitious and frighteningly adept violin pieces.

At the end the boys sang carols they had arranged themselves. Harry had a sweet choirboy voice, but we could hear the break in it. It would be his last year singing. Adam joined him for 'We will rock you, rock you, rock you' and I smiled. They both looked so innocent, but I had listened to them practising rudely with each other as they substituted the f-word, ending up rolling on the floor with raucous laughter in the sitting room.

It was here in the decorated school hall among the smell of boys and mulled wine that I saw Adam's childhood slipping away into husky awkward adolescence. I knew that next year everything would change. This time between us would fade.

He still liked to get into the other side of the bed sometimes and I didn't comment. He was growing up, becoming confident and secure. He had joined the school cadets. He was taller and leaner. He grew more like Tom every day. This year he had needed to feel close and safe, and I loved the knowledge that I had been able to give him security.

I woke at dawn on Christmas Day. I threw on jeans and a sweater, pulled an old coat from the back door and walked down into the sleeping town. I headed round the harbour and up to the island. At the top by the tiny chapel I stopped.

The sun was coming up and everything would change in an instant, tingeing the day with washed colour. The wind was so cold it took my breath away.

Ahead of me I saw a small huddle of people standing close together and snatches of a hymn reached me. It was the Christmas Day sunrise service. I stood with a little group as light edged blood-red over the sea. I thought of Tom and Rosie as the sun hung suspended in front of us, mystical and mysterious, lighting a new day. I hugged them both to me, precious and clear, as I walked slowly home to face another Christmas Day without them.

When I pushed open the back door, letting cold air into the kitchen, Bea and my sisters were sitting at the table drinking tea in their dressing gowns. I smiled. Everything was as it always was here.

My sisters hadn't seen Ruth since she was sixteen years old. They had both left home for university and a gap year when she vanished.

'Do you remember', my sister Sophie asked me suddenly as we banged pans on to the Aga, 'how on Christmas afternoon Ruth's small figure would come hopefully up the drive clutching a little present, an excuse to escape her parents and come to us?'

I stopped what I was doing. I had forgotten. The memory cut me, brought tears to my eyes. I turned away quickly, but Bea said briskly, 'Wait until you see what a lovely, successful woman Ruth has grown into despite everything. Despite those truly wicked parents.'

My sister and I smiled. Mum never used the old-fashioned word wicked lightly.

The day slid happily by and if a part of me was absent it was only Dad who noticed. Vast quantities of food and drink were consumed. The usual culinary disasters befell, which happened every Christmas. Flo was a rock, soothing

Bea, making more gravy, wiping sticky fingers. If Ruth avoided my eyes she seemed happy enough.

Adam got on well with both my sisters' children. Ruth got on a bit too well with my sister Natasha's husband, which caused a minor drama in the kitchen because too much wine had been taken. Dad raised his eyes at me and we went into the garden while he smoked his Christmas cigar and I had the odd dizzying puff.

Harry suddenly arrived in the evening and there was a lot of whispering between him and Adam and Dad, and the sitting room door was shut on us all. When we were allowed out, the dining room had been turned into a little concert hall with the chairs all facing the piano.

I smiled at Ruth. The boys were going to do an impromptu concert for her. I was so glad.

Harry played a Beethoven piano sonata. Adam played a new solo arrangement from the *St Luke Passion* on his clarinet, concentrating hard. It was haunting, and he faced Ruth and I could see her choked with pride and love. It was the most wonderful Christmas present he could have given her.

They did a little jazzy number together on the piano with Harry singing. Then Adam glanced at me quickly and what I saw in his eyes made my heart pound. He was going to do a something for me. I was standing at the back by the closed door and I leant against it.

There was a long silence. Adam held some sheet music and stood. He was nervous. Harry watched him anxiously, wondering when to begin to play. Eventually Adam nodded. He avoided looking at me as he sang. Only James and Bea knew it was the song Tom used to sing to me.

'Come away with me,' Adam sang huskily over my head, his eyes fixed on the wall. His heart was in his voice and his voice was for me. The wistful, sad rise and fall of his boy-man voice caught at my soul, created a tension in the room.

382

No one moved:

Come away with me . . . in the night. Come away with
me . . . I will write you a song . . . Come away with
me . . . I want to walk with you on a cloudy day . . . in
fields where the yellow grass grows high . . . Come away
with me . . . On a mountain top . . . I want to wake
with you . . . Come away with me in the night . . .

I was back in my house in a storm, surrounded by photographs, a fire crackling, the wind buffeting the house and Adam beside me as we pasted my lost life on to card. Tears rose in my throat. For a second I wondered who was singing to me: Tom or Adam? Adam or Tom?

I felt James alert beside me. I prayed the heightened atmosphere was inside me and not in the room.

Harry suddenly joined in and they camped it up, moving into other Norah Jones lyrics and then carols, before embarrassment took over.

I felt James relax. He pulled me to him and kissed the top of my head, then he called out, 'Mince pies and mulled wine in the kitchen!'

Everyone filed out. Ruth was talking to my sisters quite happily and I sighed with relief. One of my small nieces pulled Harry out of the room for a mince pie and I was left with Adam.

I drew in his sweet boy heat. 'Thank you, darling boy,' I said lightly. 'That was lovely.'

He grinned at me, pleased and embarrassed. 'I left out the soppier lines.'

I laughed. 'Come on,' I said. 'Or you'll miss out on the food.'

That night, when I went to bed I found a small wrapped parcel on my bedside table. *For Jenny, with love always, Adam. (Unabridged version.)* He had made me a tape of him singing 'Come Away with Me'.

The house took ages to settle down and I sat in the window

with my earplugs in, listening to Adam sing, and I loved him so much that my eyes stung. The thought of losing him made me feel sick. I felt he was mine, my own child; yet it was more than that.

We both had an acute awareness of the other; an unspoken perceptiveness for one another's moods. If I was sad or low he would try to comfort me with his guileless warmth. If I saw he was stressed by music practice or school work or overtired or bewildered by life I knew that his one solace was being with me. Often I did not even hear him slip into my bed in the dark, but I would become conscious that his breathing matched my own. Living with Adam was like having another skin, or sharing one.

I knew the danger. It was innocent. I defied anyone to misunderstand something that gave hope and comfort to us both and would cease as seamlessly as it started, but I was the adult. Adolescence was confusing enough. Tonight had shown me I couldn't blur the boundaries.

In the dining room, when I knew Adam was going to sing to me, I had broken out into a sweat in the sudden fear of him exposing us somehow to what other people would find unacceptable. It had never felt wrong, but as I stood next to Dad by the door I knew that he would be appalled by my sharing my bed, however artlessly, with a young boy. Up until that moment I had judged everything I did by my ability to tell my parents. I knew that I had to start being the parent because Adam was leaving his childhood behind.

I heard giggles from a bedroom, then a door opening and a stern admonishment to *go to sleep at once*. I smiled and got into bed as the house rustled and whispered around me. It seemed a lifetime ago since I left the house to watch the sun flare up out of the water.

SEVENTY-TWO

Antonio rang me nearly every week to tell me the news of his 'English Project', or to ask me how I was getting on, or just to chat. I grew used to hearing his voice in the early evening. He had invited Bea and James to his villa in the summer and to my surprise they had accepted.

He was impressed with Ruth. 'They are a good team, Ruth and Danielle, darling. Ruth is even more ruthless in business than Danielle.'

It was April and the gardens were full of scarlet camellias and early clematis and waxy yellow primroses. The eider duck were back and Adam spent hours on the foreshore cataloguing the birds arriving and excitedly ringing James.

For weeks it had been warm enough to sit out and have coffee facing the water. The conservatory was full of belts and bags and small ethnic tops. I was trying out different Italian dyes Antonio had found for me.

As I sat in morning sun with my coffee, listening to a blackbird singing its heart out in a garden bristling with dew and full of cobwebs lacing the trees together, I felt a flash of pure joy in the moment. The water glittered beyond the gate and I thought, *This is as good as it gets*. I sat there considering my working day.

Then Danielle rang. 'I'm flying to see Antonio tomorrow to check our first small shipment arrived safely.'

'OK. Will you tell him I have a conservatory full of belts and bags? By the way, his dyes are wonderful.'

'Are they? I am longing to see . . .'

'I've found a man and a white van, which will solve some of our problems with getting my work up to you. Flo has been hinting for weeks that I can't expect you or Ruth to travel up and down all the time, and she's right. It's fine when Ruth wants to see Adam, but I shouldn't exploit that. I can still fly the smaller batches up to you.'

Danielle was obviously relieved. 'Flo and I were just talking about that this morning. Jen . . . ?' She paused and I waited. 'Is there any chance of you coming up to London yourself, if you are ready? Flo and I would love to show you the changes we have made in the house and garden. Also, I want to show you some of our commissions. It would be interesting for your accessories. Photographing them is not the same.'

I was silent and she said quickly, 'Do not get me wrong. It is so exciting that you are working down there. Your belts and bags sell as soon as they go in the stores. It is that I miss your ideas and your input.'

Danielle had startled me. I couldn't think what to say. London seemed like another planet. I thought we had a mutual understanding.

'To see you for a couple of days would be wonderful. The girls in the workroom would love to see you. Would you consider half-term when Adam and Ruth are away? It would be a great help.'

'I don't know, Danielle.'

I heard her sigh. 'Sorry! I should not open my huge mouth.

Maybe it is still too soon. I should leave these things to Flo. Sorry. Sorry.'

I laughed. 'Don't be silly. You have a point. It shouldn't be too soon. Let me think.'

We talked of other things, then she rang off. I filled up the back of my car with orders. Three-quarters were from outworkers. A quarter of the work was not up to scratch. I had to be firm. I would not pay for shabby work. I felt happy, though. It reminded me of the time Danielle and I had started in a damp basement in Hammersmith. There was fun in starting over, in being small again; something sweet in setting things up.

I dropped some bags and belts at the shop, then drove up to the industrial estate where I had rented a small commercial unit fitted with machines and the leather tools I had sent for from London. I employed four women and two men.

One of the men had been a cobbler and the other a leather tooler. One woman was a retired dressmaker, the other had worked in textiles and had a wonderful sense of colour. Then there was a young mother who had been to art college in Falmouth, before getting herself pregnant. She was the weak link but I liked her and decided I could train her up. She had a quirky stance on design and clothes, and the imagination to invent. Maybe she reminded me of myself a hundred years ago.

I read the riot act about the shoddy work. I told them I didn't want my name behind their careless handwork. I would not produce cheap tat for tourists and they had to recognise the difference between professional craftsmanship that had a price and rubbish that would fall to bits after a couple of outings.

I stressed the importance of working as a team. They needed to check their own and each other's work. I asked them to put each day's finished products on a table by the door and I would now go through each item before it left the unit. It only took one batch of inferior work for orders to be cancelled. These items were not just going into local shops, they were going out under my label to London and to Italy until Antonio got his factory up and running.

As I drove back down the hill into St Ives, the sea glittered invitingly and I parked to walk along the coastal path for an hour before I went back to work at the house. It was a rare windless day. The air, cold above the sea, stung my face.

I thought of my conversation with Danielle and wondered if my tiny project was going to work long-term. Inferior work would harm Danielle as well as me. Perhaps I should go and work up at the industrial estate to keep a constant eye on things. I knew I couldn't. I loved the empty house. I needed silence to create. I had to be alone. That was the point of all this. If I was going to be sucked in, I might as well be back in London.

How much longer was I going to avoid the house as I left it – Rosie's room perfectly intact and our bedroom shut and gathering dust? I did not think I could ever live there again, but I couldn't avoid going back. I couldn't avoid the girls and the workroom and the hub and heart of what Danielle and I had started together.

Danielle and I still needed each other. I'd been in danger of forgetting that it was our combined designing that had given us our edge and success.

I had been touched and amazed by the letters I had received from buyers and retail outlets welcoming me back. I needed to prove to myself, as well as to Flo and Danielle, that I could produce a steady flow of work using local people, without compromising our London standards. Increasingly, as I got back to basics, I realised how much we relied on Flo to check every single piece that came out of the workroom. We had been such a tight team. We expected a lot from our workforce, but in return we looked after them like an extension of our family.

As I walked down the muddy track, past the farm where the dog always barked but could not possibly be the same dog since childhood, I made two decisions.

I would create a mini label, an offshoot, for products made here in Cornwall, find a Cornish name for the label and promote it. This might instil local pride and I could protect Danielle's designs as well as myself while I went through teething problems.

I would go up to London at half-term. Adam and I could travel together. I would stay and help Danielle and Flo while Ruth spent the break with Adam. Then Adam and I would come straight home.

I called in to Bea and James on the way home. Bea was out but I found Dad in the garden digging over the vegetable patch making conversation with a robin. I sat on the wall to talk to him.

'I've been thinking, Dad. I'm going to have to start going up to London. I can't expect Danielle and Ruth to keep coming down, can I?'

Dad leant on his fork. 'No, Jen, I don't think you can.'

I looked across the garden full of blazing old azalea bushes covered in lichen. I saw the front door of our London house. I saw Tom bounding up the wide stairs two at a time. I saw myself at the top waiting for him. I saw our huge lovely bedroom where we'd spent so many of his leaves almost permanently in bed.

I thought of the huge squishy sofa, the television in the corner. The beautiful mirror over the fireplace that Tom had bought me in Jordan; the way the flame gas fire in the old Victorian fireplace would flicker over the walls, making us feel safe and warm as we lay closeted together. I thought of the room now, devoid of him, soulless, no doubt stacked with boxes and rolls of materials: the spare room.

I saw Rosie sitting on the floor, her face full of wonder as she pulled the string of Danielle's doll and it sang to her. I dreaded going back to face the absolute finality of it all.

Dad stuck his fork hard into the ground, came over and sat on the wall beside me. 'Sometimes, the fear of something is worse than the thing itself. You've dreaded going back for so long, Jen, that it now feels like an insurmountable hurdle. I'll come with you, if it's any help.' He sighed and looked at me. 'I think it's time, darling. No one is asking you to go back to live. But it *is* your home and has been the hub of your life. You're happy here at the moment, but you're very young to bury yourself. Look at the letters you've had. Your belts and bags are very innovative and very *you*, but people want your stunning, beautiful clothes. I know you're going to design just as well if not better than you did before.'

I smiled. I hadn't realised Dad was so proud of me. I told him about my piffling little commercial worries.

'I would think', James said as we walked to the house, 'that the same rules apply whether you have a tiny work-force here or a large one in London. It's human nature to get complacent. Talk to Flo; maybe instead of having six equal workers you need to put someone in overall charge, especially if you're not going to be there all the time.'

'Oh, you are so wise, father of mine!'

'It comes with years of dealing with terrifying doctors' receptionists. Fire those who can't work as a team. Reward those who have pride in their work. Everyone needs to feel that what they are doing matters.' He grinned down at me. 'Perhaps also a little fear of the boss is no bad thing . . . An edge of ruthlessness?'

I stopped and planted my feet on the grass. 'Are you saying I can't do frightening?' I demanded.

He laughed. 'I'm sure you can, but why don't you make one of your staff a foreman of the works or manager? A Flo, in other words. Are you coming in for coffee?'

'Certainly not! I'm going home to practise being ruthless and frightening.'

James kissed me on the nose. 'I love you, daughter of mine.'

I looked at him suspiciously. Flo and Bea were as thick as thieves and I suspected conspiracy.

SEVENTY-THREE

Adam and I caught the train up to Paddington on the Friday of his half-term. I carried a leather folder of designs. Adam had brought some school work. We spread out our papers and books, and grinned at one another. Adam had never travelled first class before and took great delight in the free coffee and biscuits.

I watched him staring out of the window and knew his childlike excitement in small things would be uncool soon.

Adam had started the coursework for his GCSE exams, but this did not mean he could ease up on his music. There was pressure in being a scholarship boy and as his academic work increased, he seemed to have frightening amounts of homework and music practice.

After Christmas I had capitulated and bought a small flat television and a DVD player. Adam was very proud of the trendy television and it had caused much envy with Harry. His mother rang me and told me she was cursing me.

I had always hated the wet Cornish winters and we rushed around lighting fires, closing the curtains and settling down to watch programmes together.

We were strict during the week, but it was fun choosing

DVDs at weekends. I wouldn't sit through horror. Adam wouldn't sit through 'girlie-stuff', but we managed to compromise with thrillers.

The night before we left for London I had been tense and anxious. The days had been relentlessly overcast and depressing. Adam had come back from school tired and soaked. I lit the fire although it was May, just to cheer us up.

Adam changed and dropped his wet school clothes in a heap, thanking God dramatically that it was half-term. I toasted crumpets and we sat in the kitchen listening to the wind drive the rain against the windows and letting butter drip off our chins.

Suddenly he said, 'I want everything to stay the same. I don't want to live anywhere else. I don't want this to end.'

I stared at him, startled. He sounded like an echo of me. 'Why on earth do you think it's all going to end, silly boy?'

'Because you're working again. Because you're going up to London and you haven't been back for ages and Harry's mum says that you are too talented to stay down here much longer.'

I smiled at his stricken face. 'Adam, I need to show everyone that I can work efficiently from here. To do that I have to be willing to travel up to London occasionally, not expect everyone to travel down to me. That's all. I promise.'

He grinned. 'Honest?'

'Honest.'

I lay sleepless that night. I played the childish game of pretending I had been to London and was now safely home, like some obsessive agoraphobic. I lit a night light and put it under my incense burner, and poured in lavender hoping it would help.

I think I knew Adam would come to my room and he did. He hesitated when he saw the burner.

'I'm not asleep,' I whispered.

'Can I get into bed and talk, Jenny? I can't sleep.'

'Yes. I can't sleep either.'

He got in beside me. The wind outside blew in great gusts, the rain sounding like pebbles against the glass. I shivered and moved under the covers.

'Are you OK?' Adam asked.

'I'm anxious because I don't know how I'm going to feel tomorrow, going back into my house.'

He leant on his elbow peering at me.

'I'm afraid of testing myself after . . . my breakdown. I want to stay safely here in our odd little hut of a place. I'm a bit of a coward.'

'No, you're not. I want to stay here too, Jenny, and I've only lost someone I never knew.'

I smiled and turned to his face in the candlelight. 'Well, aren't we a couple of big girls' blouses?'

He grinned. 'Yeah.'

After a second he said, 'I'll be with you, if you want, when you put your Tom and Rosie to rest.'

Tears came to my eyes. 'Thank you, darling. I purposely picked a time when we could go up together, but saying goodbye is something I have to face on my own.' I stared at his sweet Tom-like face on the other pillow. 'Adam, I hope living with me isn't making you sad or melancholy. I hope I'm not weighing you down. I know why *I'm* afraid of rejoining the world, but are *you* afraid of anything in particular? Is something worrying you?'

He looked away. 'I'm not sad. You don't weigh me down. I'm really happy. Like I said, I don't ever want us and this house to stop being . . .'

I said softly, 'You feel like this now, but everything changes with time – life, our feelings, what we want. We're both happy here together because it's happened at a certain time in our lives. But you're going to grow up and go away and live your life, and that's how it must be.'

I reached for his hand and it curled tightly round mine. His voice was thick. 'I can't imagine being without you. When I think about it a hole opens up and I get really scared, Jenny.'

'Wherever you are in the world, no matter how old I am or how old you are, Adam, you will stay near my heart, here.' I placed our hands against my chest. 'That, I promise you, will never change.'

Adam closed his eyes tight as if to squeeze away tears. I stroked the hand I was holding with my thumb. The night light fluttered and went out, and a wave of lavender hung in the dark.

As if the darkness gave him courage, Adam began to talk, so quietly that I had to bend to hear him. 'My Auntie Violet looked after me when I was little. She used to meet me from school every day. Mum was studying on the mainland. I loved living on that island. The fishermen used to take me out on the boats.' He smiled, remembering. 'I missed Mum, but I loved Auntie Violet. She always had time to listen. She always laid tea out for when I got home. Then we moved to the mainland so Mum could work and it was OK, I knew some of the boys at the new school in Glasgow. I was old enough to walk home on my own from school by then but Auntie Vi was always there when I got home. One day she wasn't waiting by the window. I found her lying on the floor and I had to call 999 . . .' Adam's face relived the awful day. 'I thought she was dead, but she wasn't. Not quite. She'd had a stroke and she couldn't move or say anything. She never came back from the hospital. She died.' I heard the break in his voice. 'She died and left me, and I never felt so safe ever again. No one ever asked me things or listened to me like her. She made me feel real.'

I kept very still as the words poured out of him.

'When Mum married Peter I was glad. I liked him. I didn't like different men coming to the house to take her out. Then we moved again to Birmingham and it was a crap school and I *hated* it. I used to count the hours until I could go home and when I went home there was no one there. For the first time, even though I was old enough by then, I dreaded the silence in the house, like, it made my thoughts scary. I could hear the taunts in my head in Birmingham accents, like they were all in the house with me.'

Adam let go of my hand and turned and brought his knees up, moving to keep warm. His voice was husky with tiredness. 'Then you came. From the first day I met you, you talked to me. I felt weird, as if I knew you already. Then I came to live with you and it's like . . . like . . .'

'Coming home safe?' I breathed the words, they were etched so deep within me.

'Coming home safe,' Adam whispered. 'Yes. I see the light through the trees as the train comes in and I feel so happy because you are in the house, waiting.'

'Nothing is going to happen to me, darling.'

'The people you love most die.'

I said quietly, 'We can't live our whole lives afraid of losing the people we love or we miss the moments when we're all together. Losing your Auntie Vi when you were so young was terrible for you because she had been such an important part of your life. I'm sure you worry about Ruth too. It's normal to be anxious about people close to us. Go to sleep now, you're exhausted.'

Adam closed his eyes, then said in a rush, 'But I don't love you like I loved Auntie Vi or like I love my mum. I love you . . .'

'Like a sort of best friend?' I whispered quickly.

Adam opened his eyes. 'I love you because you're Jenny.

I'll always love you. Always.' His voice was vehement. His striking blue eyes gazed at me anxiously and I leant forward and wrapped my arms round him, and we rocked gently in the dark.

'I don't want this ever to end,' he whispered. 'I so love being here with you.'

I held him and said, 'But you know it *must* end, darling boy, you know it must. It's wrong.'

'It doesn't feel wrong . . .'

'No, but it is and it has to stop. You know this.' He hesitated. 'Adam, there is nothing dishonourable here between us, but if anyone knew it could be misconstrued and turned into something wicked and evil that would have terrible repercussions. Do you understand?' I asked gently.

He nodded. 'Yes.' He burrowed down close to me. 'Just one more night?'

'Just one more night, darling boy.'

I tucked the covers round him, turned away from him and he slept almost immediately. How I would miss the warmth of this boy.

SEVENTY-FOUR

Ruth thought how pale Jenny looked when she arrived at the house with Adam. Like a small ghost revisiting her life.

The girls all came streaming down the stairs from the machine room in great excitement and Jenny vanished up to the top of the house, smiling and obviously touched.

Ruth hugged Adam and missed having her own house, her own kitchen where they could have disappeared together. Adam stood awkwardly in the kitchen as she made tea and Ruth checked herself from making nervous small talk to him.

Laughter came from up the stairs and Ruth felt as she had many times in her life: that she was hovering on the outside of a lighted room.

Flo came downstairs with Jenny and produced a cake for Adam with a flourish. 'Just to prove we can do cake in London too!'

Jenny shakily wandered around the kitchen touching things and peering at notices. She looked out of the window and down into the back garden. 'Oh,' she said. 'Someone's gardening down there.'

Flo said. 'It's Will. He comes in once a week. We had to

do something, Jen. The garden had become a jungle and was depressing to look at.'

It had been ages before either Flo or Danielle had felt like going into the garden again. It seemed so much Tom and Rosie's province and their ghosts hovered. Jenny, looking down at the neglected garden, heard Tom's voice: *Look at the state of that grass! I'd better get down there first thing in the morning. That hedge needs pruning. Come on, Rosie. You sand pit, me clipping hedge. Up you come, into the garden with your old dad . . .*

'Good,' she said, turning away. 'Tom would have had a fit about the state of the lawn. Now, what can I do? Put me to work while I'm here.'

'Danielle should be back about five. She's gone to do a fitting with Marie. We thought we'd go through the Italian orders with you tomorrow, Jen, so just relax.'

Ruth picked up her car keys. 'Adam, I've got to do some shopping for tonight.' She smiled at Jenny. 'Flo's done a huge lasagne, so I just need to pick up salad and things.' She turned to Adam. 'We can go to PC World, if you like, and get that software you were after.'

Adam perked up. 'Cool. OK.'

As he followed Ruth out of the kitchen he turned and looked at Jenny anxiously.

I'm fine, she mouthed.

'Jen,' Flo said, 'come upstairs and chat. I need to check on a couple of orders and make a telephone call.'

Jenny laughed. 'I *can* be alone down here, you know. I'd like to be, honestly. I need to see to the things in my bedroom, go through my wardrobe, you know, get to grips. An hour on my own will be good.'

Flo looked at her. 'All right, lovey, if you're sure. Then it will be time for a drink.'

'Then it will definitely be time for a drink!'

*   *   *

When Danielle came through the front door she could smell Jenny's light distinctive scent. Mahler was playing softly. She did not call out as she climbed the stairs but went to the door of Jenny and Tom's room. The bed was full of piles of clothes and the windows were thrown open. The curtains were in a heap on the floor for cleaning. The wardrobes stood wide and Jenny had her face bent to Tom's dress uniform hanging inside, boots and spurs standing dusty beneath.

Danielle hesitated, about to turn away, when Jenny looked up. She straightened and smiled. 'I was just seeing if they still smelt of Tom, but they don't. Everything smells of worn clothes. The room smelt like a charity shop when I opened the wardrobe. Horrid.'

They kissed four times in the middle of the room.

'Should you be doing this on your own?'

Jenny nodded. 'Yes, Elle. It should have been done after Tom died.' She looked around. 'This is just an empty room that's being wasted. Neither Tom nor I are here any more. This room should be redecorated and changed round and used, don't you think? It's such a lovely room.'

'But, Jen.' Danielle tried to hide her dismay. 'Redecorate, sure. But it is *your* room, it always has been. It must be here for you when you come home.'

Jenny shook her head. 'No. It's time Rosie's room was redecorated too, but I'll sleep there tonight, once more.'

She looked up as Flo came into the room. 'Is that wise?'

'It's what I want to do. Come on, let's have a drink and I'll tell you what I've been thinking.'

They poured glasses of cold white wine, then Jenny led them back to her room. 'Danielle, you must miss having your own space, sharing your flat with Ruth?'

'It is fine, darling. Most of our time is up here, with Flo.'

'What about your privacy?'

Danielle laughed. 'You are asking me if it is difficult to bring my boyfriends back!'

'Yes. I thought that Ruth could have this room as a bed-sitting room and Adam could have Rosie's bedroom when he's here. When I come I can sleep in your flat, Danielle. Don't you think it's a good idea, Flo? Danielle can have her privacy, but so can Ruth. Or would they be too on top of you!'

Flo shook her head. 'Of course not. I suppose it's a good idea.' She sounded doubtful. 'I imagine Ruth does miss having somewhere of her own, but I really think you should sleep on this, just to be sure it's what you want.'

'If it makes you both happier I won't say anything until tomorrow.'

They went back into the kitchen and sat gossiping about work.

'This is like old times,' Danielle said happily. 'It is *so* good to have you here. It is not the same, Jen. It is not the same without you. We start everything, you and I, from that 'orrible basement, did we not?'

'We did! God, it seems a long time ago. I will try to come up more often from now on, I promise. I miss you two, you know.'

Jenny knew they were shocked about her decision to give up her lovely big room, which had once been the heart of the house. They feared what that decision meant. She was going to try to explain when they heard Ruth's key in the lock and they lifted their glasses in a silent toast to one another.

'We are very lucky to have Ruth,' Flo said guiltily, sensing immediately the exclusive tableau they made. She was slowly getting to know Ruth's insecurities.

'Yes. If we cannot have you, darling Jen, Ruth is the next-best thing.'

Jenny laughed. 'You know perfectly well that Ruth's business sense is an absolute godsend after me.' Her voice faltered. 'It was too perfect to last, wasn't it, the life that we all had together.'

They turned to greet Ruth and Adam as they came into the kitchen.

In the morning I would find boxes to place all Rosie's things in, but tonight I slept in her small narrow bed and let the memories come for the last time. Memories of Rosie were all happy. Sometimes, in Cornwall, I panicked when I could no longer quite recapture her laugh. Sometimes my heart thumped when Tom's face refused to crystallise exactly as I wanted it to, but I only had to go outside my bedroom and gaze at all the photographs Adam and I had put together and there they were, both with me again as clear as if it were yesterday.

The essence of Tom had disappeared from our room and it was the same here in Rosie's pretty baby bedroom. She was gone. They were gone. I could never recapture them. Leaving their rooms as they were would be a mirage with nothing real or tangible for me to hold on to.

I got up in the dark, fetched the boxes from the landing, closed the door and quietly packed up her room instead of sleeping. I held each toy and soft object before I placed it in the box. I looked at the beautiful doll's house and thought of Tom's parents faraway in Singapore. I would get it professionally packed and I would send it to a children's hospital. I would give the girls upstairs the box of Rosie's toys to go through and the rest could go to Great Ormond Street. Everything except Danielle's doll.

I took down pictures and lifted mobiles from the window. Then I made tea and got back into her bed and slept for a little. When I woke it was just a room with picture marks on the wall. I got dressed and took down the curtains. It was just a room. Yet I suddenly, childishly, thought, *Rosie and Tom will have no place to come back to now.* As if their spirits, in that violent death, were wandering the earth for peace, only to return here at night to rest.

I ran down the stairs and out of the house. I wanted to be in the park. I wanted to stop my thoughts from gathering and collecting in a dark mass. Fear drummed at my temples. I could never entirely trust my rational mind again. I longed to be home in Cornwall, watching the sun come up and listening to the curlews at the beginning of a new day.

I heard running footsteps and turned. It was Adam, clothes all awry. I stopped and he caught me up, breathless. 'I saw you run out of the house. I saw the boxes. You're not all right. You're *not*. Where are you going, Jenny?'

'I'm fine. I'm just going to the park for a walk. Really. You must go back to Ruth, Adam, it's very early.'

He stood in front of me. 'You're not fine. You're crying, Jenny. You're crying. I won't let you be alone.' He stepped towards me and hugged me fiercely to him, and my tears, hot and wet, ran down his T-shirt.

'I'm sorry,' I managed eventually. 'I'm so sorry. Look, darling, I will be OK now. You must go back. Get dressed properly and make me a pot of strong coffee. I've just got one last pilgrimage I need to do alone.'

He looked at me, then turned and walked slowly back to the house.

The park was beautiful, full of the scent of blossom. The leaves on the trees grew new and curled, emerging into virgin green. Joggers passed me with their dogs. The ducks made great wet messes on the path. I heard Rosie laugh and point, then get out of her pushchair to throw bread, while Tom and I hung on to her coat to stop her falling in. Tom threw his arm round me as we walked away back to the gates. *Oh, why don't I leave the army and become a civvie, then I can spend every Sunday with you and Rosie.*

I smiled, waiting for his laugh, which acknowledged that these Sundays were special *because* he wasn't here all the time.

Goodbye, I whispered to them both. *Goodbye.* I turned and looked back over the grass where the branches of leaves made shadows. Neither Tom nor Rosie needed rooms to house their spirits; their shadows moved with me everywhere. They always would.

Ruth heard Adam get up. She looked at her bedside clock: six thirty. What was he doing up at this time? She lay for a moment, reluctant to move out of her warm bed, and then, worried about him, she threw off the covers. She drew her curtains quietly, pulled on her dressing gown and looked down on to the overgrown garden that was beginning to take shape again.

Adam's room was empty. He wasn't in the bathroom. He wasn't in the flat. Anxious, she went out and up the stairs into the other side of the house. No one was here either, although someone was running a bath.

Ruth looked in Rosie's room and saw all the boxes. Jenny must have packed them in the night, poor thing. Had Adam gone out? Instinct told Ruth that he had and that he was with Jenny. Her stomach knotted.

Something made her go to the window. She looked down the road and saw Jenny on the opposite side with Adam. They were standing facing each other, talking; their bodies leant towards each other, intense.

Jenny lifted her hands in a small gesture of distress and Adam moved and put his arms round her. He was taller than Jenny now and they rocked together in the deserted early-morning road like lovers; like people who had known each other all their lives.

404

Fuck! Ruth's anger came streaking out of nowhere, doubling her up. *Fuck her. Fuck her. Fuck her.*

She turned from the window clutching her stomach, the pain excruciating, and collapsed into a chair, rocking. The rage rampaging through her terrified her. Coloured floaters bobbed behind her eyes, temporarily blinding her.

It was years and years since she had experienced uncontrollable anger like this. She hobbled back to her room and threw herself on the bed, giving into raw and unspeakable feelings that appalled her. *I hate Jenny and her pain. I bloody well hate her. It's always been the same: small, happy, popular Jenny. Always the centre of everyone's fucking universe. Jenny and her bloody perfect life, her bloody perfect family in their bloody perfect house. Jenny who had Bea and James and Tom and now Adam. Jesus Christ, Peter's right, I was stark staring mad.*

She was propelled into childhood again. The terrible rages that came from nowhere, that she'd had to squash down inside her, hold down with all her strength, petrified in case they escaped in an unstoppable ugly stream. Sometimes they did escape, making her inarticulate; then they had to be turned into something else, a silent dark mood which elicited sympathy and attention; from Bea, anyway.

Jenny's taken-for-granted childhood had wrought in Ruth a bitter resentment. She wanted to be Jenny. Sometimes she fantasised Jenny's death and then Bea would have to adopt her and she would have Jenny's life.

Ruth sat up, shaking. She had forgotten. She had buried and annihilated her childhood feelings about Jenny, which had swung from absolute love to blind hate, triggered by some small act or word or glance of family collusion – or, sometimes, purely by Jenny's impregnable happiness. She remembered digging her fingernails into the flesh of her arms, drawing blood, to stop the scream of anguished rage. She smelt again the toast she and Bea had made or the cake bowl she had been given to lick in an effort by Bea to cheer her. The hours she had spent in the years of her childhood in that hot, safe kitchen where nothing bad could possibly happen. *Jenny's* kitchen. *Jenny's* mother.

I wish to God I had never seen her on the train to Birmingham. I wish to God I'd never met her again. I only remembered the good times. How she made me laugh. How close we were. I had forgotten this: the green bile of envy and jealousy. I had forgotten how close love and hate are and at this moment I hate Jenny with all my heart for worming her way into my child's life. I want to run as fast and as faraway with Adam as I can. I want to carry him away with me.

Danielle called, 'Ruth! Adam and I are out of the bathroom. Flo's doing an English breakfast. We thought we'd all eat together before the day starts. Ruth, are you awake?'

'Of course! You go on. I'll catch you both up,' Ruth called.

Adam was manning the toaster when Ruth arrived after a shower and with a careful application of concealer round her eyes. 'Hi, Mum.' He grinned at her.

'Ruth, cooked breakfast? It's in the warming oven.' Flo started to get out of her chair.

'Don't move, Flo. No, thanks. I'll just have toast.'

It took Ruth a minute before she could look at Jenny. She smiled in her direction as Jenny handed her a cup of coffee.

'Are you OK?' Jenny asked quietly. 'You look a bit pale.'

'I'm fine. I didn't have the best night. Probably too much wine.'

They talked generally about the day ahead. Ruth was taking Adam off to the Eye. Jenny and Danielle were staying in to talk about Italian commissions for Antonio. Flo was meeting a friend for lunch.

406

'Ruth,' Jenny said suddenly. 'I wondered if you would like to move into my bedroom. It's so large that Tom and I used it as a living room too. I thought it might be a place where you could shut yourself away when you feel like it; your own domain. If Adam had Rosie's room when he was here, you would both be almost self-contained. You could set it up with some of his things. Of course, both rooms need redecorating. You could choose whatever you wanted. I mean, if you'd like to?'

Ruth stared at Jenny, speechless. 'But . . .'

'I've thought about it carefully,' Jenny said quickly. 'You and Adam go and look. See what you think.'

Ruth walked across the landing and into the large sunny room. Her heart soared. She could do wonders here. She could make this her own. She turned and saw Adam standing in the doorway of Rosie's room staring at the boxes, then he came to her. His face was set in an expression Ruth could not decipher. He walked into the room his father had shared with Jenny and looked around at the small ornaments still on the mantelpiece and the clothes piled on to the bed. 'No,' he said gruffly. 'It's sad. It's too sad.'

'But we could make it happy again, couldn't we? Rosie and Tom aren't any the less remembered.'

'It's as if we're wiping them out.'

Ruth looked at him. 'Perhaps you would rather not sleep in Rosie's room?' She hesitated and then said calculatingly, 'I rather think Jenny wants you to have that room, Adam. I think she would feel better if she knew you were sleeping in it sometimes, don't you?'

'Maybe,' Adam muttered. 'You really like this room, don't you?'

'I love it.' *In the room Tom shared with Jenny.* My room.

Jenny walked across the landing. 'What do you guys think?'

Adam said, 'Are you sure you want Mum to take your room, Jenny?'

'I'm sure, Adam. It would make me feel better.'

'Honestly?' Ruth asked.

She smiled. 'Honestly. Ruth?'

'It would be . . . amazing, if you really mean it, Jenny, and very generous of you.'

Jenny was always so much kinder and nicer than me. Catching me out with her sweet nature. Rarely hitting back when I was foul to her. Never telling or complaining. Catching me out with her giving. Wrong-footing me with her goodness. She still is.

Ruth moved over to Jenny. She could not bring herself to hug her, but she put her hands on her shoulders and kissed her cheek. 'Thank you, Jenny.'

Jenny's eyes met hers. Ruth blinked furiously, afraid Jenny could read what was in them, but Jenny turned away and said softly to Adam, 'I'm going to head back to Cornwall on the sleeper tonight, Adam. I just need to be home. Have a wonderful half-term, both of you. I'll hear all about it when you get back.'

Ruth watched Adam's face fall and saw Jenny shoot him a warning glance. She went to look out of the window, furious at the tears that rose painfully from her heart and ran down her cheeks with the loss of something intangible, but so fundamental that had Jenny stabbed her in the heart, Ruth could not have felt more mortally wounded.

SEVENTY-FIVE

James met me off the sleeper at St Erth station. Cornwall was being slashed by gales, that had whipped up mountainous seas. We were soaked in minutes as we made a run for the car.

'A container ship went down off Devil's Mouth,' Dad said as we drove along the causeway. 'Amazing pieces of wood were being swept ashore on the north coast. The locals descended like gannets and carted and scurried the best pieces away until Her Majesty's Customs men arrived in Land Rovers with loudhailers bellowing that anything thrown up by the wreck was government property and everyone caught with wood would be prosecuted for stealing. As if smuggling weren't in the Cornish bloodstream!'

I laughed. 'Oh, Dad, it's good to be home.'

We belted up the path into the house and I put the kettle on.

'Flo rang. She said you'd been very generous about letting Ruth have your room. I think you did the right thing. Well done, darling.'

As we drank coffee, Dad cleared his throat and said nervously, 'Antonio arrived out of the blue yesterday. He didn't realise you were in London.'

'Antonio?'

'He flew into Exeter and hired a car. He did it on a whim, thinking you were sure to be here. He's hung on to see you. It's been rather nice having him. He and Bea have been planning our proposed trip to Italy.' He trailed off, seeing my face. 'You've had enough of people, haven't you? You just wanted to be on your own?'

I nodded.

'I'm afraid you can't ignore him, darling,' he said, getting up to go. 'He's going back to Exeter tonight, so it won't be for long.'

'I know.' I sighed. 'I'll have a bath and get myself together, and then come over to Tredrea.'

I lay in the bath annoyed. I didn't like surprises. Why hadn't Antonio rung Danielle or checked first that I would be here? I could have seen him in London. I thought of his telephone calls. It was much easier to be sociable on the phone. I didn't want to be told that I should go to Italy to see for myself how his new project was progressing.

I got out of the bath and put on some Barber: *Adagio for Strings* summed up my feelings in this grey morning of dripping rain. I pulled on a huge white sweater of Tom's that came to my knees and old jeans that were too big, and tied up my hair in a scarf. I needed an hour on my own. Then I'd go and see Antonio.

I wandered into Adam's room. There was the usual boyhood mess and I picked up papers off the floor and put them on his desk. As I pulled his bed straight, some magazines slid out of the bedside table: military magazines; *Jayne* and others I had never seen before. I sat on the bed and thumbed through them, wondering where he had bought them. There was a fair amount of recruitment literature and my heart sank. It was now a different army from the one Tom had joined. The world had changed and become increasingly dangerous.

410

Unease gnawed at me. I certainly didn't want him even to think of joining because of Tom. Then I thought that this was probably just a phase because he was going to join the school cadets. It would pass.

I went into the sitting room. Adam was studying the war poets for English and had borrowed an old edition of Siegfried Sassoon that Antonio had lent Dad and it lay on the chair. I picked it up. On the flyleaf it said, *For Antonio, with love always, Sophia.* Who was Sophia? I began to thumb through it.

> *. . . And in their happiest moments I can hear*
> *Silence unending, when those lives must lie*
> *Hoarded like happy summers in my heart.*

I smiled and went out into the wet garden. On the water creek birds called quaveringly. The sun was valiantly trying to break through. The water was still choppy and out on the bar I could see angry waves. My feet sank into the grass. I sniffed the wet earth and the smell of seaweed on the wind, and it felt like a homecoming, a moving on.

I turned and jumped as I saw Antonio. How long had he been standing at the gate watching me? I felt embarrassment and annoyance. I looked a complete mess with my enormous sweater and baggy jeans, and my hair tied up like a washerwoman.

He smiled. 'Forgive me. I interrupt a meditation, I think.'

'Come in.' Self-consciously I led the way up the path.

I took him into the kitchen and plugged in the coffee pot again.

Antonio stood awkwardly in the doorway. 'I have come at the wrong time, Jenny. I am sorry.' He came and kissed both my cheeks in greeting and I felt rude and churlish.

'No. It's fine, honestly. I'm sorry I wasn't here when you arrived yesterday.'

'It was a surprise, you being in London. I should have rung first.'

'Have you been OK with Bea and James?'

'It is always a pleasure to be with your parents.'

I put the coffee on a tray and took it into the sitting room. He sat down. Siegfried Sassoon lay open on the sofa and Antonio picked it up. He shot me a look and smoothed it in his hands lovingly. 'I am glad you read this.'

'Who is Sophia?' I asked before I could stop myself.

Antonio looked amused. 'Sophia was a woman I was in love with long ago. She lived in England. We studied English together at university.'

'You have an English degree?'

He laughed at my face. 'Yes, I do.'

'It's just a surprise. I thought you would be more likely to have a business degree or to have studied fashion or history of art,' I floundered.

'I never meant to join my father's fashion business. My older brother died, so it was expected that I leave my studies and go back to Milan.'

'Just like that?'

'Just like that.'

'That must have been tough?'

'At first it was very tough. But you know, Jenny, happiness is a conscious decision. I decided to be content working with my father and I am.'

The sun was beginning to warm the room. Antonio had a facility for stillness and it unnerved me. He sat on the sofa with the book in his hand and he seemed to merge seamlessly with the room. He smelt vaguely of some aftershave. His jacket was uncrumpled and his shirt expensive. How do Italians always manage to look immaculate?

412

Dark hairs sprang from the cuffs of his shirt and over the backs of his hands, hands that were square and beautifully manicured. I had always found men's wrists sexy. I was very conscious of him in the small room. The silence grew. I opened my mouth to ask him why he was here. I looked up and met his eyes and what I saw in them made my body weak and hot. Neither of us moved. The atmosphere was stiff with sexual chemistry.

I picked up the tray and moved swiftly to the kitchen. I heard Antonio follow me but I kept my back to him and ran water into the sink.

'I came to ask you if you would visit Milan and then travel to the Far East with me, Jenny. Malaysia, Singapore . . . I have decided I must import materials from the Far East and many will be for your designs under the Antonio label. I need your advice on this.'

I turned. 'You are joking, Antonio.'

'No, I am not joking, Jenny.'

I laughed. 'I can't take off at a moment's notice. I have Adam to look after and my work here.'

'I am not giving you a moment's notice. Ruth tells me that the boy will be with her for some of the summer holiday. Bea and James tell me that the boy is always welcome there. I do not think there will be a problem.'

'His name is Adam. I see that you have arranged it all with everyone except me, Antonio.' I was furious.

'No, it is not all arranged. I would like to go next month before the holiday season, but if you feel it is impossible for you to come now, then I wait. It is no good taking Danielle. It is *your* clothes I primarily wish to promote. There is no point in going without you.'

I looked out of the window. Why didn't the world go away and stay away and just leave me and Adam to get on with our lives? Just leave us alone.

Antonio said behind me, 'I am sorry, I do not wish to upset you or make you angry. It is important for business that you come.'

I turned. 'There are other things in life besides business, Antonio.'

I thought I saw a flicker of anger. 'Indeed, Jenny, many things,' he said evenly. 'But it is business that gives us a place to live and the choice of the way in which we live, is it not?'

I opened and shut my mouth. He was right. I had a mortgage to pay and a business that needed to keep afloat in order for me to pay it.

'I know that you have Adam to take care of,' Antonio said as if reading my thoughts. 'Is it that you cannot bear to leave this house and this boy even for a short time?'

The phone rang and I moved past him to the hall to answer it. 'Jen, what are you and Antonio doing for lunch. The weather is so foul that I thought you might like to come here instead of battling into town. Anyway, I have food all ready if it's any help, darling.'

'Thanks, Mum. I'll hand you over to Antonio. I'm not sure when he has to leave,' I said pointedly.

Antonio took the phone from me. 'Bea? It is most kind. I would love to have lunch with you and James before I leave. Thank you. We will come now.'

He put the phone back and I avoided his eyes.

'You go ahead,' I muttered. 'I'll follow. I need to change. I look like a tramp.'

'No. You look intensely desirable.' Antonio smiled at me, his heavy-lidded and beautiful eyes amused. 'I do not wish to argue with you. Please forgive me for upsetting you. I see you in a few minutes, yes?'

I nodded and fled to the bedroom. As I changed I still felt indignant. How dare he question my motives for not wishing to travel to the ends of the earth with him? Suddenly, I had

414

the most amazing idea. It was so blindingly obvious I didn't know why it had not occurred to me immediately. I pulled on a skirt and sweater, ran out of the house to my car and drove excitedly to my parents' house.

As I walked into the sitting room James, Bea and Antonio all turned and greeted me a little too brightly as if I had been the subject of their conversation.

I said quickly, smiling at them all triumphantly, 'I've just had a brilliant idea. Antonio wants me to travel with him to Singapore in the summer. Adam could come with us. It's perfect! I could introduce him to his grandparents. It would be a wonderful opportunity for them to meet him at last, wouldn't it? You would have no objection to him coming with us, Antonio, would you?'

They all looked at me in absolute silence. Then James said, 'Jen, when and how Adam meets his grandparents is up to Jack and Ann Holland and Ruth, not you. How on earth do you think Ruth would feel if it were you who took Adam to meet them?'

'I'd have to talk to her, of course, but I think she would be relieved the holidays are covered. She only has two weeks in the summer. I'm sure she would see the sense in him coming. Adam is their grandchild and they're not getting any younger.' I began to falter under Bea and James's incredulous gaze. Why couldn't they see the opportunity this presented for Adam? He did not have any grandparents. I walked away and looked out at the bay below me.

Bea got up and came over to me. 'Jenny, stop for a minute and think. Don't you think that if the Hollands are to meet Adam, Ruth is the one who should be with him? Adam's name is Freidman, not Holland. You can't take Adam over and make him into another little Holland, and that is how it will seem to Ruth.'

I spun round. I wanted to cry out *but he is a Holland,*

whether you like it or not. He is all Holland. I shook as I stared at their faces full of concern. It was as if I had suggested something completely outrageous.

I turned and ran out of the house and back to my car, and drove home in the blinding rain. I parked awkwardly and dashed indoors. I picked up the phone and dialled with trembling fingers. I expected Flo to answer but it was Ruth and the relief made me almost incapable of speech. 'Ruth, it's Jenny.'

'You sound breathless.'

Get the words out.

'Antonio is here. He wants me to go on a business trip to the Far East in the summer.'

'How marvellous! Of course you must go. Look, don't worry about Adam. I'll sort something out.'

'No, no, that's why I'm ringing. You don't have to. I thought it would be a fantastic opportunity if Adam came too, to meet his grandparents in Singapore. We can plan it round your trip to Tel Aviv . . . if you agree, of course.'

I heard her intake of breath. 'No way!' she burst out. 'No way! Absolutely not. I can't believe you're asking me. Adam is staying here. If his grandparents want to meet him they can write to me, they can come to London. No way are you taking him to Singapore to fill his head with *more* of Tom's life and childhood.' Her voice began to rise. 'It's never enough, Jenny, is it? You're going to go on and on eating him up until you've swallowed him whole. My God, you're un-believable.'

I dropped the phone and ran back out into the rain. I ran along the foreshore, over the quay and on to the deserted beach. A north wind blew icy rain on to my hot cheeks. The sea crashed in great vicious waves, hissing and spraying, curling and swelling, the tips of the waves torn off in a side-ways spray. My feet sank awkwardly into the wet sand. I felt frantic. Why, why was it that what seemed perfectly logical to me seemed unacceptable to everyone else?

I did not hear anyone behind me until Antonio was nearly on top of me. He reached out to grab me as he struggled in James's heavy old Barbour. 'Jenny!' he shouted, 'stop running away.' He held on to my sleeve.

'Go away!' I screamed against the wind. 'Go away and leave me alone.'

I was soaked to the skin, my hair flattened by the rain that streamed down my face like tears. Antonio held me and pulled me firmly and with strength towards the shelter of the sand dunes. 'How can you English live in this appalling weather?' he shouted angrily.

Once up on the soft sand I could hardly stay upright and Antonio dragged me out of the wind, his breath coming in heavy bursts. When we were over the top and in some shelter from the rain and wind we stood panting, glaring at each other.

'Will you let go of me, Antonio!'

'Not until you promise to stop running and hear what I have to say.'

'I'm not interested in what you have to say. I don't want to hear it.' I pulled at my arm, furious and mortified.

He jerked me nearer as if his patience were at an end. 'Well, I am going to tell you anyway. I admired you. I did not think you are the coward who runs from the realities of her life, from the facts.'

'I'm not running . . .'

'Listen to me, Jenny. *Listen*.' He gave me a little shake. 'Adam is not your husband Tom and he never can be. Adam is Adam. You must not make him into a little husband for yourself.'

'Damn you.' I tore myself free and he let me go.

'Go then, run away into the rain. Ruin your life and Adam's

and Ruth's. Break Bea and James's hearts. What do you care, *cara*? As long as you can build your little walls to keep the real world out. Shut yourself up with a little mirror of your Tom. Your substitute child-man to replace . . .'

I lifted my hand and slapped him to stop his insidious flow of words.

He glared back at me. I lashed out again and clipped his jaw hard. He grabbed my hands and as I struggled he threw me on to the wet sand and held my hands down near my head. For a second I wanted to laugh hysterically at the ridiculousness of it, but Antonio was now as angry as I was. 'Let your husband go,' he shouted. 'Bury the man. Do not reincarnate him in Ruth's child. Love Adam, but do not try to possess him. He is not yours. It is only an accident that he is your husband's. You are playing games with people's lives.'

'That's not what I'm doing!' I screamed. 'I *have* let Tom go. I've let both Tom and Rosie go. You don't understand.'

'I *do* understand, Jenny. You *think* you have let Tom go, but you are resurrecting him in Adam. Do you not see this danger?' His voice was soft but cruel.

I turned my face away. His words stung and made me cry. Antonio pulled me abruptly upright, enfolding me tightly, talking to me softly in Italian as if I were a highly strung horse. He tried to shield me from the rain. He laid his head on mine and rocked me gently, one hand stroking my hair.

I pushed him away. 'How dare you say those things to me?' But my anger had dissipated. I was shaking with cold.

He blocked the sky with his bulk. 'I dare say them, darling, because no one else will dare. You are adored little Jenny. So loved; so spoilt. Everyone wants to spare your feelings. Well, I do not.'

He bent suddenly and kissed me hard on the mouth. He held me to him with both hands cupped round my face. Then he bent to my neck, pulled the collar of my jacket away and pressed his warm lips to my cold, cold skin.

I stifled the moan that rose up in my throat. I stopped struggling. Aroused, I felt myself responding. It felt like a dam bursting inside me. Antonio and I kissed frantically until we could no longer breathe. I wanted him. I wanted him to take me here in the wet sand with the sea pounding and the rain slanting sideways. I wanted him to take me now while I did not care and nothing mattered and I could not think. I spread my legs under him and lifted my arms up by my head in invitation. I said urgently, 'Now. Here.' I lifted my hips.

He shook his head and whispered, 'You mad English girl.' He took off Dad's mac and we lay on it. The warm feel of him made me want to weep and for a second we were absolutely still, just holding each other in a strange, heightened moment of closeness. Then he thrust into me and the pleasure was exquisite. I had almost forgotten the joy and power of sex. I cried out as I came and listened to the crashing waves and smiled as Antonio climaxed. It felt so good.

We held each other until the cold bit into our limbs. Then we straightened ourselves.

Antonio touched my nose. He looked rumpled and sexy. 'At the moment you need only my body for comfort. One day I hope you will want the man I am, Jenny.'

SEVENTY-SIX

Antonio and I flew through Milan and Rome, and I saw both cities with new eyes. It was one thing to visit as a tourist, quite another to travel with an Italian. We were here to do business but it did not feel like it. I had almost forgotten the hospitality and vitality of a country devoted to fashion and innately conscious of it from the cradle.

Antonio whirled me around during the day to meetings, wholesalers and outlets. He took me to two fashion shows and these I found the most difficult because I knew so many of the designers and the usual crowd. I managed the air kissing and concentrated on the clothes. It was a bit like returning to another planet, but one I recognised and found I could, after all, slot into again without really engaging.

After lunch we would have a siesta and then in the cool we set forth and Antonio showed me Rome. We wandered down the via Condotti, which offered the most expensive shopping in Europe: Bulgari, Gucci, Valentino, Ferragamo . . .

We met his colleagues, drank wonderful wine sitting at marble-topped tables outside on the pavements and watched the people go by, guessing their nationalities by their clothes.

I stood breathless on the Spanish Steps and took photographs. We wandered round Keats's house through rooms which had been preserved just as they were when Keats died, full of the echo and shadows of Byron, Shelley, Severn and Leigh Hunt. Antonio, mortifyingly, knew more about them than I did.

We walked together, through the Piazza di Spagna, hand in hand, and stood like tourists round the boat-shaped Barcaccia Fountain. Then Antonio took me with pride to the Basilica of St Peter. We lit candles together and kept our prayers secret in front of Michelangelo's *La Pieta*.

On our last morning in Rome I stood in early sunlight by the Trevi Fountain and I felt alive, my whole body given to the wonder of a city I had only visited briefly for work. I turned, laughing, to Antonio. 'Can this really be a business trip?'

'Certainly it is a business trip. We are doing very important survey work into what the people of Rome and their visiting American friends are wearing this year. Now, darling, you wanted to see the Sistine Chapel and then it is time to leave, I am afraid.'

I sighed. I would have liked to have seen Florence through Antonio's expert eyes. I had been with Tom for two days and it had not been enough.

Antonio threw his arm lightly across my shoulder and pressed his nose into my hair. 'Next time, *cara*. It is not a city to hurry, but to relish slowly.'

I turned to smile at him. We had stayed in a small tourist hotel round the corner from the Trevi Fountain and we'd slept and made love to the sounds of the city, afternoon after afternoon; night after night. The days were fast, yet dreamlike, not quite real, as if I might all of a sudden wake up and find myself at home.

I had rung Tom's parents to tell them about my proposed trip to Singapore, but they were about to leave for a two-month holiday with Tom's brother who lived in Australia. It was such a long way to go to miss each other and we were all so disappointed that Antonio said, 'We will go another year, Jenny. It does not make sense for you to travel all that way when they are not there.'

Instead, we were going to fly to Spain and study the Moroccan architecture and the vivid hot African colours. Antonio wanted this influence and feel to his collection. He wanted me to feel and taste and absorb it into me as I did the Cornish landscape.

From Rome we flew to Antonio's villa for two days, to rest and wash our clothes and repack. I lay beside Antonio's pool and slept, exhausted with sightseeing, meetings and nights of sex.

I thought of Adam at Tredrea with James and Bea, and I suddenly longed to hear his voice. I had seen Ruth briefly in the London house before I left for Milan. I apologised to her for being insensitive, for not thinking it through, for just assuming something I should not have done. I didn't want anything to change. I wanted to go back to Adam.

'Let's have a talk when you get back, Jenny, and clear the air, so we both know where we stand. Adam's settled with you and I'm grateful for that. I'm not about to upset him or you.'

We had looked at one another, strained and awkward. She did not want to upset her own life and a job she loved either. It was not a worthy thought and I wondered if it was ever going to be possible to be friends again.

I lay on the bed in Antonio's cool room with its Tuscan colours and rugs, and as the phone rang a long way away at Tredrea this Italian/Spanish sojourn, in the slim guise of work, again seemed trance-like, as if I had become quiescent and was being carried along like a sleepwalker in a bright scented landscape.

Bea answered the phone on another coastline, another world, and I was pulled back to my real life. Everything was fine. James had persuaded Flo to come to Cornwall to have her hip operation at the end of the month. He knew an excellent surgeon who had a space on his list. It was great news, we could all help her convalesce afterwards.

Adam was bursting to tell me what he'd been doing. He had spent the weekend on Dartmoor practising for the Ten Tors run. He was going on a school trip to Plymouth to see *Macbeth*. He and James were taking the boat out near Godrevy tomorrow because the dolphins were back in the bay . . .

It was sweet music to hear him happy. It made me smile; like a light going on. As I replaced the phone I saw that Antonio had come into the room and was watching me. He smiled and held out his hand. I moved towards him warily. He was unable to understand my closeness to Adam. He had apologised for his words, but they still hovered somewhere between us. He said something low in Italian. It sounded like a love poem.

'What did you say?'

'That I will run you a bath.'

But I knew that wasn't what he'd said.

Spain was stimulating in a quite different way. There was nothing subtle here. Colour upon colour mixed and matched; clashing and gaudy; bright and surreal against a backdrop of Moroccan architecture; arches and palaces, churches and mountains; villages and an overcrowded coastline.

Antonio drove me into an inland Spain I never knew existed; as yet unspoilt and utterly beautiful.

I took photographs of tiny villages down deserted tracks and of geraniums cascading out of windows and pouring down ancient buildings. Of children playing in scrubland in bright dresses, flashing gold jewellery and white smiles.

I studied the tiles and the decor and the filigree work on the top of doors and windows, and I sketched ideas until I could not hold a pencil. I fingered muslin and silk and heavy cotton material, weighed it in my fingers and knew the soft gold belts and light floating summer clothes I would design for next year.

It was the first time I had thought *next year*. It had been a long time since I felt the absolute joy in what I do, the promise and excitement of my own collection.

Antonio was right. It was not just necessary for a designer, or anyone, to travel, it was vital to draw inspiration from many sources and many places; to see and feel the heat and colour and people. To rub shoulders with them, to eat and breathe in a culture.

Tom and I had flown off to places whenever we could, even for a few days, but I had stopped travelling and I knew as I whirled around, sticky in hot cars, that without it inspiration and originality died. Without it you repeated yourself. Without it you grew stale. Cornwall had invigorated me, but now I had contrast and I knew the ideas that gathered in my head like a kaleidoscope would also work at home.

Antonio watched me with a constant smile on his face. On the way home I was going to stop off in Milan with him to see his new workplace and to leave some of my sketches and material samples with instructions and ideas for how they should be made up. I was impressed with his little 'English Enterprise'. The converted warehouse was spacious and cool, the women friendly and enthusiastic.

On our last night together in Milan we swam by candlelight, listening to Mozart in a huge tiled indoor swimming pool. We went back to his modern bachelor flat, full of green plants and polished furniture, and fell into bed in a heap, full of wine.

Antonio whispered soft caressing words into my neck in

Italian. They were the same ones he had whispered to me in his villa in Amalfi.

I smiled. 'You are not running me a bath this time, so what are you saying to me, Antonio?'

He held me away and looked into my eyes. 'I said, I would like to give you another child.'

The blood rushed to my face and Antonio tickled me to diffuse the moment. That night I was careful to take my pill. Sex with Antonio was like a drug. It heightened everything. It was compulsive, it was part of all that I felt and had created in the long, hot, sensuous days with him. I felt as if my body breathed and moved and glowed with life again.

He whispered after we made love that night, 'Jenny, I have loved you since the moment you walked into that restaurant with Danielle.'

I lifted his beautiful square hand and kissed the palm, then turned my cheek into it. It was a large, safe hand. Antonio was special, but wonderful sex was one thing, love quite another.

SEVENTY-SEVEN

Ruth was away doing business in Berlin when Jenny flew back to London. Both Danielle and Flo saw an immediate change in her. She was hot and weary but she exuded a glow. Her eyes and body were alight with her old vivaciousness.

Danielle, watching her, saw that Jenny had regained her relaxed, languid, catlike little body as she stretched tiredly on the sofa and in a flash suddenly knew why. She remembered that look on Jenny's face after an afternoon in bed with Tom; an irrepressible sexual smugness that was quite unconscious. Danielle wanted to laugh. Jenny was like a small, replete cat.

Antonio! How extraordinary. Anyone less like Tom was hard to imagine. Then, when she thought back to her one night with him, it wasn't so extraordinary. He was a warm and sensual lover who had obviously regretted accepting an invitation to her room. He had with tact and flattery told her gently that attractive as he found her, he always kept business and pleasure separate. Danielle grinned to herself – not always, it seemed.

She longed for Jenny to say something, but she didn't oblige and returned to Cornwall without divulging anything.

'What do you think?' Danielle asked Flo breathlessly.

Flo laughed at her. 'None of our business, young lady; but my word, lovey, she was almost the old Jenny with her infectious happiness.'

Danielle nodded. She prayed that the tension between Ruth and Jenny over Adam would not resurface, because it was a huge bore and threatened to spoil everything.

Back in Cornwall I found it hard to settle back into a routine. I felt strangely restless and found I could only concentrate for short stretches at a time. I wanted to go out and walk, lie on the beach or the grass in the summer sun. I wanted to close my eyes and let the images of the places I had seen filter through my mind like sunlight through leaves.

The sounds and smells of a different life lingered: church statues and coloured windows; the deserted cove near Antonio's villa; sprawling white bungalows with tumbling bougainvillea; the smell of spices and olive oil and tomatoes; loud cicadas.

Adam noticed my restlessness and asked me questions about my trip as we sat in the garden and barbecued sausages in the evenings. I had got some Moroccan architectural books out of the library and I tried to explain some of the influences I was bringing to my work. *When I could work.*

Speaking to Tom's mother on the phone about Adam's love of music, she had told me all of a sudden that she had won a music scholarship but had not been allowed to take it up by her mother and father. She had been living in Kuala Lumpur and, at seventeen, her parents had considered her too young to go off on her own to live in London.

'That's bad,' Adam said when I told him. 'Poor thing, she must have been gutted.'

'You said you didn't know where your love of music comes from, darling. Now you do. When I told her how talented

427

you were she was thrilled, because neither Tom nor his brother were musical.'

I was pretty sure Tom had not known about it, but he had questioned her passivity sometimes and her willingness to submerge herself totally in her sons and husband. It made me feel intensely sad. She could have been someone quite different.

Adam said, 'As soon as I'm old enough, Jenny, I'll go and see them. I hope I see them before they die. I've never had grandparents. I'm going to travel the world. I shall definitely take a gap year.'

I laughed as the misty garden filled with birdsong; his enthusiasm for life was catching. I hoped he would become something gentle, like an anthropologist or ornithologist. But if I was changing, Adam was too.

I sensed his musical enthusiasm waning. He joined the rifle club, loved the treks to Dartmoor preparing for his Duke of Edinburgh award. His binoculars and bird books were used less frequently. He fished less. He brought friends other than Harry home. He went further afield with a different set of boys. He went on early morning runs to keep fit; shadow-boxed in the garden when he thought I wasn't looking; groaned more loudly when he had music practice and piles of homework.

I was delighted. He was secure and content, and so was I. I could tell Bea and James had stopped worrying. Both Adam and I had moved imperceptibly on. It was as if we both viewed life simultaneously from a shifted perspective. The spell of our isolation within the small house was broken as we looked towards the windows and saw different horizons beckoning. Yet nothing had changed between us. It never would.

Adam was very excited about his trip to Israel to see Peter and he brought home copious numbers of books from the school library. He seemed preoccupied with the military situation out there and the plight of the Palestinians, and constantly e-mailed Peter about the injustice of Israeli politics.

'You might have to be a bit careful about voicing your views while you're there,' I warned him.

'Peter's told me that already!' He grinned at me.

Cleaning Adam's room one day I was dismayed to find that he still had a secret hoard of military magazines under the bed. I realised his interest in Tom and his army life were not fading as I hoped it would. The magazines were well thumbed and it disturbed me. I wondered suddenly how healthy Adam's preoccupation with war and weapons was. I looked around his room at all the photographs of his father: Tom for ever smiling down at his worshipping son; a man in uniform with no faults, seducing Adam with a way of life Tom had had no illusions about. Adam had not hidden those magazines from me, but he hadn't read them in front of me either. I heard the St Ives train and decided I must talk to him.

At supper I said, 'Did I tell you that Tom thought he might come out of the army and join his father's firm in Singapore?'

Adam looked at me. 'No. Why would he leave the army? He was a professional soldier. It was his job. It's what he did.'

'Yes. It is what he did, but that doesn't mean he might not have become disillusioned . . .' I hesitated. 'Adam, I saw all those military magazines in your room. I wondered if I had given you an idea of Tom that was wrong. He was a committed soldier, but constantly seeing horror and destruction and violent death in places like Bosnia and Iraq takes its toll. It wore him down. He often felt extremely low and became critical, like you, of political situations. He saw the way military life was going for the next generation: long single tours fighting terrorism, fighting insurgency in bleak hostile places; very little home life. There is no glory in war, in violence or in seeing innocent civilians mown down.'

Stupidly, I realised too late that my words were having the opposite effect on Adam. Until a young boy had seen someone blown up before his eyes or a life taken in a second, it was not possible for him to appreciate fully the horror, only the drama of imagining himself a hero.

Adam surveyed me gently. 'You sound like Peter. Of course I'm interested in wars. I'm adolescent. When you're my age wars are grimly exciting.'

I stared at him and burst out laughing. I went round behind his chair and hugged him. 'Darling boy, you're quite right. You're a revolting adolescent.'

He leant against me. 'Don't worry that you've made me interested in wars because of Tom. I always knew when I was old enough I would go and find my father, so I would have found out he was in the army anyway. I thought he must be a bad sort of person because Mum wouldn't talk about him and I was never allowed to ask questions. So when I found out who he was and what he did it was such a relief. It was so great. He was a really brave person and I don't want anyone ever to tell me any different.'

He was suddenly anxious and I sat in the chair next to him. 'Adam, there is nothing I could say that could be remotely critical of Tom. I think he was a pretty wonderful person too, but I loved him because he was *Tom*. Not because he was brave or a soldier, that's all I'm trying to say. His uniform did not define him. He doesn't have to be in uniform for you to admire the person he was.'

'I can't ever know the person he was, but I can learn everything about what he did as a soldier. It was his career and a good one. There's nothing wrong in that, is there?'

430

'No, darling. Just don't neglect your other interests. Your music and your birds. Don't remain obsessed with Tom because he was your father and because he is dead. I was in danger of doing that, you see.'

Adam looked at me. 'I'll always play an instrument. I'll always love music, but I don't want to be a musician. I'm not dedicated enough to put in the practice and there are too many other things I want to achieve.' He swung round in his chair and eyed me closely, then he said doubtfully as if it had suddenly occurred to him, 'Maybe you should have another husband. You're pretty and not old. Someone to look after you when I'm at university.'

I laughed. 'I can look after myself!'

He grinned. 'Or you could wait until I grow up and then *I* can marry you.'

I ruffled his hair. 'Eat, you silly boy. Your supper's getting cold.'

That night, as I lay in the bath, I longed for Antonio beside me. He was not a beautiful man, but God, was he sexy. It had taken me days to admit that I missed that slow early waking beside him. It was shocking how quickly I had become used to another body, even if it was only a casual sexual thing between us.

He rang me as I climbed into bed. He sounded faraway on a bad line from Paris. I felt a lurch of pleasure on hearing his voice. 'I am missing you, Jenny,' he said wistfully.

'That's nice, Paolo Antonio. I miss you too,' I said, but lightly.

He laughed. 'Ah! Both my names now, is it?'

'Well, you never seem to use your Christian name, so I thought I'd give it an airing.'

'Do I look like a Paolo?'

I giggled. 'No!'

431

He talked for a while about his day, then he said, 'I will say goodnight, my very dear Jenny.'

'Goodnight, Antonio. Take care.' I didn't say more and I felt his disappointment. I felt guilty. I did not want to hurt him. He was a sweet man and a good lover, but that was all.

SEVENTY-EIGHT

It was early September and Bea and James were in Italy with Antonio. I caught the train to London the day before they were due back. Adam and Ruth had left for Israel to meet Peter. When I put Adam on the plane at Newquay, he had been high with excitement.

'Just watch what you say, you. I don't want to have to bail you out of an Israeli jail.'

He grinned. 'Yeah, yeah, yeah . . .'

I wondered if Ruth and Peter would somehow get together again. Danielle told me that although Ruth did go out with men occasionally, she seemed more interested in work. 'As most of our male friends and colleagues are gay, it is not so easy for us single women.'

I saw she was laughing. 'Well, you never seem short of men, darling.'

'My boyfriends are not the sort of men that Ruth would go for.'

'You'll meet someone stimulating, arty *and* heterosexual one day, Elle, and fall like a stone, as we all do.'

'Do not hold your breath, *chérie*.'

I got to the London house and found Flo in an unusual

433

state of panic. She was not good at delegating and she was displacing her anxiety about her hip operation into work. We had purposely limited our commissions over the summer, knowing that Danielle would be busy in Italy, Ruth in Israel and Flo out of action. I had left the retired cobbler in charge of the unit in St Ives. So far, it seemed to be working well.

It was only when I made Flo come down from the work-room and sit and have tea with me that I understood what was disturbing her: 'An Inspector Wren rang. He tried to get hold of you in Cornwall. He wants us all to look at some photographs of men they suspect could be responsible for various terrorist activities. He says it's a long shot but he needs to know if we recognise any of the faces they've compiled of possible suspects for Tom's killing.'

My heart thumped in shock. 'It's all right, I'm not going to go to pieces. Is the inspector coming here, or does he want me to ring?'

'He wants you to ring. He would prefer it if we went to him. He said they have this machine that magnifies photo-graphs, which makes it easier for us to identify faces.'

'OK. It's a bit late to cross London now. Let's do it tomorrow before Bea and James arrive.'

Flo nodded. 'It's unlikely we'll be any help, isn't it?'

'Yes.' I felt sick and tried to hide it from Flo. 'I guess they have to go through the motions. Maybe it's just a way of showing us they haven't given up.'

Flo and I went into the police station the following day. Some of the staff remembered us and got up to greet us.

'I'm sorry to ask you to do this,' the inspector said as he shook my hand. 'But we are grateful. It is worth you both looking carefully. You should know that I will be asking all your staff to look at these photographs too.'

The photographs were magnified, accentuating every feature, pockmark and scar. There were different shots in black and white and long-lens coloured photographs on a desk.

Flo was asked to wait until I had gone through all of them first. I supposed it was so that we both concentrated. I had somehow thought all the terrorist suspects would be black or Asian, but they weren't.

The inspector watched me carefully. I couldn't recognise anyone. No one's face was remotely familiar. I went through all the photographs minutely, again and again.

I began to feel dizzy and nauseous. I realised that I desperately wanted to reach out with my hand and pin the man who wiped out my family.

'Why do you keep going back to that photograph?' the inspector asked me abruptly, pointing down at a man.

I looked at him, startled. 'I don't. I'm just going through them all in the same way. I don't recognise anyone.'

'OK,' he said. 'I'm just going outside for a moment. Please look at them all once more to be very sure. Take your time.'

I did. I looked at the close-ups and at the long shots. I leant back in the chair and blinked, then focused again. Something niggled right at the back of my mind. I tried to conjure it. I closed my eyes. I put my head in my hands. It wouldn't come. *It would not come*.

I needed to get out of the airless room or I was going to pass out. Hoping and wanting to recognise a man or men who might have killed Tom and Rosie wasn't the same thing as actually recognising him.

We got a taxi straight home. Flo poured me a stiff gin. 'You're a terrible colour, Jenny. I wish you hadn't had to do that.'

'I so wanted to be able to point my finger and say, "That's him. I've seen him before". The feeling was overwhelming. I don't think they'll ever be able to prove who did it now. He's living somewhere. He's living his life . . .'

435

'Maybe he isn't. Maybe he's already dead or maybe he's behind bars for another atrocity. Please, don't . . .'

'I'm not going to dwell. I promise you that.' I stood up, holding the brown envelope with the photographs the police had given me for Danielle to look at. 'I'm going to put these in Danielle's flat. I don't want to think about them any more. If I let them undermine me, they are still hurting us.' I lifted Danielle's key off the hook. 'Then I'll have another gin.'

'Good girl,' Flo said.

While Flo rested, I slid out with half a dozen of my belts, which I took to some select shops I knew near Kensington. They had all sold my work before and happily took the lot. By the time I got home on the tube two shops had rung and placed orders. I felt almost ashamed that it had been so easy.

'I'm not surprised,' Flo said. 'You've always had the knack of knowing what will sell at any given moment.'

I went up to the top of the house to the girls in the work-room and left them sketches and samples of materials, in case the demand grew bigger than I could manage in Cornwall.

Flo and I did some paperwork in the conservatory and then, unable to concentrate, I went and wandered around the garden.

It had been spruced up but had no real life yet. Someone had planted some sweet peas and they flowered vividly against the fence. I sat on the lawn, idly pulling daisies, but the ghosts of Rosie and Tom did not come.

I thought of Antonio. I was treating him badly. He did not deserve my cold shoulder or my polite retreat with no explanation. I thought, with a guilty pang, of all the little things he had sent me during the summer: poetry books, flowers, photos and travel books of places we had visited, all so carefully thought out to please me. He was, at this moment, treating my parents like royalty. He deserved better from me and I knew it. Yet would he retreat? Not he.

Flo watched Jenny from the kitchen window. She was glad she was old when she saw the painful working out of relationships in Ruth, Danielle and Jenny, relieved that it was all behind her.

She was afraid of this coming operation going wrong, but had told no one. It seemed feeble. She wasn't afraid of dying but of being incapacitated, unable to do a job she loved. She could not even think of retirement without an inward scream. *This* was her life, *this* her family.

She longed, as she saw Jenny struggling, to remind her not to waste a moment, but something in Jenny's restless mood prevented her trying. If she was having an affair with Antonio Flo had seen no sign, except something brooding in her.

James and Bea flew into London that night. Jenny was completely thrown by Antonio flying back with them. Bea and James had had the most wonderful time and Antonio's pleasure in their obvious delight in the holiday was transparent.

As soon as Flo saw Jenny's face, she knew that Danielle was right. Jenny was trying to be distant with Antonio and it wasn't in her nature. Flo saw the surreptitious looks she shot at him when she thought no one was looking. She was overwhelmed with gratitude for the holiday he had given Bea and James. *She's afraid of loving him*, Flo thought suddenly. *Oh silly girl. She's fighting it.* Did Jenny feel she was being disloyal to Tom's memory? Or was she afraid to love again with all the inevitable pain?

The following morning before Flo got into the taxi to Paddington she said softly, as she hugged Jenny goodbye, 'Don't waste even a second of possible happiness.'

Jenny looked at her suspiciously. 'Never mind *me*. You are not to worry about anything. Do as you're told and rest! I'll ring every day. See you next week.'

Bea and James got into the taxi anxiously, noting their daughter's stubborn look and her inexplicable reserve with Antonio. It obviously had not been such a good idea to encourage Antonio to return with them because Jenny was in London for a week.

'Oh dear,' Bea said softly as the taxi swung away to Paddington.

'Oh dear, indeed,' James echoed, feeling exasperated with his daughter.

SEVENTY-NINE

I had been completely thrown by Antonio appearing in London with Bea and James. To my dismay, Flo had offered him a bed in Danielle's flat with Bea and James. He refused, but he ate with us.

He came to say goodbye to Bea and James the following morning and as the taxi slid down the road to join the flow of traffic I was left, awkwardly, with him. I had reached the horrible point of knowing I was behaving badly but not knowing how to retrieve the situation.

I climbed the stairs with him behind me, prattled about Flo and her operation and heard myself with growing panic. Antonio followed me in uncharacteristic silence. When we reached the kitchen I saw a small tight smile on his face.

'Coffee?'

'Thank you.' He moved to the window and looked down on the garden, ill at ease, jiggling the change in his pocket. My heart contracted. I wanted to put out my hand and touch his arm in his very Italian short-sleeved shirt and say *I'm sorry. I'm sorry*. I had never seen Antonio at a loss before.

I passed him a mug of coffee and looked down at the

empty garden too. 'Hot days in a city seem a waste somehow.'

He turned. 'You are homesick already, Jenny?' His eyes were amused.

I smiled. 'Not really. Not yet.'

He took a sip of coffee. 'So, you are left alone here, holding the fort?'

'Danielle should be back this afternoon.'

We were silent. This was ridiculous. We were making small talk like strangers. I met his eyes and saw the misery in them, and I put down my mug and reached out my hand to him. He took it cautiously as if it were a Judas kiss and pulled me a little closer. I looked at the dark hairs that ran over his knuckles and shivered, instinctively bringing his hand to my cheek. He pulled me to him. 'Jenny . . . Jenny . . . *cara*.'

I buried my head in his shoulder and he held me, and we rocked together in the kitchen. He moved to kiss me. *I have to tell him*, I thought, *I have to tell him. I'm not being fair*. But his mouth was on mine and desire ignited like a small forest fire. I pressed myself against him, abandoned, grateful not to fight any more.

In a second we were in my bedroom pulling off our clothes and leaping into bed. I did not want to think. I only wanted his touch, his body and his beautiful sensuous voice urging me on. Antonio could make me melt. He could set me alight in minutes. I loved the solid heaviness of him, the feel of his square dark body. I loved . . .

'I love you, Jenny. I love you. Do you hear me, *cara*? I love you, love you . . .'

He was inciting me to a response and, although they rose in my throat, soared like a bird inside me, I could not, *would not* say those words to anyone else. I felt the tears run down my cheeks with an emotion so overwhelming that I clung to

Antonio and shook. He folded me to him like a child, pressed his lips to my hair and we slept.

I woke when I heard Danielle coming up the stairs. I slipped out of bed, swung on my robe and shot out of the bedroom into the kitchen.

Her face lit up when she saw me. 'Jenny! I thought you must be out.'

'No, I'm here. I was just going to have a shower. Mum, Dad and Flo got off all right.' I trailed off as she stared at me, pressing her lips together, trying not to laugh. I went to the mirror and my tell-tale face and smeared mascara stared back through a tangled mass of hair. I flushed and glared at her. We both heard Antonio get up and turn on the shower.

She lifted her eyebrows at me, still grinning. 'Flo rang to say Antonio was in London. Let us have a drink together and then I'll disappear.'

'Don't be silly. You don't have to disappear.'

'I am exhausted, darling, too many late nights. I am going to sleep, then I have plans for this evening. Serious partying coming up.'

I laughed as I poured us both a drink. 'You've met someone?'

She looked smug. 'Mm, Italia pilot. Seriously gorgeous. You see, darling, you are not the only one to have a sexy Italian.'

'Shut up,' I said, 'and drink your gin.'

'Oh, Jen,' Danielle said. 'I am *so* looking forward to this week with just you here. Like old times. We will have fun, yes?'

'It'll be bliss.' I held up my glass to her.

'Right,' she said, winking. 'I will take my drink to my bed. Shall I come down before I go out to say hello to Antonio? I promise to ring down first in case . . .'

'Oh, go away!' I said.

441

I went back into the bedroom and found Antonio neatly dressed. He grinned at me. I grinned back. I would say something later. *I would*. Later. It was just . . .

'Get your clothes on, Jenny. I am taking you to a very wonderful place for lunch.'

'Posh?'

'Posh?'

'Smart?'

'A little.'

'Italian?'

'Of course. Are you hungry?'

'I'm starving!'

He came and took my face in his hands. 'So am I!'

I put on a dress I had made for myself in sarong style out of some material we bought in Spain. It was a greeny gold silk that Adam and Dad had loved me in. I felt like a sensuous mermaid in its folds. I dug out some Jimmy Choos and tottered around getting used to them again. I was tanned and I felt as I hadn't felt for ages: sexy, confident. Excited.

'I cannot take you out like that!' Antonio exploded. 'Get those clothes off immediately and get back into bed where I can ravish you!'

'Don't you dare lay a finger on me, Antonio. It has taken me ages to get ready!' I shrieked.

He took my hand and we ran down the stairs. In the taxi he said, 'I am unsure if I still want to take you to this Italian restaurant run by a good friend of mine. It will be full of Italians. You cannot trust Italian men.'

'Is that right?' I said, lifting an eyebrow.

'You are very beautiful,' he said.

We ate to-die-for food in a spectacular garden with a cool tinkling fountain. The wine was delicious and Antonio's friends were easy, hospitable and amusing. I was even starting to pick up Italian. I had fun. I had such fun.

We fell into a taxi in the late afternoon and raced up the stairs like children. We tore at each other's clothes and made chaotic, giggling love until we fell into an inebriated and happy sleep, entwined in the crumpled sheets.

EIGHTY

Danielle crossed the landing and went up to her flat humming 'Love Is in the Air'. Once inside, she moved around throwing open the windows. Bea and James had stayed the night up here and they had left her a card propped against the kettle to say thank you. She kicked off her shoes, went into her bedroom and threw open the wardrobe. What was she going to wear for her beautiful Italia pilot? She smiled as she separated three dresses and hung them on the door.

She grinned to herself. Jenny and Antonio. She got herself some cold water from the fridge and went into the shower. *I am happy*, she thought as she lifted up her head and let the water cascade over her hair and body.

She pulled on her robe and wrapped her hair in a towel. Should she sleep or look at her post? She got another glass of water and sat at her table. Flo or Jenny had put her letters in a pile and there was a brown envelope beside them with a note. She pulled it towards her. She had forgotten all about the police photographs. Jenny had stuck a Post It on the front.

Danielle, the police wanted to see if we recognised any of the men in these photographs, all wanted for various terrorist activities. Flo and I went to the police station and we weren't any help at all. I think the police are just showing us that they are still actively looking. Give Inspector Wren a ring on that number on Monday just to say you have looked at them.

Elle, hope this doesn't upset you. J xx

Flo had rung and told her about Inspector Wren. She had also told her that Jenny had been violently sick when they got home from the police station.

Reluctantly Danielle eased the photographs out of the envelope. She did not want a reminder of that horrible time. It must have been awful for Jenny.

She separated the photographs and laid them out in front of her like cards. Three Europeans, two Asians and one African. Her hand stopped. The hairs rose on the back of her neck. Her heart began to hammer, her vision to blur. She got up violently and the chair fell behind her. She walked to the window and looked down on the garden.

I will walk back. I will look again. It will be tiredness, tiredness and imagination. I will be calm. It is not possible. I must be wrong.

She went into the bathroom and with trembling fingers combed out her hair, stared into her own frightened eyes. She walked back to the table and lifted the fallen chair. She looked at all the photographs and last the one by her right hand. As she stared at it her life fell away. There was no mistake. She knew who it was.

The phone rang and she ignored it. It would be Jenny. She heard the front door bang and a taxi stop outside: Jenny and Antonio going out. She was alone in the house. The blood drummed dizzily in her head like a waterfall. She stumbled into her bedroom and got into bed. She turned and pulled up her knees into a foetal position. Her teeth were chattering and she pulled the duvet up to her head. She rocked and keened with the terrible knowledge of what she had done.

The day died. Dusk filled the room. She had no idea of how long she lay, icy and motionless. She made herself go back over a sequence of events, slowly trying to comprehend her part in it. Had she been used? Or had she provided the opportunity?

Through the darkness came Tom's fury: *'Don't you ever do anything like that again. How dare you be so irresponsible, Danielle? If you want to screw around, keep to your own flat; don't you dare bring your bits of rough into our flat. Shut up! I'm not interested. You don't listen, do you? You think my job is a game I play to irritate you. I could have killed that guy. Your stupid promiscuity puts us all at risk and I won't have my wife and child put in danger by you. The door between the houses stays locked at night from now on. Do you understand?*

She had hated him. She had loathed him for humiliating her. Jumping out of the dark suddenly, scaring her and the man witless as they tottered about, drunk, in Jenny's kitchen looking for coffee. She had thought Tom liked playing Mr Tough Guy roles to impress. She had never, ever taken him seriously. Somehow she just couldn't.

She sat up with the duvet round her shoulders. Think. Where had she met O'Sullivan? Had he approached her or the other way round?

My God, he had been petrified when Tom had hold of him. He had fled down the stairs, scrabbling at the locks and rushing out into the night. Danielle had never forgotten the speed and silence of Tom or the look on his face. It had been creepy.

She had slept with this man, shared her body with him for a short intense period. He'd had a rough Irish charm. Sex was good and uncomplicated. He did not waste time with words. She concentrated frantically, heard again that Northern Irish accent: *I left Belfast in 1997. I'd had enough of British soldiers turning over my mother's house.*

One thing she *was* sure of. She had never mentioned to anyone that Tom was in the army. She put her head in her hands. Tom had been serving in Northern Ireland around that time. Had O'Sullivan recognised him that night? Or had the way Tom sprang out of the darkness made it obvious to an IRA man what Tom did for a living? Had it alerted him? Or worse – she got out of bed and began to pace. Had O'Sullivan coldly and deliberately targeted her to get to Tom? She moaned low to herself like an animal. She had casually, drunkenly, taken him straight into Tom and Jenny's home.

She had rung him the next day. Their short affair had run its course but she was worried he might cause trouble, report Tom for assault. He was the aggressive sort of man who would think of it.

'*I'm sorry that happened. Are you OK?*'

'*I'm fine, girl. I grew up in Northern Ireland under British occupation, remember?*'

Words she should have remembered. Words that should have engraved themselves on her mind. They should have jumped out at her after Tom was killed, but she had been far too busy blaming him for Rosie's death.

Danielle felt Rosie in her arms, smelt her lovely baby smell. She threw herself back on to the bed in anguish and started to weep again. Tom had been right all along. Her life had finally caught up with her.

EIGHTY-ONE

I woke and lay beside Antonio in the room that Tom and I had shared. The walls and curtains were a different colour. The furniture had been changed around. The photographs were Ruth's. The feel of the room was not the same, but in the dark the ghost of Tom still hovered.

I got out of bed abruptly, went to the kitchen, poured myself some water and drank it thirstily. I looked down at the garden. Blackbirds scuttled and called in the dusk. Ghosts were not laid so easily. They slid back without substance like a breath on the evening air.

Birdsong filled that still and empty garden, echo of a voice and a trail of laughter; a child so heavily asleep in my arms that her head felt like lead. Sadness rose and I shivered. This house and garden could never be empty of them, neither could my heart.

Something distressing hovered. What was it about this evening that felt sickly familiar – a beating in the air disturbing a hidden anxiety? I felt as if I were tracing my steps backwards. As if I had been here before.

Wine at lunchtime always made me strangely melancholy as I sobered up. I turned away from the window to make tea for my dry throat and it came to me in a rush: *I felt this thick apprehension waiting in vain for Tom and Rosie to come home from the zoo.*

I looked up and Antonio stood in the doorway, a towel round his waist. The light from the bedroom pooled across the landing and into the dark kitchen. I was glad he could not see my face.

He said softly, 'Will you marry me, Jenny?'

I stared at him, horrified and guilty. 'I can't marry you, Antonio.' My voice still sounded husky with sleep.

'Why?' he asked simply.

'I'm sorry. I . . . I don't love you.'

'No?' He came closer. 'Is that so?'

I felt my body grow hot with the thought of what our bodies had done together today. I was suddenly angry and defensive. 'I'm sorry if I gave you the wrong idea, Antonio. I'm really sorry. I thought we were having fun together. I thought our relationship was nice and casual.'

I turned and grasped the teapot like a lifeline and swirled hot water inside it. Antonio sprang towards me and the teapot flew out of my hand, hot water sprayed upwards and it crashed to the floor, breaking its spout.

Astonished, I met his eyes.

He was furious. 'Casual! My feelings for you could never be mistaken for casual. Let us be truthful here. How then, do you think of me?'

I floundered, stunned by his anger and he said, 'Good enough in bed. Not good enough for marriage? Am I right?'

'No! No, Antonio, it's not like that . . .'

'What is it like, Jenny?' He came and took my arms, shaking with the effort of not raising his voice. 'Tell me what it is like.'

'I'm not ready. It's too soon . . .' I said frantically.

'It will *always* be too soon. You are still in love . . . you

449

are still obsessed with a dead hero. How could I think you could possibly love an ordinary mortal like me, a dull Italian businessman?' He laughed without humour, let go of me and moved towards the door, his body still stiff with rage. 'No one else will ever be good enough. No one on God's earth can compete with a man you won't bury. Well, good luck with your life, Jenny. I have had enough.'

As I stood there the phone shrieked into the silence, making me jump. I went and picked it up. 'Hello?'

There was no answer and then I heard a little whimper. 'Who is it? Adam?'

'*Aide-moi*, Jenny.' The words were a whisper. 'Jen . . . *Aide-moi* . . . forgive me . . . I . . .'

'Danielle? What's happened? Where are you?'

There was a rush of whispered French, repetitive, hopeless. I couldn't understand her. 'Elle, speak English, I can't understand. Just tell me where you are. I'll come, wherever you are, I'll come now.'

'Forgive me, *chérie*. I go now. I need to hear your voice.' She reverted to French again, the words rising and falling like an incoherent litany.

I shouted, 'Antonio! Come quickly,' but he was already beside me. 'It's Danielle. I can't understand her. I don't know what's happened or where she is.'

Antonio took the phone and tried to calm her. '*Danielle? Qu'est-ce-que tu dis? Calme toi, parles anglais.*'

He listened and I watched his face grow anxious. 'Darling, listen, tell me where you are. It *does* matter. Nothing can be so bad, nothing. Oh . . .' He turned to me. 'She has gone. I do not know what is wrong, Jenny. I do not know what has happened, but I think it must be bad.'

Danielle never spoke French. I took the phone and dialled 1471. I expected it to come up as her mobile but the number was unobtainable. I closed my eyes. Danielle had been so

450

happy. What on earth could have happened in a few hours? She would not be this distraught over a pilot standing her up. I shivered, terrified she had been raped.

We stood in the dark house, Antonio and I, and disaster hovered everywhere, so tangible we could have reached out and felt its clammy hand. Into the silence came the sound of something falling from above. Our eyes met and we ran up the stairs.

Danielle's door was locked. Frantically I ran back down and snatched up the spare key from a dish on the landing, and with fumbling fingers we turned the key, only to find that the door was on the chain.

I called, 'Elle, please let us in, darling. Whatever's happened, it will be all right. Elle . . .'

There was no answer. Antonio started back down the stairs. 'I am going to have to try to kick in the door. I need my shoes.'

I kept calling to Danielle through the gap in the door, but the silence inside was absolute.

Antonio rushed back with his shoes on. I stood out of the way as he levered himself against the top of the banister rail and kicked at the hefty door. It hardly gave. Sweating, he kicked again and again until the frame splintered and we could reach in and unlock the chain.

I flew into the bedroom. Danielle was not there. I heard Antonio cry out. I ran through the sitting room. Danielle was hanging in the passage between the bathroom and kitchen where we had put in a skylight and new wooden beams when we converted the flat. A small stepladder lay upturned on the floor underneath her. So did the phone.

Frantically, Antonio got the stepladder, and climbed up and held Danielle's body slack while I got a knife. It was hard for us to hold her and to cut her down. We all fell on the floor and we laid her down, loosening the flex round her

451

neck with shaking fingers. She was warm and there was still a faint flutter of a pulse. Antonio breathed into her mouth. We rubbed her chest as if we could prevent her heart from stopping, then Antonio ran and phoned for an ambulance.

I held Danielle's head on my lap, stroked her lovely blue-black hair and murmured words of love I hoped she could hear. We sat each side of her talking and holding her for ten minutes until the medics arrived. We stood away, then, while they worked on her. I clutched Antonio and we prayed, although we both knew in our hearts that Danielle had gone.

I saw the brown envelope on the table with one photo-graph on top of it. I saw my name on an envelope and Inspector Wren's on another. I stood looking down on it, my heart icy with dread. I stared and it came back out of nowhere: the man's shoes. The man wore strange shoes with a paler piece of leather in the middle like a golfing shoe. I had seen them before: the man with Danielle in our flat in the dark, the night Tom heard them in our kitchen. In the half-light I had caught the odd flash of white leather on his brown shoes.

'I'm sorry,' the para-medic said. 'I'm afraid we're too late. There is nothing we can do. The lady's dead.'

'Jenny,' Antonio said, 'you must stop crying. You must try to stop now. You will be ill.' He handed me a brandy. We were sitting in the dark sitting room.

'What was Danielle saying to you in French on the phone?'

Antonio's voice shook. 'She said, "Forgive me. I am fright-ened of dying alone."'

I got up and went to the window. The last police car was turning in the road and leaving. A carpet of lights spread in front of me, shimmering into the distance: people in their houses safe and asleep.

452

'Did we get there in time? Would she have known we were with her?'

'I hope so, *cara*.'

I used to look out at this view at night when Tom was somewhere in London doing something covert he could not tell me about. I used to look out from the top of the house as I stitched clothes together and I wondered how many people gazed back out of faceless windows of tower blocks and houses, feeling alone but comforted by the knowledge that other lives were going on out there, side by side with theirs. Within that shimmering mass of flickering lights, little births and deaths and tragedies and celebrations were being enacted.

'I lied,' I said without looking round. 'I lied. I felt I was betraying Tom. I was afraid of loving again, of being hurt. But I do love you. I *do*. I don't want to be in this rotten, shitty world without you, Antonio. I don't.'

I turned and saw that Antonio was crying again too. He held out his arms to me and I went into them.

Damien says, 'Northern Ireland was my first posting with Tom. I was a corporal. We were both pretty young and green. Despite the ongoing peace process it was still a violent and lawless place. We did three tours out there back to back. We were fed up to the teeth of being there. Weary to death of constantly being spat at and stoned for picking up thugs with no political ideal except murder and mutilation; sick of the drug running and bomb planting; of young soldiers losing eyes and limbs and life; sick of it all.

'One night Tom and I are called out of the garrison late. A routine patrol have found a young lad thrown in a ditch. He has been kneecapped and so badly beaten up his body looks like an open wound. He is sixteen. His crime? His grandfather is a retired Garda officer who had gone to the

453

security forces to give the name of a member of the IRA who was controlling and terrorising a whole neighbourhood, extracting his own form of revenge for anyone he deemed was fraternising with the security forces. The man's name was O'Sullivan.

'Tom and I call for back up and go and pick him up in a bar. He is well away and cocky with it. He swears he has been there all night and a hundred people swear he has too. We haul him out none too gently. In the interrogation room he laughs at us, says we can't touch him, he has hundreds of witnesses. And anyway, why are we getting worked up about one skinny Catholic youth who is probably drug running and deserves broken knees?

'Tom is called out and told the boy just died. We tell O'Sullivan. He shrugs. No skin off my nose, he says, but it might teach his grandpa a lesson. He grins. You scum can't pin his murder on me and you know it. I'll walk out of here and you can't do a thing. Not a fucking thing.'

Damien pauses. 'I'm not excusing what Tom and I did. After twenty-four hours we had to let him go. We followed him in an unmarked car and picked him up again before he got to the pub. We drove him near to where he'd beaten the boy to a pulp and we beat the living shit out of him. Then we left him in the middle of nowhere. "We've got a whole police station that says we never left the premises," we tell him. "You can't prove a thing. Not a fucking thing."'

Damien and I stare at each other. 'Did O'Sullivan pick Danielle up because he found out where Tom was living? Or was it chance that Tom jumped him in our kitchen and he recognised Tom or his voice?' I ask.

Damien hesitates. 'The pub where Danielle met O'Sullivan is a pub where Irish construction workers go to drink. It's possible it was chance, Jen, but Danielle would have only to mention the name Holland in relation to you or Tom for it

454

to ring bells for O'Sullivan. Danielle was a gift. He waited a long time, but he got his revenge.'

'It could have been you too,' I whisper.

Damien stands up. 'I wish it had been,' he says. 'I don't have a wife and child.'

EIGHTY-TWO

I walked over the cliffs, round past the island towards Porthmeor beach. It was early and no one was about. The tide was out and seaweed, smelling of fish and ozone, covered the flat rocks at the end of the beach and dried in the morning sun. Seagulls wheeled and screamed over my head, guarding their young.

I sat on the rocks looking out to sea. Disembodied engine noises and voices came out of the mist from the fishing boats heading home. I wrapped my arms round my curving stomach as if to protect it. I thought of all the times I had played here in the rock pools with Ben and my sisters. Bea and James had seemed omnipotent. I had a charmed and protected childhood. Nothing terrible had ever happened until Tom died.

I was about to take a huge leap into the unknown. There were no guarantees. I could never be sure that those I loved would not be grabbed from me in a moment.

Flo was going to buy my house on the Saltings. Her hip had healed but her heart never would. Ruth had left for Israel to be with Peter, then they were both coming back to England together. Adam was going to be a weekly boarder and go to

Bea and James for the weekends. It would be easier to work for his exams in school, he said. He asked if he could sleep in my old room.

The house in London was up for sale. We had closed down. The business was transferring to Italy. Two of the girls were coming with me; the rest had to find work elsewhere.

Danielle told me so little about her life: tiny snippets, wounded places she shared with her dry wit, which forbade pity, in the early hours of the morning as we completed a commission; a stepfather who, I suspected, violated her as a child; a mother who never listened.

Despite her talent and looks, Danielle never felt her body was sacred. She wanted to leave her French life behind her. Flo, and Rosie and I in the London house were her life, her family.

I was going to design under a new Danielle label. My things had been shipped to Italy, where Antonio waited for me. We would marry there in a month or so.

The tide had turned and it began to come in fast towards the rocks. Soon I would feel my child moving inside me.

I thought of leaving Adam with a strange disbelief. When I had told him about Antonio he had gone white. 'Oh, no! I'll never see you, Jenny.'

'Yes, you will,' Ruth had said quickly. 'Italy is a hop. You can go and visit Jenny whenever you are welcome.'

'That is always,' I said, smiling at Ruth. We had never regained our former intimacy, but she seemed relaxed over Adam now. A future with Peter had changed her completely. And, of course, I'm leaving; Adam would be in the care of Bea and James. It hurt, the thought of moving on without him. It cut like a knife.

I closed my eyes. There was a little whispery butterfly movement inside me, a suggestion of life, of hope and a future. When I looked up, Adam was threading his way surely towards me. I smiled. He always knew where I would be.

EIGHTY-THREE

Antonio, standing on the veranda of the house, watches Jenny and Adam make their way down to the beach. The two small boys, Paolo and James, walk between them, and Adam carries baby Danielle. It is a late afternoon in August and they have all just got up from their siesta to swim. Antonio is trying to work, but it is difficult to concentrate. He is restless and reluctant to admit the cause.

They have not seen Adam for some time. Not since he passed out of Sandhurst and was posted to the north of England with his regiment. He and Jenny have been taken aback by his confidence and maturity, and his increasingly more marked resemblance to Tom. He is becoming the mirror image of the man she fell in love with.

To Antonio's shame, it is this that undermines him. Each time Jenny looks at Adam now, he can see how it must have been with Tom. He sees her revelling in this tall, blond Englishman and he feels a seeping jealousy, a growing resistance to Adam's presence here, in a way he'd never done when Adam was younger.

He cannot pin down his exact unease but he sees in Jenny's unqualified pride in Adam the boy's power to hurt her in his single-minded intent to expose himself to the same sort of danger as his father. Antonio knows Adam cannot have told Jenny yet where he is being posted or she would not look so happy.

He sighs, puts his work away and walks down the steep path to join them. Laughter drifts up from the beach and Antonio smiles cynically to himself. Maybe it is just a case of old stag, young stag. Adam is brimming with youth and excitement, and beautiful still. Antonio is not a man used to feeling jealousy. It is unlike him. It is the long hot summer, he thinks, and this coming fashion show. He must not let any youth spoil his happiness.

Ellie runs to him. She is the light of his life. At two she is just like Jenny, with masses of dark curly hair. He lifts her, throws her into the air and catches her as she squeals.

Jenny calls, 'Hi, darling. Are you finished?'

'I have given up for today. It is too hot.'

The boys call out to him to come and swim. They are fooling about in the shallows.

Adam looks up from his book and grins. 'Hi, Antonio. Glad you've given up trying to work.'

'Would you like to water-ski when I've had a swim?' Antonio asks, feeling guilty about his unworthy thoughts.

'That'd be great. Shall I go and get the gear from the boat-house?'

'Good idea.' He pulls Jenny up. 'Come, little whale of mine, and wallow in the shallows with me.'

Jenny makes a face at him. 'Cruel. Cruel, but true.'

She lowers herself into the sea and splashes water all over herself. Antonio watches her looking down at her protruding stomach with something like surprise. This really should be their last child, but how Jenny loves being pregnant.

Jenny checks Ellie's armbands before she moves deeper

into the water to swim. 'It's the only time I feel light at the moment, when I'm in water,' she calls out to him.

Antonio throws the boys up and lets them plop down into the water with a yell, coming up coughing and spluttering. He smiles at Jenny's dreamy pregnant wonder at the lightness of herself in water as she swims back into the shallows. He sits down next to her while the two boys run off to find Adam.

'You know what?' Jenny says, floating nearer so their feet touch.

He smiles. 'What do I know?'

'I am so, so happy, Antonio.' She laughs and looks up at the blue sky. 'Blissfully happy.'

'If you are trying to get round me for more children the answer is Basta! Basta! No more.'

'Oh, shame!' Jenny says.

As Antonio swims out to the mooring for the boat, he sees Adam sit down beside Jenny in the water. He hears her suddenly cry, 'Oh, no, Adam!' So Adam has told her and cast a shadow on their peaceful afternoon.

Ruth pushed the double pushchair along the creek path from the cottage. There was a swollen flood tide and she could see Peter fishing on the bend by the wooden bench. Rachel and Leah were clutching bread to feed the swans. Two old herons were perched high in a small scrubby tree. They looked ridiculous, like partridges in a pear tree. The twins covered their mouths with their small hands and shrieked with laughter. Ruth felt a flash, a second, of joy so complete it made her dizzy.

Swans sailed silently and majestically down on the incoming tide, skimming the water like gondolas. Under their wings the water sparkled. Behind them was the backdrop of ancient woodland and here, on the path, no one.

She had come here as a child to escape her parents. She had come as a moody, troubled teenager. She had come as a young restless parent. Now she was here again with a second chance. She had swapped a soaring career for late motherhood and she was loving every single moment of it.

Jenny had rung last night and Ruth had understood why. It was a reaching out, a call for solidarity. In a way, it was worse for Jenny than it was for her, having to watch Adam eagerly following in Tom's footsteps.

Jenny had invited them to stay, once the new baby had been born, and Ruth had accepted. She knew that Jenny was always going to be part of Adam's life. Ruth had not relinquished Adam because she had the twins. She had learnt to let him go, choose his own way, because she must zealously guard the life she now had. She and the twins waved at Peter, and he waved back.

That night, as we lie side by side, I say to Antonio, 'Adam told me this afternoon that he is being posted with a rapid response team to the Pakistan border in Afghanistan next month. The papers say it's becoming one of the most dangerous places on earth. He couldn't bring himself to tell me or Ruth until now.'

'It is his life. We cannot go through this again. Adam did a degree because you and Ruth thought he would grow out of the army. Well, he did not. He has chosen his career.'

'I know,' I say. 'I know, Antonio, but I'll always feel responsible. I'll always feel . . .'

'That it is to emulate his unknown father that drives Adam forward to danger?'

'Yes.' My voice sounds small, Antonio's sounds weary. I should keep my fears to myself.

Faraway we can hear the sea and a new moon lights up the room.

'Jenny,' he says. 'There is something I must say to you. I do not think you will like it.'

I turn, surprised. 'What is it?'

'You told me earlier how happy you are.'

'I am. I am, but Antonio, it is not something to say out loud too often.'

'Then please, I ask you, do not resurrect this thing you have with Adam. I say to you, once long ago, let go of the boy. I ask you again. I ask you now, let go of him or you threaten our happiness together.'

I search his face. 'How do you feel threatened?'

He hesitates. 'Adam is Tom's child and special to you. I understand this. I have always understood. But once he took over your life, he became an obsession. I am afraid this might happen again.'

I open my mouth, but he lifts up his hand. 'Let me finish, *cara*. Now that Adam is trained and out in the world, are you going to follow his career with close scrutiny? Are you going to scan the English papers avidly, jittery over some trouble spot he might be sent to? Are you going to imagine the poor boy's death every time he is posted? Life has no pattern, my darling. History does not always repeat itself. You are right to guard your happiness, we all are. It cannot be taken for granted, but because you lost all that you loved once does not mean that tragedy strikes every time you are happy. You do not have to have a child every year as an insurance against loss.'

He places his hand on my stomach. 'Hundreds of soldiers go to dangerous places. Some die. Most do not. Who are you to decide that Adam may get hurt or killed? Who are you to pre-empt his fate? Why do you not decide instead that he will live happily, marry, have children and come out to visit us all his life? Is this not the better way to live, my darling?'

I am silent. I meet Antonio's eyes. He is extraordinarily perceptive. I trace his mouth with my finger. 'Don't feel threatened by my past, Antonio. You know how I feel about you and our children. I love my work, my life, but most of all, I love *you*.'

Antonio smiles and bites my finger. 'Then I say no more. I sleep contented. Goodnight, you and baby number four.'

I lie awake, thinking. Antonio has nurtured my security and happiness so tenderly and now he feels vulnerable. He senses danger and a need to protect our life together. I have been taking for granted the strength and quality of his love. I almost missed something essential: Antonio's ability to love without judgement.

Sorrow rises in me. I want him to know I understand. I move as close as I can with my bump and he falls asleep against me with the moon streaming like butter over the covers, making a passage of light across the polished floorboards.

I wish it were not so, but there are things I can never tell him.

I believe there *is* a pattern to all things and that I can never break this pattern. I can, with all the power in my body, try to protect those I love. But I know that some things are preordained. I have always had an instinctive fear that Adam will gamble with his life, nudge his fate a certain way. Antonio has made me realise that I must live each day as if this were not so.

I think of Ruth and Peter with their twins. I think of James gone, and Bea and Flo seeing out their old age together. I think of Adam and I cannot bear to think of a world that he is not a part of. I can't, despite all that I have, be sure it would be worth living.

I turn over carefully. I think of the duplicity of love. All the things we say to those we share our lives with and the damaging complex feelings we can never share. It is a lonely thought, for it means that love is never wholly truthful.

Antonio dare not reveal his true feelings about Adam, he just bravely fights them. I cannot say to Antonio that whatever truth lies embedded in me is not to do with my love for him or the children, but with a whole life that was wiped out in an afternoon.

Was I ever entirely truthful with Ruth? I wrapped the truth cleverly from myself and made it acceptable; but then so did she.

'I don't deserve you,' I whisper to the sleeping Antonio. 'You are too good for me.'

He is not asleep and he laughs. 'Will you stop dwelling on your wickedness and go to sleep?'

It is Adam's last Sunday with us. The day is baking and airless. I am lying inside on the sofa with the french windows thrown open for any breeze. Antonio is down on the beach with the children and the au pair.

Tomorrow we return to Milan. Adam comes into the room and joins me. He has been down the hill to the village for the English papers.

'Look.' He grins at me excitedly. 'There's a huge article on you in yesterday's colour supplement.'

I laugh. 'It's the time of year for the fashion writers, darling.'

The sun sizzles outside on the veranda. The noise of cicadas rises and falls in crescendos and diminuendos. I feel languid and heavy as my time comes.

Adam moves around the room restlessly, unable to stay still. In a few days he will be in Afghanistan. I know that nervous pacing. It means he wishes he were not going at all. It means he is excited and fearful and anxious to be gone. It means he does not want to leave me.

465

My child kicks hard and I shut my eyes against the glare of the day.

'Is the baby moving around?'

I nod sleepily. I would like another girl.

'Can I feel the baby?' Adam asks suddenly, coming to rest beside me.

I open my eyes and I see Tom with his hair flopping over his left eye. I smile and lift my top and place his hand on my stomach. I watch his face as the child moves in a strong little squiggling movement, then turns a little, changing the shape of my stomach. I can see Adam is astonished by the independent movements of this person not yet born.

His hand is warm on my skin. He is struggling with some deep emotion. His eyes are a vivid, startling blue. 'I wish you had waited for me. I wish *I* could have married you, Jenny.'

He is half smiling, trying to make a joke. Sadness crosses his face like a small shadow. He leans forward and places his head on my stomach to listen to the pulse of life that beats beneath my skin. His arms encircle me. He is very still.

I place my hand on his cheek and stroke with one finger the fair hair that grows almost white in front of his ears. I say gently, 'Remember what I said to you once. You will always be a part of me, however old I am or faraway you are. That won't change, ever.'

Adam's tears cool my flesh. This is very hard.

'I love Antonio, darling, and you will find a young girl to love. You will bring her here to meet us all. You will have children and I will love them because they are part of you. This is how it will be.'

Adam is weeping for he knows not what: for a wistful fulfilment of a thing intangible; an amaranthine love; for a visceral sense of loss caught achingly under the ribs and in the darkest moments of a night.

The pressure of him moulds with the weight of my child. I cannot tell where Adam ends and I begin. He is beneath my skin and in the pulse and beat of my blood. His head bent to my child and my hand in his hair are as natural and unsullied as his warmth had been in my bed. He is familiar; he is known. Time cannot change what has an everlasting life of its own.

Adam begins to hum softly and tears rise in my throat, for all that I lost, for all that I have. He hums. His breath like a butterfly kiss on my bare brown stomach, his mouth pressed intense against my skin.

Come away with me . . . in the night . . . I want to walk with you on a cloudy day . . . on a mountain top . . . in a field of blue . . . I'll never stop loving you . . . I want to wake with the rain falling on a tin roof with you . . . Come away. Come away with me . . .

My darling boy.

ACKNOWLEDGEMENTS

My thanks, as always, to Susan Watt, and to Katie Espiner for encouragement and patience; to Jane Gregory and her lovely team; to my friends, for love and support, especially to Jenny Balfour-Paul, who let me use her lovely poem and Broo, who give me much needed e-mail companionship, inspiration and laughter; to Margaret and Laura, who unknowingly found the right word and deed at the right time.

I am grateful to Paul Smith, headmaster of Truro School, who found time to show me around his stunning school on an A-level result day. Any inaccuracies are mine.

Last, but certainly not least, my love and thanks to Tim for forbearance and food parcels delivered with four footed friends to whom a deadline means nothing.